OBEDIENCE

The Guild Book One

NICHOLE M. WILLDEN

-Dedicated to Amanda-
You helped me rekindle my belief in myself

A Note Before Entering The Guild

Obedience, The Guild Book One by Nichole M. Willden deals with topics that may be triggering to some readers. This book delves into the experiences and psyche of an underage girl trapped in a dangerous secular cult. It attempts to capture an experience of being in the world but separate from it. Additionally, it has content about emotional and physical abuse, bullying, indoctrination, martial arts, weapons (including handguns), threats, teen identity crisis, and physical and psychological violence. If any of these topics could be triggering for you, this may not be the best book for you to read at this time.

The author and publisher do not condone violence or abuse to anyone, especially minors.

Chapter One

Emma halted as soon as she trudged into the house. Leader was home. She could feel his presence. Whenever he was home from prolonged business trips, he was a cancer that took hold and metastasized immediately, pressing the infection of his presence into the rest of the House.

Fingering the black-dyed tips of her formerly blonde hair and tugging at the shortened hemline of her school skirt, Emma tried to slip past his office to the stairs without being seen. There was little chance he was away from his office. He seemed to reside there and, in the brief periods when he was at home, he never seemed to sleep. The stairs that represented her escape seemed much farther away than usual, as if Leader's large presence forced the building to expand.

"Emma," his melodic voice, at once hypnotizing and reproachful, caught her before she managed three steps. Her wide blue eyes were devoured in his gaze. Her body stopped abruptly and she turned toward him—a sunflower to its god.

"Sir," she whispered. Words tripped over themselves in her mind as she attempted to find an acceptable greeting. "Welcome home."

The left brow slowly rose on his forehead, the only movement in him. Emma was small and weak and insignificant in front of his towering scrutiny. Rather than allow the sensation to sweep her away, she rose to her full height—a foot south of him—and squared her shoulders. Blue eyes met penetrating black.

"It's important to blend in here," he reminded her in that same stern melody. He did not raise his voice at all, but he somehow seemed to shout. Her fists tried to clench but she restrained them.

Selecting carefully from her trained vocabulary, she answered, "I do not understand the importance of sitting in a blender with these people." Informative, complete, and hardly defiant at all. Emma was pleased.

Leader was not.

"You know this is where I have the Family stationed. So, regardless of your ignorance, you will do as I say." Also informative. And not just a little threatening.

When words tried to escape in a volley back at him, she resisted. It would never do to get him angry. She had only ever seen him at a simmer.

His gaze did not so much as flicker away, but Emma found she could no longer meet it directly. Instead, she was drawn to the black hair above his unyielding brow, dancing slightly in the breeze from an overhead vent. The same gust rippled the fabric of his gray silk shirt and brought the clean scent of linens and aftershave to Emma's nose. His black suit jacket hung loosely on the back of his desk chair, not in motion and yet somehow as sinister as the rest of him. Clothing that knew, somehow, they belonged to Leader and, therefore, could never tamely hang in a closet or drape on a chair. Although his jacket was off, his narrow gray tie was still in place, and the thin leather belt in his belt loops. He looked like a man about to descend on a quavering boardroom rather than at rest from business.

"What is it you will do?" Leader asked, snagging her gaze once more with that seductive, venomous tone.

At first, she did not comprehend his meaning, but then she realized it was a trick question. There was only one kind of answer to a question like this: "I will Obey," she said in perfect semblance of humility.

He nodded and looked away, forgetting her immediately. He settled himself in his desk chair and opened his laptop with a practiced lift of his perfectly clean fingers. Emma remained on his threshold a few moments more, entranced as she always was by Leader. There was no way to ignore such a man. A total eclipse that casts a shadow for miles across the ground could not demand as much attention as he did. His shadow eclipsed her courage.

When at last she tore herself away, his distracted tone called her back.

"Have Ilene bleach that atrocious color out of your hair. Adjust your hemline to a respectable length. And strip that polish from your fingers. You're supposed to blend in to the suburban Utah culture, not front a gothic rock band." He did not even have the courtesy to raise his gaze from his computer.

"Yes, Leader," she whispered and gave her fingernails a quick glance. Before he could say more, she hurried away, her steps heavy but somehow soundless, as though he had stolen away even her will to be noticed.

She moved several steps down the hall and leaned back against the wall with a long breath. She fingered her rough split-ends and mourned the loss of the harsh black color. It was completely wrong for her skin tone and, more importantly, for her superficial Utah cover. But it had been a mark of defiance, a little pin in the voodoo doll of Leader's captivity of her. But, like all things, Leader removed it from her grip. Theft of a bottle of hair dye stolen from an unfortunate girl's open locker was not even Emma's crime. The crime was that Leader had given her an image to maintain, and blonde was part of that image.

She pushed off the wall and moved toward the stairs. As she suspected, no one noticed her. Even Scott, Emma's direct superior who was seated on the steps to the second floor, did not look up as she approached. He leaned forward, his forearms on his knees, with an expression that suggested he was waiting for his doom. In his right hand was a pink slip detention paper. This was the kind of paper given at their school to misbehaving students who were expected to return it signed by their parents. Emma did not envy Scott's forthcoming conversation with Leader. Trouble at school did not compare to trouble with Leader.

Emma slipped past him, then crept down the hall to the storage closet to find bleach and nail polish remover.

The acrid smell of bleach surrounded Emma when she was finally permitted to escape to her private room. She closed the door behind her, and was alone at last. Breathing in the sanctuary on a pained sigh, she allowed her eyes to slide shut.

A full day at school of being jostled in halls, sneered at in the lockers, and generally ignored in class took its toll on her each day. She always came home exhausted. Leader in the House, though, could drain her energy reserves in moments. Yet still she had to attend to her homework, chores, and possibly an evening training session before she could climb into the very enticing bed across the room.

Emma had always had her own bed, but she never had a room of her own before the Family moved to Utah. It was by no means something Emma would have designed herself, but she did not care because it was private. The bed was four-poster glossy white with yellow satin sheets and sunflower bedding. The vanity dresser was also glossy white. It held a mirror framed in white with sunflowers stenciled in yellow around the edges. Photos clung to the mirror with tape and tacky, as if she had placed them there herself. She hadn't. Emma did not recognize anyone in the photos. She had no friends; she moved too often to make any meaningful connections in school, and she got along with no one in the Family.

Beside the window, which looked out onto the landscaped front yard and the quiet street, were framed pieces of childish artwork that bore her young signature, though she was relatively certain she was not the artist. The only recollection she had of bringing home artwork was when she had drawn a portrait in kindergarten and brought it home to excitedly share it with Leader.

"See?" she had crowed to him, dashing into his office and waving the picture around excitedly. He had been on his red phone, the corded one that sat on his desktop, completely out of place among the sterile white of everything else. "I drew our house. See? The teacher said she loved it! See? See?"

But Leader slapped a hand over the receiver and shouted, "Amos, get this child out of here!" He looked at Emma then and glanced at the paper in her hand. "Do you think I'm interested in your being an artist? I'm not." And without another glance, he returned to his phone call.

Emma slid the picture behind her back and allowed herself to be led away by gentle Amos. He had complimented the picture and said he would hang it on the fridge, but she answered stoically, "I'm not interested in being an artist."

Despite her comment, Amos had hung the portrait up. It taunted Emma for several weeks before it was removed from the refrigerator. She never saw it again. She never asked about it again. After that, she never brought another art project home; she threw them away at the school door.

There was also a scrapbook between bookends on her plain white desk full of photos she had not taken or arranged. And a shelf with several trophies she had not earned. In some ways, Emma felt that decorating the room with trophies, artwork, and photos was taking their job of "blending in" much too far. No one outside the Family would ever be in her room. The pretense, rather than being homey, was isolating. But Emma ignored her discomfort at the duplicity in favor of having a space of her own.

She tossed her backpack on the chair by her desk and, even though it was well made, it gave an ominous creak under the weight of her textbooks. She was used to the weight of a private-school education, but her dainty little chair was not. She sighed and flopped down on the bed. There was no time, really, for lying around. According to the clock on her bedside table, it was already after four. Monique would be home at five and would expect a favorable report of finished homework and completed chores. But it was impossible for Emma to move now. Leader's presence in the House weighed her down more than even her books could.

She was so heavily disappointed! Dyeing her hair, though risky and unnecessary, had been a choice she had made for herself. True, she had done it with an ill-conceived plan of striding in to show it off to Monique, with the full knowledge that it was temporary. Emma never considered the possibility Leader would be home to see it first. The prank was for Monique. She was the person who had snapped at Emma this morning during breakfast, "You do not need to make friends at school!"

Monique's lack of understanding, her completely unsympathetic approach to Emma's isolation at school, incensed Emma. The bile of rebellion caught in her throat and she seethed all the way to school, and all the way through her first and second periods. All she could think about was how she had confided in Monique that she hated her new school, and she did not feel she belonged there.

"I have not made a single friend!" But Monique had obviously not cared about that. Black hair and fingernail polish had been a statement, an attempt to control her own isolation. If she had seen it, Monique would have quirked her famous eyebrow—a portentous sign of imminent danger—but she would have probably let it go with an eyeroll and a "suit yourself." Leader's reaction was crushing because he did not even recognize it as mutiny.

Emma's cell phone rang. She sat up in alarm; it never rang. The phone was an accessory Leader had given her to complete the extremely fake image they attempted to create in their new city. She was meant to be the rich, privileged, but ultimately well-behaved daughter of a wealthy businessman. Modest, religious, and Obedient. Obedience was her only responsibility in the Family, but it taxed her every moment.

Confused, she got off her bed and walked over to her backpack on the chair. She retrieved the ringing phone from the right pocket. There were Family orders about cell phone use, but Emma could not remember offhand, because it was knowledge she had never needed before.

She studied the phone, looking for an answer button. There were no words to indicate which button was the right one, so she touched the screen over the green button shaped like a phone.

She pulled her phone up to her ear and spoke hesitantly. "Hello?"

"Hi. Is this Emma Harris?"

The caller was a young woman, but not anyone in the Family. She had a valley accent. As a scholar of languages and accents, Emma could hear the tiny nuances that identified her location. She was a Utah County girl through and through. But Emma did not know who she was.

"Who's asking?"

"Oh, sorry!" The girl's voice dropped to a conspiratorial whisper. "I would have texted, but my mother made me call." Then back to her conversational tone, "I'm Cara Winters. I'm in your biology class."

Emma could not verify the girl's story. She did not know any names of the girls at school because she mostly avoided them. Whenever she tried to have a conversation with kids at school, she became flustered. She never knew what to say. The topics they discussed never seemed to have anything to do with her life. They talked about movies and extracurricular activities, parties, and crushes. She understood nothing except the Family's expectations of her.

"How did you get this number?"

Cara answered unconcernedly, "I got it off the official school roster. My mother volunteers in the office occasionally. I know it's a gross violation of your privacy, but I really needed to ask you a question."

The idea that it was a violation of her privacy meant nothing to Emma, because there was never any privacy in her world. She was intrigued. This girl's question had been important enough she had asked her mom to go through the trouble of looking up her number on the school roster. Even though Emma hadn't known her number was on a school roster, finding it had shown some ingenuity. Of course, ingenuity was dangerous for people at the bottom of Leader's chain of power.

Cautiously, Emma asked, "What's your question?" She glanced toward the door, but if anyone was listening from outside, she could not tell. She comforted herself with the idea that Leader was safely ensconced in his office downstairs.

"I'm having a birthday party tomorrow night at my house and I wanted to know if you wanted to come."

Emma was shocked. She knew all about parties, what they were, why people had them, but she had never actually been to one. No one had ever invited her to a party. People invited their *friends* to parties. She did not know Cara Winters. She would not have been able to pick her out of a group of school girls if Leader pointed and said, "Which one is Cara?" The thought of Leader made Emma wince. She could not go to a party. Leader would never let her out of the House for a frivolous party.

"I can't," Emma explained. "My father doesn't allow us to go to parties."

"That's kind of silly." Cara sounded like she was smiling. Her voice took on a condescending tone that Emma knew well. Leader and everyone else in the Family used that tone with her. "It's not a keg party or anything. We are just going to watch some movies and eat cake."

Really confused now, Emma stared at the phone in her hand. It could not produce answers to the swirling questions in her mind. The only people she spoke to at school with any regularity were the teachers who greeted her at the beginning of each class, and her biology lab partner. Cara was not her lab partner. Emma could not imagine she had made such a good impression in classroom roll calls that this girl really wanted her at her birthday party.

"What is it you really want? My biology homework, or something?"

Cara replied, "It's just a party. Will you be attending?"

"No" was the correct answer, but Emma could not say it, because she had a strange sensation of longing. She wanted to go to the party. She wanted to hang around with silly school girls, talking and watching movies. Emma had only ever seen one movie in her life. It was an old rendition of "The Scarlet Letter" in her English class, but it had fascinated her. She knew newer movies were more interesting and had better acting, so it would probably be enjoyable. The cake she would have to pass on, since she could never compromise her health with sugar and processed foods. She did not actually know what she would say to the girls from school; she had nothing in common with them. Interacting with them was daunting, but she was curious about what it would be like. She was intrigued by the idea of making friends. Hope blossomed from the pit of her stomach, springing to life in the hole left behind by the scent of bleach.

"Look!" Cara's voice altered to scathing, dropping out of the sweet tone Emma now realized had been pretense. Her real tone was impatient and reminded Emma of home. "My mom said I had to invite you because you're new and lonely. It's not my idea, okay? She told me last week that I had to give you an invitation, but I didn't want to. Now she is saying that if I don't ask you I can't have the party, and my friends are all planning on it."

That made a kind of sense to Emma. It certainly explained the reason for this call. Emma did not understand why Cara's mother was interested in her loneliness at all. It could possibly just be a tactic to convert her to their religion or something. People in this valley tended to be aggressive proselytizers. She had been approached several times at school by kids who wanted her to take a "release time" from school to go to some kind of super-specific Bible study. She had always rejected them because in her life there was no "release time" from academics. Academics and Obedience were her life.

"Listen, I already told my mom you are coming, so it's important that you do. Tell your dad that it is for biology homework or something and I will see you tomorrow night." The phone clicked, and Emma looked at it in shock once more. The words "CALL ENDED" flashed across the screen.

Emma was puzzled by the entire interaction, not sure what had happened exactly. Cara seemed to think Emma was to blame for this, but it was a personal issue. If Cara had lied to her mother—Emma could not imagine lying to Monique!—then how was that Emma's problem?

She put the phone down slowly on her lap and sat back against one of her white bed posts. Emma tried to think rationally about it all. The party would probably just be a bunch of girls from school she had avoided for weeks. It would probably be a lot of conversations about topics she did not understand or had no interest in. It would be mindless giggling and whispering, like in the halls at school. Inane, that's what it would be. But Emma wanted to go anyway and find out for herself.

Her phone buzzed again, but this time it was not a call. It was a text message with an address, followed by the words: **6ish dont B L8**. She memorized the address, and then deleted the text. She also deleted her call history, which had only the one number. No one ever looked at her phone, but if Leader suddenly took an interest in it, she didn't want him asking questions about this call until she decided what she was going to say about it.

Chapter Two

"Emma!" Monique shouted from downstairs.

In shock, Emma turned to look at the clock on the wall. She swore. Monique was home early today. That almost never happened.

"Coming, Mother!"

She tossed her phone onto her dresser, then thought better of it, and tucked it into the top dresser drawer under some clothing. She ran out of the room.

Monique was perhaps one of the most beautiful people in the world. She had long black hair that was always in an immaculate style. Her eyes were an almond shape, and her lashes long and thick enough that she did not need makeup to enhance them. She was as tall as Leader, although she was slender and more graceful. The grace was deadly, though, as she was skilled in many forms of martial arts and held to no creed about the misuse of it. Monique frightened Emma in ways she did not fully understand. And yet, she preferred her to Leader.

"You studying?" Monique asked in a clipped-short manner she used with everyone except Leader, as if she did not have time to formulate complete sentences or listen to unnecessary answers. She did not even give Emma time to answer. "Dinner will be with my colleagues tonight. Bathe and dress."

Leader stepped from the shadows to stand beside Monique, looking Emma over with speculative eyes. They were black pools of contemplation, and they again weighed and measured her. Emma felt her throat constrict. Did he somehow know about Cara's call?

"You will want to appear like a daughter we can brag about," he informed her in a slow and musing voice. He looked her up and down, and Emma felt dread in her stomach that he would find something wanting. "You need to be a girl who refused to join the cheer squad because it seemed too cliquey and the uniforms are immodest."

If it had been only Monique, she might have rolled her eyes, but she did not dare to roll her eyes at Leader. "Yes, Father, Mother." Her tone slipped into acerbity before she could stop herself. "I will wear a pink cardigan, a ribbon in my hair, and pearls, if it pleases you."

Monique's eyebrow rose on her forehead. It was the only warning Emma needed. Leader's contribution to the threat was a simple hardening around his eyes. It made Emma's breath catch in her throat. Her mind grabbed frantically for words that would meet their mutual approval.

"Did you have some specific wardrobe in mind?"

Monique's arms crossed beneath her chest and she shifted into a cocked stance. Tiny muscle movements in her face hardened her even more than her lecturing tone. "We are a wealthy family living in the River Bottoms on Tenth. You have designer clothing and an attitude of superiority, mingled with a need to appear angelic. In *this* Family, however, you have only one responsibility and that is to be Obedient."

Emma swallowed. "Yes, Mother. I will pick out something suitable and be ready in thirty minutes."

Monique turned and looked Leader in the eye. "Do you smell bleach?" she asked quizzically. Leader's eyes smiled a little. He put his hand on Monique's arm and led her away. He turned the conversation toward some other business. Emma was both relieved and annoyed that they had already forgotten about her. She sighed, even though she never expected them to be anything but what they were. For all her life they had made threats and pronouncements and then talked on to each other as if she ceased to exist.

When she had been in the second grade, she had come into the den one day. Questions she had been developing for weeks at school had swirled through her mind and she had naïvely asked, "Are you my mom and dad?"

Leader looked up from behind his computer, both brows raised expectantly. "Do you *need* a mom and dad?"

As a six-year-old, Emma had not known how to answer that. She shrugged and said, "All the other kids have a mom and dad."

Monique snorted. "All the other kids have an average intelligence. Are you hoping to be like the other kids? Stupid and insignificant?"

She shook her head emphatically and answered the way she had been programmed to answer. "No, ma'am."

"Right," Leader had said firmly, and returned to his computer as if the discussion was over. Monique had likewise returned to her work while Emma just stared at them both in confusion. That may have been the first time she thoroughly felt her insignificance.

Emma hurried up the stairs, pushing her thoughts towards her leaders behind her, hoping their conversation wouldn't turn back to bleach. She went to the shower, thinking exhausted thoughts about an evening with them together. Leader's business took him away most of the time. He was rarely home, so when he was, she found his presence unnerving. On top of that, she could not imagine why Monique had agreed to bring the Family to dinner. It was a waste of good training time for Emma, and it could not possibly help Monique at work. She was working for a law firm that had begged for her. And why wouldn't they, when her fake resume had been so impressive? None of her colleagues had any idea she was not a lawyer because Monique was so good at playing her part. That was what it meant to be a part of the Family. It meant playing a part and creating an image. Emma just did not know why.

She hurried through her showering ritual. She quickly shaved her legs and scrubbed her body. She double-washed her hair, hoping to reduce the smell of bleach. After showering, she moisturized with her $200 bottle of lotion. It probably worked like a $5 bottle, but that was not the point. It was part of the image, part of her part.

Wrapped in a bath sheet, she wound her hair in a towel and then crossed to her room to choose clothing. The styles here were strange. It was as if everyone wanted to be wearing the newest styles but could not for the immodesty factor. They altered the styles then. In keeping with that ridiculous trend, Emma selected a sleeveless yellow sundress and a white baby tee to wear under it. She smiled to herself, because wearing a shirt under a sundress defeated the purpose of wearing a sundress at all. But it was in keeping with current Utah trends.

She found a pair of white strappy shoes at the back of her pristinely organized closet. She removed the tags from the shoes and placed them on her desk. Rooting through her vanity drawer, she discovered a rainbow of expensive nail polish. She carefully painted her toes yellow with white dots. People would notice that she was coordinated from head to toe, but it had to be done nicely or they would expend extra thought. She was wealthy enough she should have had professional manicures.

Walking with a toe separator between her toes, she minced to the vanity and dried her hair. When she failed to get her hair to rat up big and ridiculous the way the girls here did, she chose to pull back the middle front and pin it on her head, then she parted and braided her hair from the nape of her neck. She felt ridiculous with all of the volume she had created on top ending in two braided tails, but it did seem like something an ex-cheerleader would do.

From her drawer of organized jewelry, she selected a pair of dangling earrings and a necklace. After a quick study of herself in the vanity mirror, she added heavy eyeliner and cherry lip gloss.

The next step was to pack a purse. She never carried a purse because her backpack had everything she could ever need. But today she minced into her closet and selected a purse that was much too small to be practical or even fashionable, and she dropped in her lip gloss, school ID, and her phone from beneath her panties in her top drawer. And not too soon.

"Emma!" Monique snapped through the intercom system. "Downstairs, immediately!"

"Yes, Mother." She grabbed her shoes, ripped the toe separators from her feet, and raced toward the stairs.

At the bottom of the stairs, they waited for her. Leader narrowed his eyes slightly at her when she dropped onto her seat on the bottom step to pull on her sandals. She wisely did not look up at him, afraid her outfit or general demeanor would not meet with his approval. There wasn't time to change now. She tugged her shoes on, latched them carefully, and rose to her feet. She avoided his watchful eye.

Scott was nearest her when she stood. He was dressed well in slacks and a long-sleeved t-shirt from one of those fancy boy stores in the mall. His Disney-kid longish hair kept sliding into his eyes and he moved his head to get it out of the way. He was the perfect image of her brother: hair only slightly darker blond and similar eyes.

He shot her an annoyed look from the corner of his eye. It was an expression she knew well on him. He was constantly annoyed with her. It was an inescapable displeasure which Emma had endured for as long as she could remember. Even her earliest memories of him, when she was perhaps four years old, included glares, jabs, and insults. When his superiors were around, he kept it mostly to glares. But not today.

"Glad you could finally join us, Your Highness."

She did not answer him. In her elementary school years, she had discovered that nastiness for nastiness would never work in the Family. If Emma had retorted with a snide comment, she would be scolded for not showing due respect. If she physically lunged at him, as she had half a mind to do, she would be punished for breaking the Aggression Compact. Ignoring him was her best option; the worst she could be accused of was inattention, and anyone who knew her knew she was always paying attention.

"Don't be snide, Scott," Monique interjected as she strolled into the room, eyes and tone blistering. "Until you are required to shave your legs and deep-condition your hair, you do not get to complain about how long it takes a woman to get ready."

Adam nudged Emma with a snort and whispered, "She called you a woman," as if it was the most hilarious statement in the world. Emma looked straight ahead and ignored him, too. He wasn't cold animosity as Scott was. He was rather more taunting. His talent was in delivering comments that belittled or made her feel insecure.

Adam, like Monique, was an unparalleled beauty. The girls fawned over him at school. His hair was the darkest of the three children, nearly black, clean cut and well-styled. He had a dark skin tone and almond-shaped chocolate eyes. He was half-a-head shorter than Leader and Monique, but currently taller than both Scott and Emma. That wouldn't last, Emma was sure; he had stopped growing and they had not. His torn-up jeans belied the "presidential candidate" image his collared shirt and short-cut hair created. He had a smile in his eyes, but to Emma it would always be a wicked smile of the boy who had laughed at her when she had brought home her first misbehavior note from her teacher. His dark, laughing eyes would live forever in her memory along with the wooden spoon Leader used to reinforce good behavior.

As usual, no one said anything to Adam about his comment. He could generally get away with anything.

Monique sauntered toward Leader, hair pinned up and held with a golden clip. Diamonds dangled from either lobe and a matching necklace graced her collarbone. She wore a black cocktail dress with wide straps. It ended partway down her thighs. She carried a gold handbag that precisely matched her strappy gold shoes.

Leader tilted his head as she approached him, and she leaned to kiss his cheek. Despite the enchanting red lipstick, there was no residue left on the side of his face. Watching them interact, it was hard to believe they were not a perfect married couple. Him in his three-piece suit, her in her little black dress. She could be his trophy wife and he her adoring husband. But that wasn't it at all. Every time they left the House to do business, she kissed him that way, but there was no affection in it. It was a ritual that always went the same way. She kissed him, he nodded at her once, she straightened his tie needlessly, and then he nodded toward the exit. Emma did not know why they did it, but they always did. Every time.

"We will take the Lexus," Leader stated. That was Monique's car, but Leader would drive. Leader always drove.

"I'd be happy to drive myself," Adam suggested innocently. Emma agreed with his sentiment, though she would never speak up about it. She would much rather ride with hateful Scott and callous Adam than Leader and Monique. Together, they were like a steel train—cold, unfeeling, and unstoppable.

"I will not repeat myself," Leader said in a voice that implied his words were obvious. He did not look at Adam, but the rebuke was implied: *Don't trifle with me.*

Sufficiently smothered, Adam changed the subject, "Do you have specific instructions?"

Leader exchanged looks of impatience with Monique, who quirked a thin brow at Adam. "We will take the Lexus," she said slowly, in a tone meant to communicate that Adam was an idiot for not realizing those were the instructions. Leader led her through the door with a hand on the small of her back, as if there was nothing more to say about the matter. Adam rolled his eyes once they had walked away.

"Do you believe them?" he asked Scott. Scott shrugged. Emma could believe them. She understood that their superiority would always be diminishing for those beneath them. They held all the answers to the questions Emma, Scott, and Adam wrestled with each day, and they shared nothing.

Adam grabbed the door to the garage before it could swing shut. He ordered, "Let's go!" and held it open for them. When Emma tried to comply, Scott shoved her aside and walked past her. Adam followed on his heels, and Emma was left to snatch the door herself and bring up the rear. Even though Adam was playing the part of her brother, he was not her brother; he was her superior. She sighed at his back.

The silver four-door Lexus, which was supposed to be the family car, was parked in the driveway. Leader opened the passenger door for Monique and the two of them were doing the annoying mind reading thing they did—looking at each other, sharing smiles and expressions that could have meant anything. Of course, Emma could not prove that they read each other's minds; it was not supposed to be possible, but Emma did not put anything past the two of them. They seemed to think similarly, except Leader tended to be menacing and deliberate where Monique was quick and fierce.

"Middle," Adam commanded Emma. He need not have said anything. Emma knew already that she would be sitting in the back in the middle, because it was the least desirable seat in the car and she held the lowest rank. But she said nothing about his command.

She got in the backseat of the car and scooted to the middle. After a glance from Leader through the rearview, she fastened her safety belt. Adam and Scott climbed in on either side of her, buckled, and sat back against the designer leather seats. They jostled Emma on either side until she scrunched herself as small as she could get, folded her arms long across her crossed legs and drew her shoulders inward. Leader's gaze seemed to be on her the entire time he reversed out of the driveway and pulled into the street. Emma carefully kept her head down.

Chapter Three

"What are your goals?" Monique asked him once they were under way. She removed a handgun from her gold bag and opened the chamber to check for bullets. Emma had seen guns in the House before—most of her superiors seemed to have them—but the sight always made her uncomfortable. It dried her mouth and her brain swarmed with questions like fire ants out to protect a hive. *What could Monique possibly need with a handgun at a cocktail party?*

"I intend for us to blend in and charm them. Ideally, I would like to be invited to a family dinner before the evening is through, but I'm not idealistic. Use your wiles and see if you can win their confidence."

A mischievous smile tugged at Monique's mouth as she tucked her gun back into her handbag. "If I managed to win *your* confidence, they should not be much of a problem."

Leader replied to her sass with a dangerous chuckle but said nothing.

"Adam," Monique said, voice changing from liquid charm to the quick authoritative voice she always used with the lower ranks. "My boss has a daughter near your age. See how far you can get her to commit to you. She has a boyfriend, but win her heart if you can."

"In one night?" Adam was amused by the idea. So was Emma, but, of course, she would never say so.

"Of course not," Leader contradicted in his scathing tone. "Tonight, you will only plant the seed. I hardly expect you to work miracles, even if you are pretty enough to capture all young girls' hearts."

Emma thought she would never understand the humor in the Family. Monique and Leader made playful comments to one another all the livelong day, but God forbid anyone else have an enjoyable time!

"Scott," Monique's sedulous instructions continued. Scott did not acknowledge her. He did not so much as lift his head. "You are not to be sullen during dinner. Dial up the computer obsessions and attempt to dominate conversation. Butt in where you ought not to be. Especially try to get anyone talking about the backwards security filters. All we need is one way in, and Amos can tell us the life story of everyone in the room."

"Henshaw is my main target," Leader spoke up in that musical voice. "If he is who I suspect he is, Scott will not have any success. I do not want him to overshoot and lose focus on our objective."

Monique replied with flawless deference, "Yes, Leader." Her clipped tone returned when she went back to addressing Scott. "Don't prod so hard that you make others suspicious. Just be a regular technology enthusiast and ask a lot of questions. Is that clear?"

Scott drew a breath as if preparing to speak, but he let go of it and slumped even farther in his chair. Emma thought it was risky that Scott failed to answer Monique's question, but she did not even seem to notice. She glanced at Leader and the two of them conversed again without ever speaking. She finally looked forward toward the road and true silence fell in the car.

After several awkward moments, Emma cleared her throat and spoke softly.

"Do you have instructions for me?"

Leader caught her eye in the rearview mirror, black pools of displeasure. The car decelerated dramatically, and he pulled to the side of the road. After flipping on the hazard lights, he turned in his seat to peer at her with menacing black eyes. "You need to *listen*, Emma, or you will have very long and painful years learning Obedience in this Family."

Emma was stunned silent and still by his rebuke, and further stunned that he had felt he needed to pull over to the roadside to do it. Without noticing what she was doing, she pressed herself as far from his gaze as the seat would allow.

"I already told you what I expected out of you," Leader went on, his harsh musicality reaching into Emma's stomach and tying knots there. "I will repeat it now for the benefit of this mission and for no other reason, although I warn you that repeating myself is a tedious affair and I will not make a habit of it:

"You are to behave as a modest, straight-A daughter we can brag about. You are to *blend in* in this society. Be a girl who would not join the cheer squad because it was too cliquey, and the uniforms were immodest. Is that clear enough for you, or will I need to repeat myself *yet again*?" The threat in those words chilled Emma to her core—frozen butterflies dropped like dead weight against the bottom of her belly.

Hurriedly, she shook her head and whispered, "That won't be necessary, Leader. I remember your instructions." She looked down at her hands and tried to control her mortification. She had not realized that the instructions about how she should dress applied to the entire evening.

When his hand reached between the seats toward her, Emma saw it in her peripheral vision. She tried to press herself into the seat some more, but she was already as far from him as she could get. It was not nearly far enough. As if there was no obstacle, he grasped her chin to lift her face, drawing her gaze back to his. It devoured her.

"You are to refer to me as 'Father.'"

His reminder vibrated through the air between them. She heard it, but she also breathed it in and tasted it. She felt it, like lashes against her skin. No wielded wooden spoon could have been as terrifying as this velvet tone.

She forced her voice to produce sound, but it came out as a whisper, "Yes, Father." His grip was painfully strong, but not as if he wanted to hurt her. It was the natural grip with which he held onto the things he owned. And the grip of his hand was not nearly as strong as the grip of his eyes.

He relinquished both at once and turned back to the wheel. As he signaled to take the car out into traffic, he pointed an accusing finger at Monique. He said nothing, but again they seemed not to need words to communicate with one another. She nodded, as if accepting blame for Emma's ineptness, and then sat back against her seat and looked out the side window.

"I will be more direct in my instructions," she assured him, but she sounded angry. That did not bode well, Emma suspected. It suggested Monique would be intensifying her discipline regime. Emma would have to resist the temptation to dye her hair or paint her fingernails again for a while.

Once they were underway again, Scott shoved Emma to get her out of his way, then Adam pushed at her, as well. She was once again forced to sit forward so they could spread out. Leader watched it all in the rearview but said nothing. Emma refused to meet his gaze.

"I hardly expect we will have them in the palms of our hands before the evening is finished," Leader told Monique. His tone had returned to moderate intensity. The change was so vast, it was difficult to believe this was the same man who had spoken so severely before. Emma found herself wondering, as she always did when he was home from his business trips, if he had multiple personalities. Or perhaps he was bipolar. She kept her thoughts to herself, though, because her heart had still not returned to a normal rhythm.

"They are very proud of the hold they have, trivial as it is. We can subdue them tonight, but they will see us coming, Leader."

"Only if they are who we suspect they are." He did not reprimand *her* for calling him by his title.

"They *are* who we think they are," Monique insisted.

Leader raised his dangerous eyebrow at her, just as she often did with the Juniors. "Cockiness is not the same as Confidence, Monique. You ought to remember that."

Emma was always curious about what the Senior members in the Family were talking about. They had entire conversations Emma did not understand. All of their conversations confused her. She kept her eyes down, but she listened intently, hoping they would let something slip that she could make sense of.

"I am *Confident* they are who we think they are. Everything adds up. And just in time, too, because if their deal goes through, we're screwed. And I, for one, am tired of pretending we are not who we actually are."

Leader's smile seemed teasing, but his tone was dark. "Your Confidence is adorable."

"When we are on our way home from this highly successful endeavor, I would like you to recall that you said those words to me." She was not smiling. Her voice was calculated and cold.

"Lighten up," he ordered sharply. "It is my responsibility to question your assertions."

She snorted. "I think most of your responsibilities are self-appointed."

"Careful," he sang back at her. The warning must not have concerned her, because she rolled her eyes. The last time Emma rolled her eyes at Leader, he had slapped her face. Now she was careful to do it behind his back.

"Turn here," Monique prompted him as they approached an intersection.

As he flipped his blinker on, he raised a brow at Monique. "Telling me how to drive now? Really?"

She smiled but kept her eyes ahead of her, on the road. "Not telling you *how*, Leader, telling you *where*."

He chuckled. Emma studied his face in the mirror, memorizing the dancing shadows on his features as the lights shone across them from overhead street lights. Besides the exceptional beauty they all shared, he could have been just anybody. He could have been any man driving his family to a party. There was nothing particularly remarkable about him. He did not emanate power or demand worship. He could have been a regular guy, until he met her eye. It was his gaze that enthralled her; powerful, direct, passionate. She tore herself away from it with no little difficulty. She was grateful when his gaze did not pursue her but fell instead on Scott.

"Scott, have you perked up yet? You have a part to play tonight." He was harsh again, like an abrupt squall at deep sea.

Scott said nothing, which in Emma's opinion was a dangerous decision, but it did not seem to affect Leader. His attention was on driving. The car pulled through another light and into the parking lot of a country club.

He parked in one of the insanely wide parking stalls. Even if someone had been trying, they would not have been able to ding another parked car with slamming doors. Leader had been lucky to get a spot near the building, since the tiny country club lot was nearly full of expensive cars with personalized license plates. Perhaps luck was never in it, though, because Emma had never known him to park in the back lot of anywhere.

"Adam," he instructed, before clicking the unlock button. "Do your part well, because the daughter might be the key to this whole thing." He looked over his shoulder to acknowledge Adam's affirmative response. But instead of exiting the vehicle, he turned the sharp gaze onto Scott. "Perk. Up."

Emma never actually felt sorry for Scott. He was vicious toward her, so she felt no need to spare him any good thoughts. But seeing him come under Leader's threatening gaze made her the tiniest bit nervous for him. He was expected to be Obedient, just as she was, but also Diligent in all circumstances. He had already brought home a pink slip which would be seen as a failure to be Diligent, so he did not stand a chance of escaping Leader unscathed today. But if he continued to be disobedient, it would be so much worse for him! Fortunately, he Obeyed.

"Yes, Father." He sat up and pushed the brooding expression away.

Leader did not respond, like he often did with Emma. Once he had gotten the desired result, he promptly forgot about Scott and moved on. He climbed out of the car and pocketed the keys. While he walked around to open Monique's door, she turned a furious glare on the three children in the backseat.

"No mistakes," she warned them. She lingered especially long on Emma, and only broke away because Leader opened the passenger door.

Monique put on her smile like it was a mask in a play. She reached a hand out to Leader and let him lead her from the car. He drew her out and then closed the door. Adam and Scott were not so gentlemanly. Scott closed his door right after he got out and Adam almost closed his in Emma's face. She caught it with her hand and glared at his back. By then Leader had walked around the car. He caught the door from her, pulled it open, and reached a hand out to assist her. Not meeting his eye, she accepted his hand and let him pull her out. He closed the door and clicked the lock on the key ring in his pocket. Emma smoothed her dress and controlled the emotions on her face to cover her frustration with the boys and conflicting emotions about Leader.

"Come, children," he called, taking Monique's arm and leading them toward the clubhouse.

"Who talks like that?" Adam scoffed, loudly enough for his skepticism to be heard by all. He did not hesitate to comply, though, and, as always, he was not reprimanded for his disrespectful commentary.

Chapter Four

The clubhouse was a white brick building with large windows and vaulted ceilings. The glass doors were framed with light and flowers, and a professionally created and mounted poster on an easel declared the party was in the ballroom. They walked through the door held open by Leader, and then followed him across the main entrance into the candlelit ballroom. It was filled with floral decorations and people dressed in evening finery. Emma was infused with smugness when she saw that she was not the only young woman present in a baby tee and sundress. She so had these people figured out.

"Ah, Monique!" cried a man near the entrance. His suit was Armani and she could not identify his shoes except that they were probably outrageously expensive. His hair was styled in a faux-hawk, and he wore eyeliner. *He is a major homo,* Emma thought.

"I am so glad you could make it," he said in his doting tone, hugging Monique and kissing her on either cheek. Then he sized up Leader. It was kind of amusing to watch this flamer check Leader out as if he were leaning against a bar counter. "And who have we here?" he asked, emphasizing each word in the annoyingly flirtatious way only gay men could properly achieve.

"This is my husband, Eric," Monique answered, flashing a bright smile. Although this was not the first time she had heard them use this specific alias, Emma had no idea if his name was actually Eric. She had always referred to him as "Leader." Monique turned toward him, wrapping a sensuous hand around his arm. "Eric, please meet my colleague, Donald Aaron."

"Nice to meet you, Donald," Leader said, putting his free hand out.

"Pleasure," the other man said, shaking Leader's hand. "We *love* your wife. She is the up-and-coming lawyer in the firm. Adorable and incredible."

Leader turned his perfect smile on Monique. He bore such a look of adoration that it took Emma a moment to remember he was acting. "She is incredible," he admitted, voice as thick as honey. He looked back at Donald, and the electricity alive in his black eyes momentarily stunned the gay man silent. This was the gaze that made the masses part when Leader walked among them. His gaze held his power over Emma and everyone else in the world.

"And gorgeous!" Donald choked and recovered. He presented Monique's dress as if she were a prize on a game show. "Is this the new Marc Jacobs?"

"It is," she admitted, posing for Donald's benefit. Then she wrapped herself around Leader's arm once more. "Eric selected it."

They had a nauseating conversation about clothing for several minutes. If Emma had not been so disgusted with their mockery of love, she would have been amazed at how well Leader could pretend to be interested in something as dull as Monique's dress. After far too long, Donald finally noticed the three other people standing in the doorway.

"Are these your children?" He gave a gasp that Emma supposed was meant as a compliment.

Leader presented them. "These are three of our four children," he said. "Lara, our eldest, is on a date tonight. This is Adam, Scott, and our baby, Emma." Donald shook their hands as they were introduced, and they murmured polite words to him.

"Four children," Donald said in a scolding tone. He raised his brows at Monique. "How did you never lose your figure? It's a modern miracle."

Emma investigated the ballroom to avoid scoffing aloud. She doubted Monique had ever had any children. Less a miracle; more a total deception. Even if she did have children, Emma was not one of them. It was genetically impossible for them to look so dissimilar if she were. She could possibly have been Leader's spawn, but Emma was certain that was also not accurate. She belonged to neither of them by blood. The Family bond was tighter and more demanding than a genetic one. Monique laughed politely and moved with Leader into the ballroom, away from Donald.

"Insufferable," Leader hissed behind a smile.

"Isn't he?" Monique replied, smoothing the front of Leader's jacket as any loving wife might do. But it was just to get close enough to say, "Every day I want to murder him."

Leader laughed—a party laugh for the benefit of anyone who might be watching—but his words were stern. "Do not do anything stupid."

She gave him a vicious smile. "I never would." Her eyes flashed dangerously.

Leader stood that way with her, locked in her gaze until she lowered her eyes, deferring to his superiority. He turned on his "children" then. Snapping his fingers impatiently, he said, "Go, go, go. No mistakes."

Emma watched with longing as Adam and Scott both escaped into the mass of party guests. She knew better than to follow. Her part included an element of being a child to brag about. That meant she needed to be on hand as a reference for her "parents" to show off.

After they left, the evening was a blur of introductions and polite conversation. Emma was hugged, kissed, complimented, mooned over, and often completely ignored. But she played the part well. She patterned herself after a couple of girls from the school. She was aloof, flirtatious, and coy by turns.

"Your daughter is delightful," a young man said from beside his wealthy, pompous father. "Perhaps you would permit me to dance with her."

No, no, no... She begged Monique in her head, but it was Leader who answered.

"Not on your life, young man. Your reputation precedes you." Leader encircled Emma's shoulders with a protective embrace. "My Emma is too young to be dancing with some wild, handsome rogue."

She could have cursed, because now she would *have* to dance with the boy. Leader had set her up to rebel. She pushed away from him and practiced her best annoyed expression.

"Daddy, I do not need you to protect me." She flashed the young man a winning smile and lied, "I would be happy to dance with you." Leader chuckled when the boy shrugged apologetically at him and led Emma away. Behind her, she could hear Leader talking about how children grow up too fast and learn to cop an attitude.

"My name is Benjamin," the boy said. He had brown hair and blue eyes, and was probably two or three years older than she was. "I do not know if my father remembered to mention that. He gets wrapped up in conversation sometimes and forgets I am there."

She let off a small scoff. "I know the feeling," she agreed. "My father and mother—perhaps especially my mother—often trip right over me at these parties. I was actually left behind once before when they failed to remember that they brought me along."

He laughed. "You're lying."

She smiled but did not reveal that her story was actually true, although the details were changed. Leader left her at a school function without telling her where he had gone. It was not so much that he had *forgotten* her as that Adam had been picked up by police and needed his attention more than Emma needed him at the school function. The trouble was that no one remembered Emma until several hours after the school had closed. Instead of causing trouble for the school staff, she pretended to leave with some other kids, but had hidden in the dark behind the school dumpster for hours. In Queens. She was lucky she hadn't been killed.

"My father left me once without telling my mother to take me home. When she left, she assumed I was with my father," Benjamin told her. "Self-absorbed bastards." His words should have been softened by the smile on his face, but she thought she could see real pain in his eyes.

"Anyway, my name is Benjamin. And did I hear your mother say your name is Emma?"

"Yes," she replied. "Emma Harris of the River Bottoms Harrises."

He laughed. "Then I am Benjamin Stillwell of the Alpine Heights Stillwells."

She smiled at him and was surprised to find it was a genuine smile. She was surprised she was having a good time. It had never crossed her mind that she might go to this party tonight and enjoy herself. It was business. But Benjamin was rather pleasant for a pretentious, spoiled, rich kid.

"Where do you attend school?"

"Avanair," she answered, glancing over his shoulder at Monique who watched them from across the room with a scowl. That wasn't pretend. Emma looked away before she could motion to her, and was pleased when Benjamin spun her into the middle of the dance floor.

"Wait, you go to the prep school up the canyon? Smarty!"

She rolled her eyes at him playfully. "Where do you go?"

"Mountain Park. You know, the big pretentious school you can see from the freeway after the point of the mountain?"

"That's a school?" she teased. "I thought it was a resort, with all those paved walkways and flowering gardens. What do you study? Aromatherapy?"

He scoffed. "Mountain Park is a pretty penitentiary, is what it is. The garden and all of that are to attract wealthy parents of the unfortunate kids who are doomed to spend their lives trapped behind those stone walls. They would probably put bars up on the windows if it wouldn't spoil the architectural design."

Emma laughed at the idea and patted him on the shoulder as if to console him. "Poor little rich boy at his fancy resort school."

His mouth dropped open in a disbelieving scoff. "You can ditch at Avanair just by climbing over their walls! If *I* want to ditch, I basically have to swim across a moat and fight off a dragon."

Ditching school was a completely foreign concept to her. She knew other kids did it sometimes, but she had never even considered it. School was her work and contribution to the Family. Academia was her job, and Leader was a harsh taskmaster. But she considered it for the sake of argument.

"You could just...not go, I guess," she offered him speculatively. "I couldn't get away with that because I ride to school with my brothers, but if you don't..."

Benjamin shook his head at her. "Rookie. You have to go to your first class. If you're not on the roll, they'll call your parents."

Oh. She hadn't thought about that. Avanair was very strict on attendance. Without a doctor's note, students who failed to attend school could be disenrolled. Emma shuddered at the thought of how Leader would handle that kind of misbehavior.

"Emma!" Monique's distinct call broke through the dancers all the way from the side of the dance floor. Emma stiffened.

"My mother is calling," she told her dance partner. "Excuse me." She tried to pull away from him, but he would not relinquish her so easily. He tightened his hold and gave her a playful smile.

"Don't let her bossing pull you off the dance floor until you're ready." His smile was intoxicating. She could feel herself getting drunk by it. A glance toward Monique sobered her up, though. The woman had murder in her eyes, and her arm was looped loosely around the handbag where she carried her deadly weapon. Emma had never actually seen her pull a weapon in public, but she didn't put it past her.

"There is no sense in upsetting my mother," Emma told Benjamin. "She can be extremely...excitable."

He chuckled at that. "Very well. She beckons, and you immediately respond, like a dutiful daughter. She has you quite well trained, doesn't she?" He turned to lead her off the floor like a gentleman. "You're a goody."

The emotion that bubbled up from the pit of her stomach was unfamiliar to Emma. There was displeasure at his gentle accusation, but not the same kind of displeasure she had from Scott's hatred or Adam's taunts. This was more personal.

"I'm not a goody," she argued. "Whatever that means. I just don't see the sense in upsetting my mother and forcing her out onto the dance floor to humiliate me in front of this big crowd."

He stopped walking to look at her thoughtfully. He smiled again. "And you think she would do that?"

Emma raised her brows at him. "She would *definitely* do that."

"So, it's noble, what you're doing. You're keeping her from creating a scene and embarrassing herself and her colleagues, and you're sparing my tender emotions." Before she could argue with his outrageous interpretation, he gave her his disarming smile, and added, "You are a goody."

She pulled her arm away from his. "Then you must be a baddie."

He laughed and, before she knew what had happened, he had taken her arm again and led her off the dance floor. He inclined his head to her once, then to Monique, who returned a violent scowl.

"A pleasure," he said, then turned and walked away before either of them could reply.

Chapter Five

Monique watched, glittering fury, as Benjamin strode away. "Having fun?" she snapped, but as always, she did not wait for an answer. "They are getting ready to serve dinner and your father wants you to sit with him. He's across the room with Mr. Henshaw. Do you see him?"

She said yes. She could never *not* see Leader when he was in a room. His electric presence magnified her fears and shocked her to silence. It beckoned her with an insistent glow, like insects into a zapper. She knew she would be fried by him, but she struggled to resist the urge to draw nearer. Emma could pinpoint him in any crowd at any venue. He locked gazes with her from across the room, and she felt compelled to move.

"Go to him," Monique allowed. Then at the last second, she grabbed Emma's arm above the elbow. It jerked Emma out of Leader's gaze and forced her to look at Monique. She hissed, "Stay away from Benjamin Stillwell. I think he's trouble." When she sauntered away, returning to her party smile once more, she left Emma behind with bruises forming on her arm. Emma glared after her retreating figure before she caught herself and adjusted her expression to keep with her character. Benjamin had been polite and a welcome relief from the tedious conversation of the adults. But she need not have mourned the loss of him. He was nothing, because Monique was her senior and had given her a direct command. She could not disobey Monique without a countermanding order from Leader.

Emma wove through the crowds, keeping a look out for Benjamin so she could avoid him as she had been commanded. When she reached Leader's side, she touched his arm to let him know she was there without interrupting his conversation. He reached up and patted her hand on his arm in acknowledgment. Then his hand slid across her back and came to rest on her opposite shoulder. It was a cage, but to the outsiders it just looked like a loving father cloaking his daughter with affection.

"I have been nothing but proud of my wife," Leader was saying to one of Monique's colleagues. "She comes home each day ecstatic about her accomplishments at work. I can honestly say I have never seen her happier. Don't you think, baby?"

That was at her. She glanced up at him uncertainly but recovered quickly and smiled. "Yes, Father." She looked at the other man. "She has been able to talk of nothing else. It all seemed terribly tedious to me, but she loves it." The man laughed at Emma's tone of forbearance.

Leader squeezed her shoulder in a brief crush of pain for her negative spin, then flashed his flawless smile. "If only I could drum up as much enthusiasm about work." Effortlessly deflected.

"What is it you do?" the other man asked.

Leader took a sip of the cocktail in his other hand before answering. "I'm the editor for an online magazine."

In her years as his subordinate, Emma had heard him assign hundreds of job titles to himself. He had been a doctor, a priest, an accountant, a correspondent, and multitudes of other positions that he always seemed to know and understand on a deep enough level that people accepted him at his word.

"How is that?" the man asked, evidently enthralled with the conversation. Emma wasn't. She allowed her mind to wander, although Leader's grip did not relinquish her. She attempted to appear as if she was listening, but really she was looking for Benjamin Stillwell. She could stay away from him and still wonder about him.

When dinner was announced, the man nodded politely to Leader and made an excuse that he needed to find his family. It was probably just to get away from the mind-numbing discussion of online magazine marketing troubles. Leader smiled until the man disappeared into the crowd. Then his congenial expression faded, and he turned too slowly to look at Emma. He said nothing aloud, but the ferocity of his rebuke was there in his black eyes.

Monique's timely arrival saved Emma from cowering. Leader removed his hand from Emma to escort his wife to dinner. They were a handsome couple, and many eyes stole jealous glances their direction. Emma fell into step behind them, keeping her distance because she wanted to, but still close enough to hear if one of them should mention her.

The grand dining hall had wooden tables covered with perfectly white linens and floral centerpieces. The chandelier overhead was made of hundreds of crystals and tiny lights. It gave the room a magical glow, like the light from hundreds of fairies, bouncing off the windows and ballroom walls. The magic was somewhat spoiled by the pressing throngs of fancy-dressed people. Leader had no trouble navigating through the crowd; they parted as he walked through as if he were royalty. Emma wasn't certain they even realized they were doing it.

Through a gap in the crowd, Emma caught a glimpse of Scott. He had evidently recovered from the sullenness that had kept him silent in the car; he laughed and talked with a crowd of older men at a table across the room. One of the men slapped him playfully on the back, and Emma found herself scowling until she corrected it. She could not imagine how anyone could get enjoyment out of Scott. Even playing a part, she despised him.

Before reaching her chair, she spotted Adam at a different table. He sat too near a young woman who gave him a coy smile. It was not at all discouraging. *Slut*, Emma said in her head, but her face did not betray her thoughts this time. She was controlled and Obedient.

Leader and Monique led her to one of the tables near the front of the room where the bandstand was. The ensemble band on the stage was playing a simple instrumental piece that she identified as soft jazz. It was by no means as fascinating to her as the music she had heard at school assemblies or the occasional forbidden snatches of radio in the car when Adam drove to school. The jazz was light and meant as background, but it intrigued her. Her first day in junior high school she had heard the band play and had dallied in the hall to listen. She missed a full class period before she was caught by a hall monitor. She had not gotten distracted on purpose then. Music just intrigued her. It did so now, as well, and it took Leader clearing his throat to remind her of where she was.

He had already pulled Monique's chair and now held Emma's for her. Blushing a little, she folded herself into her seat as gracefully as she could muster. She unfolded her napkin and placed it in her lap, then folded her hands there, as well. She tried to copy Monique's movements but did not have her dangerous grace.

Black and white clad servers walked through the aisles between tables, filling water glasses and pouring wine. Emma watched Monique and Leader carefully in order to match their movements. A serving woman poured wine into Leader's glass, but before she could fill Emma's, Monique stretched a beautifully mani-cured hand across it.

"None for our underage daughter, please," she told the serving girl in a sweet tone that could have killed. When the girl flamed to her hairline and moved away, Monique shook her head at her boss in the chair beside her. "Really, how hard a job is it to pour wine?"

Henshaw, a thick man with neatly trimmed gray hair and a mustache, chuckled agreement about the server's inadequacy. But then he peered hard at Emma beneath his gray brows. "Tell me about this daughter of yours, Monique. She doesn't look a bit like you."

"Emma?" Monique laughed, sultry and amused. "No, I'm afraid she took her Daddy's genes and left mine by the wayside." She gave Emma a fond look, even going so far as to touch her head affectionately. Emma had to restrain herself from pulling away. "Em's our baby." She looked back at her boss with raised brows. "She's not at all like her troublesome brothers."

"Oh?" Henshaw barked a laugh. "They give you trouble? I have a tough time believing you let anyone give you trouble."

Monique laughed again. "They could try the patience of a stone, I think. But our sweet Emma never gives us an ounce of trouble."

Lies! Emma tried to stay out of trouble, but that did not mean she had not seen her fair share. Sometimes it felt like she received the brunt of every problem in the House and was the most trouble of them all. Monique and Leader were stellar actors, though, because even Emma got sucked into their story, trying to imagine what it must be like to have mischievous brothers and be her parents' favorite.

"Emma is a delight," Leader added. "You know, she has had a 4.2 grade point average all through school." He patted Emma's knee affectionately. "She has been offered a prime scholarship to Brighten Boarding School in Michigan."

Henshaw blinked in surprise. "Really? That's a prestigious school, young lady. You should be proud." Emma only got a chance to smile before the man turned his questions back to the adults. "When will she go?"

"I am not sure I am willing to part with her, frankly," Leader answered just as Monique tried to speak. She gave Leader a practiced glare.

"Her scholarship is for next year," Monique informed the table. Then sternly to Leader, "And we are sending her, Eric. This is the opportunity of a lifetime."

Leader nudged Emma under the table, and she flashed a smile at Henshaw. "They have been arguing about this since I received the notification about my acceptance to the school."

It was true she had received a scholarship to the Brighten Boarding School, but what they failed to mention was that Emma had applied in secret. Monique had been furious with her when the acceptance arrived. She made Emma sit in the room while she called Leader and explained the situation to him. He diverted his business itinerary to pay the school a visit and turn down the scholarship on her behalf. And then he had come home to deal with her personally. Thinking about it still made her tremble, so she tried to force it from her mind.

"Are you going to attend an Ivy League university?"

"Sarah Lawrence, with any luck," Emma replied.

"Harvard or Yale," Monique contradicted in her stern voice.

"Or something closer to home," Leader suggested with an affectionate pat to Emma's knee. "There's no need to ship you off to the other end of the country, Emma. It would be best for you to stay close to home." Emma looked up at him and gave a smile she hoped Henshaw believed was affectionate, even though meeting Leader's eye was always arduous for her.

"Well, I can see she is her Daddy's girl," Henshaw crowed. Emma nearly sighed with relief. "I was exactly the same way with my daughter, Eric. I have sons, but it's your daughters who steal your heart away. Am I right?"

Leader slung an arm over Emma's shoulders and gave a squeeze. "Too true. I'll never forget my little Em, the way she wrapped her arms around my neck for the very first time." He was far too good an actor. His voice sounded reminiscent, and Emma felt for a moment that she could remember a time when she had been enthralled enough with him that she had wrapped her arms around him. But she had seen him play dozens of roles with flawless accuracy. She sipped at her water to dispel the images she created, angry at herself for giving in to the little fantasy family they created here this evening.

"Where is your daughter now?" Leader asked, scanning the room.

Henshaw put on a dejected look, though it was all in fun. "She went overseas to school at Oxford."

Leader winced. "That's a long way."

Henshaw nodded. "Married an Englishman and moved to London."

Leader winced some more. Then shot a look at Emma from the corner of his eye. "Maybe Emma will go to the U." Henshaw laughed out loud.

"Go Utes," Emma said, but dryly and without any enthusiasm. The University of Utah would probably be where she did attend college, if they stayed in Utah long enough, because she could not imagine Leader allowing her to get so far away from the Family as an eastern school.

Monique leaned across the table and touched Emma's chin. "Don't you listen to them, Emma," she said. "I will see to it you get into a school that deserves you. Not some local state university." She cocked an eyebrow at Leader. "Honestly! As if I would ever let her attend a local school. I may as well send her to a community college."

Leader shrugged. "A degree is a degree."

"Says the Princeton graduate," Monique declared sarcastically to her boss.

Henshaw offered Emma a conspiratorial smile. "They do this a lot, don't they?"

No, she thought. To her knowledge they never talked about her unless she was in trouble. But she didn't say that.

"Every day. After a while you get used to it and it just becomes senseless background droning. The first minute they aren't looking, I will print off pamphlets about Oxford. It seems to me your daughter knew what she was doing."

Henshaw laughed, completely charmed by her. Emma smiled in response, pleased that he had bought the entire charade. She now understood why Leader and Monique wanted her to be a daughter they could brag about. Henshaw idolized his daughters. They wanted to build common ground with him, and children were always a convenient common ground. Or they wanted her to distract him. She had no way of knowing which, since her only instructions were to be a well-dressed, well-behaved girl.

A salad plate was placed in front of her. She knew from the numerous forks at her place setting that this would be a multi-course meal. She watched Monique and copied her movements. Since they did not resemble each other in appearances, she attempted to sell their relationship through mannerisms.

"How old are you, Emma?" Henshaw asked after he had a chance to try his salad. He snapped his fingers and passed the plate to a server in disgust.

"14," she answered.

"Not until next month," Leader argued. "Stop trying to age yourself prematurely."

She shrugged at Leader. In actuality, she would be fourteen in a matter of days. She did not know if he was just playing parts now or if he really did not know her birthday. It was possible, she supposed. Birthdays were of no importance in the Family. They passed practically without acknowledgement every year. It was a day that held little significance to her; a passing of time that meant nothing except it made her change her answer to the question, *How old are you?* The first year she even realized she had a birthday, she was turning ten.

"It's close enough to say 14," she argued playfully, acting her part. "Honestly, Father."

"Honestly, you are 13 until next month," he insisted.

Henshaw laughed again. "You sound so much like my Lindsey, it is startling. She was always trying to age herself, grow up too fast. Just wait, Eric! Wait until Emma has a boyfriend. That's a dire change..."

Henshaw trailed off when Leader bolted to his feet. The man's gray eyebrows turned downward in surprise. Leader was no longer laughing or acting, his face was a thunderhead.

"Eric," Monique tried to soothe him. Emma felt cold stones forming in the pit of her stomach again. Why was he upset at the mention of a boyfriend? Emma had never had the least interest in boys. In fact, besides her inane lab partner, the only boy Emma had ever talked to was Benjamin Stillwell on the dance floor.

Leader did not let Monique speak.

"Excuse me." He backed away, even forgetting himself so far as to allow his cloth napkin to slip to the ground under his feet. He strode from the room, commanding far too much attention from the crowds again. They whispered about him after he walked out of the room.

"Did I..." Henshaw gestured toward the exit, "...offend him in some way?"

Monique forced a smile. "No, no. He's not that excitable. I mean, God knows he'll meet any prospective boyfriends at the door with a shotgun, but I think he's prepared for that."

Henshaw chuckled a little, but his formerly good humor had paled. He looked around for something to do, saw his empty setting, and picked up his wine cup instead.

Emma had an awkward feeling of unease. Perhaps Leader's abrupt exit had nothing to do with this party or the part they were playing at all; it was too sudden to be acting. He was too good an actor to make this kind of mistake. She was relatively certain their goal had been to put Henshaw at ease. This certainly had not done it.

"Emma," Monique recalled her attention. "Eat your salad."

"Yes, Mother."

Emma picked up her fork and flashed Henshaw a smile.

"Tell me about Lindsey," she invited him, tugging him back to their objective. He blinked at Emma and finally smiled in return. With little prodding, he was back to talking about his Oxford-educated, English-wife daughter. Emma nodded along and listened attentively, except occasionally when she noticed Monique was lost in thought.

Chapter Six

"I did my best!" Adam snapped at Monique from the passenger seat of the Lexus. She was driving with her eyes focused straight ahead and her lips pressed tight. From the back seat, Emma watched their interaction, knowing that Monique was not actually angry at Adam, even though he had failed to meet his mission objectives. The stress in her eyes was for the fact that Leader had never returned to the party after his abrupt exit.

"I will not listen to excuses," she replied tersely. She pointed a finger at Adam accusatorily. "If your Confidence faltered and you couldn't close the deal, I will not listen to you whine about it. You had a mission and you failed. Have the Confidence to admit your failure."

"She wasn't interested!" Adam snarled. Emma was accustomed to his taunts, but not his anger. He generally managed to temper his impulses. "I practically threw myself at that stupid girl. She laughed and flirted as if she was interested, but in the end, she just wanted a dance partner until her boyfriend showed up. When he finally did, he threatened to kill me."

"And you were scared?"

Adam scoffed because of course he wasn't scared. He had been Guild-trained after all, which meant he had spent his life preparing for any kind of attack or aggression. The other young man would not have stood a chance in a fight. Adam swore at Monique in his fury and slunk into his seat.

"You watch your language!"

Adam's answer was fouler than his previous statement and Emma winced. It was such a dangerous thing, disobedience. Obedience was the first Skill introduced in the Family, and it continued to be expected forever. Emma had years of lectures in her head about Obedience. Leader's most famous words echoed in her mind every day: *"Obedience is not a gift you give to your superiors. We persistently require it because it is the gift you give yourself, and it keeps you safe and focused."* His directive was the ruler against which she measured her every word, action, and, often, even intention. She could not imagine ever having the guts to deliberately disobey Monique or Leader. She could not even remember a time when she had seriously considered it.

"Adam, don't you—"

"No!" Adam railed, losing the last of his reserve. He slammed his fist against the door. It was a hard strike; he was lucky the airbags didn't deploy. The Family was full of violent people. Every day they had martial arts training on top of regular strength and resilience training. They were disciplined harshly, expected to Obey without question, held to absurdly exacting standards; it was enough for anyone to become violent. It made sense to Emma why Adam would get upset enough to react violently and disrespectfully, but it started her heart racing on his behalf.

"I did what I was told to do. I seduced that girl. It's not my fault she did not go for it. It's not my fault her boyfriend ousted me. What was I was supposed to do?" He slammed his fist against the door again. "Push him out of the way and demand the girl sleep with me?"

"You were only supposed to plant the seed tonight," Scott reminded from the backseat. A little too quippy; he was celebrating success with his mission for the night.

Monique snapped, "Shut up!" at Scott at the same time Adam jerked around in the seat and tried to hit him. Scott dropped below his hold, diving across Emma's lap. Adam's flying fist nearly contacted with her face, but she moved just in time. Though she had been taught to respond with blocks and return aggression, she could not keep herself from screaming.

"Turn around!" Scott roared at Adam, grabbing his arm and trying to force him into the front seat. Adam caught hold of Scott with one hand and slammed his head forward into the seat. Emma drew herself into her knees against the back seat as the Aggression Compact flew all to hell. Scott and Adam threw punches in the confined space, each managing to make contact with the other. In most families, that would probably have been enough and even adrenaline would not have made brothers continue to fight one another once they had each thrown a real punch or two. But resilience training made for dire fights in the Family; no one would stop just because they were in pain.

Monique shouted one order, but it was lost in the pandemonium. The car screeched to the roadside and slammed into park. From seemingly nowhere, Monique's handgun was there in the middle of the grappling arms and legs, trained on Adam's temple. She clicked a bullet into the chamber.

"*Stand down!*"

Self-preservation worked on him. He lifted his hands toward the ceiling of the car, releasing his hold on Scott. Scott slunk back against his own seat, breathing heavily from rage and exertion. The car was full of their silence. Pulsating terror raised the hair on Emma's arms and the back of her neck. Adam's chest heaved, and Emma was certain it was fear for his life.

Monique's voice was cooler when she spoke again, but still too loud in the heavy silence. "Form 28!" She lowered the gun but did not put it away.

Adam did not move a muscle. In his peripheral view, he could see the gun was no longer trained on him, but his hands did not lower, and he continued to stare straight ahead.

Emma knew the forms up to number 73—the one she was currently trying to master. They were focus techniques and movement methods she had been taught as part of her martial arts training. Everyone in the House learned the forms, advancing in complexity and stamina as they built on previous movements. The forms could be strenuous, time consuming, and sometimes painful, but always required centered focus. It made sense to Emma that Monique would require Adam to form, because it would force him to calm down. Unfortunately, instead of immediately Obeying her, as he ought to, he let out a raging breath and lowered his arms. He made no move to comply. He slouched back against his seat and stared straight ahead at the street sign directly in front of the parked car.

"Now." Monique's voice had cooled to a dangerous degree, and her gaze on Adam never wavered. The fact that she was warning him was surprising for Emma; she thought he should not take it lightly.

Adam glared straight ahead, rebellious. "We are on the side of the fucking road!"

Monique only blinked at him. She did that when her subordinates stated the obvious. She had calmed to a simmer now and Emma was relatively certain she was more dangerous in her simmering wrath than her outright rage. The time passing felt like a flexing rubber band, stretching tighter and tighter while Adam's mortal danger increased.

The band did not snap. Adam snarled some foul comment under his breath and shoved the car door open. He slammed it shut behind him as he stalked off the roadside into the brush. Emma lost sight of him in the darkness. Monique, as graceful and stately as ever, unfolded herself from the car, taking her keys with her.

"Stay here," she ordered before closing the door. Emma and Scott were left alone in the car.

As if the presence of their superiors had been a plug in an overfilling tub, their exit drained the car of its tension. Slowly, it diminished until the heat of antagonism was gone, replaced by the chill of the early autumn night. Now that she felt relatively safe, Emma unfolded herself, putting her feet back on the floorboard and adjusting her seatbelt so it wasn't choking her. She watched Scott pick himself up from the seat.

Adrenaline from the fight left him, and he let out the slightest groan. Probably from pain; he had been hit multiple times, and at least once in the ear. He straightened with some effort and then tugged for a few moments at his seatbelt until he had it around himself securely. He let his head fall back against the headrest, and he looked up at the dark ceiling above them—beyond it, really, into his thoughts.

Lights from passing cars lit up his chin and the sockets of his eyes. In those streaming lights, Emma caught glimpses of him as a little boy. He had helped her up once when she had fallen on the pavement in front of their elementary school. She had been in kindergarten, he in second grade. He had seemed so strong then, grabbing her under the arms and hauling her to her feet, snatching her backpack from the pavement and pushing it into her arms. Her little girl tears leaked over her eyelids, and she had murmured, "I'm okay," to ease the tension in him. The eyes that had stared down at her in concern back then were the same ones that gazed up at the ceiling now.

Scott turned to glower at her in the dark of the back seat, and Emma's memory filled in. The concern in his eyes back then had been for himself rather than her. He had shoved her down on the concrete as soon as Leader's car drove away up the street. Then, when Scott had realized he could get into trouble for hurting Emma, he helped her stand back up. Even ten years ago, he hated her.

Emma still felt the need to ease the tension between them, like she had at the kindergarten door so long ago.

"Strange party," she told him, keeping her voice neutral and soft. He grunted but that was all. No effort. He did, however, turn and look away, peering out into the darkness beside the road. He was probably searching for Adam and Monique, bored and tired like Emma.

After mentioning the party, she found her mind wandering to the three enjoyable minutes of the entire affair: her dance with Benjamin Stillwell. Normalcy was a rare luxury in the Family, but for the few minutes she had danced with Benjamin, she felt like a normal girl. Practically everything he said was in teasing, but she remembered it with fondness rather than annoyance. Even the term "goody," which in the moment had pricked her, now seemed endearing. She let her mind wander to the playful smile on his lips and the dance of challenge in his blue eyes.

Scott's eyes were blue, as well. She compared them in her mind. Benjamin's warm; Scott's icy. Benjamin's twinkling mischief; Scott's glittering hatred. Strange that eyes the same basic hue could elicit such different responses from her. Benjamin's eyes made her curious and soft; Scott's eyes made her cower.

"Do you think you did a decent job tonight, Scott?" Emma asked innocently, trying to dispel the dredges of resentment that still floated around them like a foul smell on the wind.

"Shut up, Emma. You don't always have to fill the silence."

Emma sighed but Obediently said nothing more. She had not been trying to fill the silence, she had been trying to busy her mind and urge it away from forbidden thoughts of Benjamin. He had treated her like a real girl, like she could be a regular person in a real family. But it wasn't true. Here she would always be the bottom of the chain of command.

A menacing buzz made them both start. The accompanying ringtone squawked from within her purse. Scott grabbed for the bag, but she beat him to it, snatching it from the seat and jerking it into her lap. He could simply have demanded to see it, but he didn't. Instead, he scrutinized her while she reached into the purse and removed her ringing cellphone. Her heart raced as she stared at the number flashing on the screen. It was Cara again. Emma's heart started thumping again, as it had when Monique pulled her gun on Adam. Maybe harder than that, because this time, she was the one in danger. When she had been in the privacy of her room, she felt safe entertaining the idea of a party, but under Scott's watchful eye she knew she couldn't. Normal girls in normal families did not pull guns on one another to restore order. In normal families, brothers did not watch sisters with such greedy suspicion in their eyes. Her phone sat in her hand, flashing up at her, pulsating like a strobe, lighting up the interior of the car every other second. The ringtone was the loudest sound in the car, besides Emma's heartbeat.

"Answer the damn phone, Emma!" Scott shouted, his voice louder than the ringtone and her heartbeat combined. She Obeyed, because it was her first nature to Obey without thinking.

More confident than the last time she had answered her phone, Emma touched the correct button and said a hoarse, "Hello?"

Scott shook his head and muttered something about Family phone etiquette. But since she did not know what he was referring to, she only swallowed.

"Emma?" Cara said briskly through the receiver. "This is Cara."

"I know. What do you want?"

Emma recognized that her tone was a little hostile, but she did not know how else to react with Scott glowering at her suspiciously. She would have been suspicious, too. No one had ever called her before. She had never seen any of the others in the House take social calls. Business calls, sure; calls from others in the Family, absolutely; but not social calls!

Cara did not even seem to be phased by Emma's cold tone. "Okay, so I want you to meet us in The Commons tomorrow at eight."

"What? Why? Who?"

Scott's eyes narrowed, and he seemed nearly ready to lunge for the phone, tense like a coiled spring.

"OMG, Emma! My friends are meeting in The Commons tomorrow before school. Are you going to be there or not?"

Emma's first response was "not," but then she got curious. "Why?" What could Cara possibly want with Emma that she would invite her to sit with her friends? It was probably just to appease her mother some more, which was fine with Emma. She didn't care what Cara's motives were, but she did feel she had the right to know about them. It wouldn't matter if she wanted Emma there to help cure cancer, Emma would never be able to convince Adam and Scott to take her to school early. Usually they showed up right on time to avoid the tardy bell.

"You are about the most tiresome person I know!" Cara gave an exasperated scoff. "Eight o'clock. Don't be late."

There was a click and then a tone. When Emma looked, she saw the words "CALL ENDED" flashing across the screen again. Cara was rude, always hanging up abruptly that way. Emma stared at the phone as if it could produce a reason for her to behave in such a way, but it was silent, and after a moment, it was also dark.

"Your boyfriend?" Scott's scathing voice attacked her, and her head jerked up. She glared at him in the darkness, but it was from fear rather than anger. Her voice was tight when she answered him.

"No."

Scott snorted. "Who was it?" The dangerous glint of curiosity had returned to his eye. It was as if he knew she was thinking about going to Cara's party. As if he knew she was doing something not entirely honest. Heart beating so hard now that she could feel it in her throat, she formulated a lie.

"They called the wrong number."

She was surprised how easily the words came to her and rolled off her tongue. There was no real reason to lie to Scott. She could have explained that Cara was an annoying girl from school who was completely unrelated to Family business. She could have said Cara's only interest in Emma was predicated on her desire to have an idiotic party. Period. It ought to have been easy to say aloud, but Emma did not want to tell Scott about it. This was the first time Emma had ever been treated like a regular girl before. She did not want to give it to the Family. But Emma had never lied to a superior before; the thrill of it was terrifying.

Scott would have said something, but the passenger front door opened. Adam climbed in, and Scott turned away from Emma to watch him with no little anxiety. Though Adam had not been at forms long, he looked considerably calmer, even when he glanced askance at Scott in the back seat. The two of them exchanged a long tense look before Adam faced forward and buckled his seatbelt.

Monique opened the door and folded herself into the driver seat. Without a word or a glance at any of them, she started the car and pulled back into traffic. She looked focused, as if she too had been at forms and was now re-centered. Gone was the terrifying woman who had drawn a gun and placed it aside her subordinate's head.

Scott broke the focused silence. "Emma's boyfriend called." His innocent tone could not have been more calculated to destroy the mood in the car.

"What?"

Monique's brisk tone had returned, and along with it was a severe glare in the rearview.

"You have a boyfriend? Why didn't you report this, Emmalyn? Who gave you permission to engage in—"

"No!" Emma shouted in desperation. "I do *not* have a boyfriend, Monique. I swear. It was just a wrong number. It was just..."

Monique studied her, and Emma felt herself drawing inward from terror. She had lied to Monique. She had never lied to Monique before—had never even been tempted. The studying gaze made Emma's stomach clench and she almost blurted the truth and begged forgiveness. She would have, if her throat had not constricted with terror. In the next instant, though, Monique raised a stern brow at Scott and returned her attention to the road.

Scott smirked as if pleased with himself. Emma could not even look his direction, because she was afraid the deception would be all over her face and he would begin to doubt her. Emma's face was hot, but her belly was ice that she feared would never thaw. She sat perfectly still all the way home, fearful that at any moment Monique would look back and read the guilt on her face.

Chapter Seven

Monique parked the Lexus in the second garage, next to Leader's BMW. As soon as she shut the engine off, Adam jumped out and strode into the House. Scott was only a beat behind him and seemed to be trying to catch up to him. Monique stalked them as if they were prey, remembering finally at the door of the garage to reach the key remote behind her and click the lock button.

Emma had not moved. The dome lights clicked off and Emma finally felt she was able to breathe at a normal rate. Her heart began to beat at a normal rhythm. She stifled her desire to weep, unlocked her door, and climbed out of the car. She manually locked the door and walked through the dark garage to the door to the House. She stood there with her hand on the cool, painted wood, willing herself calm.

When she walked into the House, Monique was emerging from the office with a menacing strap dangling from her hand. Emma froze in step. But Monique only walked past her. "To bed," she ordered, and she climbed the steps to the upper story, swinging the strap as if it were not a weapon at all.

Emma did not trust herself to answer, but she was relieved at the permission to escape to her private room. She crept past the study, where Scott was already buried in his textbooks, and slipped beyond the kitchen door, finding relief when her foot at last touched the bottom step.

"Emma." Leader's musical voice beckoned her to the kitchen, and she felt her heart jump in a painful and unnatural way. She seriously considered continuing up the stairs and claiming she had not heard him. But the idea of lying to Leader sent chills up her spine. She physically shuddered at how he might respond to lies. Obediently, her foot slipped back onto the wooden floor, and she shuffled into the kitchen.

Leader leaned against the counter, watching Emma approach with one good eye. His other eye was swollen and red. He had obviously taken a serious hit to the face. The front of his suit was torn, and his shirt was stained with blood.

Yet he looked at ease and in complete control, as always. Thoughts of her recent falsehoods raced away amid her concerns for him, and she sped to his side.

"What happened to you?"

A smile sprouted on his face and he lifted a hand to touch the underside of her chin with a gentle tap. "I'm all right," he assured her. He nodded toward the stools beside the kitchen bar. "Sit down and tell me about the party."

Stepping reluctantly away from him, she pulled the nearest stool and sat down. "Who hit you?" It couldn't have been anyone in the House, because they would only have struck him on the mats, and he wasn't wearing training clothes.

"He tripped on the stairs," offered Waylon from the stool beside her. Though he appeared to be engrossed in a textbook, his ironic tone gave evidence that he was listening to their conversation. He was currently working toward a doctorate, although Emma had no idea in which field.

The fingers of one manicured hand drummed on the countertop lightly, and he studied the book with intense interest in his brown eyes, though he did occasionally speculatively glance up through his lashes at Leader. He was supposed to be Emma's uncle, but his Brazilian brown hair and eyes were as likely to be her blood relation as Monique's half-Japanese.

"Careful," Leader warned him in that musical lilt.

Julianne strode in carrying a bag of medical supplies. In addition to being Fourth in the Family power chain, she was a doctor. Emma's only illness that she could remember, and every injury, had been attended by Julianne at home rather than in a medical facility. Her skeptical voice berated Leader, just as he had Waylon.

"*You* are the one who needs to be careful, Leader. What were you thinking, going out all on your own?" She hopped up onto the counter, sitting beside him. "You're lucky you weren't killed."

"I doubt it was luck," Waylon piped in again, but in a low tone.

Emma's eyes widened at the mention of Leader getting killed and she gripped the edge of the marble countertop.

"Who was it? Are you okay?"

When Julianne tried to dab at his lip with an antiseptic wipe, Leader swiped her hand away, snatching her wrist into a firm grip. He gave her a fierce glare that had nothing to do with her doctoring. Like he did with Monique, he communicated silently. The hardness around his eyes made Julianne sigh and she mouthed an apology, though Emma had no idea why.

Leader smiled over at Emma in reassurance.

"It was nothing, Em. And I daresay I will survive it." He then quirked a demanding brow at Julianne. "Won't I, Doctor?"

Julianne waggled her brows at him and slapped an ice pack against his eye, not gently. "I might be able to give you a stronger diagnosis if I knew the cause of your injury."

Leader answered with a dangerous chuckle, and pulled away from Julianne, holding the ice pack himself. "I fell down the stairs."

"Of course, you did, Leader. Right onto someone's crowbar." She opened her medical bag and began rummaging.

Leader smiled but turned his attention back to Emma. "How did the evening go after I left?"

She shrugged one shoulder and shoved away thoughts of their car ride home. She focused on the good news.

"It seemed to go well. Mr. Henshaw loved me. He loved us all, I think. After you left, he never stopped talking about his daughter, and he and Monique talked about the possibility of getting together for some kind of family dinner."

Leader nodded thoughtfully. "I'll have her give me a full report. How did Monique handle my abrupt exit?"

Emma was not sure how to answer that. "She did not explain it to anyone. She seemed ... a little distracted. But Mr. Henshaw did not seem to notice."

Waylon chuckled and looked up from his book in surprise. "I hardly believe she allowed herself to become distracted. She is unshakable."

"Watch it," Leader warned him, sharpness back in his tone. It softened again when he looked back at Emma. "Did anything unusual happen tonight at dinner? Anything out of the ordinary?"

She wanted to say that she did not feel qualified to answer that question, because she was no judge of what was usual or normal. Every day was a new experience for her with no previous point of reference from which to draw wisdom. However, she did not think Leader would be pleased with that answer. He waited with a sharp look of expectation.

"Not that I noticed," she finally admitted. "Dinner was fine; it went off smoothly."

"You're sure?"

Her heart beat, because she suddenly wondered if the call from Cara counted as "out of the ordinary." But she calmed herself down and answered, "I'm sure, Leader."

"Then it's not them," he told Julianne with confidence. He looked toward the ceiling with a sigh. "I knew it. They're slippery, but they can't be in two places at once."

She murmured, "Monique is going to be pissed as hell."

He dropped his chin to stare hard at Julianne for a moment, then he nodded as if in agreement over Monique's reaction. He smiled then and crossed the kitchen to touch Emma's cheek with a soft hand. "You are probably tired, Em. Go get some sleep."

She was painfully curious, but Obedient. "Yes, sir."

He grunted when Julianne began unbuttoning the front of his shirt. He pulled away from her. He glanced over at Emma again.

"When do you have to be at school tomorrow?"

Emma's throat constricted again. She clutched at the counter top to stop her hands from trembling. This was her chance to tell him about the calls from Cara and ask him about the party. It was her chance to admit that there had been no wrong number calls. As she stared into the dark tunnels of his eyes, she imagined how he might react to the fact that she had lied to Monique. Even leaning against a counter with a cut in his lip and an icepack against his eye, he was dangerous. His question filled her ears, then the room, and it pushed against her like a tidal wave.

She locked her knees to keep her legs from trembling. In as natural a voice as she could manage, she said, "Eight. That will give me time to complete the homework I did not finish today."

Without appearing to notice her discomfort, Leader nodded. He fully accepted her lie. "Fine. I might as well drop you off on my way to the airport. We need to leave by ten after."

Emma did not trust herself to answer. She ducked her head, ears burning with the shame of the lie. She pushed herself away from the counter and, despite the jelly-like feeling in her legs, she managed to walk to the exit without falling.

"Good night, Emma."

For a moment, they were the only two people in the world. Unable to resist him, she looked back over her shoulder and stared up into his magnetic black eyes. His farewell pulsed in the room between them, caressing her with its rare touch of warmth. They were like a real family right then. He was a father wishing his daughter good night. She sucked in a heavy breath and pulled in her lower lip, as well. She bit down hard, to remember herself, and him.

They weren't a family. They were an organization that demanded Emma's Obedient compliance. The lie on her tongue was still a ten-pound weight, but she swallowed her terror.

"Good night, Father."

Chapter Eight

"Good morning, Emma," Amos greeted her as she walked into the kitchen. She had made record time training, showering and dressing; Amos was usually at work by the time Emma came down to breakfast. It helped that her school had a uniform policy, so she never had to think about what she would wear. Her white and black plaid skirt was the proper length for school this morning, and her white Peter Pan collar blouse was starched and pressed. She had even properly knotted the tie at her throat and put on real black pantyhose instead of knee-high socks. She had to sit in a car with Leader all the way to the school; she intended for it to go as smoothly on her side as possible.

Amos was making breakfast, a task he thoroughly enjoyed. He tossed a thin pancake-like food into the air and caught it on a serving plate. Giving Emma a triumphant smile, he put the plate down in front of the seat at the bar. The way he behaved, it was sometimes surprising that he was just beneath Monique in seniority. It would have been within his rights to be as demanding and dispassionate as she was, but he wasn't. Amos was a ray of much needed sunshine in the House. Generally soft-spoken and kind-hearted, he always tried to ease Emma's way. All her memories of him were fond.

"Good morning, uncle," she greeted him as she sat up to the bar in front of the plate he had placed there for her. She examined the plate as he added berries and cream to his creation. It hardly seemed like something she was allowed to eat. "What's for breakfast?"

Amos gave her a mock-glare for the doubtful tone of her question. "I'm making crepes, if it pleases your highness. If not, you can pour yourself some cereal."

"Really?" That was a shock. The House diet was restrictive of sugars and unnatural colors and flavors. Cereal was never permitted as an acceptable meal, since it was unhealthy for the body. Yet several brands were always in the cabinet, as though anyone outside the Family might need to come into the kitchen and browse through the cabinets. There was no reason she could think of why someone would need to do that, but she had stopped questioning those types of inconsistencies years ago.

Amos laughed out loud. "Of course not!" He put a shake down in front of her. This was more what she expected to find at the breakfast bar in the morning. The shake was standard daily fare containing vitamins, minerals, and daily fiber. Everyone in the House had one every morning after Training.

"Thank you," she said with a smile.

Amos' beautifully arranged plate of crepes with berries on top and some white cream filling oozing onto the china looked more appealing than cold cereal could ever be, and it was certainly a healthier option. Unless it was all-natural, perfectly balanced, and healthy for the hardworking body, he would not have been permitted to offer it to her. He watched in anticipation as she took her first bite. Heavy, like healthy fare always was. She swallowed hard and gave him a wan smile.

"Thanks," she said again, unwilling to tell him the truth and risk hurting his feelings. As soon as he turned away back to his cooking, she traded her fork for the shake, and drowned the aftertaste of the crepe.

"Morning, Amos," Leader greeted as he strode into the room. He hardly seemed to be the same man who was sporting injuries and under a doctor's care only the night before. The coloring around his eye was mostly gone, and he walked with as much self-assurance as ever. He offered Emma a quick nod, but that was all. Apparently, the man who spoke sweetly and touched gently was likewise gone. Today, he was Leader from apron-toed loafer to woven ground-stripe tie. Even the slight scent of his aftershave had the smell of supremacy.

As if he was not dressed to meet royalty, he leaned back against the counter on his elbows, creating a long diagonal line to the floor with his body. He watched Emma drink her shake until she was nervous enough under his gaze that she put the glass down. He glanced at her plate, so she retrieved her abandoned fork and put more of the unsweet, health-heavy crepe into her mouth. She tasted nothing this time except his surveillance.

"Breakfast, Leader?" Amos asked, offering a shake to him. Leader only shook his head to decline, but his gaze never left Emma. Swallowing got harder with each bite. Panic had that effect on appetite. What could be so wrong about her that he needed to watch her relentlessly? Her fingernails were clean, her hair bleached, and her skirt was acceptable blending-in length.

She wanted to ask him if anything was wrong, but the question caught in her throat alongside the crepes. She had lied to him last night. She had lied to Scott and to Monique, too, but it was Leader who mattered most; he was the one staring her down with savage intensity.

Amos dipped his toes into the tension.

"I got a sense from Monique's eagerness in this morning's Summit that we had reason to worry about detection by unwanted third parties. I intend to go on hyper-watch today. Nothing should be able to slip past me."

Emma knew that the senior members in the Family hierarchy met each morning before dawn, but she had never been invited, and had certainly never volunteered to get up that early. Training already started before sunrise as it was.

Amos continued to make plates of crepes as he chatted in Leader's direction. Emma's heart swelled with gratitude for his interference.

"I do not mean to reinvent the wheel, or anything like that, but our security is a major concern to me at a time like this. I scoured the Cortex for hours, and all I saw was paltry evidence of a movement in this district. But nothing substantial. I almost wish for air raids and gutter strikes. At least they were direct. These sniping, backroom, shadow-assaults are an insult to my intelligence. Not to mention my patience."

If he intended to grasp Leader's attention, he failed. Emma cleaned her plate and emptied her glass under the man's inflexible gaze. Amos glanced between them several times. He cleared his throat and approached Leader directly.

"If you have any ideas, Leader, I would be happy—"

Leader's hand shot into the air in a silencing gesture, and, Obediently, Amos ceased speaking. He stopped a foot short of Leader in a holding stance until Leader's hand dropped.

"I have Confidence in you, Amos, and very high expectations. Your incessant prattling has not obscured for me the fact that you have once again failed to do your job. I expect Refinement from you, or have you already forgotten?" That was certainly a threat. Emma could always hear the threat behind Leader's musical words. "Do not bore me with the details of your ineptitude."

He never even looked at Amos through the melodic insults. Amos, always good natured, shrugged as if they had been having a playful disagreement. He returned to setting plates and pouring drinks, utterly devoid of concern.

Emma desperately tried to emulate Amos' carefree air. Leader was not fooled. Neither was he diverted. His unveiled disapproval made her squirm in her seat. What did he know? What had he discovered? She had to forcefully swat down the urge to start apologizing and begging for his mercy.

She dared to glance up at him through her lashes. His unwavering gaze did not seem to hold any disapproval, yet he did seem to be waiting for something. Had she forgotten to do something? What could it be?

"Leader?" she asked, hoping he would give her a hint of why he was standing there staring down her and her breakfast.

He stood up to his height. "Finished? We need to be going."

Emma let out a relieved sigh. She was just being paranoid! He had been waiting to drive her to school and that was all. "Let me just clear my plate," she gushed from relief. But Leader said no.

"Amos will get it. Get your things and come quickly." He strode out without another glance at either of his subordinates in the kitchen. She stared after him, relieved, and annoyed with herself.

"He was just standing there waiting for me?" she whispered the partial question at Amos.

He leaned to grab her plate and gave her an encouraging smile. "Better hurry on." Which was no answer at all.

Obediently, Emma left to gather her school things. She passed the parlor where she saw Adam doing basic forms under Monique's scrutiny. He never even winced, though the marks of a recent beating were evident across his naked back. Emma averted her eyes and shoved down her fear. This was nothing to the terror she felt in the car last night when Adam lost control and Monique lost her patience.

She kept her head down as she crossed Scott's path on the steps. Attempting to make herself smaller, she held her breath and leaned into the railing as she passed him. He shoved at her anyway, even though she was not in his way. Her ribs banged on the stair railing and she stifled her cry of pain; it would only have brought him satisfaction. He marched on down the steps without a backward glance. He was not dressed for school, to her relief. That meant she would not have to sit in the car with him all the way to school, using up some of the oxygen he surely felt belonged to only him. He wore his martial arts uniform instead. He was probably being punished, too, for breaking the Aggression Compact last night. Little did their superiors know that he showed off-the-mats aggression on a daily basis.

Emma retrieved her backpack from her desk chair and heaved it onto one shoulder. Attached to the shoulder strap was a sticky note with the words Homework incomplete? We will discuss this. –M written in Monique's brisk handwriting. Emma let out a sigh of complete despair. How could Monique really have expected her to finish her homework yesterday? The day had been packed to the brim. The note gave a satisfying crumple as she waded it up. Monique would never accept her excuses, and the Aggression Compact disallowed Emma to take any physical action against her. She tossed the note into her wastebasket on her way out of the room.

When Emma opened the door to the garage, she found Leader was not alone. Yet another member of her dysfunctional family stood beside the car with him. Ilene kissed him rather passionately, pressing one palm flat against his chest while the other grabbed a handful of his face and neck. Emma turned her face away, cheeks flushing slightly.

Most kids would have been horrified rather than embarrassed if they walked in on their dad kissing some other woman. But Emma had no idea what the relationship dynamics were between Leader and Monique aside from that they posed as loving spouses out in public. Their attraction for one another was nauseatingly obvious to everyone out there, but she had never seen them show any regard for each other at home. They spoke like partners in business, rather than partners in love. Emma could not blame Leader if he found Monique less attractive than Ilene. Monique's overwhelming beauty was dark and fierce and intense; Ilene was a classic first-rate knockout, with silvery blond hair, blue eyes, and a captivating smile when she deigned to show it to anyone.

"Do you know when you will be back?" she whispered at Leader.

"No. Probably not soon, if everything goes as planned and Amos gets his act together." His tone was soft in a way Emma had rarely heard from him. Just once, in fact, could Emma recall him speaking to her as sweetly. She had begged to be kept from school in sixth grade, and he had resolutely refused, thinking her claim of not feeling well was a lie to get out of her duty. She had fainted at school, having come down with a wasting strain of flu. He had spoken gently to her then and rarely left her side while she recovered. She could still feel the cool weight of his hand on her forehead when she thought about it.

Emma peeked over her shoulder to get another look at the mellow version of him. He held Ilene's face in two hands and kissed her again.

Ilene, who was always arctic disapproval and placid rebuke to Emma, was warm summer breezes in Leader's hands. "Do you have to be gone so long? Things do not go as well when you're absent."

Leader's brow rose, but rather than dangerous, he looked playful. "Monique is perfectly capable of handling the situation here without me; god knows she's aching for me to be gone for good." He kissed the tip of Ilene's nose. "I could be gone for good and probably no one would even miss me."

Ilene gave him a kind of playful glare and planted a quick peck on his lips. Then she shrugged and tore herself out of his embrace. "You're probably right," she agreed, matching the playfulness of his tone with mischievous indifference. In total rejection of her disinterest, he grasped her bottom and pulled her forcefully back against him.

"I'll be back before Monique can declare herself Leader," he promised darkly. She chuckled, but he kissed her silent. Sharpness edged out all playfulness when he snapped, "Stop lurking, Emma, and get in the car."

Emma started, recovered, and tried to walk nonchalantly to the passenger side of Leader's BMW. She climbed in. Leader did not open his door yet, and he spoke so softly to Ilene that Emma could no longer hear their goodbyes. She pulled out one of her text books and began scanning it as she waited. She considered turning on the radio, but she did not intend to anger Leader unnecessarily with trifles like music.

Chapter Nine

After an annoyingly long wait, Leader got in. His mood was cold, and she was grateful she had decided against turning on the radio. Behind them, the garage door grated open, and Leader backed the car out, down the cobbled driveway, and into the street. Emma kept her eyes in her textbook, focusing on finishing as much work as she could. If she finished her homework before class today, Monique would likely go easier on her. But concentrating on her studies was hard when she was alone with Leader. It was unsettling being alone with him. She never knew what to say or how to act. He could behave remarkably like a caged animal, at once docile and the next minute eating your face off.

"Emma, put the book away," he commanded, never taking his eyes from the road. He drove out of the neighborhood before the admittance gate was even completely up.

Obediently, Emma tucked the book back into her bag and settled against the seat. If he wanted her attention so he could converse with her, he made no indication. After an awkward, long silence, he only said, "Buckle." She flushed with embarrassment. She *never* forgot to buckle her seatbelt!

Hating herself, she reached up and pulled the belt across her lap and clicked it into place. She settled back against the seat once more, wishing she were like the camouflaged creatures of the wild that could transform themselves to suit their surroundings. If she could take on the gray hue of his leather seats, for instance, so he forgot she was in the vehicle with him, she would feel much better.

For a few minutes, they rode in silence. He never reached for the radio dial since radio, like television, was viewed by him as an inexcusable waste of time. Time was more precious than food and money, and he was death on the waste of any of it.

Emma hoped they might manage to drive the entire way without speaking. He maneuvered the city roads without ever looking at her, and she wondered if he had, indeed, forgotten she was there. But after Leader merged into traffic on the freeway and climbed up to speed, he glanced her way.

"Monique mentioned that you gave an impressive performance last night."

Emma's throat constricted. *He knew!* He knew that she had lied to Monique, that she had lied to him. She was doomed! His voice had the tone of small talk, but Emma was not fooled. Leader never engaged in idle chatter; it would have been a waste of time. Since Emma's tongue had become a lead weight, and she had no intelligent excuses come to mind, she said nothing. She grappled with her shattered thoughts, trying to grasp at any monosyllable he would find acceptable.

"I was pleased with how you managed yourself with Henshaw while I was there," Leader continued. And Emma blinked in confusion. *Henshaw?* "He was certainly charmed by you. I am impressed by how easily you fold into character. You estimated his adoration of his daughter quickly and accurately and anticipated his response to your every word. It was commendable performance; I agree with Monique."

Emma swatted down the last vestiges of panic and focused on finding any intelligent response. Was a "thank you" or a "you're welcome" more acceptable?

"What is your opinion of him?"

Emma shot Leader a startled glance. Was he seriously asking her opinion? No one ever asked for her opinion! Five or six years ago, Thomas had asked her what her favorite color was. That was the last time she remembered anyone in the Family asking for her opinion. And she had not even been able to answer him because she had never thought about a favorite anything before.

Emma cleared her throat to shove away her shock. "I thought he was very ..." she paused, desperately trying to locate a proper adjective from the library of words in her mind. The words *pompous, insufferable,* and *dull* had volunteered themselves first, but she resisted. Instead she gasped, "Reserved."

Leader nodded, assimilating her claim without either agreeing or disagreeing.

"How so?" It was such a benign question, very like the way a father would probe his daughter about a school social event; half-heartedly.

Again, Emma had to resist snide answers. "He was open enough about his daughter and his wife. He made a good show of being a family man, but it was almost too forced. It was like he was concealing the real man beneath the pretense of a concerned father and husband." She turned and looked out the side window at the businesses just off the freeway. She could have easily been describing the man sitting beside her right now. She uneasily changed her focus.

"I thought he seemed like he was expecting Monique to make an excuse for your sudden departure. He brought you up plenty of times, but never mentioned your absence directly. I thought it seemed like too obvious an attempt to hold himself back. But he constantly watched her, and me, for any break in our restraint. Almost as if he was watching us as closely as we were watching him."

Leader made a thoughtful sound, and when Emma glanced at him, his gaze was anything but benign. He met her gaze for a searching moment, then he returned his attention to the road and merged into the carpool lane.

"Why would he conceal the truth?"

Emma schooled her features before she let show her exasperation for the interrogation. "I hardly know, sir. I do not understand why he might conceal his true self. Perhaps I see it in him only as a reflection of myself."

"Oh, really ... A reflection of self. Spoken like a psychologist." His tone was amused but transformed quickly to dark curiosity. "Do you hide your true self, Emma?"

The dangerous question chased the oxygen from the car. She choked on it, struggling for an answer he would find suitable. She writhed with the desperate need to turn their conversation off of her.

"Of course not."

"Of course not," he repeated slowly. She saw from the corner of her eye that he studied her longer than he ought, since he should have been watching the road. His tone, if possible, was even more dangerous when he said, "That was a trifle too glib, even for you, Emma." She avoided him by looking out the side window at the traffic they sped past.

"Look at me."

She squeezed her eyes shut and attempted to calm herself quickly, then she Obeyed. He had just complimented her on her acting skills. She employed those skills when she looked at him; she radiated innocence. Silently pleading with him to accept the pretense, she locked her gaze on him.

Leader looked at her only long enough to say, "What is it you hide?" He then turned back to the road and the increasing commuter traffic.

Every reply she constructed was wrapped in three or four layers of disrespect and disdain. She had to forcibly shove them aside and snatch in the dark for any acceptable response. Questions could be precarious, but not as much as the truth.

"What could I possibly hope to hide from you, Leader?" It was both flattery and deflection. He wasn't fooled. She had hardly expected him to be.

The flash of darkness in his eyes could have been amusement or fury; she had no way to decipher it since he immediately looked away again. It did dry her mouth, though, and pull her back from the dangerous precipice of boiling sarcasm.

"You can't hide from me."

She tried to bring moisture back into her mouth, so she could answer carefully, "Why would I want to?"

With the grace of a serpent, his gaze slid over to her once more. She had been careful not to be sarcastic that time, but he seemed even less pleased now than before. He spoke with the same serpentine grace as he moved. "You should just ask me about it."

Emma puzzled over his injunction. It was so broad. Ask him about *what*? Mr. Henshaw? The Family? Politics? Hiding in plain sight?

She had a thousand questions she could ask him, but she thought he was expecting something specific. He could not actually be offering to answer *any* of her questions. He never answered her questions. Her mind reverted to another time he had prompted her candor. She had been in middle school then, in a bout of rebellion. After trying to run away to find her real parents and being captured by Leader before she had even made it out of the school parking lot, he had trapped her in his sterile car just as he did now.

"What did you think you were going to find?" he had asked her in his darkly musical tone. "Where did you think you were going to go?"

Emma had tried to cover her face with her hands, to hide her frustrated tears from him. Trying to deflect him, she had answered, "I don't know." It had basically been true. She had not known exactly what she was looking for, nor even where to start looking. But he knew she was deflecting.

Cooling significantly, he had prompted, "Ask me."

A little encouraged, Emma had asked, "Who were my real parents?"

Leader had snorted and, though it softened him out of his cooling anger, it did not bring Emma any comfort or satisfaction. "A foolish question."

Enraged, she had screamed at him, "How is that a foolish question? I know you're not my father. Where did you get me from? Who are my parents?"

With a heavy shake of his head, Leader had looked toward the ceiling, muttering *"We are surrounded by fools and grumblers,"* in Mandarin. Returning to English, he had demanded, "If you ever expect to be taken seriously, you are going to need to turn your focus on issues that truly matter in this life."

This had only enraged Emma further. "This is the issue that matters to me: to whom do I really belong?"

Leader had steered his car to the roadside, but Emma had not allowed herself to be cowed by this maneuver. She had been too angry. "You don't get to keep pretending I belong with you. I know! I know I'm special. You are working too hard to conceal me, and that means you're hiding me from someone. You can't fool me! Who do I belong to?"

Leader had parked by this time and, as usual, he had grasped her chin in a hard grip. "You belong to *me!*" he had snarled at her. "You *are* special because I selected you and brought you here! If you keep looking outward for a place to belong, you will always find only emptiness. And don't speak like an uneducated boob: *To whom do I belong?* Not, 'who do I belong to?' You're not an idiot."

She had screamed wordlessly at him from frustration, jerking from his grip and slamming her fists into the dashboard to let out her anger. It did not work, though, because he snarled another demand. "Ask me something worthy of you."

She snarled profanities, but that only earned her another reprimand to speak intelligently. And another injunction to ask him. Emma had not been able to rein in her fury. "Where did I come from?"

"That doesn't matter," he replied coldly, not even raising his voice now as he waited with what appeared to be eternal patience.

"Why me?"

"Why *not* you, Emma? You're very promising sometimes, present moment excluded."

Clenching her teeth on her rage, she snapped back, "Who is my family?"

"Do you *need* a family? What good is family doing any of your friends or classmates?"

She had continued snarling questions at him, but every question she asked had been turned back on her. By the end of the raging conversation, she had been so confused she could hardly think straight. As he pulled his car back into the road, his parting shot had been, "Foolish questions receive indecorous answers." Emma had never been tempted to ask him again about her life before the Family. She avoided asking him anything at all if she could help it.

She was a few years older and wiser now. The car was different, his suit was different, and the outside scenery was different, but it felt painfully similar. Emma did not take her eyes off Leader, because he had commanded her to look at him, but her hands fidgeted with her skirt. The longer she kept him waiting, the more uncomfortable the silence felt. It draped over them like wet wool blankets.

"What should I ask you about, Leader?"

The sharp look she got in response was as suffocating as the silence had been, and she wanted it back!

"I might surprise you," he answered, tone dancing. If it was meant to be reassuring, it failed. It was as calculated as everything else he ever said to her.

"You always surprise me," she snapped back. Too fast. She had not meant to speak through her emotions again. She turned away from him, staring hard at the road, and sputtered, "You never surprise me." The contradictory statements pranced around the car, taunting her.

"Well, which is it? Do I surprise you or don't I?"

She glared at him. The taunt in his voice mirrored the one in her head. It made her answer truthfully. "Both."

He nodded acceptance of that impossibility. "And you don't think other children have the same dilemma with their fathers as you have with me? Contradictory emotions and unusual circumstances?"

Her initial response of *You're not my father!* had to be reined in. She answered calmly and carefully. "I suppose they do. But I defy anyone to produce a set of circumstances as unusual as mine."

Leader smiled, breaking the heated tension between them. "That's fair. The Guild is not much like a family. There are so many more rules."

Emma glanced quickly around; although it was impossible anyone had heard him, since they were alone in the car. But she was nervous about his use of the word "Guild." Several years ago, she had removed the word from her working vocabulary. Leader had commanded them to replace it with the word "Family."

"I do not remember life before the ..." She omitted the forbidden word, since she had been ordered not to use it.

"Naturally," he answered with a serious nod.

"But my *current* life has taught me to hide. I hide my true self all the time. So then why would you ask me if I hide, when you know that I do? When *you* are the one who taught me to do it! When you are the one who expects me to do it so well that no one on the outside will know I'm hiding at all! And why, also, would you say it had impressed you that I was successful? Were you expecting me to fail with Henshaw? And, if so, *why* were you expecting me to fail? You were the one who taught me to do what I did!" She bit off her tirade and glanced nervously at him.

He watched the road. "So, you're saying that I ought not to have complimented you on the success of your mission last night, because I was the one who taught you act? Come to that, you may be right, and all compliments should go to me for my excellent training."

Emma rolled her eyes, then froze when she realized he was watching her. Had he seen her?

"Very astute of you to realize I had misplaced my compliments, Emma."

He was being an ass. The conciliatory tone nudged her toward anger, but she kept a tight rein on it. The sarcasm she could no longer restrain. "I'm actually trained mostly by Monique, so if you must give your compliments away, it is to her."

Leader's voice dropped to a conspiratorial whisper, "And who do you think trained *her*?"

Emma met his eye with a sarcastic retort on the tip of her tongue. The blaze of dominance residing in those black eyes reminded her of their relative positions; it cooled her fire. She broke the gaze and looked again out her side window. A few moments of breathing and not talking would bring her back to equilibrium, wherein she could manage the onslaught of emotions she always felt around him.

He gave her some time. He studied the road, and the hundreds of brake lights ahead of them. Morning traffic was worse than anything except afternoon traffic. And evening traffic. Emma prayed that everyone would get out of their way so he could drop her off at the school and this torturous conversation could be over!

"Am I just part of an illusion to make people believe that we are a regular family?" she asked into the stillness. "Or is there some other significant thing I should be doing?"

Leader shot her a searching scowl. "Every member in the Guild has a personal responsibility. You are 12; your responsibility is Obedience. The Junior Guild, numbers 7 through 12, are novices. You are learning the skills you will need for when you enter the Senior Guild. For now, you learn, you grow, and you Obey. Those are your responsibilities."

Emma sat back against the seat and watched traffic. It was a litany she knew all too well. She had been hearing it for as long as she could remember. Obedience. Obedience was her one responsibility. It was her one contribution to the Guild mission.

"Fine." But it wasn't fine. What if she did not want to contribute anymore?

"Stop being petulant, Emma. I feel the air of rebellion around you. You have spent a very long time studying the art of Obedience, and you're tired of it. You are looking for a change, because you are changing. You may be dangerously smart, but you're a hopeless liar."

She glared at him for that, because he had no idea how good a liar she could be. Hadn't she lied to him only yesterday? And Monique? And Scott? And how about years of masking her true feelings, hiding her hatred, restraining her disdain?

"Fine," she drawled again, but this time the word dripped with the scorn she always concealed. "I am looking for a change. I hate it here! In Utah, in the Guild, in all of it. And I want to know if I actually belong somewhere. I want to know if I had a family before I came to the Guild." She should not have admitted that. She should not have used the forbidden word. She should not have let him bait her. But she had, and it was too late to go back now.

He looked at her for a thoughtful moment. Then he nodded. "That's better. Real, at least, and self-contained." He looked back at the road. "And the answer is no. You did not have a family. You were made for the Guild."

She never knew what to think about the things Leader said to her, things like this. She was usually awed or confused, but today she had the terrifying feeling that he was lying to her. From her mind, she jerked forward the image of a woman kissing her head. Her smell was clean linen and clean sweat. A soft smile played at her lips, and she held Emma in a tight embrace. When Emma focused on it, she could almost remember the woman's face. There was too much emotion attached to the memory for Emma to deny it. She felt a connection to this woman that she did not feel for Leader, for Monique. She wanted to believe that woman had been her family, back before the word "family" became a meaningless, insignificant word, like "love."

"The Guild is your family."

Emma ignored him. The Guild was her fate, but it was not her family.

Chapter Ten

L eader finally exited the over-crowded freeway and wove the BMW through morning traffic on the canyon road. Emma's school was up the canyon a little way. No way could the fancy private school sit down in the valley with the common, mediocre public schools! The canyon elevated it for its status, so rich families could feel their children were getting a superior education. The benefit of the canyon was that it offered a beautiful drive in the early fall, before the leaves fell off the trees. Emma liked to watch the world changing before winter came. It was nice to see that it was at its most beautiful when it was dying.

"What's on your mind, Emma?" Leader prompted too soon. Oh no, she would not give him the satisfaction of having access to her thoughts. She tried to divert him.

"Would it be okay if I joined a sport team or the drama club or something?"

Leader smiled to himself in the knowing way he often did. "Does your school even have a drama club?"

Emma thought about that. "No, but it has a girls' basketball team."

Leader shook his head. "No. Sports will put you in an aggressive position of competition. I cannot allow you to get competitive."

"I could be good in competitive sports." She attached too much hope to this request. If he allowed her to play basketball, she would have somewhere to belong at school. It would not be as awkward. She was a year advanced in school, so she already felt out of place. Basketball could help her find a crowd and a distraction. Monique had flatly refused to consider it. It was dangerous to go over her head and ask Leader, but if he conceded, Monique would be forced to allow it. And Emma just knew she could be good at sports.

"No doubt, but the answer is no."

That was the end of the argument. But Emma felt desperation clawing at her breast. She could not let this go without a fight. "*Why?*"

Leader was not fazed by her frustration. He quoted at her in that musical tone, "'Aggression shall be closely monitored and carefully concealed within the Guild. Guild members shall not engage in public displays of aggression, including organized sports, talent demonstrations, heroics, and other activities which may interfere with or impede the Guild Mission.'"

Emma leaned an elbow on the car door and rested her face in her hand. To keep from snapping profanities at her Leader, she bit down on the fleshy part of her hand until she was collected enough to speak without fury in her tone. Disrespect, she could not account for.

"Am I *supposed* to make friends? Because it seems to me that kids who 'blend in' have friends and are involved in extracurricular activities. What is the point of trying to blend in if when I come home, my 'father' restricts me from joining the basketball team and my 'family' has a dysfunctional meltdown on the roadside?" She did not look at him to see how he took her tirade. She watched out the side window as the BMW pulled into the school drive-through.

Leader parked the car, then reached over and patted Emma's knee. It lacked true affection and served only to mock her pain. "Tell that little story to your peers and see if it can't make you some friends."

Emma glared up at him. She was relatively safe now, since the school counselor was standing on the steps to the school, and the campus police were monitoring the parked cars like spiders in a web. She felt safe enough to snarl, "What does that even mean?"

Leader wasn't concerned. "I mean, they will probably be able to relate with your whining teen angst." He reached past her and opened the passenger-side door. "Out."

Emma shoved his arm away and tried to escape, but he captured her thigh in an iron grip, and when she peered up at him, his eyes were sharp. Time for disrespect and petulance was over; his dominance had returned with full force.

"Be very careful," he cautioned, black eyes drilling into her mind. The words permeated through her rebellious annoyance and settled against her skin as completely as a sunburn. She extracted herself painfully from his gaze and his grip and stepped out of the car onto the loading zone sidewalk.

She pulled her backpack up onto her shoulder and backed away from the car. She wanted to turn her back on him and escape into the school, but his steady gaze pulled her attention back to him. He leaned across the passenger seat and grasped the door handle of her door. With one last dark scowl, he said, "Have a good day." It was not a glib greeting from parent to child. It was an order from superior to subordinate. She waited until she was walking through the school gates toward the commons area entry doors before she rolled her eyes.

A giant copper-plated eagle statue dominated the commons area of the school. Cara and her friends were seated beneath it on the stone dais. They were just one of the many groups assembled in the room, but they were in prime space to be seen by everyone. Several of the school cliques were there, including some of the girls from the basketball team she was forbidden to join, the cheer squad, and some of the school council. Emma moved toward Cara and her clique of spoiled rich kids. She tried to become invisible, but people always stared at her. Wherever she went, the gazes of the masses found her.

"Emma!" Cara summoned, waving a hand to motion her over. The commanding gesture was as bossy as anyone in the Family could do, and as unnecessary. Emma could not have missed her since she was set up in the center of the room. But Emma quickened her pace to join them in the hope of shaking the following gazes.

"Why did you invite her?" one of the girls in the group hissed as Emma approached, not quietly enough for Emma to think she meant it to be a private comment. It received a couple supportive snorts and not a few unfriendly glances.

Cara answered with an unconcerned shrug, "My mom made me." She pointed to an empty space at the edge of the dais. "Sit," she ordered, then immediately turned her back to Emma. The other girls did not forget her as easily.

"Why would your mom make you invite her?" Brinley sat in front of Emma in homeroom and had never even spoken to her before. It was a mystery to Emma how the girl should have such a decided dislike for her.

"I don't know. It's probably her Good Samaritan act for the year. She noticed Emma at the pep rally last month and asked me why she doesn't have any friends. Like I know, right? Maybe because she's super weird, and never speaks to anyone, but whatever! My mom is so annoying." Cara glanced over her shoulder at Emma, a glance that explained to Emma exactly how big an intruder she was in this clique. It was a familiar feeling because it was what she felt when Leader and the others talked about her as if she was a nuisance they had to put up with. They always did that right in front of her, too.

"Anyway, she told me I had to invite Emma to the party. I thought she would forget about it, but apparently not. So, Emma has to come tonight, or my mom will cancel the party. Which is so stupid, since it's supposed to be *my party.* I should be able to invite anyone I want to. It's just so ..." she tossed up a hand in an abrupt gesture to stop, like a crossing guard to encroaching vehicles. She shook her head in disgust. "I can't even talk about it."

Brinley interrupted her, rushing in to rescue Cara from such an unpleasant topic of conversation, "Anyway, so I was thinking we could get ready before the party at five. Do you want to do it at your place?"

"Yes!" Cara insisted, brightening again now that she wasn't discussing Emma's intrusion. "I want to see what you're all planning to wear. I've invited everyone important, so we need to be serious about our choices."

They continued making plans in which Emma took no part, since she was not invited to participate, and was not actually a member of Cara's cohort. She pulled her textbook out of her backpack and returned to studying. This way, if Monique asked her about her morning, she could truthfully tell her she had been working on homework. It was not absorbing, since she had read the textbook through once already, on the night it had been issued. Her tenacious memory did not allow her to forget many things she read. Yet the online class schedule called for her to read certain chapters before class, and Monique was more inclined toward the letter of the law than the spirit of it.

"Emma, *what* are you doing?" asked one of the girls in a scandalized tone. Emma slid a finger into her place on the page and looked up to address the complainer. The girl was one of those who had no reputation except by association to Cara Winters. Emma studied her, preparing to speak, but Cara did not give her a chance.

"Put your books *away*, Emma! God! Could you be more annoying?"

Turning back to her cronies, Cara abused Emma as idiotic and clueless. Emma slid the book into her backpack under the scrutiny of the initial complainer rather than the queen bee. Cara was too busy lamenting Emma's inclusion in the party and her social circle. As soon as she had put away the offensive textbook, they all forgot her again. Their party preparations resumed with no input from her at all. Not that she would have had any significant input, seeing as she had never been to a party. Except missions, and she did not think that was likely to be the same kind of experience.

Emma used her moment of idleness to look around the commons area. She spent almost no time in here; the Guild did not permit idleness in general, so the concept of a common area to hang out with friends and connect with cliques was usually out of the question. So much for blending in. The longest amount of time she had spent in the commons area previously was less than the minute it cost her to cross to the main corridor.

The room was massive; easily large enough to hold the entire student body. It had overhead skylights to bring in natural light. Spotlights also shone onto the black and white school banners hanging on the walls. One wall had randomly placed copper-plated bricks set in beside the red bricks of the wall. The copper-plated bricks were etched with names of people who had donated money to the school. She wondered idly if any bricks were Leader's aliases. He had given plenty of money to the school before Emma, Scott, and Adam had enrolled. She knew that because the dean of the school had greeted them personally on the first day, lumbering out of his office to shake their hands. And no one did that unless a great deal of money had changed hands. Overall, the room seemed to be a massive tribute to some architect's imagination, a monstrosity of useless space and bizarre lighting. She felt small here, and out of place. Even Leader's car seemed preferable.

"What are you wearing?" Cara's waspish question interjected through Emma's thoughts.

Glancing in confusion down at her black and white plaid, Emma tried to imagine what about it was offensive to Cara. "My uniform."

The girls laughed out loud. It was laughter Emma knew well: derisive school-yard cackling at her expense. Cara joined the laughter, and then rolled her eyes at Emma. "Not right now, you idiot. I mean what are you planning to wear *tonight*?"

Emma blinked at Cara, shoving down the immediate violent reaction to being called an idiot. She was not now nor ever had been an idiot. The most appropriate word for her current state of misunderstanding was *ignorance* because she had never experienced anything like this before. Instead of attacking Cara, she tried to imagine in what universe she would need to plan a wardrobe for watching movies and eating cake. Cara tapped a finger against crossed legs with expectant impatience.

"Jeans and a t-shirt?"

A long pause followed in which she faced seven blank expressions. They were trying to decide if she was serious or not. One of the girls broke the impasse with a vulgar comment. Cara addressed Emma like she was a classless moron. "Are you joking? There are going to be *people* at this party. People with eyes."

The rebuke was in a tone so similar to Monique's that Emma averted her eyes and admitted, "I did not realize this was going to be a fancy party. I thought it was just movies and cake. Didn't you say it was movies and cake?" She glanced up at Cara, who gave an exasperated sigh and rolled her eyes toward her friends.

"Of course, that's what I *said*, because my mom and dad were in the room. I have to play it cool, or they won't allow me to have a co-ed party. They're ridiculously old-fashioned about some things. But half the school is going to be there, so you can't show up in jeans and a t-shirt."

Brinley interjected, "Okay, whatever, she's close to my size. I will bring clothes for her." The gesture of her hand was meant to placate Cara. When she pointed at Emma, though, there was no calmness about her. "You be there at five, Emma, so I can get you ready." Back to Cara, she softened, "Thank goodness she's pretty. This could have been a real travesty."

"Do not let her embarrass me!"

Emma thought up several nasty retorts to Cara's concerns that she would be an embarrassment. The truth was that, in looks alone, Emma outshone them all. Perhaps they knew and that was why they treated her so coolly. Years of Guild tutelage had taught her how to speak in scathing enough words and tones to eviscerate regular non-Guild civilians. It would have been rewarding to let loose after her morning of frustration. She resisted, though, because Leader's warning about aggression danced across her mind as soon as she contemplated violence. Besides, she did want to go to Cara's party.

"I'm not sure I can get out of my house by five. That's before dinner, and my parents will not let me. I can just dress myself."

Cara glared at her. "Everyone at school is going to know I invited you to this party, Emma. If you show up in an outfit that looks like it was picked out by some blind nun, *I* am going to look bad. Be at my house at five, and if I don't like what you're wearing, Brinley can dress you." She turned away and promptly forgot about Emma again. This time Emma made no argument. She spent her time trying to figure out what she was going to tell Monique that would allow her to get out of the house without an escort.

Chapter Eleven

Emma sat outside school on the steps with her knees crossed. It was 4:30. She had already completed her homework, had read her English book again, and now she was waiting. No one had picked her up from school. Usually she rode home with Scott and Adam, but neither of them had even come to school today. Emma tried to call Monique, but she wasn't answering her phone. Even the house phone—which was usually manned at all times by Amos—went straight to voicemail.

Cara's party had completely slipped from Emma's mind, replaced by the terrifying idea that the Family had forgotten about her. Again. The teacher parking lot had emptied slowly in the past hour, and it would only be a matter of time until the custodial staff locked the gates for the night. When that happened, Emma would have to sit out by the road. This was not a pleasant thought and Emma could not make herself think about it. Someone would remember her before then.

Emma considered the possibility that she was being punished. She did not know why she would be, unless Monique had discovered she had lied to her about the call last night. A disconcerting fluttering in her stomach reminded her that Monique was a hands-on educator; it was not her style to punish by ignoring her subordinates. Emma's heart pounded hard and she wished she *was* being punished. At least then she would know they had thought about her and realized she was missing. The idea that they had forgotten about her was a much bigger and scarier possibility in her mind, and one she liked less. Being forgotten meant she was not worth thinking about.

"Emma Harris?"

Emma glanced over her shoulder at the woman who had called her name. She was tall in heels, with natural brown hair tied up into a professional bun. She wore a pencil skirt and a peach button-down blouse. Emma recognized her as the school counselor, Ms. James. Emma had seen her plenty of times in the halls and common areas at the school but had never actually spoken to her. Emma avoided speaking to the adults in her school with as much dedication as she avoided speaking to the other students.

"Yes," Emma answered, guarded. Leader had warned her about school counselors before. *They are trained to pry*, he explained to her. *They will use your emotions to confound you and your words to condemn you. And if they don't condemn you for speaking out of turn*, I *certainly will*. He told her that after the first time she had talked to a school counselor, when she had shown up at school with a bruise under her right eye.

"It's 4:30, Emma," Ms. James said in a concerned tone. The tone was probably meant to show concern for Emma, but she just assumed the woman was concerned for her own evening plans. Emma had not considered it, but Ms. James probably had to stay until all the students departed. As uncomfortable as that thought was for Emma, it was a relief to think she would not be shut out of the school gates and left by the roadside. "Have you tried calling your parents?"

She had tried Monique many times with no luck. She had not called Leader because it was Monique's responsibility to organize her schedule. It was Monique's job to see that Emma was picked up from school. Leader did not deal with the day-to-day business of the House; it had never occurred to her to call him. In fact, Emma could not recall a time when she had a reason to call Leader. He was rarely home and even when he was, Monique was stricter, meaner, and less compliant; she would not thank Emma for going over her head to Leader because of a little tardiness.

"I am sure my mother will be here soon. She probably just got caught in traffic." It would never do to upset Monique.

Ms. James gave a sad smile only professional shrinks and doctors can give and said, "Come inside, please, Emma." She backed toward the door and opened it. That gesture said it all: she was not going to take no for an answer. Emma rose to her feet, pulling her backpack onto her shoulder, and uncomfortably followed the counselor into the school.

As they came into the entryway, the woman stepped up and walked alongside her down the hall.

"This is the latest I have ever seen you stay at school, Emma. Did you join the Chess Club? They just let out a little while ago." All extracurriculars got out by four o'clock; it was in the student handbook.

"No," Emma answered curtly. She had not joined the Chess Club because Leader would not let her join any extracurriculars. Not that she would be interested in Chess Club, anyway, she realized. It was sports she wanted; something physical.

"Well, this is a late afternoon for you, isn't it?"

Emma chose not to respond to such a benign platitude. Obviously it was a late afternoon or they would not even be having this conversation.

"Were you able to get some studying done? Or reading? When I'm stuck somewhere unexpectedly, I like to pull out a book and read."

Emma lifted her eyes to the woman's face, studying her critically. She was a pretty enough lady, better than any of the other teachers at the school by a longshot. She was probably accustomed to her beauty and her charm working on students, loosening them up. But that would never work on Emma. She had too much experience with Leader and Monique, and they were the most beautiful people in the world.

Again, Emma said nothing in response. She did not want to give the woman any words that could condemn her, as Leader warned her counselors would do. Emma lengthened her stride toward the administrative offices, speeding her pace.

Most of the desks were empty now that the staff had all gone home. It was the quietest Emma had ever seen the offices. Usually there were no less than four secretaries, a half dozen students, and parents and other educators milling around. While none of the lights had been extinguished, the place seemed somehow darker without so many people to bring it life. Ms. James indicated Emma should sit in one of the waiting chairs along the walls, then went behind a desk and turned on a computer. Emma did not sit.

"Have you tried calling your mother?"

"Yes, ma'am." Emma looked away from the woman's prying eyes. She read the motivational posters on the walls, wondering idly whose job it was to create these posters for kids who would probably only read them to avoid talking to educators and counselors.

Ms. James called her name, so Emma peered over a shoulder at her. Before the woman could ask any more questions, she offered, "I also called my house but there was no answer."

That had been bizarre enough to make her uneasy. There was always someone home to pick up the House phone. Always. What were they all doing that no one could be bothered? What were they all doing that they did not notice Emma was missing? She shoved her rising panic down into the pit of her stomach and turned away to continue her perusal of the office signage.

"What about your father?"

Emma stiffened at the mention of Leader. Her tone was too interested, like she was just waiting to pounce on dysfunction in a student's life. Fearing she would betray some of her frustration or fear, Emma made her voice as light as possible.

"My father is away. When he dropped me off this morning, he was headed to the airport."

The counselor's eyes intensified, but her tone remained light, "Let's just give him a call, hmm?" She picked up the office phone and, glancing at the computer, typed a number into the phone base. She must have had access to the school contact roster from that computer. Emma would have liked to protest, but she could not manufacture any compelling reasons not to call. At least, not reasons she could share and still maintain her cover.

Placing the phone up to her ear, Ms. James gave Emma a slight smile. Emma could barely hear the ringing through the receiver from this distance. Then she heard a voice but couldn't make out the words.

"Hello, Mr. Harris," Ms. James said in the professional voice all educators seemed to cultivate. "This is Ms. James, the school counselor at Avanair Preparatory ... Yes, that's right ... I hope I'm not disturbing you. I am calling because Emma was not picked up from school today ... Yes, I have her right here ... Of course. Please hold for a moment." Her eyes focused once more on Emma and she smiled. "He would like to speak with you."

Emma felt as though her legs had turned watery. She had to think through the motions of walking as she approached the desk. The counselor offered the phone to her, then watched her with those intense, unnaturally interested eyes. As casually as she could manage, Emma brought the phone to her ear.

"Father?" she asked into the receiver.

"Emma, are you all right?" He sounded concerned. It was such a contrast to the tone of his dismissal of her that morning that she doubted for a moment it was him. "Emma?"

"Yes, sir, I'm fine," she assured him. Aware of the counselor's presence, she carefully worded her explanation for the call. "I tried to call Mother, but there was no answer, and no answer at the House. I'm sure she's just stuck in traffic ..." Emma moved away from the counselor slightly—as far as the coiled cord would allow—and dropped to a whisper, "Or she maybe got busy and ... forgot about me."

The pause after her words made her worry that he was angry with her, but when he spoke again, his tone was as controlled and musical as ever. "I am sure there was just confusion about who was meant to pick you up. No one forgot about you. You are an important part of my Family. It is unacceptable for you to be left at school all afternoon, as if your time is not important."

There was a tightness to his final words that caused Emma to shrug away from his displeasure. She tried to lighten herself of the fear of his disapproval. "I did not waste any time, Father. I got all my homework done while I was waiting and reread most of my English text." Emma became acutely aware of the counselor again when the woman shifted her movement and the chair creaked. Emma dropped her voice to a whisper. "I don't have your number in my phone or I might have called you sooner, before the school could get involved."

"Don't worry about that," he replied coolly. "I'll take care of the school. And why, in the name of hatred and peace, do you not have my number? Amos ought to have taken care of that for you when he issued your new phone." Emma did not admit that she had removed his number from her phone last time he had come home. It had been after he had punished her for insubordinate speech. She had had no recourse and removing him from her phone had seemed the best retaliation at the time. Not, Emma thought reasonably, that she would ever have called him today if the choice had been hers.

"When we hang up, I will call your phone and I want you to save my number. Amos should have fully programmed that phone for you before he gave it over. This should never have happened!" Emma winced away from the crackling fury in his tone. Amos would probably get the sharp edge of Leader's tongue later, but not even protecting Amos was inducement enough for her to come clean when Leader was this angry.

"Yes, sir," she replied, but she wasn't sure if she was answering his instruction to save his number or replying to assuage his anger. "Do you know where Mother is? Is she on her way?"

"She's in a meeting."

"Oh." Emma's shoulders itched with the feeling of Ms. James' scrutiny. "Can *you* come get me?"

"I'm in Vermont. But I'm sending a message to Monique right now. She will be there soon. This should never have been allowed to happen and will not happen again, all right? Let me talk to the counselor. And Emma? I will take care of this."

"Okay." The word was just a wooden object falling off her tongue, trying to clatter away his anger. She could not understand why his voice was so intense or why his anger seeped around his words into her soul. Hardly feeling the woodenness of her arm, she handed the phone back to Ms. James. "He wants to talk to you."

She was certain her words sounded as wooden as her mouth felt, but she couldn't help it. She walked back to the line of chairs and this time seated herself. She looked again at a motivational poster on the wall, but she did not actually read it. All she could hear was the tone of Leader's calm wrath filling up the room with the breadth of it. It muted the world around her, draining it of its tone and color. Everything paled because Leader was angry.

Ms. James talked with Leader for a few minutes of polite and professional conversation. Most of the time she was typing at the computer, so she could hardly be paying him the attention he deserved. Somewhere in the distance in her mind, Emma was aware of her own annoyance at that. How could the counselor do anything else except listen to Leader, hanging upon his every word like a root clinging to the soil during a hurricane?

Ms. James shut down the computer and hung up the phone. Then she smiled at Emma.

"He says he will call your mother at work. You and I can just wait here in the office, okay?"

The light tone was in such contrast to Leader's that it jerked Emma forcefully back into the moment. It was as if the woman thought she was a five-year-old. Emma deigned not to reply except to cross her legs and fold her hands on top of them.

"How are you liking Avanair?" Ms. James asked in a conversational tone. "You're quite new here."

Emma detested comments like that—ones meant to sound interested and involved but were actually just telling someone a fact about themselves that was common knowledge. Might as well tell her she's a girl or she's a blonde. It was a manipulative comment meant to make her open up. Counselors were full of those kinds of observations. Things like "You seem upset" when someone is crying, and "That must have made you angry" when someone just got pulled out of a fistfight.

Emma answered in a detached tone, being as polite as possible while using as few words as she could manage. "It's a fine institution."

Ms. James tried to make more of her manipulative small talk, but Emma was not in the mood. She answered the questions with little more than sounds from her throat. She removed her phone from her backpack and stared determinedly at the screen. She hoped this attention to her phone, mimicked from Emma's observations of her schoolmates, would deter the counselor. It did not work.

"Where did you come from?"

Emma's eyes jerked up. It took Emma a moment to realize the counselor was asking about her previous schools, and not referencing the existential questions Emma frequently asked herself.

"From whence did you come," Emma said quietly. It was rude to correct people on their grammatic phrasing; she wanted to kick Leader's teeth in when he did it. But the correction was out of her mouth before she could stop it.

Ms. James smiled as if she was not at all perturbed by Emma's corrections. "Which school had the privilege of calling you its student, before Avanair?"

Emma let out a sigh of exhaustion.

"Honestly, I don't know." She did not exactly whisper, but the quietness of her tone was in direct relation to how tired she was of this small talk. She had endured hours of it today, following Cara around like a dedicated crony between classes and even at lunch. Brinley had insisted she join them, so she looked like she belonged, and it would not be so confusing when she showed up at the party.

"All private schools start to blur together after a while. When I leave here, I probably won't be able to remember Avanair, either."

Emma glanced at the clock on the wall, watching the hands creep closer and closer to five. It was approaching the time when she should have been at Cara's house to dress. It was a stupid thought, one that she struck down with a furious blast of self-loathing. But it reappeared a few minutes later when the minute hand marched steadily onto the 12.

"Well, that's too bad," Ms. James answered, still trying to pull Emma into conversation. "I would have hoped this place might have an impression on you. Have you made any friends?"

Emma snorted. Friendship was such a ludicrous idea. Emma could not even get along with the people in her own House, people who lived, trained, and learned alongside her. How was she meant to relate to people on the outside? Especially as she was not permitted to join any teams or clubs.

"No."

"I thought I saw you with Cara Winters today. Could that become something, maybe?"

Emma stared straight into the counselor's face, intending to respond rudely. But something in the woman's eyes halted her. An intensity she only associated with Leader and Monique. Interest, certainly, but deeper than professional curiosity. It unnerved Emma. She balanced her tone.

"I don't think so. They're just being … nice." The word did not in any way apply to Cara and her accomplices. It was well-chosen, though; it backed Ms. James off.

"I'm sure that's not true. You might give Cara a chance. She seems to be well-liked."

Emma blinked at her. Cara was not well-liked. She was feared. But Emma had to play her part now. Ms. James' keen interest had rattled her out of her self-absorbed misery.

"Maybe," Emma demurred, giving the counselor what she needed to back off.

As promised, Leader called a few minutes later. When the phone in her hands rang, it broke the awkward silence that had fallen in the room. It startled Emma and the counselor both. But she scrambled to answer.

"Monique is on her way," Leader promised her, but his voice was extremely cool. "Wait in the office until she gets there." He paused, and his voice softened—as soft as solid rock could be. "Are you sure you're okay?"

His concern surprised her. "Yes. How soon will she get here?"

"She will be there right away, Emma. She's in the canyon already. Save this number, do you understand? And if this ever happens again, you call me immediately. Don't wait until you're alone with the counselor at five o'clock at night. Do you understand me?"

"Yes, sir." She understood that he, like Emma, did not trust school shrinks. He hung up and she obediently saved his number into her phone directory again.

"He seems very worried," Ms. James said with a smile, seating herself in the chair beside Emma.

"Yes," Emma answered, sliding as far from the counselor as her chair would allow. "He's very protective of me. I'm his baby."

"Well, that's nice sometimes, isn't it?"

Emma did not want to talk. Not about Leader or anything. Not with a shrink, so she said only, "Yes," and then clamped her teeth closed over everything else.

Chapter Twelve

In the deep silence, Emma heard Monique as she entered the school. Her six-inch heels made a distinct clacking on the tiles that Emma could recognize anywhere. It echoed through the empty school hallways all the way from the entryway door. Additionally, she was talking into her hands-free headset, engaged in a conversation which, by her tone, was less-than-pleasant. Monique was clearly furious. Emma feared that anger would crash down on her head when Monique entered the office through the glass doors. But Monique seemed only relieved when she laid eyes on Emma, pausing halfway into the room to study her with troubled eyes.

"Hang on," she snapped into her headset. She crossed the room to Emma, holding out a hand in a beckoning gesture. "Emma, I'm so sorry, honey. I got caught up at work, and I—"

Emma jerked to her feet and said, "Can we just go?" The continued scrutiny of the school social worker was unbearable; she wanted to be away from those too-interested eyes. Emma hauled her backpack onto one shoulder and marched past Monique into the hall.

"I'm sorry to inconvenience you," Monique told Ms. James inside the office. If it was meant to be an apology, it missed. Her tone was too dismissive to be apologetic. "This has never happened before. We had crossed signals today."

"No, no," Ms. James answered, waving her hand in a calming gesture. "It is fine, Mrs. Harris. Really. The extra time gave Emma and me a chance to get to know each other a little bit. But if you have a moment, I would like to speak to you, if I may. About Emma."

Emma spun back in alarm. Monique was also surprised, but she responded gracefully. "Of course." She waved Emma out of the office and snapped the door shut.

Waiting outside the glass doors, Emma worried about what Ms. James might be saying to Monique, or what she might know. She had eyes all over the school;

was it possible she knew about the Cara Winters party? Or did she just want to tattle that Emma had been rude and reticent while waiting in the office? It wasn't exactly the way she was supposed to behave if she was trying to keep up the role Leader had assigned her while on mission in Utah. If Ms. James mentioned something about her behavior, she could get into serious trouble for jeopardizing their image here.

While Leader was away, Monique was responsible for the House and, if she wanted to, she could quite easily make Emma's life unbearable. In Emma's opinion, it was almost worse to anger Monique because she was *always there*. Leader at least disappeared on business trips most of the time, so his anger was always short-fused and hot. Monique could smolder for days.

Emma stood near enough to the door to try and listen in, but Monique's and the counselor's voices were only soft drones. At least no one seemed angry. Although, Monique raged cold instead of burning hot.

Monique breezed through the door only a few minutes later, sweeping Emma ahead of her through the commons area and toward the exit. She seemed no angrier now than she had before the short meeting. She tapped a button on her phone and started talking again into her headset, as if her conversation had not been interrupted by a few minutes' conversation with Emma's school counselor. If not for her hand on Emma's shoulder, she might have forgotten Emma completely.

"It's not like that! What was I supposed to do, tell her to shove off and leave us alone? I don't think—" Monique gave an exasperated sigh and fell silent. It was Leader then; he was the only person who ever could silence Monique when she went on a tirade. Her grating frustration was obvious in her every movement, from the way she slammed the door open and ushered Emma through, to the ferocious way she remote-started and unlocked the car. Emma tried to make herself small as she opened the passenger back door of the Lexus, tossed her bag in, and skulked into the front seat. She buckled her seatbelt and sat back against the leather seat. Not wanting to draw Monique's eye, she turned her gaze out the side window and shrunk down to make herself appear smaller.

Monique got in with her normal deadly grace, and though her face was emotionless, the way she shoved the car into gear spoke volumes of her vexation. As soon as she had pulled away from the school, she clicked a button on her phone and removed the headset. Leader's voice came rasping through the car speakers.

"I do not have to tell you the importance of my time in Vermont, Monique. If I thought you could not handle everything in my absence, I would have postponed the trip."

"God, Leader! It was a simple mistake," Monique argued. It was a dangerous thing, arguing with Leader, though Monique seemed to do it every day. "I *know* Vermont is important. I have everything well in hand. I am sorry that nosey counselor thought it was necessary to disturb you about this." She finished that off with an expletive that was probably meant to describe the counselor.

"You watch your language!" Leader's voice rang through the vehicle. Emma winced at the ferocity of the tone. "And don't you dare blame the counselor for being concerned. It is her job to be concerned. If you were doing your job, she wouldn't have to be concerned about Emma. Really, Monique, this is inexcusable. You're my Number Two! I should be able to rely on my Number Two but, as always, I have to do everything myself."

Monique's eyes squeezed shut. She pinched the bridge of her nose with her fingers and took a deep breath. When she opened her eyes, she exited the school driving lane and merged into canyon road traffic. In a forced calm, she assured him,

"I have everything under control now, Leader. You can go back to your conference."

"Don't you dare condescend me, Monique. I'll be on the very next flight home. I want to talk to you about this up close and personal." The line clicked and then there was silence.

Monique swore under her breath and gave a disgusted shake of her head, but she did not look worried. She never looked anything but perfectly calm. The way she weaved dangerously through traffic, though, suggested she was not as calm as she let herself appear. Emma tried to disappear into the seat, wishing to stay out of sight and, thereby, out of mind. Monique was a force to reckon with when she was angry.

"You okay?" Monique asked, glancing at her from the corner of her eye.

Emma did not look her direction. She just answered, "Yeah."

Monique, as always, was intense. "I'm sorry about this, Emma. I thought I made it clear to Ilene that she was supposed to come get you today."

"It's fine." Ilene had probably decided to ignore that particular order. On her best day, Ilene ignored Emma and pretended she did not exist. She was not ruthless or unkind like Scott and Adam, but she had little patience for the children in the House. "It's not like I was hurt or anything. I just had to stay at school a little longer than normal. I got my homework done."

Still, she did not look Monique's direction. She feared that if she looked at her, Monique would see the depth of her pain over being forgotten. It was not the first time she had been abandoned. Emma watched the trees go whizzing past on the side of the road.

"Ilene has never ignored me before. I am sure it is just a misunderstanding." Emma could feel Monique's gaze again, a penetrating, searching gaze, if brief. But Emma did not return it. "You should have called me."

"I did," Emma snapped. She kept her eyes averted, but she forced herself calm. When she spoke again, she was considerably more detached. "There was no answer. I called several times."

When she dared a glance at Monique, the severe woman was watching the road. Emma went back to studying the trees. She did not want to think any more about how Monique or Ilene or everyone had forgotten she existed and abandoned her at school all afternoon. She was tired with making up excuses for them. "Self-involved" was the only reason she wanted to think about now. She was angry, but only because she had lost her chance to find a way to Cara Winters' party. If she had been picked up from school on time, she might have been able to create some kind of believable excuse, and Monique may have let her go. Also, Leader would have stayed in Vermont, and she would not have had to deal with him for at least a few more days.

"I was on a conference call. Don't you have my work number?"

"I am fine, Monique!" Her tone lost its calm disinterest. She shot a severe glance at the older woman, catching her quick searching gaze. "I'm hungry and tired." A sudden thought jumped into her head, and she added, "And now I'm late for my Biology study group with Cara Winters. You are acting like I was nearly killed or something! I'm annoyed, but I'm fine." She held her breath, choking on the lie, but also basking in the feeling of thrill that accompanied lying to a superior.

Monique made a sound in her throat but kept her eyes on the road. "You have a study group tonight?" Unlike Monique's normal brisk tone, this was slow and musing. Emma focused on normalizing her breathing, though her throat tried to constrict.

"Yes, with Cara Winters and some of her friends. I was supposed to be there at 5, but ..." she presented the clock in the dash, which read 5:17. "Evidently, I'm not going to make it." She bit down on her teeth, jaw creaking as she waited for Monique to punish her for lying.

"Why didn't you tell me about this study group?"

Emma thought she could feel her heartbeat in her toes. She let out a breath, hoping it sounded like a sigh rather than the gush of fear it was. The fluttering or worry in her stomach, like the flapping of tiny wings, made her scramble for a response that Monique would find acceptable. Something that would get her out of trouble and conceal her lies. However, she found that the lie was growing in her brain, coming easily now she had started.

"Cara just told me about it yesterday. I didn't even know the specific time until today. They are the most hopeless group of worthless sloths—of *course* they would leave it to the very last second."

Monique raised one stern brow, looking at her doubtfully, and Emma almost lost her nerve and confessed. She went for a little more honesty.

"I don't know how these things work, Monique! Study groups and social gatherings ... I don't know how to do any of it. Cara was the leader. She organized it; I just listened to her instructions."

Monique drew a measured breath, returning her attention to the road. She swerved into traffic, cutting off a vehicle who intended to ignore her blinker. Her tone returned to its regular brisk pace. "How long will you be?"

A blossom of hope filled Emma, though she was careful to hide it.

"I have no idea. A few hours, probably, if I know how unfocused these girls are."

Emma had hardly expected it to work. She half-thought Monique would declare she was a liar and spend the remainder of their car ride listing all of Emma's faults. Lists of punishments came into Emma's mind, and again she felt a rise of panic. However, Monique had taken the lie: hook, line, and sinker.

"Where does she live?"

Emma had to think fast. "4950 West Pine in Orem."

Monique gave a brisk nod. "All right, Emma. I will drop you off there and you can call my cell when you're finished."

Emma stared at her, shocked at how easily the lie had succeeded. Monique was going to let her go? To a gathering with people who were not part of the Family? It seemed almost impossible. Her studying gaze caught Monique's eye then and the woman turned to look at her. Emma jerked her gaze back to the window. She knew that one look at her face would give it all away. She hoped instead that Monique assumed Emma was still angry about being picked up late. The truth was, Emma was delighted now about the mix up, because it had given her the courage and the means to convince Monique to let her go to Cara's.

"Fine," Emma answered coldly, as if she did not care. In nervous excitement, she watched I-15 traffic out the passenger window. She thought forward, toward the party at Cara's. And she planned some specific words she could say about the "biology study group" and how they had gotten nothing of substance done. Then Emma would insist she would ask the teacher to be removed from the group, that way Emma would not have to answer awkward questions if Monique ever wanted to know what had happened with her group project.

Chapter Thirteen

Monique dropped Emma off in front of a four-story mansion in the gated community on Pine. It was probably the ugliest monstrosity of a house Emma had ever seen. It seemed to be taking over the street, it was so large and sprawling. Emma grabbed her backpack from the back seat, nodded to Monique, and walked purposefully toward the front door. She walked slowly, waiting until the Lexus turned a corner before she changed course and took off running. She had given Monique a false address, but Cara's house was only one street over on Maple.

Cara's house was nearly as large as the mansion where Emma had been dropped off, but it was of a more modest and attractive design. Every light in the house was on and the house was decorated with balloons and banners that said **Happy Birthday, Cara!** Emma walked up the steps in the landscaped yard and knocked on the giant wooden doors.

Brinley opened them with a bright smile. She was dressed in a black strappy camisole, white slacks that were extremely tight on her, and an expensive scarf around her neck. Her makeup was way too dark for her complexion, and her hair had been curled and pulled up in a messy bun. It was too sexy a look for a 15-year-old girl.

Her smile dropped away immediately. "You're 30 minutes late!"

She hauled Emma inside. "And still in your uniform? You're killing me!" She gave Emma no time to look around the mansion; she hauled her up the nearest floating staircase to the wing that was Cara's room. Cara's entire clique was there getting ready for the party, putting on makeup as ridiculous as Brinley's, and outfits as sexy. Emma looked around the room in wonder. She had been overjoyed with her own room at the House, but her room could have fit five or six times inside Cara's room, with space to spare.

"Finally!" Cara snapped in exasperation as she came from behind a dressing screen. She wore a dress that may as well have not been there at all for how tight and short it was. Her hair was down in massive ringlets, and her makeup was light and attractive.

"What happened to you?" Cara demanded of Emma, but she did not wait for an answer. She pointed a bossy finger at a massive pile of clothing and coats on the bed. "Brinley, get her dressed before anyone shows up and sees her looking like that."

Brinley pulled Emma toward the bed. This bed was large enough that half the girls in the school could probably sleep on it comfortably. Idly, Emma wondered where they found bedding for it.

On the bed were piles and piles of clothing. Brinley grabbed Emma's backpack and shoved it onto a pile, ignoring Emma's protests. She selected a few pieces and held them up to Emma, only to discard them onto another pile. Nothing she said made any impression on Brinley; she might as well have been talking to Adam or Scott for all the care Brinley paid to her opinions. After a few tiresome minutes standing silently while Brinley sighed and fussed over the "Ridiculous lack of acceptable clothing," Brinley finally shoved a pinkish dress into Emma's hands and said, "Put this on. I hope you're freshly shaved." She was, because she shaved every day before school since she had to wear the stupid pleated skirt.

Brinley did not indicate a bathroom or a dressing room where Emma could dress. The other girls in the room did not bother to seek out a modest space. And Cara was once again behind the only dressing screen. Brinley snapped her fingers at Emma to urge quickness. So, after another embarrassed glance around the room, she stripped right there. She was more modest about it than the others, but Brinley still managed to see a large bruise across her ribs.

"What the heck?" Brinley demanded, jerking the dress out of her hands so she could get a better look at the contusion. "Someone beat you?"

"No," Emma said patiently, pulling the dress back into her grasp. "I was kicked in the ribs doing martial arts."

Brinley blinked at her. "Martial arts? Really?" For a moment, Emma thought she had impressed the girl. But then Brinley laughed and rolled her eyes. "You are such a colossal bore."

She shoved Emma away and then turned to another girl to laugh and make jokes at Emma's expense. Emma did her best to ignore them. She dressed, and then submitted to Brinley's manhandling. She zipped Emma in, all the time abusing her for not knowing how to wear this kind of dress, and for not taking off her bra, which she had to do to wear this kind of dress. Emma had never been in public without a bra since she started wearing one in seventh grade. Losing it made her feel even less secure than she already felt. Brinley laughed harshly at her when she reluctantly unhooked it and pulled it off.

"What are you even doing here?" Brinley snapped with another roll of her eyes. Emma was trying desperately hard not to ask herself that same question. She was as far out of her element as possible.

Brinley pushed her in front of the full-length mirror and adjusted the dress on her, pulling in some places, smoothing in others. It was not "pinkish," Brinley informed her. It was dusted rose, and the tie around the middle was mauve. Emma looked at herself and doubted. She looked ridiculous, like a little girl dressed in her mother's Sunday dress. Not that the dress was too big or too small, it just didn't seem to fit her. Brinley did not care about that.

"It looks awesome on you. Thank goodness you don't have boobs yet."

Emma took offense at that comment, since she thought she had a very nicely formed set. But she said nothing, because it would do her no good to respond to a bully's criticisms. She had spent her life mostly ignoring them.

Her dusted rose dress had no sleeves or straps. The zipper held it up, tight as the thing was on her body. The mauve tie across the middle of the dress did not make her feel any more secure. The hemline was not quite halfway down to her knees, but she did not dare pull it down any farther, or she might expose her chest. Brinley's comment made sense; Emma, too, was glad she was not any bigger in the top. There would have been no way to keep the dress up if the zipper did not cinch her in completely.

All the dresses in the room were as immodest as hers, which surprised her. She had assumed these girls were religious, modest girls, like so many at school and in this valley. Only two of the girls were wearing clothing that covered shoulders and hid their thighs. It seemed a contradiction to what Leader had told Emma about this place. He had cautioned her to dress modestly last night, because modesty was an element of the part he expected her to play. But he had insisted on it because she was meant to blend in. In this crowd, though, blending in meant dressing like a hooker.

Brinley stepped into another room that appeared to be a closet. When she returned, she carried a pair of black heels. She dropped them at Emma's feet. "Wear these."

Emma pulled them on. She had never worn heels this high before, but she had seen Monique in them every day. To the best of her ability, she copied Monique's movements, with little success. This time, though, Brinley did not seem to notice. Emma did as well as any of the other heeled girls in the room.

Brinley made a spinning gesture with one finger and ordered Emma, "Turn." Emma made a careful circle, presenting herself for Brinley's inspection, and the girl nodded, accepting her own handiwork. But, of course, her opinion was not as important as the queen's.

"Cara, how's this?" Brinley asked in a tone much sweeter and more entreating than she had ever used with Emma. She waited patiently for Cara to finish her own business at a mirror, then presented Emma with the flick of a wrist. Cara gave a curt nod of approval and ordered, "Makeup."

Brinley sighed in annoyance, but she obeyed. She shoved Emma toward the vanity, kicking aside discarded clothing, shoes, and purses. The vanity was a permanent fixture in Cara's room—a mirror the full length of one wall, with four stools set in the floor at perfect intervals, and counter and cabinets for just this sort of dress-up party. Brinley commandeered a stool from a girl who allowed herself to be pushed aside without an argument. She gestured toward the stool, and Emma looked at it uncomfortably.

"I can do my own makeup," she insisted, but Brinley only rolled her eyes at her and pushed Emma onto the stool. Reining in her urge to smack the bratty expression off Brinley's face, Emma conceded. She had already come this far; she figured she might as well let Brinley do her worst. She made no protest when Brinley selected the colors and started making her up. There was no going back now.

After a few minutes of Brinley's officious orders to "close your eyes" and "look up," she was startled when Brinley abruptly turned the stool to face the mirror. Emma hardly recognized herself. Her makeup was dark and smoky, like Brinley's, and there was glitter everywhere, including in her hair, which Brinley was taking a brush to. It was nice not to recognize herself for a few minutes, Emma thought, since she was not supposed to be there, and would get into serious loads of trouble if Monique found out about it.

The flurry of girls getting ready around them increased in number and fervor. More and more girls joined them, and Emma wondered if anyone dressed at their own houses or if it was standard opocedure to get dressed at the host house. Cara's clique was still at the hub of activity but now they were surrounded by about half the girls from school.

Brinley did not have time to curl her hair, which she lamented and blamed Emma for. "You should have gotten here on time!" She did dump about half a gallon of product on it, pinned it up with probably a million bobby pins, and tied a pink ribbon around it all. Emma thought the entire ensemble looked nice. A little like a prostitute, but nice.

Brinley abandoned her with an order, "Don't embarrass Cara." She went back to the clique with whom she really belonged. Emma was elbowed out of the stool and away from the mirror by frantic latecomers.

With a hundred girls in there, Cara's room seemed much smaller than when Emma had entered it half an hour ago. The girls talked to each other about everything from menstrual cramps to boyfriends. They laughed at jokes Emma did not understand, said mean things about girls and boys Emma did not know, and talked about the hottie Algebra teacher. They dressed multiple times, sharing and exchanging their things. They helped each other with makeup, hair, dress choices, shoes, and everything Emma could have imagined. Emma would not have known how to insert herself, even if she had been welcome. She wasn't, of course; that would have embarrassed Cara. She was in way over her head. She started to wish she had just told Cara no and not come to the party. In all this jumble of girls, would Cara's mother even have noticed her absence? Emma backed out of the frenzy.

She had no desire to stay in Cara's room in this jumble of girls who looked at her like she did not belong there. Which she absolutely didn't. Not sure what to do, and being jostled no matter where she stood, Emma escaped from the room. She planned to go downstairs and take a quick look around but found herself wandering into another trap. The party had already started. Music blasted from the speakers in the walls, boys were everywhere, and there was more talking, laughing, and joking about things she did not know anything about. Also, there was alcohol. She could smell it, but she could not see where it was. So much for movies and cake!

When some people spoke to her, she tried to respond, at first. She quickly realized, however, that she did not know what they were talking about. By their leering smiles, she thought it must have mostly been inappropriate chatter, so she stopped answering. The music was so loud she was not sure she heard them all correctly, anyway. She started pointing at the speakers when people spoke to her, saying only, "Music!" as her explanation for not responding politely as she pushed past them.

"Hi!" shouted an older woman, snatching at her arm to catch her attention. Emma tried to point toward the speakers, but the woman did not wait for an answer. "I'm so glad you could make it, Emma!" This was obviously Cara's mother, though there were few similarities in their features. For instance, she had a polite smile. She gestured around. "You have a good time. Okay? Make some friends!"

Emma smiled. "Thanks." She did not know what else to say because she was not really glad to be there, overwhelmed as she was, but she felt like she should be polite.

The woman was gone through the throngs of people as quickly as she had appeared. Emma felt very alone. She looked around with a sigh. She thought maybe it would be worth Monique's wrath, if only she would pick her up and take her out of here. But her phone was upstairs in her backpack, and there was no way she was braving the crowd up there again.

Chapter Fourteen

Someone grabbed Emma's hand and jerked her through the crowd. She panicked for a moment, fearing it would be Monique, come to find her. But there was a break in the throngs, and the person whose hand surrounded hers turned to face her and smiled.

"I thought that was you beneath all that black eyeliner," he said with a grin.

"Benjamin Stillwell," Emma said, shocked, and not a little relieved. "Of the Alpine Heights Stillwells. What are you doing here?"

He laughed in answer and shook a scolding finger. "What are *you* doing here, Emma Harris of the River Bottoms Harrises? *My* father works with Mr. Winters, and our families are old friends. You're the one who appears to be out of place."

She nodded and found herself telling the truth. "Cara only invited me because her mother told her she had to. She was pretty unhappy about it, actually. She doesn't like me."

He rolled his eyes, and Emma felt a thrill of relief that he shared her annoyance over Cara's assertions. "She's intimidated by you because you're so beautiful. She and her friends aren't used to having competition."

Emma smiled softly, cocking her head to the side. "You think I'm beautiful?"

He seemed surprised. "Of course, I do! I mean, I thought you were beautiful at the party last night. You don't look like yourself tonight." He winked when she blushed in embarrassment.

"Yeah, I let Cara's friends dress me."

Benjamin grinned. "They're silly girls. You were the most beautiful girl in the room last night." He glanced around and then said, "Look around you, Emma. Every man in the room thinks you're the most beautiful girl here." She glanced around as she had been instructed. Many of the boys in the room were staring at her, but people always stared at her.

"They watch me because I'm so awkward," she answered, shaking off his compliment.

He shook his head at her, mock seriousness on his face. "Not true. That's not the way it works. When girls are awkward, guys avoid looking at them. When they're beautiful, guys stare. True, they probably all want to get in your pants, but it's still a little flattering, right?"

Emma stared up at him, unsure. "Is that why you're talking to me? To get into my pants?" When he laughed heartily at that, she asked, "No? Just being nice?"

He gave her a sly grin. "Seventy percent nice thing; twenty percent pants."

She scowled. "You're missing ten percent."

He gave her an innocent shrug. "So, I'm ten percent a mystery."

Then he looked around the room. He had an advantage of height she didn't have; he could see over the tops of people's heads. To her it was like a maze of endless bodies all around her. He began pulling her after him and, not knowing where else she would go, she chose to follow him.

"Do you want something to drink? The kitchen is this way." He indicated with his hand toward a congregation of people.

"I don't think it's a good idea to drink anything here. I can smell alcohol."

Benjamin laughed again. "Come on, Emma! You can open your own drink, so you know no one tampered with it." Emma mused it was probably too late to worry that Monique had told her to stay away from Benjamin. She had already lied to Monique and disobeyed her. Besides, she liked to be around Benjamin. He treated her like a regular person.

The crowd parted around Benjamin, and Emma was uncomfortably aware of the eyes of the people on her. He had been right that they stared at her. She tried to imagine them in the way he had instructed her—as admirers—but it was hard when for so long she had assumed everyone watched her because she was a weirdo.

In the kitchen, Emma opened a can of soda. She had never had soda before, so her first swallow made her nose tingle and caused her to choke. Benjamin laughed at her as she tried to recover. She did her best not to acknowledge his laughter, but she put the soda down with every intention of not picking it up again. She grabbed a bottled water instead because she knew that would be safe. It tasted strongly of minerals but was a vast improvement on the soda.

"You're really kind of peculiar, Emma," Benjamin said with a smile to take any sting out of the words. He tapped his soda can against Emma's water bottle and said, "Cheers!" She smiled in response.

"Is this what all birthday parties are like?" She watched some boys push and shove at each other on the other side of the kitchen bar, in a way that may or may not have been playful.

"Not really. Usually there is some structure and perhaps a theme. But the Winters like to push the boundaries of popular society. They throw a shindig on the slightest provocation. It usually involves more people than fire codes allow, loud music, and an open bar."

Emma was confused. She thought most kids at her school, or their parents at least, were religious, and that this kind of party was a violation of their beliefs about social conduct. In the school cafeteria, she had heard kids talking about the evils of caffeinated beverages. Wasn't beer even worse? Leader thought it was. To her knowledge, the only time anyone in the Family had a drink was at a social function where they were trying to blend in and be polite. But even at the party last night Monique had not touched her wine; it was not healthy for the body.

"I know," Benjamin whispered near her ear. "It is a little hypocritical to profess to be one thing and behave differently." She glanced up at him in alarm, and he grinned. "We all have our faults." She smiled. It was eerie how well he could determine her thoughts. She wondered if her expression gave her away. Benjamin was a closed book on that score.

"I just thought it was a little strange that there is such a good turnout. My father doesn't even allow us *near* alcohol." She looked around again, this time spotting Brinley leaning against a young man in what was probably supposed to be a dance, but it looked as if they needed to be alone for what they were doing. "He would be horrified if I was dancing like that or doing ... basically *anything* that people are doing here."

Benjamin took her hand and lead her through the crowd once more. He had to shout to be heard while saying, "So, what you are telling me is that your father does not know you are here."

She was startled by that, and her face gave away her guilt. He laughed. "It's fine. Most of the kids here did not have permission to come. And the few who did probably have parents who do not know what kind of party it is. If you look around, you can even identify the kids who did not know what they were getting themselves into. You can watch their internal struggle with right and wrong; it's all over their faces." He laughed again. "That's my favorite pastime at parties."

She allowed herself to be pulled along, smiling. He led her into the colossal living room where presents were on a decorated table. She swallowed because she had never even thought about bringing a gift. Benjamin saw her unease again and put it to rest.

"Forget about it, Emma. You were a pity invite, and anything you would have given her would have been donated to Charity Industries, anyway. She most likely won't even open them. The 'help' will do that."

Emma wondered what it would be like to think so highly of yourself that you did not even bother to open your own gifts. On second thought, she wondered what it would be like to get gifts at all. She did not remember anything that was given to her unless she needed it for a mission, even her clothes. She and the rest of her Family were restricted from accepting gifts.

The two of them settled on an empty space on a couch and began making comments and observations about the people around them. When Cara finally made it downstairs, there was cheering and wolf-whistles. Emma had to admit she looked fabulous. Her dress was different than the barely-there tight one she had been wearing upstairs. It was green and flowing, and modest in comparison to what many of the girls were wearing. The most prominent part of her outfit was the tiara she wore, set with stones that looked like diamonds and emeralds. They probably weren't actual gemstones or the tiara would be in a vault somewhere.

Once Cara joined the party, it seemed to revolve around her and gained a little more structure. Her parents toasted her 15-year-old soul, and her father invited young men to dance with her, if they could be gentlemen. She was absolutely glowing when a boy asked her to dance and the music changed from the penetrating rock to something soft and slow.

Emma settled back, content to watch rather than participate. She imagined what it might be like to be some man's daughter and have him kiss her on the head the way Cara's father did. And have him throw her a giant birthday bash. And make her into a spectacle in front of the whole school, in a good way. She imagined, but her level of imagination was thwarted by the idea that Leader and Monique did not care about her enough to even acknowledge her on her birthday.

"My parents forgot to pick me up from school today," Emma quietly admitted to Benjamin beside her. He turned from people-watching and gave her a concerned look. "Yeah. They forgot about me. I sat on the steps for two hours, and then the nosey school counselor made me wait in the office. She called my father in Vermont, and he had to get ahold of my mother. She picked me up after 5."

"Jesus, Emma! That's ridiculous. How did they forget about you? Don't you have brothers that go to your school?"

"They were not at school today." She shrugged. It was strange how much being left at school affected her. She had been neither surprised nor dismayed about it at the time. It was just watching Cara with her family made her jealous. She was jealous of Cara's right to feel important. Emma had no right to feel important; her family was set up as a chain of command, in which she was positioned at the bottom. She would never be able to feel important or like she was special. Even if Leader threw her a party, it would only be a part of some scheme or mission and not about Emma at all. Emma wanted something to be about her.

"I'm sorry, Emma," Benjamin said, and he sounded empathetic. "I know how you feel. I can't tell you how many times I was forgotten or left behind."

"Yeah," she said, softening. "You said they left you at a party one time."

He scoffed. "They lost me at Disneyland and were not even concerned. I was picked up by Social Services."

Emma let out a long breath. "That is outrageous," she said, but she whispered it, shocked as she was that anyone could be so thoughtless.

"No more outrageous than your mother forgetting to pick you up from school for two and a half hours," he replied, tone tinged with anger. "It is infuriating because it is like they do not even think about you. Like somehow you're an afterthought."

Emma nodded, amazed at the accuracy of his words to describe her emotions. "That's it exactly." She looked away. She felt a sting in her throat and eyes. She could count on one hand the amount of times she had cried in the last five years. She could not believe this was bringing tears to her eyes.

"Hey," Benjamin whispered. He pulled her face around with two gentle fingers and looked her in the eye. Then he hugged her. "It's okay. They are assholes."

Emma remembered Amos hugging her, comforting her once. He had come upon her when she had failed to advance a belt in her martial arts training in what was considered a reasonable amount of time. Leader had watched her perform for all of five minutes before he declared "fail." He had said it to Monique, but Emma felt the full sting of the failure. And then when Leader had left the room, Monique gave her a ferocious reprimand and left her in tears. When Amos came in, there was nothing he could say to contradict Monique's disdain, but he had embraced Emma. He held her in his arms until her tears dried and her determination returned. That was the only time she remembered a hug that was not just for show. Emma allowed Benjamin to hug her.

After she recovered and apologized for crying—to which he responded severely that she need not apologize—they talked about mutual experiences. They shared stories about school and difficulty making friends. She talked about moving to Utah, although she avoided saying anything about where they came from as it was "forbidden conversation" outside the Family. They laughed together about living up to parental expectations and her difficulty with siblings. For the first time in her life, she felt like a regular kid having a regular conversation.

Chapter Fifteen

As the evening wore on, Emma never even thought about the passage of time. It was Benjamin who finally mentioned it. "So, where does your father think you are?"

She turned, suddenly alarmed. "What time is it? I told my mother I was at a study group."

Benjamin shook his head with a little laugh. "Rookie mistake. No one holds a study group on Friday night." His laughter died when he noticed how concerned she was, and he checked his phone for the time. "It's almost 9." Emma sprang to her feet.

"I have to call home," she announced, panicking a little. She had not thought this through, she realized. Monique was probably getting concerned. Maybe she had even tried to call, but Emma had left her phone in her backpack, upstairs in Cara's room. Emma turned and tried to push through the crowd, but Benjamin grabbed her arm.

"Emma, it's okay, all right? I'll take you home. My car's just outside, and I can drop you off a few houses away. You can tell them one of your friends gave you a ride."

Emma knew there were problems with this plan, but it seemed like the best option she had now.

"Thanks. I have to change and get my backpack. It's upstairs."

"I will wait right here," he answered and let her go.

She pushed through the crowd, but was again stopped, this time by a different boy. She did not recognize him, but he said, "Hey, new girl," so she assumed he was from her school.

"Dance with me," he ordered.

"I can't," she answered and tried to pull away. He wouldn't let go of her.

"Come on," he said, tightening his grip. "We would make a great—"

"I can't," she repeated and jerked her arm away.

He grabbed her again and this time he was not gentle. "Hey," he growled. He grabbed her by the backside and pulled her forcefully against him. "It's just a dance."

Emma was aware of Benjamin approaching. He grabbed the other boy's shoulder and firmly said, "Let her go."

The boy shoved Benjamin away, but he came right back, fists up. Emma tried to take advantage of the diversion to get away, but the boy's grip was too firm. He was not going to let her go.

Unfortunately for the boy, Emma calmed down. She calmed her mind and her body, and the forms automatically began. Using form 38, she freed herself from his grip and shoved him away. When he came back, she moved into form 51, a hit to the groin, which he blocked, and then to his kidney. She knew her self-defense like the back of her own hand. Despite being half his size, she had nearly 10 years of martial arts training behind her, and that greatly increased her chances of destroying him if he tried to touch her again.

He tried, but now he was angry and needed to save face. He came at her with his arms wide, as if to bear hug her or perhaps knock her to the ground. She slammed her hands against his shoulders to stop his momentum, and then she linked fingers behind his neck and shoved his head into her raised knee. He managed to break free, but he stumbled back. She stepped back into a defense position, ready for anything. The crowd around them now was pulling him away, trying to tell him he had had too much to drink and that he couldn't go around picking on a teenaged girl. He broke away from the people and lunged at Emma again. She dodged him and did a flying kick to his head. It fell short, glancing off his shoulder. because she was in a dress and it restricted her range. She moved into another attack form but was interrupted by a command that echoed above the blaring music.

"Stand down!"

Everyone in the room turned to see Leader and promptly moved aside for him. Emma Obeyed his command automatically, stepping into a ready-and-waiting stance. She did not dare look at him. Her mind, which ought to be clear during any type of formation, began to race. She could not imagine how he had located her or how he had returned so quickly from Vermont. She did not know what she would say to explain herself. She started thinking up lies that removed blame from her, but nothing would hold up. If she had gone to study group and found out it was a party, she should have called Monique right away. And what about the fact that she had told Monique a different address? There was no way to get out of this with a lie.

Leader grabbed her antagonist by the shirt and shoved him away. "Go home."

It was said in such a powerful tone that the boy stumbled back and shoved his way through the crowd. He looked back only once at Emma, with fierceness in his eyes, but she thought maybe she detected fear, as well.

Leader advanced on Emma. She wanted to run the other way, but she did not step out of her stance. She had learned from the time she was a small child not to step out of her stances until commanded to do so. Leader grabbed her chin in his rigid grip and tilted her face to look into his eyes. The look there frightened her more than any look he had ever given her. It said he was prepared to destroy her if she made the wrong move.

"Emmalyn," he said in a tone to match the expression of his eyes. "What are you wearing?" He pulled away from her and looked around. Someone had shut the music off and there was relative quiet around them. "What are you doing here?" he asked and looked back into her eyes. Cara and her parents were moving in now to find out what had disrupted the party.

"It's a party, sir," she answered, even though she suspected he was not looking for an answer.

"Where is your phone?" he asked next. Mr. Winters tried to speak to him, but Leader never looked away from Emma's eyes.

"In my backpack, upstairs."

Leader looked at her for a long time and then he stepped aside and pointed toward the stairs. "Two minutes." Without waiting for another second, she dashed away. The crowd parted around her as she took the stairs two at a time.

Behind her she could hear Mr. Winters saying, "It's just a little party, you know. No harm done."

But Leader's only response to that was, "I am taking my daughter home." His judgment was clear to them: he thought the Winters were irresponsible parents and a terrible influence over youngsters. Emma suspected that he was not judging them at all, but they certainly would think so, listening to his tone. Emma was certain he was plotting what he was going to do to her when she got back downstairs.

It took her too long to find her backpack, and her uniform was lost in the jumble of clothing. She considered bolting through a window, but where would she go? What would she do? *No!* she told herself firmly. It was time to stop running on impulse. She grabbed her backpack, slung it onto her shoulder, and turned to march downstairs. She checked her phone once before she got downstairs, just to see how many calls she had missed. She was surprised to see she had missed only one, from the house phone. Not that it gave her any relief.

Leader was waiting for her at the base of the stairs. He grabbed her arm above the elbow and hauled her through the crowd. She did not resist him. The crowd parted ahead of them. To Emma, it was just a sea of faces until she saw Cara. She thought, maybe for an instant, Cara looked concerned but then Emma was out the door and being hauled up the street.

Leader's BMW was parked in the middle of the street. He dragged Emma toward it then opened the back door behind the driver seat and shoved her in. She pulled her feet and arms out of the way just as he slammed the door shut. Pulling herself erect, Emma dropped her backpack on the floor and buckled her seatbelt. She did not dare look up. She could feel Monique's eyes on her from the passenger seat. She did not need to see the fury to know it was there.

Leader got in and shut his door sharply, though in the awkward silence Emma noted that he had not slammed it. He shoved his car into gear and drove off with his tires squealing on the pavement. Emma sat as small as she could in her seat, but it did nothing to take away the fear of her impending doom.

Monique tried to speak once, but Leader stabbed an accusing finger at her and she fell silent. The car ride was the longest and most painful ride of Emma's life, even though it was only a couple of miles to her neighborhood. She had only the company of her own thoughts and her ragged breathing. Over those loud sounds, she could not even focus on Leader or Monique. In her misery, they might not have even been there. All she could think about was how foolish she had been.

Going to the party had been a small crime compared to breaking her cover. Attacking that drunk boy in the middle of a room full of people! There would be some questions about that back there. She imagined people surrounding Cara, asking about her crazy ninja friend whose father could dominate a room without saying a word. They would want to know why Cara had invited such a freak to her party. And Cara would probably tell them the truth: her mother had made her. And instead of blending in, Emma was standing out in every student's mind. And they would tell their friends. By Monday, the whole school would be talking about it.

"It's important to blend in here," Emma heard in her head, in Leader's musical tone. It hammered at her, getting louder and louder. She tried to silence it, to no avail. His voice in her head only got louder and faster, uncharacteristically violent.

Her eyes slid shut, but that only hurled her into darkness with his raging words. *"It's important to blend in here."* Her heart would not stop racing.

Leader parked in the first garage. Emma's eyes popped open, and she drew a gasping breath, wondering in the back of her mind how long she had been holding her breath. Leader got out without a word and snapped his door shut behind him. Emma was alone with Monique. Afraid to look at her, Emma's eyes followed Leader as he stalked into the House and slammed the garage door behind him. Trembling slightly, Emma peeled her gaze away. Unwillingly, they moved with their own determination to Monique.

The woman sat in the passenger seat with a hand on her face, a thumb on her cheek and the rest of her fist covering her mouth. Her eyes blinked once slowly, then again. For a moment, Emma's terror for this silence swept her back into a frenzy of words, but this time it was Monique's reprimands she heard in the darkness of her mind, whispers that tore into one another to be heard. Monique was never silent about mischief or disobedience. She was never silent! Monique always had something to say. Wishing she would break her silence, and at the same time terrified she would, Emma continued to watch her.

The graceful turn of Monique's head was one of the most menacing movements Emma had ever seen from her. But the look in her eyes was not the reprimand Emma had expected. It was too distant, too concerned or disappointed to be a reprimand. Monique gave Emma a long, searching look. Then, without a word, she too exited the vehicle. Emma made a sound in her throat suspiciously like a whimper. She had never rendered Monique speechless before. No good could come from this. Like a shadow, Monique walked across the garage and through the door, trailing Leader.

Emma was slow to follow. The weight of everything they had not said slowed her down. She dragged her backpack up to her shoulder, opened the car door slowly and got out. The overhead light in the garage went out, and Emma stood in the silent darkness, feeling small. Alone, but not in a pleasant way. She gently closed the car door and moved toward the House in the blackness of the garage. The ribbon of light beneath the door beckoned to her, but she was not sure what she would find on the other side.

The locker room was also dark, although the light from the hallway spread into there. She could see well enough to leave her backpack on the lockers by the door. Stepping soundlessly onto the carpet in the hall, she crept past the offices, hoping she would not run into anyone else between here and the safety of her room upstairs.

"Emma!" Leader's voice cracked from his office. She froze and squeezed her eyes shut, trembling. She had never heard quite that tone in his voice. All musicality had fled the House. Taking a steadying breath, she stepped into his office.

He stood behind his desk with his back to her. This was new, too, and she didn't like it. At least when he was seated at his desk on his computer, he seemed too distracted to pay her any real attention. He ordered, "Close the door," over his shoulder, again with the hard edge in his voice that chased away its usual musicality. Obediently, she closed the door as softly and silently as she could and stepped forward, taking her customary place in front of his desk.

When Leader turned around, Emma felt even more frightened than before. His eyes no longer looked murderous, just calm and black, mirroring the pools of despair in her stomach. If she had expected his rage to be ferocious or loud, she was wrong. It was as dark and controlled as every syllable he ever uttered, and every movement he ever made. Grace at its most deadly.

With a jerk of one hand, he freed his belt from its loops. Emma's stomach fell even more at that ominous gesture. She had been struck before, by Monique, many times. Pain was part of the learning process in the Guild. But it had been several years since Leader had raised a hand to more than give her a sharp smack in reminder not to be petulant or caustic. Her heart pounded ruthlessly against her ribcage, but it was not until he said, "Take it off," indicating her dress, that she panicked. She now desperately wished she had taken the time to find her uniform in Cara's room.

Leader was not a man to be kept waiting, so she Obeyed. Trembling, but controlled, she pulled the dress over her head, and let it fall in a puddle on the floor. Using her arms to cover her chest, and she knelt slowly on the floor and bowed her head.

The first strike across her shoulders took her breath away and made her lose her balance. She caught herself with her hands on the rug, took a breath and sat back up. Leader waited for her, and then he struck again. And again, and again. Emma lost track of the number of times the belt snapped across the tender flesh of her shoulders and back. The pain escalated quickly, but it was the silence of it that hurt most. Besides the crack of the leather implement, Leader was utterly silent. His punishment was crueler than anything Monique could have conceived. For a regular girl in a regular home, this treatment would be considered child abuse. That idea crept across her brain more than once. It was chased away by the raw recollection that she was not a regular girl, and this was far from a regular home.

Emma tried desperately to keep from crying, but she couldn't. Weeping was the only way she could cope with it. She broke into audible cries within a few minutes, hating herself for giving him the satisfaction.

She was not sure he was finished for a few moments after the belt stopped coming. The pain was so intense. It was not until he said, "Tell me what your responsibilities are in this Guild," that she knew it was over. The musical lilt of his voice had returned.

It was terribly difficult to wet her mouth enough that she could speak, but she managed to squeak out, "To learn, to grow, and to Obey," through her shuddering sobs.

"Good," he answered, musical tone light and distant, as usual. "I was afraid you had forgotten. We will discuss this at length tomorrow. Go to bed."

Emma used all her strength to get to her feet. She kept her arms across her chest, choosing to abandon the dress on the floor. She opened the door, escaping the oppression of him, and ran. She did not look back, because she already knew what she would see. Leader would be leaning nonchalantly against his desk, belt dangling from his hand. His pitch-black eyes would stare harshly back at her with zero compassion or affection.

Chapter Sixteen

The first sensation she had upon waking was that she was surprised she had fallen asleep at all. Last night she had lain in her bed, absolutely raging with pain. She desperately tried to find some kind of comfort, even though she knew there was none for her. Waking in the morning, however, proved she had slept at least a little.

"Get up," Monique said, already at her bedside. The woman touched her head to get her attention, stroking a hand through her hair to push it out of her face. Emma was grateful Monique touched her softly, and on her head rather than her shoulder or back.

Moving proved to be a challenge but Emma managed to get up to her knees in the bed.

"Leader wishes to see you right away," Monique told her, all brusqueness returning as if the event of last night had not happened at all. There was no more silence or fury in Monique. Only expectation. She strode out of the room, calling over her shoulder, "Best not to keep him waiting."

Emma Obeyed the covert order to hurry up. She found a lightweight t-shirt in her closet and a pair of workout pants that would not injure her welted and stinging back. When she crossed the room to dress, she got a glance of herself in the vanity mirror and looked away again immediately. Her eyes were swollen from crying, and her entire backside was striped red from her shoulders to the small of her back. She was surprised it wasn't bloody. It felt like it should be bleeding.

She dressed as quickly as her straining muscles would allow, brushed her teeth, pulled her hair up, and washed her face. When at last she had no reasonable excuse for delaying, she walked down to Leader's office. She was grateful when she met no one on the stairs or in the halls. She did not think she could bear to face anyone. By now, they all knew she had lied and been beaten harshly for it. Nothing they could say, either in commiseration—which was unlikely—or condemnation, would be palatable to her.

As she approached the office, Emma halted. She heard Monique's voice, angry and soft, dressing Leader down in direct contradiction to everything Emma knew about her. Monique was Leader's Second, his first and fiercest champion.

"She is just a child, Leader. A smart, young, *lonely* child seeking a place to belong. A less-harsh approach works well enough with her; you hardly have to beat her into oblivion."

Emma was shocked to stillness. Monique was defending her.

"Don't you dare tell me how to run my Guild," Leader answered at his coolest, colder than he had even spoken to Emma last night. It chilled Emma and made goosebumps rise on her skin. "I am surprised, Monique, that *you* even have the balls to talk to me about this. What I did to her is nothing like what I plan for you, for letting this all happen in the first place." It was a threat that Monique brushed away entirely, though Emma felt a tremor of terror on her behalf.

"*I* have been in the Guild for almost 40 years; I am accustomed to your ruthless severity," she replied hotly. "Emma is only a baby!"

"Emma is not a baby anymore! She made calculated decisions yesterday, foolish choices that put my Guild in danger! She put her*self* in very great danger! I was as gentle as I could be."

"You lost your temper," Monique snapped back, ferocious as a mountain feline.

After that, the office descended into silence. Emma froze outside the door, fearing she might hear Leader's belt come free of its loops again.

Monique leaned out of the room and levered a glare at Emma stalled in the hall. "Get in here." Even if she had been defending Emma to Leader, her tone was no softer than it ever was to Emma herself. She grasped Emma by the arm and jerked her into the room. She shut the door softly and leaned against it, crossing her arms like a sentry. Not that Emma could have left Leader's presence without his permission, anyway.

Leader was seated at his desk behind his computer, in his customary position, giving his computer screen more attention than anything else. Leader did not look up, but with an idle hand, he indicated a chair where Emma should sit. Emma eased herself down slowly on the chair, careful not to sit back far enough to let her back touch the chair.

She stared at Leader, not confident she recognized him today. He was dressed in his customary full three-piece-suit with the same distant expression in his eyes. He ought not to be a stranger to Emma, but the man she had met last night had taken precedence in her mind. She was not sure she could ever perceive Leader in quite the same way again. In contrast, Monique was wearing a full workout suit, complete with a matching zip-up jacket. And her expression and stance were exactly what Emma would have expected at any time.

Up against either of them, Emma felt underdressed.

After a moment, Leader looked up. His eyes were as calm and compassionless as yesterday before the storm of his punishment. It frightened Emma all over again. He sat back in his chair, folded his hands on top of the desk, and said, "Emma. I am going to ask you a series of 'yes, sir/no, sir' questions which I will expect you to answer truthfully. Do you understand?"

Emma nodded. "Yes, sir." He gave an abrupt approving nod.

"Did you tell Monique yesterday that you had a study group meeting?"

Emma glanced at Monique quickly before saying, "Yes, sir." Her stomach began to churn all over again. Hadn't they already taken care of this with the ruthless beating?

"Did you give her a false address for this supposed study group?"

Emma drew a pained breath. "Yes, sir—" She would have gone on, but Leader's hand shot into the air to stop her.

"Did you have an actual study group you were meant to attend?" Although his tone never changed, Emma felt like this was a more dangerous question.

"No, sir."

"When I took you to school early yesterday, was it so that you could get your homework done?" She was startled by this question, because how could he have known?

"No, sir, although—"

He stopped her again with a finger in the air. "Yes, sir? Or no, sir?"

"No, sir," she answered, defeated.

He raised his brows at her. "Well, you have created quite the web of deception about this party, haven't you?" He did not wait for an answer. "Did you understand what I meant when I instructed you to be modest and to blend in?"

"Yes, sir." She did understand. Many of the people in this city had a popular culture surrounding an organized religion's standards. She was supposed to be perceived as one of those people: modest, chaste, sheltered, and innocently judgmental.

"Did it occur to you that by attending that party last night, you not only disobeyed me, but you also thwarted the mission I gave you?"

She had to think about that one for a moment. She did not know how to answer.

"I don't know," she dared more words than "yes, sir" or "no, sir."

"Perhaps for the sake of this investigation it would be best for you to elaborate," Leader allowed, musical warning tingeing his tone.

"I knew I was disobeying your orders, sir. I knew you would be displeased and that I would get into trouble if I was caught. But my mission did not cross my mind. So ... No, sir?"

He nodded. "That's a problem." The words were loaded with threatening content. He stood up. Afraid of what he would do, Emma slid back against her chair only to jerk forward again when her back came into contact with it.

But Leader turned away from her, giving his full attention to Monique. "I gave you Emma and all the Junior Guild as wards, Number Two. You are meant to instruct them in the Guild Laws and Skills. If you had done that properly, Emma's mission would never have slipped from her mind."

Emma could not believe Monique was being blamed for this. It was really not her fault Emma had lied to her. She had lied to Leader, too. He could not blame Monique unless he found himself equally culpable. Of course, Emma said none of that. She wasn't suicidal.

Monique did not attempt to divert blame. She only nodded at Leader, accepting his accusations with good grace.

"Monique, I have entrusted you with a great deal of responsibility," Leader went on firmly. "I expect my Guild to run like clockwork even when I am not here. I have trained you well enough that you should be able to live up to my expectations. I should never have felt the need to come home from Vermont, Monique. I should have been able to trust you to keep things going without me."

Again, Monique only nodded. She did not say one word in her own defense.

"This causes me a great deal of concern over my Guild command structure," Leader lifted an accusatory finger and pointed it at Monique. "*You* are causing me a great deal of concern. *You* are the person whom I should be able to trust above all others, but I cannot when the Junior Guild runs amok, and the children endanger themselves and the local population. Do you understand why I cannot?"

Monique nodded once more. "I understand, Leader, and I submit to your authority."

Leader studied her for a moment, then he turned to Emma. He jerked his thumb back toward Monique. "*That* is perfection right there, Emma."

Emma was shocked. She was pretty sure he had just accused Monique of imperfection, and now he was declaring she was perfect. Emma could never keep up with him.

"That is perfect compliance, perfect submission, perfect grace ..." He rose from his chair, walking around the desk in measured steps. "One day you will have the opportunity to behave as Monique does. One day, if you ever make it as far as she has." The threat in his words was unmistakable. Emma dropped her eyes and stared at her hands on her knees, avoiding his grasping gaze.

"Do you know when Monique learned how to be Obedient?" Leader moved to stand directly in front of Emma's chair, looking down at her imperiously.

Emma shook her head, not daring to look up into his eyes. "No, sir."

"When she was Twelve in the Guild." Leader dropped into a squat in front of Emma, capturing her gaze as he came. "It is when we all learn to be Obedient. Monique is responsible for teaching you the value of Obedience, which she will now do without fail." He shot a significant glance at Monique, and then said to Emma, "The sooner you learn the lesson, the better your life will be."

Emma looked into her leader's eyes. She felt the taste of rebellion in her mouth, but this time she could not stop it from coming out. "I thought you already 'taught' me about the value of Obedience last night when you beat me within an inch of my life."

Leader stood up with slow grace and peered down at her. "You are mistaken." He leaned back against his desk and crossed his arms. "On several counts. The only person I have ever beaten within inches of life is Monique. Perhaps one day she will share the story, and you will not be able to pity yourself anymore." Emma shot a glance at Monique, but the woman gave nothing away. Emma suspected the story was not one she would enjoy. "Also, last night you dealt with *me* and, as I have already said, it is Monique's responsibility to teach you about Obedience. My responsibility is to protect my Guild." He moved in the space of a blink to Emma again, close to her face and menacing. "You endangered my Guild. You endangered yourself, and you *belong to me.* You endangered my mission, and your mission, and my Guild's Mission. You should be thanking the lucky stars that stayed my hand last night or this little collection of bruises you have today would have felt like nothing."

When he backed off, she whispered, "Yes, sir." She was effectively cowed. She would never sneak or tell lies or endanger the Guild again. It was not worth risking his wrath.

"Monique," Leader said, turning to face his Second. "I promised Emma I would speak to her at length, and I always keep my promises. You may go. I will send Emma to you when I am through with her."

Monique stepped off the door and said, "Very well, Leader. I will be training. Send her to me in the training suite, if you please."

Leader nodded, but when Monique left, he followed her out of the room. When they were down the hall a sufficient distance, they whispered to one another in tones low enough that Emma could not hear.

Waiting was nearly as painful as talking privately to Leader. When he had promised her that they would speak at length, she had hoped he might forget. And then, when he had prepared to dismiss Monique, Emma had allowed herself to briefly hope that they already had the "at length" conversation, despite its brevity. She wanted to get away from him long enough to calm herself down and try to recover from his cruelty. He obviously did not want to give her that opportunity.

CHAPTER SEVENTEEN

W hen Leader returned, he had a breakfast shake, which he deposited into Emma's hand with a peremptory command to "Drink this." She Obeyed, of course, since it was her responsibility to Obey.

Leader grabbed a book from the glass-fronted shelf behind his desk. It had worn old leather covers, faded and stained in several places. He carried it reverently in his hands as he returned to her. This time he took a seat beside her and held the book for her to see. There was no title on the cover.

"This is a volume of the Guild Book, Emma." His voice softened with the reverence he must have felt for the book. "It is a book with the names of all the people throughout time who have been members of this Guild. All the previous Leaders kept records, as I do now." He indicated his computer as the place he kept records. "They placed their thoughts, struggles, and triumphs in this book."

He opened the book, but shielded her from reading it with a strategically placed arm. He flipped carefully through the pages until he came to the page he wanted. Reading, he said, "'I can never be too careful that my wards know the Guild; the Guild, my passion and purpose. I can never be too careful, for they are subject to the meager and paltry passions of the world in which they dwell.'"

He looked up at her. "That was a Leader near the time the United States was founded." He immediately returned his attention to the book, so he missed the skeptical expression Emma had to quickly wipe off her face. He flipped more pages. "'At last, I see I have done my work well! Twelve has learned the finest lesson I could ever teach him. He has learned to protect the Guild over himself.'"

Leader looked up at her as he closed the book. He tapped it with his hand. "Leader from when I was the Twelve," he informed her. She blinked. She had never thought about his ever having been the bottom of the Guild. But of course, he had been. Where else would he have come from? One day perhaps Monique would be Leader, and the person who was Twelve then would never know her as Monique at all.

"Here is the dream, Emma," Leader said, tapping the book again. "The dream is that I can teach you to protect the Guild because it is your purpose, and not because you fear the consequences."

Fail! she declared in her mind at him. She hated the Guild, and the only reason she did anything was because she was afraid of what would happen if she refused. She was never allowed to question! Never allowed to think about her motivations. But after last night, she knew: She did what she did because he would hurt her if she didn't. She did not know what would happen to him that would make Monique Leader, but when he was no longer a threat, Emma would not do anything for the Guild. She would escape so fast, no one would know what had happened to her.

"That cannot happen in one day," Leader said, almost as if he knew her defiant thoughts. "But I have all the time that I need." There was definite weight in those words, as if he were threatening her.

He returned the book to its place on the shelf. Placing a paper on a clipboard, he grabbed a pen, then returned to the seat beside her.

"I am going to illustrate the stages for you. The stages it takes to get to the point where you have passion for your purpose." He paused a moment, thinking, and then amended his statement, "The stages it takes to convince me that you know and understand the principle of Obedience and will apply it in your life without hesitation."

He wrote a large **1** on the page. "Number one, I establish my authority." He wrote the word **authority** on the page. He continued writing the key words as he told them to Emma.

"Two, I remove all your comforts. Three, I give you as many opportunities as it takes for you to prove you understand. Four, I instruct you in all the things you need to know to succeed. Five, I establish a challenge for you. If you succeed, I have done my duty, and I write an inspirational quote for some Leader in the future to use as an example for his subordinates. If you fail, we start over at number one." He put the paper into her hands, removing the now empty glass from her and placing it on the desk. "This paper is for you to keep. I know the process by heart."

Emma imagined herself throwing the paper away in the wastebasket at school, because she did not think it would ever be important to her. But then she imagined what might happen if he ever wanted her to show it to him again and she did not have it.

"What is number one?" he asked.

Sarcastically, she thought, *Didn't you just say you knew it by heart?* But of course, she did not say that. "Establish authority."

Leader stood up to pace the length of the room. "I think that is fairly well established. One can never be too sure, but here's what I am going to do." He looked at her. "I am going to demonstrate faith in you. I am going to assume that all our experiences together, especially recent activities, have proved my authority. If not, I will be able to tell, and I can always find ways to show you later."

Emma did not dare to look at him for fear her eyes would tell him she needed him to establish his authority again. If last night had not done it, what could?

"Number two?"

"Remove comforts," she replied after consulting his reference page. This was the one that made her want to cringe. What did that mean? What more could he do to make her uncomfortable? She was as uncomfortable as she could imagine. She had been uncomfortable all her life.

He smiled. "Yes. That's a daunting one, isn't it?" He sat beside her again. "That will be a process starting with this conversation. There are things you need to know that will help with this." He grabbed her chin and turned her face to look at him. As accustomed as she was to his manhandling, she tried to resist. His powerful grip insisted and her resistance faded. "How did I find you last night, Emmalyn? How did I know where you were? How did I figure out that you were lying and scheming?"

Emma thought his questions were rhetorical, but he appeared to be waiting for an answer. "I don't know," she admitted in pinched staccato.

"Of course, you don't," Leader answered, his voice tinged with condescension. "But I am going to tell you, because I have the feeling that until now you have been pretty comfortable." He pulled his hand away and not too soon. She looked away to hide her forbidden rebellious thoughts.

"Long before Amos gave you your phone, I had a tracking device installed in it. It is state-of-the-art, Emma. I could find you at a neighbor's, in Tahiti or on the moon. Do you understand me?" She turned her head slowly to look at him. Her incredulous expression faded away as his words and tone made her realize he was not teasing her. She did understand. She understood that all she had to do to get rid of that kind of surveillance was to conveniently lose her phone. But then Leader leaned forward and touched his forehead to hers. "And just in case anything ever happens to your phone, I have a tracking device embedded in your spinal cord," he whispered. "You can never get away from me."

It worked. She was uncomfortable, the most uncomfortable she had ever been in her life.

Leader wasn't finished. He walked to the desk to pick up his own phone. He handled it for a moment, pressing buttons.

"All of your phone calls are recorded and sent to me," he continued calmly, as if they were discussing the weather. "They are transcribed so all I have to do is read the transcript to know what you are planning." He turned his phone around, showing her an email on it. What she saw in the email made goosebumps rise on her arms and legs.

Emma: *Hello*

Miss Winters: *Emma? This is Cara.*

Emma: *I know. What do you want?*

Miss Winters: *Okay, so I want you to meet us in the Commons tomorrow at 8.*

Emma: *What? Why? Who?*

Miss Winters: *OMG, Emma! My friends are meeting in the Commons tomorrow before school. Are you going to be there or not?*

Emma: *Why?*

Miss Winters: *You are about the most tiresome person I know. Eight o'clock. Don't be late.*

Leader watched her read the transcript. Emma could not keep the shock off her face. He was serious. He really had her conversations recorded.

"If you knew what I was doing, why didn't you stop me?" she demanded, getting angry and trying desperately not to show it.

Leader snatched his phone back from her and placed it on the desktop. "That's not the way it works. I'm not going to rescue you from all your bad decisions; just the ones that endanger my Guild." He leaned against his desk again and gave her a piercing look. "But be sure to understand this, I will see to it that you answer for all your disobedience and indolence."

Emma shook her head slowly, trying to dispel the gloom and the hatred. She leaned forward on her knees and put her face in her hands. She could hardly believe this.

"If you have the power to stop me, why don't you do it?" She glared up at him. "It is obvious you have the control, why don't you just *make* me do what you want? God!" she swore. She stood up and shook her head at him. "You are really ..." she did not know a word bad enough, but she had to get away. She spun abruptly, reached for the door handle, and pulled the door open.

He was too fast for her. He came behind her, pushed the door closed, and caged her between his arms. He had her pinned and trapped. She would never have been able to outmaneuver him even in the best of conditions. The fear kept her from thinking clearly and took her breath away.

"I don't do it because I don't want to," he said into her ear. Her knees nearly buckled. "And I don't have to do anything I don't want to do." She squeezed her eyes shut, but it did not stop the tears from springing to her eyes. "Do you understand?"

"Yes, Leader," she said, and relief came. He backed away from her.

"Did I give the impression I was finished?" he asked, returning to his desk where once again he leaned at his ease. "I'm not. Sit down."

She thought about trying to escape again, but what good would it do her? Even if she did get away from him, he would be able to find her without any trouble, and she had no idea what he would do to her when he got her back. She sat down.

She scrubbed furiously at her tears, but Leader ignored them. "I haven't even started talking about the surveillance," he said in a chipper voice.

Emma looked up at him. "I have seen your surveillance cameras. They're all over the House." She found a small triumph when his eyes widened until she realized it was amusement instead of surprise.

He reached behind him and turned his computer screen around, saying, "Those weren't the ones I was talking about."

The images were crystal clear, as if they were filmed by a television crew. It was her school, specifically her classrooms, her locker, the restrooms ...

She could not keep herself from moving toward the screen to get a better look. The places were empty, and the lights were all out, but it was definitely her school. Leader pushed a button on the keyboard and brought up a control panel. He typed in a series of numbers and symbols, and suddenly the view changed. It was one of her classrooms, from several angles, filled with students and a teacher interacting. He had her school days *recorded*! Emma did not look at him. She did not want to see the satisfaction that was probably all over his face. She had no idea he watched her this closely.

"You might like this feature," he said, pressing another button. Once he pressed it, Emma could hear what was going on in the room. It was her English class from several weeks ago. She remembered the lesson.

Emma looked away. She was starting to feel sick now.

"And that's not all."

"I doubted it would be," she answered numbly. She sat back down in her chair, completely overcome with defeat. She had been under the illusion that she had some control over her life, at least at school. What a foolish, childish fantasy!

"Do you have a thorough grasp of my authority now, Emma? Do you have a better understanding of my role in your life?"

"You are the prison-keeper and the slave master," she replied, cold and calm. She did not dare look up from her hands. "And I guess I am one of your minions." Silent, furious tears slid down her face, and she did not even have the desire to wipe them away. If he always had a camera on her, then she had no tears that were a secret from him.

She watched him nod from the corner of her eye. "Not a perfect analogy, but it's a start. All I really want you take from this is that you have no way out. Plotting and hoping for a way out is futile. It's a waste of your time and education."

She was crushed already. He did not need to rub it in. "How would I ever get away? Why would I ever waste my hopes on this? You hold all the cards."

He nodded slowly at that, capturing her eyes with his authority and ultimate dominance. "Yes, I do. Even the ones you think I don't."

Right now, Emma could not think of anything he did not control, except her emotions. She clung to that. She even said to him, "You cannot make me like *this* or the Guild or you. You can't."

His dark smile crept slowly across his face. "Your partiality is not required. Only your Obedience."

She tried to keep her composure in the face of his derision. His matter-of-fact, simple tone filled her with despair.

She swallowed, sat up straight, and took long breaths. But the emotions were too strong to be ignored. She found herself bending over her knees, sobbing, her entire body shaking with tremors of despair. And Leader just stood there, leaning against his desk, silently watching her be stripped of all her comforts.

Chapter Eighteen

Emma wiped sweat out of her eyes and stood up to stretch her back. The muscles ached as she straightened, unaccustomed to the strain caused by crouching for prolonged periods over a sink. Everywhere she had ever lived had had a dishwasher to perform the task of washing dishes. Before today, she had never had to do more than an occasional rinse.

Chores seemed to be a routine punishment for misbehaving teens; Emma had heard complaints and chatter about this from kids in school. Emma's family was unfortunately more vindictive than an average teen's. She was not permitted to do chores that would be of any immediate help or overall influence. For the past hour, she had been scrubbing oven racks. Not that oven racks did not need a good scrubbing now and again, but it did not make or break household harmony. Additionally—and this Emma was certain was the true reason she had been assigned this tedious chore—no one was likely to notice the oven racks had been scrubbed.

She reached a water-wrinkled hand to the small of her back and pressed against the muscles, wishing she could ease the ache. Then she bent back over the sink and the wire rack she was scrubbing. It would not do her any good to be caught standing still. If she stretched for too long, she might be accused of idleness. Monique's Training session this morning had taught her about the evils of indolence and other undesirable attributes.

"Are you standing over there on the edge of the mats because you need a lesson on the evils of indolence?" Monique had demanded when Emma entered the Training arena that morning and stood for several moments watching Monique's forms. She had not meant to be lazy; it's just that Monique was an impressive martial artist, and Emma learned nearly as much watching her as listening to her instructions.

If Emma's earth-shattering conversation with Leader had not been so fresh—the tears still glistening on her cheeks! —she might have responded in defense of herself. But Emma had only apologized and bowed herself onto the mats. And the lesson went downhill from there.

"Why are you here?" Monique had asked immediately, and then again and again throughout the lesson. Unfortunately for Emma, she had not known that there was only one right answer.

"Because Leader dismissed me to Training."

Monique swept her feet from beneath her, catching her by the shoulder on the way down. She captured her legs, entwining them with her own, and almost gently guided her onto the mats, forcing her into a hold made more painful by the recent welts across her shoulders and back.

"You have one responsibility to this Guild, little girl," Monique hissed in her ear. "If you don't know what it is by now, I have the daunting task of correcting that." She released her and shoved back from her. Emma, alarmed by the force in Monique's movements and the ferocity in her tone, shied away instead of stepping into a ready stance. Therefore, Monique's second attack hit her when she was not expecting it, knocking her onto her back. Despite Emma's yelp of pain, Monique pinned her in position.

"Why are you here?" Monique asked her again, face only centimeters from Emma's, eyes boring into Emma's with expectation.

On a shuddering breath, Emma said, "Leader told me—" But Monique flicked her in the side of the head with firm fingers and Emma cut off.

"Not now, not here, not on the mats. Why are you *here*, in the Guild?"

The implacability in her eyes was as compassionless as Leader's had been. Gone was the woman who had defended her to Leader that morning, the woman who had told him he was too harsh and that he'd lost his temper. Monique had her mind on one answer and Emma was expected to figure out what it was.

"I don't know," she admitted when Monique seemed unlikely to move away without her answer. Monique leaned until her forehead pressed against Emma's, staring forcibly into her eyes.

"That's a problem," Monique whispered at her.

It took Emma nearly an hour of forceful training to realize that Monique was waiting for her to say, "I'm here to Obey."

As Number Twelve, Obedience was Emma's primary responsibility to the Guild. Yet Monique had not been finished with her even after Emma flawlessly responded, "I'm here to Obey" to every sneak-attack demand, "Why are you here?"

They ran through her entire expanse of training forms, including her most current acquisition, which had not yet been perfected. Since Piper—Number Seven—was generally responsible for her Training, Monique called her in and made her kneel to one side and watch. The red-haired young woman was as stoic as ever, although she occasionally found Emma's gaze with a grave expression in her green eyes. She seemed to be silently pleading with Emma to form correctly. And Emma certainly wanted to! Every time she slipped, Monique made her run the Block—the discipline course around the edge of the Training room—or start all over.

"She's still learning it," Piper had said, coming to Emma's defense once when she had failed to execute her form perfectly. Monique's finger pointed to the Block for the fifth time. "I haven't taught her the crossover yet."

"Your ineptitude as a teacher does not excuse hers as a student," Monique answered as she set the time for the Block and nodded Emma to begin her fifth run.

When Emma finally executed her form perfectly, she let out a sigh of relief. But Monique still captured her by the upper arms and pinned her forcefully against a wall. "Why are you here?"

The intensity in the woman's eyes could be matched by Leader's only. Tears pricked Emma's eyes again in exhaustion from the forceful training session and pain of contact with the wall.

"Obedience," Emma replied immediately. To her own frustration, her voice trembled. Monique leaned forward again, placing her forehead against Emma's, far too close to be natural or comfortable.

"Obedience," Monique murmured, and Emma spent a confused moment trying to remember if she had said the word wrong. But then Monique dismissed her to take a shower and get dressed for the day. "Find me in twenty minutes. I have some chores for you to do. Keep you busy so you can't develop lies and make mischief."

It seemed such a benign threat; Emma had gone to shower in relief, not even considering the words. But as soon as Monique assigned her the first chore—washing off the patio furniture which would just get spotted and dirty again in the next rain—Emma realized her Obedience was going to be tested. Over nine hours of useless chores followed.

"You got beef?" Monique had asked during the fifteen minutes she allowed Emma to pause for dinner. The question had referred not to the meal, but to Emma's attitude.

Unable to resist, Emma answered truthfully, "These chores are pointless. I wish I was a regular kid in a regular house where they would make me mow the lawn and do the laundry and be done with it."

The spark of something like amusement danced in Monique's eyes, but her tone was as hard as ever. "They're not pointless. I told you to do them. And what's your responsibility?"

Emma had been getting that question all day. "Obedience."

"Yes, Obedience," Monique answered. "After you finish eating, I want you to go through the House and organize the linen closets. The towels can be placed in color order and organized according to size." Emma stared at Monique for too long in disbelief. The woman grasped hold of her ear sharply. "Did you misunderstand me?"

"No!" Emma cried out. "I understood. I'll do it, Monique."

"Yes," Monique replied, voice menacing and cold as a Canadian winter. "But *why* will you do it?"

Emma pulled against Monique's hand, trying to pry herself free. When it did no good, she answered, "Because my responsibility is to Obey."

Emma dried the last oven rack and returned it to the top oven. She emptied both sinks, wiping them clean and dry. She had not seen Monique in a couple hours. After the linen closets, Monique gave her a list of chores to keep her busy and then disappeared into the Offices for the evening. Oven racks had been the last chore on the list.

Emma rested for a moment, laying her face against the cool marble countertop. She let her eyes slide closed. Muscles in her neck and back eased out of their strain. Her breathing slowed, and her mind tried to pull her from consciousness.

"Emma?" Amos asked, moving into the kitchen from behind her.

Emma jerked upright, blinking the sleep from her mind, and spun around. "Yes, sir?"

He quirked an amused brow at her use of formal language, but all he said was, "You okay?"

She nodded. "I'm fine, uncle. Thank you."

Amos studied her for a moment, eyes narrowing. He said, "Sit down."

Emma shook her head, denying the need to rest, despite her crushing exhaustion. "I can't. I have to report to Monique."

Amos arched his brow and pointed a firm finger at a bar stool. His tone was mildly scolding when he insisted, "I said sit." He was higher in the Guild than she was—Number Three. So, she Obeyed.

She moved around the bar to the stools and sat down on the nearest one. Her aching back and legs seemed to give a sigh of relief. Emma slumped, resting her head on her hands, elbows propping her up.

As Emma got situated, Amos removed the rag from her hand and tossed it unceremoniously at the glistening sink. He moved to a cabinet across the kitchen and fished through it for a bottle of what looked like pain relievers. From another cabinet, he extracted a dark container with some kind of liquid in it. He returned, placed the liquid container on the counter, and opened the pain reliever.

"This is the good stuff," he said cheerily, giving her a compassionate smile. "But it will knock you out something fierce, so you are going to need to go to bed soon."

She glanced at the clock on the microwave flashing 10:24. It was likely she would be sent to bed soon. Her bedtime was usually around nine. She took the three pills from his hand and popped them into her mouth. He handed her a paper cup with water to wash them down.

Taking another paper cup from the dispenser beside the bar sink, Amos half-filled it with the brown liquid from the other container. The smell of it was putrid. Emma shied away.

"What is that?" she asked, afraid he would make her drink it.

Amos grinned at her obvious concern. "It is a soothing agent. I know Leader took a belt to you yesterday, and I know how he uses one. Put this—" he handed the paper cup to her, "into your bath water tonight and soak in it. It will do wonders in the way of soothing the welts. And it doesn't sting."

She smiled at him. He was always gentle with her. Taking the cup gratefully, she said, "Thank you."

He halted her when she tried to stand up. "I did not excuse you," he said, again smiling. "Sit down and take a breather."

"I think that is the opposite of what Monique expects me to do," Emma answered, but she stayed seated. "I am so tired."

Amos leaned forward over the counter in front of her and touched her face softly with the back of his hand. "I can see. You do not look well. Maybe Julianne should take a look at you."

She hastily shook her head. "No. I am well. I'm just tired, is all."

He stepped back, studying her, and nodded. "Fine. But if you still look unwell tomorrow, I will tell Julianne I think you're ill."

She nodded. "I'm sure I'll be fine."

He jumped up to sit on the counter across the kitchen but still facing her. As always, he wore jeans and a shirt with the name brand printed in huge letters across the front. He dressed like he was 20 when he was actually middle 30s. Even his hair was in the shaggy, boyish haircut that no grown man should try to sport. Emma thought it was endearing, though.

Amos watched her, almost expectantly, and said nothing.

After a few minutes in the expectant silence, she softly asked, "Amos? You're in charge of security, right?"

He nodded. "Among other things."

"So, you know about all the surveillance?"

He quirked a brow at that. "Naturally. Did you have a question about it?"

Emma just sighed and shook her head. "Not really. I just wanted to know if you knew about it ... if everyone knows about it."

Amos gave a sly smile. "Usually everyone finds out when they are at Twelve or Eleven. I remember when it was new information to me, and back then the security regime was not as expansive as it is now. *I* am responsible for surveillance now, so it is immensely improved. Also, it helps to have access to better technologies."

Emma stared hard at him for a long time, trying to wrap her tired mind around what he was insinuating. When she could bear it no longer, she blurted, "So, *you* set up all those hidden cameras?"

"I make sure they get put up in all the right places, yes. It is one of the things I am best at, deciding where to place a camera for optimum exposure to a room."

It was too much for Emma to bear that Amos, whom she tolerated better than all the others, was one of the people responsible for her imprisonment. She lowered her face into her hands and drew a deep breath.

"I see that dismay, Miss Emmalyn Harris," Amos chided. "But you do not understand everything yet."

Emma glared up at him. "What? What am I meant to understand? My house and school are under 24-hour surveillance, my phone is bugged, and my spinal cord has a microscopic tracking device in it."

"Tracking is not *all* that thing is programmed to do," Amos said, in a quiet voice that was almost a caution to her. It did not make her feel better.

"Do you know what?" he was talking softly, conspiratorially. "All those things, the surveillance and the tracking and all that ..." He looked around as if checking to see that no one else was listening. It was all show, she knew, because Leader walked into the room, and Amos continued in the same tone. "...It's all for your protection."

Emma barely heard him, she was working so hard to avoid Leader's gaze as it swept the room. She could not avoid him, though. He approached her.

"Did Amos tell you to sit down?"

She nodded, opting not to speak to him. Amos had told her to sit, but he might still be angry about it. She was supposed to be in punishment, after all.

"Good that you Obeyed."

CHAPTER NINETEEN

L eader lowered his brows at Amos as he turned his surveying eyes around the room. "Is that the vile smell of your soothing concoction, Number Three?"

"Of course, it is," Amos replied with an innocent shrug. He winked at Emma unconcernedly. "I gave it to Emma for her bath tonight. And before your nose picks up the scent of prescription drugs, I should tell you I administered a powerful painkiller, as well. She needs to be able to rest."

"Your gentility will destroy this Guild one day," Leader said, but he was smiling when he said it. Emma did not think he was angry, although the smile at his lips did not seem to reach the dark intensity in his eyes.

"You won't be around to see it, Leader, so you need not worry about it," Amos answered, hopping off the counter, utterly unconcerned about Leader's cautions.

"Is that an excuse you expect me to accept for teaching the young ones to be soft?" was Leader's amused reply. Again, no amusement seemed to shine through his eyes.

Amos made a facial shrug and leaned across to pat Emma's hands on the countertop. He grasped one of them in his own, folding her fingers around his.

"Not soft, Leader. Pliable." He kissed her hand sweetly and returned it to the counter. When he turned to face Leader, he had no more apology in his tone or manner than before, "And I bet more resilient than if you had her to yourself for training."

Emma shuddered at the idea of training with Leader without the relief of others to distract him. Leader's quick glance caught her pained expression. He descended on her like a hawk, grasping her chin in his unrelenting grasp.

"Not an amusing idea?"

She only shook her head in answer, not trusting herself to speak to him.

"Maybe that's what it will take to bring you into line: training with me alone."

For too long, she stared at him, afraid and hating him for it. When she could restrain her words no longer, her anger restricted them to a hoarse whisper.

"I will do as you say, Leader. I have done as you said. I am atoning for disobeying you and for lying to Monique." She wished she could shout her protestations, filling the room with her fury at the unjust treatment, but she did not dare raise her voice to him. "Tell me what else I must do and I'll do it, Leader."

She regretted her words as soon as she saw the challenge in his eyes. He backed away from her and motioned toward the china cabinet with his hand.

"Set the table," he ordered. She blinked. That was all? All he wanted was for her to set the table?

"Was I unclear?" Leader's voice cooled and his eyes darkened. He did not need to move nearer to her for her to feel his anger pressing further into the room, like ink spreading across a white carpet.

"No, sir."

Emma sprang from her stool. She hastened to the china cabinet, but before she could open it, he chided her, "Do you know *exactly* what I want, Emma?"

She did not successfully keep confusion off her face as she peered over her shoulder at him. He had leaned against the counter with his arms crossed, watching her with an unreadable expression. When she continued to stare blankly at him, he raised one brow. It was too near a threat for Emma and she blurted, "What is it you want, Leader? Exactly?"

Amos gave a stiff nod in the background, but Leader's glance in his direction made him shrug and leave the room. She envied him the freedom to walk away from Leader's threatening gazes.

"I want a formal setting for six, with white lace tablecloths and blueberry china on the formal dining table."

"Yes, sir."

She knew place settings well. She had been setting table in the Guild House for as long as she could remember. She collected the tablecloths first and carried them into the dining room. Leader followed her, but only to stand in the doorway staring at her.

Having him watch her perform such a mundane chore was intimidating, as if it was a life and death affair. He said nothing. He remained in the doorway as she walked back and forth between the formal dining room and the china cabinet in the kitchen. She carefully placed every pretentious piece of silver and folded every delicate cloth napkin. When she finished, she looked to him for approval but saw only a stony expression.

"What centerpiece are you going to use?" he asked after it was clear she did not know how to proceed.

She hurried to cabinet to retrieve two candlesticks, but before she removed them, she looked back at his stony face and asked, "What centerpiece would you like, Leader?"

His nod may have been approval, but his voice was still cold. "The candlesticks will do fine."

She placed the candlesticks on the table then stared at the beautiful place settings. After wiping an imaginary smudge from a wine glass, she looked up at him. "Will this serve you, Leader?"

He studied her a moment, not even glancing at the table, and nodded. "Dismantle it."

Emma started in surprise. He did not intend to *use* the place setting? She did not argue, though. This was hardly the most pointless chore she had completed today. Immediately, she began dismantling it with a prompt, "Yes, Leader." She went through the arduous process of returning all the chargers, plates, and glasses to the china cabinet, wrapped and ready again for the next dinner party. She returned silver to its drawer, and refolded tablecloths and napkins.

"Set it again," Leader said as soon as the final wine glass was tucked carefully into its hanging slot in the cabinet.

Emma glanced his way but did not hesitate to Obey. "Yes, Leader."

She began again. Her exhaustion made it difficult to concentrate on the minute details, but he never spoke to her unless the task was complete. Then all he said was, "Dismantle it" or "Set it again." In the hour that passed under his eyes, she lost track of how many times she set and unset the table. She lost track of how many pieces of silver slipped through her tired fingers and had to be washed, how many wine glasses she nearly dropped on the tile floors. Her legs began to feel numb from exhaustion, but she did not slow. She did not hesitate at his commands. She always promptly answered, "Yes, sir," and did as she was told.

Finally, she looked up before he could tell her to set the table again and she asked, "Why am I to keep doing this, Leader? Is there something I am doing wrong? Do you have any corrections for me?"

Leader pursed his lips.

"Yes," he drawled.

Relief washed over her that there might be an end to this. But Leader's correction was, "Questioning me is wrong. This exercise has nothing to do with the setting, although I am sure it would pass a home economics test. This is simply an exercise in Obedience. You set the table because I tell you to do so. You dismantle it because I tell you to do so. If I want you to spend your life doing it, you do so. But above all you *do not question me.*"

Emma sighed and struggled to keep her composure. "How am I expected to learn anything if I am not permitted to ask questions?"

Leader sprang from his post against the doorframe so quickly, Emma visibly started. Directly in front of her, his voice was firm but not harsh. "Asking questions is different than 'questioning.' Questioning is a precursor to treason. It is your way of telling me, in all your 13-year-old wisdom, that what I asked you to do is not important. You do not know my mind, so you do not question me. Is that clear to you?" His face was so close; she could smell mint on his breath. His eyes were twin pools of intensity. Under that strong gaze, she could do nothing but stare at him, wishing she had the strength to look away.

"Yes Leader. Thank you for clarifying." She pulled her gaze away with some effort, settling her eyes on Monique's form across the dining room in the shadows of the stairwell. There was no comfort for Emma in the realization that Monique had joined him to punish her. She had been giving Emma pointless chores all day. The two of them together were a deadly combination.

Leader lifted Emma's face with one finger, drawing her gaze back to him again. The liquid intensity of his eyes, for a moment only, seemed like affection. But Emma dashed that idea away ruthlessly when all he said was, "Set the table."

Emma immediately turned and went back to work.

Monique moved out of the shadows, crossing the dining room to stand beside Leader. Her leaders conversed in murmured whispers in a language Emma did not know yet. They could have been talking about the weather for all the expression in their voices, but Emma caught her name several times. And even if she could have misunderstood that, Monique's gesture toward her was pointed. A sharp word from Leader silenced her, and then the two of them stood in the doorway like silent sentries set to watch an untrustworthy slave.

Monique stepped away from Leader, coming into the room. She moved closer to Emma until, when Emma suddenly stumbled from exhaustion, Monique was able to catch her before she lost her footing. Emma said nothing, just pulled herself from Monique's grip and moved on to complete her task. Behind her, she heard the sentries break their silence again.

"She needs to be in bed, Leader."

"She will go to bed when I feel I have taught her adequately," Leader replied in his icy tone that left no room for argument.

Somehow, Monique found room to argue. "She's a child, Leader."

He cut his eyes at his Second. "I know exactly who and what she is, Monique. I have no question in my mind about Emma." He held up a hand at Emma when she finished putting away the final piece of silver, pausing her before she could start over. The brunt of his attention went to Monique. "You need to know that I hold you responsible for the lack in her education."

Monique raised her brows, "So you've said."

His jaw creaked with strain as he clenched his teeth, staring hard at her. "The Junior Guild is your responsibility, yet Emma has been neglected. I will not neglect *you*, Monique."

The threat in his tone was overly obvious to Emma, but Monique did not seem to notice. Or didn't care. "What would you have me do, Leader? Beat her senseless to prove I'm stronger? Keep her up all hours of the night setting a table to test her fortitude?"

Leader raised one brow slowly, stepping closer to Monique. "Maybe *you* ought to set the table for a while."

Monique's expression challenged Leader's threat. She closed the distance between them and pointed with one finger until she tapped the tip of his nose. "I always Obey you, Leader. But if you wish to punish me for questioning your methods, we have all night."

One of his brows rose slowly. Emma would have squirmed under that gaze, but Monique did not back one inch. Finally, Leader nodded at her and stepped back. His musical tone was dismissive and had none of the threat in them Emma had heard only moments before. "Take her to bed, then come see me in the office. You and I can discuss my methods at length."

Emma squirmed on Monique's behalf, but Monique only smiled after Leader's retreating form. She shook her head, wrapped up in her own thoughts for a few moments. All her brisk ferocity returned when she looked at Emma.

"Well, come on, child. To bed."

The relief Emma felt nearly took her consciousness, and Monique had to catch her once more.

Chapter Twenty

Emma grabbed her lunch bag from the counter with a nod of thanks to Amos for making it. He grinned and gave her an encouraging wink. He knew her weekend had been tough, with the abusive justice of Friday, the painful Training and endless chores of Saturday, and then a Sunday filled with more Training, more chores, and hours upon hours of setting the table under Monique's watchful eye. Looking at Amos' grin, Emma wondered how he managed such high spirits after spending his life in the Guild. She did not ask him, though; she was not sure she wanted to hear about his experiences. Instead, she returned his smile and walked out of the kitchen.

She slid past Leader's office on the way to the garage, not slowing down. His door was closed, but she knew he was in there. She could feel his presence, like a malevolent gaze on her back. Lifting her head, she stared into the visible camera high on the wall above the garage door. She nodded to it deferentially, as if nodding to Leader himself, and walked on. *How many other cameras does he have hidden?* she wondered. But she forced herself to stop thinking about that. She had spent all weekend thinking about almost nothing but that.

In the last garage, Adam already had the engine running in the little red Honda they drove to school. He and Scott were outside the car, leaning against the hood. For a moment, she wondered if they were trying to commit suicide, running a carbon-monoxide-producing vehicle in a closed garage. When she drew nearer, though, she saw they were only smoking a joint. Scrunching her face up and drawing her shoulders in, she stared hard at them, trying to comprehend their idiocy. She could not conceive of any reason they would risk smoking anything, much less an actual drug, on House property. It seemed so unnecessarily foolish.

When they noticed her, they both started and Adam dropped the small, white rolled paper on the ground.

"You're like a snake, Emma, you know that?" Scott snapped. She ignored his comment and stepped toward them. She could never argue with Scott because he was an angry juvenile, like she was, and probably for the same reasons. He deserved her compassion.

She squatted and retrieved the joint, examining it in her fingers. Both boys stared warily at her while she did. They were wondering what she would say, how she would respond to them destroying their bodies with illegal substances. They were wondering if she would immediately turn and tattle on them to Leader. Lifting her eyes, she stared up at them through her lashes. For a moment, she enjoyed their discomfort; rather, she enjoyed the momentary control she had over them. Even Scott was silent. Adam stepped forward at last, holding out his hand to take the joint from her, dark eyes watching her nervously.

"Emma, give that to me," Monique's voice rang into the silence, utterly calm. Emma jumped this time, her heartbeat taking up a rapid pace. Monique strolled up between the two boys. Her manner was as brisk as ever, as if she had not just caught them all exchanging drugs. Adam dropped his outstretched hand and backed away as if the joint were a weapon. Emma met Monique, who retrieved the joint and crushed it in her hand. When she turned on a heel, looking up, her eyes swept past Emma toward the two boys.

Scott jerked his head toward Emma and said, "I don't know where she picks up these filthy habits, Mother." If his tone was meant to be teasing, it missed.

Emma's mouth dropped open in shock. He was trying to blame *her*? She had walked in on them, innocently headed to school, and now he was trying to blame her for his stupid choices? Emma had never been tempted by drugs—would never do something so dangerous for her body! Much less do it in the House, on a school day, when Leader was home.

Before she could retort, Monique slapped Scott with the back of her hand. It had been an almost careless gesture, but Scott turned away, reaching up to cover his face. When Monique spoke, though, it was to Adam. "Was it yours?"

Adam looked at her darkly and shook his head. Monique's answer was, "Good thing 'integrity' is not a Guild Skill, isn't it?"

There seemed to be a threat in her words, but her tone, as usual, was mild. She dumped the ruined joint into Adam's hand and said, "Go give this to Leader and see if he has some insights for you on Guild Skills."

Adam did not answer. He only looked down at what was left of the joint, and for a moment Emma wondered if he was considering trying to salvage it. But he walked away toward the exit with a purposeful stride, Obedient if not altogether honest.

Monique leaned in through the open car door and turned the engine off, removing the keys. "We'll take the Lexus," she informed them.

"You're driving us?" Scott demanded, pulling his hands away from his face to accost Monique with his raging question.

"From now until the end of time," Monique answered dryly. She used her head to nod toward her car, indicating they should precede her. Emma went without a thought. "I think it would be best if I took a personal interest in your life, as I have Emma's this weekend."

Emma ducked her head, pretending not to hear. Even when Scott stood still, demanding answers, Emma felt the painful urge to Obey, especially since they were now discussing her horrible weekend. She walked away toward the Lexus on the other side of the garage. Monique's call stopped her. "Haven't I taken an interest in your life, Emma?"

Emma turned slowly around, thinking uncomfortably about the past two days. "Yes, Mother," she answered, although "interest" would not have been her choice of words.

"What is your duty to the Guild?"

"Obedience."

"And yours?" Monique asked as she turned her dark gaze onto Scott.

"Diligence," he muttered.

"Do you know what sorts of behaviors violate 'Diligence?'" Monique demanded. She had stepped closer to the young man, looking down at him like a sparrow at a worm. She answered herself before Scott had a chance. "Imprudence, heedlessness, and inaccuracy." She glanced over her shoulder to pin Emma with a deliberate stare. She raised her voice slightly. "Did you hear my words, Emma? One day, your duty will be Diligence."

"Yes, Mother," leaden words falling out of her mouth. Leaden words that had been force fed to her all weekend. She turned and walked away. Emma had had enough lessons since Friday, and she did not want anymore.

She climbed into the backseat of the Lexus, which was unlocked, and buckled her safety belt. Resting her head against the window, she wondered what today would be like at school. After two days of rigorous training and instruction under Monique's less-than-tender care, Emma did not want to face any more problems.

School held no peace for her now she knew Leader was watching. And the half of school who attended Cara's party had seen her create a giant scene in front of everyone, so Leader was sure to be watching how she dealt with the humiliation. Somehow, Emma was expected to return to school and to her mission of blending in, even though she had no chance of blending in after the spectacle she had made of herself Friday night.

She had been devastated when she realized Leader still intended her to return to school.

"What am I to do about my mission?" she asked Monique yesterday after another forceful Training session, when she had been told to go study for school. "There's no way I'm blending in now."

Monique said, "That's something you're going to have to work out, Emma. You broke it; you fix it." Emma seriously contemplated asking Leader to put her in a different school. But then she had seen him in the study, flaying Piper with his silver tongue, making her tremble on her knees in front of him. And Emma changed her mind. She decided she would rather deal with an entire school full of whispers and jibes than brave asking Leader to change his plans.

When Monique and Scott got into the car, a few minutes had passed. Scott had an even stonier look on his face, if possible, and the rising image of a handprint on his cheek. Monique must have struck him again with an open palm to leave that kind of mark. Emma sat small in her seat.

With a peremptory command to fasten seatbelts, Monique drove out of the garage and pulled into the street. Scott and Monique continued a semi-heated discussion on the way to school but Emma ignored them. She was too tired to engage in trite conversation, and she honestly did not care what Scott's issues were. She had too many of her own to deal with. She needed no part in any other drama.

Through the window, Emma studied the monstrous mountains in the early light of morning. It was cool enough that white clouds surrounded the tops, making it seem like the mountains were exhaling cool autumn air. A flock of some dark birds made their way south in a strong V formation in the distance. Nature always seemed so free and enchanting. Like the idea of magic from a children's story book, freedom was a brilliant impossibility.

The peace of nature was broken when her phone gave a short double ring. Monique's eyes caught hers in the rearview, deadly serious. Under that gaze, Emma fumbled to retrieve her phone from her backpack pocket. She unlocked it. The text message that presented itself was from Leader. All it said was: **Have a good day at school**.

Emma stared coldly at the message. She wished she could believe it was the benign greeting it seemed, but she knew better. Leader fully intended to live up to his promise to discharge all her comforts. Yet he could not make her feel worse; she was already as dismal as possible after her weekend under his thumb.

"Who is it?" Monique asked sharply.

"It was Father, wishing me a good day," Emma answered truthfully, glancing up through her lashes at Monique's gaze in the rearview.

Monique quirked a brow at her as if she did not believe that, but she didn't challenge Emma's claim. She could have asked Leader for the transcript if she wanted to be sure Emma was telling the truth. Emma pulled her gaze away. They drove on in silence.

Once at school, Emma collected her belongings from the car and stepped out onto the sidewalk. With a furtive look around, shoulders hunched, Emma searched for anyone from Cara's clique. Although there were some people who pointed at her and whispered to each other, Cara and her cronies were nowhere in sight. The muscles in Emma's shoulders relaxed slightly.

"Emma, Scott," Monique called from the car. Emma leaned down to see Monique's face, dark eyes filled with an intensity Emma generally associated with Leader. The Second said, "Make me proud today." These were words any mother might say to her children as she dropped them at the front door of their school, but when Monique said it, it was an order. She wanted them to know that their choices reflected on her.

"Yes, Mother," Emma immediately replied. Scott gave a slower but just as dutiful response.

"Don't forget this," Monique added, passing a dry-cleaned bundle through the window, and the pair of black heeled shoes Emma had worn the night of the party. "They're going to need to be returned to their rightful owner."

Emma had completely forgotten that she had borrowed clothes for the party. In fact, she had done her best to forget about the party completely. Face flushing with the heat of shame, Emma snatched the bundle from Monique and hugged it to her body, hoping to hide it from prying eyes.

Emma nudged the car door shut with her shoulder and stepped back onto the curb to let Monique drive the car away. Scott stood beside Emma on the curb, watching Monique's car drive out of the carpool lane, the heat of rebellion and frustration in his eyes. He glanced at Emma, catching her staring at him, and made a rude gesture with his hand. He snorted and strode away from her toward a collection of other angry-looking young men.

Chapter Twenty-One

For a few moments, Emma considered staying outside. The cool morning air chilled her still-flushed cheeks, and out here she would not have to face Cara. She would not have to try and come up with an apology for ruining the girl's party. She would not have to create a story that would allow her to maintain her cover, and still explain her break from character at the party. She might have liked to stay outside, but one glance around her showed that people were still staring, still whispering and pointing. She would not be able to avoid her responsibilities by hiding outside for a few extra minutes. Her resolution to get it over with drove her inside.

The commons was bustling with early arrivers. A few boys played catch with a football in one group, and girls in another watched them and laughed and whispered behind hands. A co-ed group sat next to the giant statue reading from a book of scripture, speaking to one another in reverent voices every few passages. All around the room were couples breaking the PDA school standards, leaning against each other kissing, or wrapped in each other's arms. There were loners reading books or completing homework. One person, a young man, was drawing with a pencil on a large pad of paper across his lap.

Cara's group of minions was as easy to spot as it had been last Friday. They were under the eagle statue, near the scripture readers, and not maintaining a respectful quiet, as if they were the only people in the world who mattered. Emma would have liked to avoid them, but she knew what she had to do. Leader expected her to maintain her cover, and that meant she had to confront Cara's group and try to explain her actions. Surely Monique had given her the dry-cleaned dress and polished shoes to return as inducement to force this confrontation. If Emma had really wanted to avoid it all, she could have left the bundles in the office lost and found. But besides being cowardly, it was not Obedient. Monique had told her to return it to its rightful owner. Straightening her spine, Emma let the bundle against her chest go slightly, so she was holding the dress by the hanger printed with a dry-cleaning logo. She turned to face Cara and her cronies.

At that moment, Cara, amid her group, looked up and spotted Emma at the edge of the room. For a brief beat, they shared a connected gaze. A bizarre electricity seemed to connect them. To Emma's ears, even the loudness of the commons room quieted. The authority of Cara's gaze—so like Monique's during Training—could not hide the barest expression of concern.

Breaking the spell, Cara lifted a hand and beckoned. Emma drew a breath to give herself time, even though there could be no preparation for this encounter. Emma had no point of reference from which to gain insight. She had never embarrassed herself or the Guild in such a public setting before. She had never ruined a young woman's birthday party before. She had no idea how to behave now. But she took a step, answering the beckoning wave with action.

"Hi," Cara said in a neutral tone. She stared intently at Emma, studied her as if she had never seen her before now. Perhaps she hadn't; Cara tried very hard not to see her last week, annoyed by her presence and frustrated with the necessity of inviting her to her birthday party. Emma avoided her gaze.

"Hi." The word sounded hollow, but she did not know how to give her voice any expression now. She pretty much spent all her energy trying not to imagine what Cara must be thinking about. Emma felt the gazes of the other five girls, but she avoided eye contact with them all. "I have your dress." She pushed the plastic-wrapped dress toward Cara with one hand, and the shoes with the other. "It's been dry-cleaned."

"It's Brinley's," Cara replied in that same neutral tone. She passed the dress and shoes into Brinley's open hands.

"Thank you for letting me use them," Emma told the statue's feet. It was easier to speak to the inanimate features of the room than to face the accusing gazes of the young women.

"It's no trouble," Brinley answered. Emma's gaze jerked up in surprise at the sincerity in her tone. Brinley stared hard at Emma, but she was not angry. Her eyes looked concerned, if anything. With a quick sweep of her gaze around to the others, Emma realized none of them were angry or accusing. Like Brinley, they were only concerned. Cara's face was the stoniest of them, but even in her, Emma thought she saw what she had seen as Leader had torn her from the party Friday night: compassion.

Emma itched a little under their scrutiny. She tried to back away, but Cara grasped her arm and held her in place.

"Are you all right?" Her tone was somewhat hushed, although it lacked any actual emotion. "Your father seemed angry."

Confusion washed over Emma as she studied Cara's stony face. She let her gaze slide down to Cara's hand wrapped tightly around her arm. Her gaze kept moving, slipping first to Brinley, whose wide eyes were by far the most expressive of fear. Then she looked at Sarah, at Madeline, and to each of the others. There was no anger in any of them. They were not angry at her for ruining the party or fighting with a boy; they were concerned about what her father had done to her after he had forcefully removed her from the Winters' mansion.

It was such an unexpected response that Emma was at first not sure she was interpreting it correctly. Concern was not a foreign emotion for them; she could see the echo of compassion in their eyes as if they had experienced this sort of thing before. They looked sympathetic, as if they understood the weekend she had had. They did not, of course, but Emma realized that, by their expressions, most of them must have had a similar exit from a similar social gathering.

"He was angry," Emma answered truthfully. They continued staring at her after she spoke. She blinked, unsure what they were waiting for. Cara's brows lifted a bit, questioning, and Emma realized they were all waiting for more. They were waiting for her to tell them about what had happened to her.

Emma cleared her throat. "I ... uh ... It's against my family standards to attend parties ..." She cleared her throat again. "Those kinds of parties, I mean: alcohol, boys, the complete absence of any theme or control ..." She met Cara's gaze. "My father is used to being in control."

The deep-seated compassion in Cara's eyes gained a bit more warmth, and she gave the barest of nods, as if Emma had confirmed something she had been wondering. Emma shrugged, tearing her gaze away from Cara's to look up at the statue, wondering if some of Leader's cameras were stationed there.

"I bet it must drive him crazy when he can't control things; when instead he has to watch from a distance as all of his carefully engineered plans wash away." Emma felt smug. She knew Leader had wanted her to be uncomfortable at school today. He had been counting on her having to waltz in here and defend her cover.

When Emma brought her attention back to the clique, she saw some confusion in their faces, so she forced a smile. "I'm right as rain."

"Right as rain?" sneered a young man who moved into the space between two of the girls. He was one of the kids who had been playing catch. Now he carried the football under his arm and grinned at Emma, brown eyes teasing. "I think the last person I heard say 'right as rain' was my great-grandmother." He chuckled, but Emma did not think he was being malicious. There was no malice in his tone.

"Go away, Jonas Jensen," Cara said, her tone dripping with disdain. "Leave her alone." She pushed at his shoulder, trying to dislodge him from the group. He was bigger and stronger, though, so she could not move him. Cara turned and rolled her eyes at Emma. "All the boys thought it was incredibly sexy how you beat the snot out of Bryan McCormick. I guess they never realized before that a girl could hold her own." She shot Jonas a murderous glare. Jonas did not seem to notice or care. He stepped up beside Emma, sliding a companionable arm across her shoulders.

"I was disappointed that your father came and ruined the show," Jonas said, grinning down at her. "It looked like it was going to have an impressive ending."

Emma shrugged the boy's arm away and stepped to one side. "My father saved that young man from being hospitalized. I'm not pleased with what I did. It was not my proudest moment."

Jonas smirked. "It wasn't Bryan's proudest moment, either. He'll never live it down. Beat up by a 90 pound little girl." He chortled. His teasing started to rub Emma the wrong way. He did not understand. None of them understood how serious it was for her to have formed in public against an unarmed civilian. There were very strict rules against it! One of the most important edicts she had learned in the Guild was the Aggression Compact, part of which was a commitment not to use her training to injure an unarmed civilian.

"He never stood a chance," Emma insisted, speaking firmly and with absolute certainty. Part of Leader's fury had been that she had placed herself in a situation which required her to violate the Aggression Compact. "My father saved his life."

Jonas laughed again, louder this time, as though Emma were joking and not speaking in earnest. Emma looked up at him in exasperation, but Cara did not give her a chance to speak.

"Your father seemed irrationally angry."

Emma, very aware of the cameras that could be anywhere—and were probably everywhere—shook her head. "I knew better than to try and deceive him." She shrugged.

"What happened to you, then? You get grounded?" Jonas wasn't concerned like the others. His tone was more intrigued than anything.

Emma did not know what the word "grounded" meant when it was not applied to electrical devices or aircraft. But she guessed by context that it was some sort of punishment. She thought she could even remember hearing some girl complaining in the locker room about being grounded because she was sassy to her parents.

"I spent the weekend doing a lot of chores."

That was an understatement. Sunday alone she had set the table 63 times in a row while Monique watched and said nothing but "Do it again." It had been a massive waste of time for them both, hours passing in which no studying, no work, not even any conversing could be done. Unless Monique saying periodically "Why are you doing this?" to which Emma had to answer, "Because you told me to and I'm Obedient" counted as meaningful conversation.

"Chores," Brinley murmured, but her eyes betrayed some serious doubt.

"If I had a dad like yours, I would be thanking my lucky stars the only thing he did was make you do chores," Madeline put in, weighted words aimed to get a reaction from the others. It mostly worked. They nodded and made agreeing sounds.

"But you're not grounded?" Jonas asked pointedly. His dimpled smile loomed dangerously close to Emma and she backed away again. "If you're not grounded, maybe I can take you out some time."

Emma glanced around when the girls scoffed. Cara and Brinley rolled their eyes. He ignored them, looking only at Emma, grinning, waiting for an answer.

"She *is* grounded," Scott snapped, shouldering his way into the group and shoving Jonas away from Emma. He had had more years of Training than Emma; he was just as deadly a weapon as she was. "But even if she *could* go out, she wouldn't go with you, Jensen! Stay away from her."

"Scott!" Emma snapped, flushing in shock at his interference and anger. He had hardly ever acknowledged her at school before. "I can handle this myself."

"She proved that," Jonas put in, recovering his footing and returning to slide an arm around Emma's shoulder with leering smile.

Scott shoved Jonas again, and this time it sent him staggering back a few paces. "Stay away from my family, Jensen!" Scott roared, taking a step toward Jonas and pointing a dangerous finger at him. "Just stay away from Emma!"

"Jesus, Scott!" Emma snapped, grabbing Scott's arm to hold him back. She was astounded by his outburst; it had caught the attention of the entire commons room. This was the opposite of blending in. "Let it go. He's just being friendly. I can take care of myself."

Scott turned his full anger on her, jerking from her grip like it burned him. "Oh, you can? Like you did last time? Took real good care of yourself and made all sorts of trouble for everyone!" His fists were clenched at his sides. "You have no respect for who we are. If you did, you would understand you have no business even talking to these …" He gestured furiously around the room. "… ignorant bastards!" His gaze returned to Emma with force. "Do you even realize what you've done? He's never going to let up now. He'll never relent."

Emma widened her eyes at him, shaking her head slightly in disbelief at his blame. Slipping into Mandarin, she said, *"He was never going to relent, Scott. He's not capable of relinquishing control."*

He roared, "You made it worse!"

Emma jerked back from him with a defiant scoff. "I'm so sorry if I got in the way of your weed-smoking parties!" Scott's troubles could not be blamed on Emma; she would never stand for it when she had her own burdens to carry.

Scott's hands sprang to Emma's shirt. His violent attempt to drag her close to his face was greeted with gasps from the girls around them. "Don't you dare shout at me, Emma! You've got nerve speaking to me at all! Because of you, he's watching over everyone's shoulders. He's wound as tight as a fucking spring, and I—"

His cell phone rang, stopping his tirade short. He shoved her away from him with an expletive and the muttered threat, *"I'm gonna kill you."* He snatched his phone from his pocket and stalked away.

"This is Scott," he said calmly as the phone got up to his ear. He had moved beyond earshot before he spoke again.

Emma stared after him, smoothing down her collar he had displaced in his manhandling. He had always hated her, had always gone out of his was to hurt her, but he had never outright threatened her or attacked her in public before. She turned to see the shocked or disgusted looks on the faces of the kids surrounding Cara. Her knees weakened. She had no idea what to say to them.

"Freak," Sarah muttered, shaking her head. Emma did not know how to respond. Cara saved her.

"He's a little intense," Cara said doubtfully. She met Emma's eye. "Probably a lot like your dad."

"Yeah." Emma nodded. "Probably."

Her words made Brinley cringe a little, but Emma did not know why.

Jonas straightened his jacket and came back to the group. "I didn't mean to upset your brother," he said in a normal—not leering—tone of voice. He looked after Scott, who was still stalking away toward the front school doors. "I'm sorry I upset him."

"You didn't." She shifted her school bag on her back, adjusting herself back into her school mindset. "I've got to go to class." She had also seen the nosy school counselor across the room and intended to avoid her at all costs, especially if the woman had caught any sight of Scott's manhandling.

"You aren't coming on the Freshman Class field trip?" Brinley asked in surprise.

Emma knew her face must have twitched with uncertainty, because Cara smiled her normal superior smile. She was the queen bee again in an instant, tone slipping into its most condescending.

"It's the Capitol Building field trip. They make the freshman class go every year and talk to the 'leaders of our local government.' Remember?"

Emma did. They had announced it at the beginning of the school year. Leader told her the field trip was pointless and she had no reason to attend, so she had not even given him the permission form to sign. She now reached into her bag and pulled out her planning binder. At the back of the binder behind the tab labeled **important school documents** she found the permission slip with her teachers' disclosure documents from the first day of school. She withdrew it and scanned the page. Cara smiled a dark little smile and proffered a pen. Emma glanced around, certain that Leader was probably watching right now.

He never said I couldn't *go,* she reasoned to herself. *Only that it was pointless.*

Without focusing too hard on her racing heart and suddenly dry mouth, she forged his signature across the bottom of the page.

"Nice," Cara complimented. There was no condescension in her tone now. "You know, Emma Harris, I think you're starting to grow on me." The other girls laughed. Emma was not certain, but she thought maybe she was making some friends.

Chapter Twenty-Two

The warning bell rang overhead, and Cara snapped her fingers at the dress and shoes in Brinley's hands. "Put these in your locker and let's get to homeroom."

The group was dispersing. Jonas already rejoined his football friends, and the crowd of onlookers was falling away. Emma pulled her backpack up onto her shoulders once more and nodded to Cara and the other girls. She would have stepped away from them, but Cara caught her by the arm again.

"Where do you think you are going?"

"My locker," Emma answered truthfully.

Cara widened her eyes at her. "Not by yourself, you're not. Where is it?"

Emma blinked in surprise, because she was pretty sure Cara's authoritative question indicated some concern for her well-being. Did she think Scott would show back up to make good on his threat? Except Cara had probably not understood his threat, since he had cursed it at her in Mandarin. No ... With a little shake, Emma made an alarming realization. Somehow, after walking into the commons today expecting to be a pariah, Emma had joined Cara's clique.

"It's okay. My locker is just right around the corner."

Cara motioned with her head for Emma to go and released her, but then the entire group of girls walked beside her. Emma kept expecting them to peel off, head toward their own lockers and their own homerooms, but they stayed with her all the way. Cara stood right beside her when she reached her locker and began putting in the combination. Her eyes darted aside a few times, checking to see if they would move on, but they didn't. Cara took up an imperial stance, leaning slightly against the locker next to Emma's, all the while talking to her drones like she was presiding over her royal court.

"Uh ... You don't have to wait with me," Emma told her, when she fumbled with her combination for the second time.

Cara snorted. "Believe me, you are glad we're here. You need protection." Unnerving thoughts of Scott faded away as Cara explained. "Jonas Jensen is not the only idiot who is going to get all chummy with you because you kicked McCormick's ass. Every guy who was there thinks you're a sex goddess, and every guy who wasn't is going to want details."

She rolled her eyes over at her friends. "High school boys are so juvenile. A girl protects herself from a smarmy little asshole, and suddenly they think she's the Tomb Raider." Emma did not understand what raiding tombs had to do with defending herself, but she did see that Cara was right about the student body's interest in her. Everywhere she looked, people watched her. The jocks and popular boys smiled and nodded at her, grinning suggestively. Girls watched her uncertainly. Some had judgment in their eyes and some had concern. Still others watched her as if they did not know what she would do next. Leader would be mighty unhappy that she was this much of a spectacle. She would never blend in this way.

When Emma finished at her locker, they walked in congress toward Brinley's locker, only another set down the corridor. Emma felt awkward hanging out next to Brinley as she put in her combination and opened her locker. It was a lot more decorated and disorganized than Emma's sterile one. Brinley shoved the clothes into it and slammed it shut again.

The procession took Emma all the way to the door of her first period class.

"Meet us in the bus lot after first period," Cara ordered Emma and Brinley. Then she and the rest of her drones walked down the hall and took the stairs up to the second floor. The school bell rang, but Emma could not take her eyes off Cara's retreating form.

"She risked being late for class so she could walk me to my locker," Emma murmured in disbelief.

Brinley stood beside Emma in the doorway, looking after Cara. She turned her gaze on Emma slowly and shrugged. "It's her way. Although, I've got to say, I never thought I would see the day Cara would go from complete dislike to friendship in one day."

Emma could not read her tone, so she said nothing. She stepped into the classroom, out of the way of some other students trying to get in before the tardy bell rang. Brinley followed her.

"It's not in her regime to turn outcasts, you know, or care about people in general."

"I don't know what I'm supposed to say to that," Emma admitted.

"Yeah," Brinley said, nodding. She halted Emma in the aisle between two rows of desks. "That's what's so annoying about you, Emma. You really are just an innocent girl. Genuine and straightforward." She shook her head slightly and walked on.

"Get up," Brinley told Anna, the girl who was seated in her usual chair next to Brinley's. Anna seemed confused, but she slowly collected her things and stood. She turned to look around the room, searching for another seat. Emma had moved to her customary seat behind Brinley's, but Brinley snapped, "What are you doing, Emma? Sit here." She pointed to the chair Anna had vacated. When Emma hesitated, Brinley rolled her eyes, "Don't be obnoxious, Emma. Sit down." Emma obeyed, leaving Anna to occupy the desk behind Brinley's.

While she applied fresh lip gloss, Brinley watched Emma from the corner of her eye. She tucked her compact mirror into her purse and turned in her chair, facing Emma directly.

"You got in a lot of trouble Friday night, didn't you?" Brinley's eyes were narrowed, like she was studying a specimen in a jar.

Emma stared blankly at the other girl for a moment. "Yes," she finally admitted. There seemed to be no reason to lie to her. It's not like Brinley was asking for details that would blow her cover. In fact, if anything, Emma was solidifying her cover by pretending her parents were normal people who got pissed when their kids lied to them and snuck out. Letting her eyes fall away, Emma watched the homeroom teacher collect the role and get ready for the day.

"A *lot* of trouble?" Brinley demanded. Emma drew a breath and allowed her eyes to briefly close in remembrance of Leader's form of justice.

"Yes, Brinley, a lot."

Brinley nodded as if they were agreeing on something. "I knew it," she said smugly.

Emma quirked a brow. "I told you of my own free will, Brinley. You don't have to go all … private detective." Brinley rolled her eyes in answer.

"Good morning, students," Mr. Johnson said, like he did every Monday. "I sincerely hope you had a good weekend. When I call your name, please indicate that you are in attendance and disclose your intentions for the field trip today. For example, 'Mr. Johnson, I will be attending the field trip for my own educational benefit' or 'I decline the educational opportunities of this field trip and will instead spend my borrowed time catching up on my late research paper in the Study Hall.'" He began calling the names on the role immediately, so Brinley sat back against her chair.

When the teacher called Emma, she answered, "Present."

Mr. Johnson pulled his reading glasses down his nose slightly and peered at her over the top of the rims. "And your intentions for the field trip, Miss Harris?"

Emma hesitated, which gave Brinley the chance to say, "She's coming, Mr. Johnson."

"Is that so, Miss *Harris*?" he asked, not taking his eyes off Emma as he waited for her to answer for herself.

She looked up slowly and nodded. "Yes, sir."

"Very well," he said, and pressed his glasses back up his face to continue calling role.

Before he finished, Emma's phone rang, startling everyone in class. The school rule against cellphone use in class was extremely clear in the student handbook; it was a zero-tolerance school.

Mr. Johnson removed his glasses and folded his arms across his chest. "Whose is it?" he asked sternly.

Emma's breath caught in her throat but not because she had gotten caught with a cellphone at school, but because she just knew it was Leader calling. He had probably been watching her on his creepy surveillance and heard her say she was headed on the field trip.

Certain she was right, but needing to see it, Emma reached into her vest pocket and removed her ringing phone. The word **Mother** flashed across the screen, and Emma's face contorted with confusion.

"I sincerely hope, Miss Harris, that that is the President of the United States calling," Mr. Johnson declared. "Although that will not save confiscation of the phone and a demerit against your behavior record."

Emma rose slowly. "It's my mother," she admitted. She moved into the aisle and walked to the front of the room. His words finally sunk in as she reached the desk. "Does this demerit mean I will not be permitted to attend the field trip today?" The only reason Monique would have called after school began is if she wanted Emma to get into trouble.

"First offense?" he asked quietly, lowering his voice so he could not be overheard by other students. Emma nodded. The teacher studied her with narrowed eyes for a moment then said, "I'll make an exception today."

He nodded toward the phone in her hand, which had finally gone to voicemail. "Turn it off and put it in my basket." He nodded his head toward a basket labeled **Forbidden Paraphernalia** sitting on the oak-top desk.

Emma pressed the button on the side of the phone until the screen turned dark. A tiny thrill of defiance shot through her as she placed the phone in the basket. Phone tracking disabled? Check!

The teacher returned to calling names. Emma gave her darkened phone one last look, then returned to her seat. At least she would be able to tell Leader and Monique that she had not disobeyed them. Neither of them told her she could *not* go on the field trip. She knew they would still be angry, because walking out of this school meant escaping their surveillance. How could they watch her when there were no cameras where she was going?

Chapter Twenty-Three

Emma slid to the back of Cara's pack as they moved through the Capitol Building. She was already exhausted from another day spent in their company. She was not accustomed to being a part of a group; it was more tiring than spending her time all alone like she usually did. She was used to falling into her own thoughts and using the world only as fodder for her imagination. She was not comfortable being *on* all the time.

Brinley fell back whenever Emma did, walking beside her at the back of the pack, matching her slower stride. Emma did not understand why Brinley felt the need to walk with her the entire morning, but she was grateful. Brinley did not speak to her much, leaving her free to observe others and focus on her own thoughts. Then, whenever Emma was at risk of being swept away with worry about what Leader would do to her when she got home, Brinley spoke up.

"I can't believe *this* is the Freshman Class field trip!"

And Emma was brought back from the precipice of anxiety to answer Brinley's complaint. "It's supposed to be educational."

Brinley scoffed. "One field trip this year and we have to go to the Utah State Capitol Building. Seriously lame."

"I think it's interesting, to be honest." Emma's comment was more to quiet Brinley's complaints than out of honesty. She had never been to the capitol building before, so even though it was not full of excitement, it was new to her. She thought the local government was a fascinating study. In fact, the entire concept of a republic, in which leaders were appointed by the vote of their constituents, was appealing. Before today, Emma never paid much attention to the government of the land of the free; it never seemed to have anything to do with her. Their tour guide had shown them some of the assembly rooms and the courtroom. It intrigued Emma: an entire government run by the people. Seeing it in action gave her some hope for her future. The rebellion in her heart, fortified by her successful flight from Leader's surveillance, allowed her to hope.

"Interesting?" Brinley asked doubtfully, sliding a hand onto her hip in defiance. With her other hand, she gestured at the portraits on the wall, at the crest embedded into the stone underfoot. "Seriously?"

"I mean," Emma went on, tone slightly tinged with exasperation, "a free government designed for the people is an interesting idea. Two-party systems with checks and balances ... It ensures no one person can be a supreme ruler."

Brinley narrowed her eyes at Emma. "Supreme rulers like your dad?"

Emma startled at the exposure of her inner thoughts. She busied herself studying a portrait on the wall, not allowing Brinley any confirmation for her speculations.

"I know he hits you, Emma," Brinley whispered, grasping Emma's arm to hold her back from following the student group. Unable to shake her off, Emma turned a blank expression on Brinley's too-concerned face. Concerned, but also knowing, she had a glint of experience in her eyes. "I saw the bruise on your ribs the night of the party."

"That was an injury from martial arts," Emma explained, pulling away from Brinley's grip. "I did a weave when I should have blocked. And it wasn't even him, it was my brother." She and Scott had been sparring last Friday morning, Training under Thomas's supervision. Scott pivoted coming into an attack, and Emma misinterpreted his movements. She weaved into his sudden kick instead of blocking. Emma had been knocked roughly to the ground while Thomas's cry to stand down was still leaving his mouth. As much as Scott seemed to enjoy jabbing Emma in the ribs or shoving her on the stairs, he had not been pleased that Emma was hurt on the mats.

"I thought she would block!" he cried in panic, face stricken with horror when Emma rolled in on herself, wrapping her arms around her body. He screamed at Emma, "Why didn't you block?"

Thomas shoved him to his knees for stepping out of his waiting stance, but it had not silenced Scott. "Why didn't you block, Emma? What is the matter with you?" It had been a shriek of terror. It awarded him a snarling lecture from Thomas, who shoved Scott's forehead into the mat. "Calm down!"

Emma would have bet her sanity Scott had not meant to harm her. But when she tried to say something to him, he glared over at her as if she had deliberately allowed him to hurt her. Julianne was summoned before Thomas would let Emma move. Then he took Scott away into a private training room and left Emma to Julianne's ministrations.

"It was an accident. My aunt is a doctor. She checked to make sure nothing was broken. I'm fine."

Brinley nodded but she looked doubtful. She stepped away to study the mural on one wall, quiet, but shouting her doubt with every miniscule movement of her face and body. Emma let out a frustrated sigh, pursuing her to insist again that the injury had been an accident. But when Emma stepped up beside her, Brinley spoke first, in a quiet tone that nevertheless silenced Emma.

"I once told Cara that the bruise on my face was a result of falling asleep in the shower and hitting the edge of the tub when I fell."

Emma winced at that but carefully kept her face turned away so Brinley could not read her discomfort. Her situation was night-and-day different from Brinley's. Brinley was suffering child abuse at the hands of her own family. Emma was not even permitted to be a child, and abuse was never in it. Abuse was far too mild a word for Emma's life and training.

"It really is a martial arts injury."

"Of course, it is. And I fell in the shower."

Brinley scoffed and stepped away from Emma. Emma pursued her again, following her out of the main corridor into the State Reception Room. It was empty now, as the rest of the field trip had moved to the upper level. They violated one of the rules they had been given before exiting the bus: Stay with your group!

The reception room had a roped-off viewing area where Brinley stood, looking resolutely at the fine furnishings and draperies. The docent already explained it to their group when they passed through it several minutes before. Emma liked it empty better: she could imagine the room's history all on her own then. She wondered if, when the building had been built, there had been a Leader and a Guild. During Leader's lengthy conversation to remove her comforts, he implied that the Guild existed since the foundation of the United States. Emma had not truly believed him, but it did make her wonder.

Emma stepped up beside Brinley, placing a tentative hand on her shoulder. Brinley shrugged it off forcefully, but she met Emma's gaze with a harsh glare. "Can you confidently say your father never hurt you? He never hit you so much that you had trouble sleeping? He never beat you so that you were too sick to eat anything?" Brinley shook her head and looked back at the gold-plated moldings the docent had been so proud to show off to the group earlier. "You never had to pretend your injuries were self-inflicted?"

Studying her own thoughts, Emma drew a heavy breath. When Leader had taken his belt to her Friday, she imagined she was the only girl in the world who received that sort of harsh punishment. She never thought regular girls in real families might have to deal with abuse and playing a part. Humbled by their shared pain, Emma touched Brinley's arm again. The girl glared at her, but Emma could see the pain buried beneath that anger.

Before this moment, Brinley had always been the obnoxious Cara crony in Emma's homeroom. This might have been the first time Brinley ever admitted to being hurt by her father. She gathered the strength to talk about it, but only because she thought Emma shared her pain. And Emma did. This weekend was not the first time Leader had taken an implement to her, and he was by no means the only disciplinarian in her House.

Emma had had the sharp edge of Monique's tongue more than her hand, but Monique had hit her, too. So had Julianne and Thomas, although much less frequently. Amos was the only adult in the House who had never struck her, at least not that she could remember. Emma never acquainted the treatment to "child abuse" before. Not really. Because she had not considered herself a normal child with regular rights. She belonged to the Guild and to Leader, and so the child abuse assemblies and "Just tell someone" slogans at school never seemed to have anything to do with her.

"Okay," Emma admitted, nodding in acceptance. Leader wanted her to blend in and try to appear like a normal girl, even after her disastrous removal from Cara's clandestine party. He probably had not meant for her to admit to being abused, but what was she supposed to do? This was the most obvious path. It was the best way to make everything fit together. "He hit me. He's done it before."

She met Brinley's pained eye, sharing a silent moment of absorption. Emma had the prickling feeling of being watched again, even though the school and Leader's surveillance was a long way behind her. Emma felt certain Leader somehow heard her betray him. Her fear about that leaked through her eyes, and Brinley reached out a hand to touch her arm. Commiseration, Emma thought, and shook her off.

"What does it matter? I can't stop him."

Brinley nodded, relief washing over her features. She whispered, "I know. It's impossible to even think about."

This was what Brinley wanted, Emma realized: a friend to share her woes with, not someone to fix the problem. Brinley seemed to gain a sense of weightlessness, as if she had shed the yoke of bricks she spent her life carrying. Emma envied her. Sharing Guild secrets did not take her weight away; it added more strain to her labor.

"What about Cara?" Emma asked, glancing through the doorway to the corridor, where Cara and her posse were reassembled. They were looking around, probably searching for the girls who had disappeared from their group.

"Oh, no," Brinley insisted, shooting a troubled look through the doorway, lest they be overheard. "Cara's never been punished a day in her life. She can do no wrong in her house."

Emma expected that, but she had not anticipated the overwhelming jealousy that washed over her at hearing it. What would it be like to be important?

"Keep to the group," the grumpy history teacher snapped as he came into the room behind them. "We have been searching for you two." Emma and Brinley apologized, saying that they had gone in search of restrooms and gotten distracted. The teacher hurried them along to join the others. Cara widened her eyes in exasperation as they approached. In Emma's view, Brinley transformed from a troubled girl using hushed tones and wide eyes into a spoiled, haughty brat with a superiority complex. It was who Brinley had always been to Emma before today. It was only a mask. Just like Emma, Brinley put on an act when she walked through the school doors every morning. She hid her true self away underneath layers of attitude.

Cara rolled her eyes at Brinley's snapped explanation that they had gone to the restroom, then the group continued following the history teacher. He lead them to the upper level stairs, to the Supreme Court. Emma fell to the back of the pack again, but this time she did it to give herself a few moments to breathe away her fears. Brinley might have been satisfied with their shared experiences, but Emma could not conjure such emotions. Brinley's darkest secrets may have wormed their way into the light today, but Emma's were far from surfacing. Being beaten by Leader was barely a secret, much less a dark secret.

Chapter Twenty-Four

"Emma?" hissed a voice from behind her. Emma panicked, certain it would be Leader or Monique come to collect her and bring her home to face the pain of further disobedience. She froze on the bottom step, scanning the faces of the people in the corridor, searching for an angry face. When she found the caller, her fears melted away and she smiled. Benjamin Stillwell.

He hurriedly gestured to her to join him behind the column. Glancing up at her group, led by a docent and followed by a history teacher staring at his cellphone, she considered her options. She let the group continue up the steps and she backed away. Her quick steps brought her into his embrace before she realized she was being hugged.

"Hello, Emma," he exclaimed in surprise. "Fancy meeting you here." He backed away, looking down into her eyes with a grin.

Emma threw on a crooked smile. "It's good to see you so soon, Benjamin Stillwell." She looked past him at the empty corridor and then lowered her brows at him. "Where did you come from? Who are you with?"

He gestured behind him at the crossing corridor. "Restroom. I don't know where my group went. We're on a class field trip, but I was late to school, so I had to drive myself." He shrugged innocently. "My teachers were not thrilled to see me show up here, since apparently you are supposed to check in at the school and ride the bus on field trips." He gave a playful shrug, as if he had not known about the expectations before today. When she only gave him an arched look, he grinned, "I don't know about you, but I don't love the bus."

"We rode the bus," Brinley's waspish voice entered their conversation. She appeared at Emma's shoulder with a doubtful look on her face.

"Oh, sorry." Emma cleared her throat and backed away from him. "Brinley, this is Benjamin Stillwell. Benjamin, this is Brinley Taylor. She goes to my school."

"How do you do?" he asked, extending a hand to shake Brinley's. She took his hand, but her superior attitude kicked in and she studied him down the end of her nose.

"Where's your class?"

"I don't know," he admitted, glancing around the halls. "They are around here somewhere." He tucked Emma's arm into his own and said, "I will stay with you until I find my class. They're the ones in the ugly uniforms."

Emma rolled her eyes. "Every high schooler here is in an ugly uniform. It's private school day at the capitol."

He gave an innocent shrug and smiled. "Good excuse to hang out with you, I guess, Emma." He smiled apologetically at Brinley. "I have another arm, if you want."

Brinley shook her head and lengthened her stride to pass them up. "Maybe if I was living in the eighteenth century," she snapped back at him. But Emma did not care if walking arm in arm was old-fashioned; it was nice.

"So, is it your annual class field trip?"

He laughed, although nothing she had said was funny. "Actually, it's a history field trip and I'm not even in history this term." He laughed again. "I conned Old Landry to let me go anyway, because it was time I had a day off for good behavior."

"Landry is the history professor?" Emma asked. She was surprised, as she had been the other two times she talked with him, that she was so interested in his life. She had never been interested in the kids at her own school. Interest was vulnerable, because if Leader put the kibosh on a friendship, it was so much harder if there had been real interest.

"Old Landry is the Dean," he corrected and gave her a wink. "He and I see a lot of one another."

She shook her head in mock disappointment. "You're a troublemaker."

"Well, I had to have some sort of flaw," he replied with a shrug. "Otherwise I would be the whole package."

She rolled her eyes at his mock bravado. "That would be intimidating."

"You should join me."

She gave him a skeptical look. "What? Become a troublemaker? I'm a well-behaved, cordial, excellent student any teacher could be proud of and any dean could ignore. In fact, I doubt if my headmaster even knows my name."

"Headmaster Murphy knew me well, too," he answered with another shrug. "He saw me every day. He probably keeps a picture of me in his wallet next to his grandkids."

She missed the joking. "You used to go to my school?"

"Yes," he drawled. "I have served my time in *every* private school in the area. My father said if I can't make it here, he'll send me to military school."

Military school could not be any worse than her home, Emma thought. It would be preferable to going home once Leader found out she had skipped out of educational opportunities at school to go on a pointless field trip. But Emma smiled and said, "Yikes," due to the social convention of agreeing even when you don't agree.

"Like I said, this school is just a fancy prison," he answered with a shrug, and the haunted look in his eye suggested he was not really joking this time. She longed to lighten the mood.

"Not much of a prison, I would say, if they lose you when you run to the bathroom."

He laughed out loud at that, and the former heaviness surrounding him faded away.

Ahead of them, through the glass doors leading to the parking lot, Emma spotted her school group. They must not have spent any time in the Supreme Court if they were already headed back toward the buses.

"Lunch time," Emma told Benjamin. She was a little sad to separate from him, but as they walked through the doors and out onto the sidewalk, one of the teachers spotted her on Benjamin's arm and scowled.

"Young lady," she called sternly, waving her toward the other students. "Stay with the group!"

"I had better go," Emma said, glancing up at Benjamin apologetically. Then she grinned playfully, adding, "I wouldn't want to give her any reason to know my name."

He smiled, but then his voice dropped to a conspiratorial whisper. "Screw her. Screw them all. Wanna get out of here?"

Emma jerked back in surprise. "What do you mean?"

Benjamin grabbed her arm and pulled her close again. He leaned toward her, forehead nearly touching hers as he whispered firmly, "I mean, I drove here, and it's lunch time. You could get your friends to cover for you, and you and I could go on our own field trip." He jerked his head the opposite direction. "I'm parked over there."

Emma contemplated it. With knots in her stomach and painful memories of Leader's fury, she considered Benjamin's proposal. She wanted to say yes, but Monique's firm order to stay away from Benjamin overpowered her need for rebellion. She shook her head. "I don't think it's a good idea. What if my father comes looking for me and I'm not here?"

His brows rose in amused surprise. "You have some reason to think he followed your class on its field trip today? Doesn't he trust you to stay with the group?"

"Of course, he does," Emma replied, glancing toward Cara and her posse. Not that anyone should trust her to stay with the group, since she had already proven she could not be trusted in that regard. "But he did not exactly say I could *come* on the field trip. And if he finds out I forged his signature on the permission form, he will be over here in a blink."

Benjamin laughed out loud. "Harris, you surprise me! Who knew you could be such a badass, skipping school to go on an educational outing?" He shook his head at her, teasing her for what he considered to be a silly waste of rebellion.

"I am going to be in huge trouble," Emma shot back. "If I leave the field trip with a boy ... A boy my mother already warned me of ..." Her hand jumped to her mouth, thumbnail caught between her teeth. She *wanted* to go with him; that was the trouble. She wanted to go and not think about the consequences. But Monique's anger, and Leader's rage, filled her mind. Her heart thumped painfully against her chest.

"What's the worst that could happen, Emma? If you're already in trouble, what's a few more crimes to the list?"

Emma stared hard at him, and then back at the teacher who was calling to her again and beginning to move her direction. "I can see why you're well known to your dean."

She pulled away from him and let out a heavy sigh, "All right. I'm going to go tell my friends, so you won't be accused of kidnapping. And I'm going to get that teacher off my back. I'll meet you at your car."

"I'll drive around," he replied with a grin. Then he winked and added, "The black Dodge truck."

He slipped away just as the teacher approached to demand that Emma rejoin the group.

"Yes, Mrs. Hayworth," Emma meekly answered. "Sorry." The teacher stayed beside her, looking back in concern at Benjamin as he strode off on his own. Emma kept her eyes forward and moved toward the buses. When Hayworth stepped away from her, walking back to a small knot of teachers beside one of the buses, Emma hurried to where Cara's group was situating themselves. They were arranged on the grass beside one of the cement walls, each opening a lunch bag or box. Emma caught Brinley's arm before she could settle herself on the ground. She pulled her a few feet back. "Hey, I'm going to leave with Benjamin."

Brinley's eyes widened. She shook her head with urgent jerks. "Is that a good idea? How well do you know him, Emma?"

Emma shrugged. The answer was not very well. She lied. "We're good friends. He drove up here himself, so I'm going to leave with him. I'll have him take me back to the school before final bell. Okay? Will you cover for me?"

"Emma," Brinley insisted urgently, grasping her arm in tight fingers. "I don't think—"

"Let her go," Cara interrupted, popping her head into their conversation. The expression she shot at Brinley was exasperated. She rolled her eyes before turning to give Emma a tight smile. "I'll cover for you, Emma. You should go. Have fun."

"Thanks," Emma answered, but Cara's collusion did not bring her any comfort. If anything, it made Emma more nervous. Brinley's face, full of dark concern, was what caught Emma's eye. She did not think Emma should go; she did not trust it. But then Brinley jerked her head to the side, telling her to leave. Of course, she could not contradict Cara right in front of Cara's own face. That was the power Cara Winters held over the people in her posse.

Despite the hammering in her heart, Emma looked right and left, studied the teachers until she was certain they were too occupied to notice her, and she slipped away through the crowd. She let herself be carried from her own school group by slipping into the middle of another schools' red-striped uniforms.

"Be careful," Brinley called after her in a hushed shout. Emma waved back at them once the red-striped kids had moved beyond her. She saw Cara gesture for her to go, but Emma studied Brinley's concern-tightened lips for a moment before she ducked behind a cement wall. A moment before the teachers turned to look that direction.

Emma crouched and ran the length of the wall. Then, peeking back toward her own school buses, she saw the teachers were occupied. She ran. The sidewalk was open to the teacher's view, but there was enough foot traffic around Emma that she was able to blend in until she rounded the edge of the building.

Now out of sight, Emma slowed her speed, looking around for Benjamin. He told her he had a black truck, and she skimmed the side parking lot for it a bit frantically. She feared that any moment a hand would close on her shoulder and she would look up into the eyes of a furious teacher. Or worse: Leader.

With a sigh of relief, she saw Benjamin's black truck parked next to the curb a few meters up the lot, its hazard lights flashing. With another nervous glance over her shoulder to dispel the ghostly impression of Leader's fingers on her shoulder, Emma strode toward the truck. Benjamin was in the cab of the truck on his cellphone, speaking in angry little bursts she could not make out exactly. He saw her through the passenger window, smiled at her look of concern, and hung up his phone with an unconcerned tap to the screen. He leaned across to open the door for her.

"My mother," he admitted as he shook the phone in explanation. He placed it on a patch of rubber on the dashboard meant to hold it in place. "My school called her when the roles went to the office and I wasn't checked in for the day." He gave an innocent shrug. "The price of driving yourself to the field trip, I guess."

Emma dragged herself onto the seat and tugged the door shut behind her. A little nervously, she said, "I didn't ask."

She buckled her seatbelt before looking him in the eye. He had one brow raised in a sort of amused confusion. She clarified. "About the phone call ... I didn't ask about it. You don't have to tell me anything."

He reached across the cab and squeezed her shoulder in a brief, warming grip. "I know you didn't ask, Emma. I was just being friendly. It's kind of rude to be on the phone in front of someone and then not tell them anything." He chuckled. "My, my! Someone has hurt you." He touched a button to turn off the flashers as he put his truck into drive. He flipped a U-turn in the parking lot and headed toward the exit. He merged into traffic on the street. "I can see that I will have to watch what I do and say around you. I'm sorry if my explanation made you uncomfortable."

Emma felt a wave of guilt cascade around her. Desperately, she shook her head. "No, Benjamin. It's all right. I'm just not used to people sharing, is all. In my life, no one says anything they don't absolutely have to. No one knows anything unless it's pertinent to their ... schedule." Her lips pressed together, and she turned her head away to look out the window. She had almost said *mission*. She barely caught herself in time to change it to *schedule*. The carelessness of it almost made her ill.

When she glanced his way again, she saw an expression of concern in his face when he tugged his eyes from the road to study her. She brightened, smiling at him.

"Where are we going?"

"How much time do you have?"

She shrugged. "None, really. But I'm already out and breaking the rules. I may as well go all the way."

"Uh-oh," Benjamin laughed with a rueful shake of his head. "I'm rubbing off on you."

"I have to be back at school before the final bell so I can be picked up. If I'm not there when my mother drives up, I'm going to be in more trouble than I want to imagine."

Benjamin smiled, eyes twinkling mischief. "A few hours of freedom," he replied triumphantly. "Harris, I am going to teach you how to ditch school the *real* way. No educational outings for you, madam."

Emma settled back against the seat. She smiled to herself to try and lessen the sick feeling in her stomach. That had to be because she knew she would get into serious trouble for this. Yet, right now it seemed a price worth paying.

Chapter Twenty-Five

"Go-karts," Emma said doubtfully, staring through the chain-link fence at the strange looking cars on a miniature track.

"No, Emma. Not 'go-karts,'" Benjamin said, mimicking her voice with far more disdain that she had used. He thrust his fist into the air and announced triumphantly, "Go-karts!" as if he were a superhero and go-karts were the power behind his abilities.

Emma laughed at him. "Well, look, Mr. Go-Kart Man!" She pointed at the wooden "CLOSED" sign over the entrance gate to the go-karts. "They're not even open right now." She looked back over her shoulder at the empty Fun Center parking lot. No one was here today. The place looked abandoned, perhaps for the coming winter.

Benjamin shrugged innocently and walked backward toward the gate anyway. "Come on, Harris. Wouldn't want to leave you in the dust."

"Is that your clever way of suggesting I'm slow, or I'm scared?" Emma challenged.

Benjamin shrugged again. He crooked one finger to summon her closer. She gave him a doubtful look as she approached the fence. If he wanted her to climb over and break in, she would not do it. No matter how attractive his mischievous smile was, she would not break the law. Leader would kill her. "How do you propose to get through the locked gate?"

The mischievous smile blossomed on his face as he removed a key from his pocket. He dangled it in front of her eyes. "How about a key?"

Emma laughed at him. "Oh, you're a *nerd*," she said as if she had made a giant discovery. "You have a key to your very own obsession."

"Some people would say it's very cool, you know." He glowered at her playfully as he turned the key in the lock.

"Other nerds?" She slipped past him through the gate, then spun around and waggled her brows at him. "Come on, nerd!"

"Sometimes I don't know who you are, Harris," he chided her with playful scorn. "From serious to flirtatious to butt-kicking in an instant. Quicksilver."

She paused in alarm at his words, heart thumping. She attempted to read his expression, trying to see if he had started to figure her out. Had he discovered that she was only playing a part?

Benjamin only smiled. "Don't worry!" He tapped her under the chin with a firm finger. "I like it." He walked into the go-kart arena, leaving her staring after him with a heavy sigh.

He crossed the track toward a rickety shed where the cars were stored. Another key from his mysterious key ring opened the shed to reveal two rows of old go-karts shoved in tightly. Emma followed him into the shed, silently scolding herself for her previous fears. The Family had taught her to be distrusting, but she had no reason not to trust Benjamin.

From the collection of beat-up karts, Benjamin dragged a blue one out of the shed and to the starting line. Next, he retrieved a green one and dragged it up beside the other. "I got it," he teased her, lifting a hand as if to ward away an offer to help him. "No need to assist." She smirked at him. When he finished, he brushed his hands together and smiled at his handiwork. He motioned toward the karts.

"Which would you like, Harris? Your choice."

"I don't have the slightest idea how to drive one of these. Whichever of them can't be demolished by my horrific driving skills will be the best candidate."

He shook his head. "See the tires on the sides of the track?" He motioned to two rows of tires lining the edges of the go-kart track. They had been painted white and made unceasing lines on either side of the paved kart track for as far as she could see. "Those are there to keep you from demolishing anything." He leaned down and shoved squarish keys into the ignition of both cars. The sound of their tiny engines was unbelievably loud. She barely heard him say, "But just for good measure, take the green," with a twinkle in his eye.

She climbed into the torn leather seat and settled her feet in the slot. The vibrating machine numbed her buttocks almost immediately. Her hands went to the smoothed-over rubber steering wheel. She pressed the pedal under her foot and the kart shot down the track. Frantically, she turned the wheel to keep from running into the line of white painted tires.

"Wait!" Benjamin shouted to be heard over the roaring vehicles. As soon as she let off the pedal, the car slowed down. The brake stopped it with a jerk that nearly threw her out of the kart. Benjamin came running down the track carrying a couple of helmets. One, tucked under his arm, was black with orange flames down the sides. The one dangling from his hand by a strap was pink with white stripes.

"Cheater," he accused as he approached. He shook his finger at her. "Bad girl, breaking the rules." He held out the pink helmet for her. "You have to have this."

Looking doubtfully at the pink and white helmet, beat up and stained from frequent use, she replied dryly, "I hope you don't expect me to wear that"

He became serious and leaned forward to try and place it on her head. "I doubt your father and mother will thank me if I return you to them broken."

"First of all," she replied, dodging his attempts to place the helmet on her head. She held up a hand to stop him. "My parents are never going to know about you. Second, I'll take this one." She reached past his hands and snatched the black helmet from under his arm with a grin.

She smashed it onto her head and snapped the strap underneath her chin. He scowled at her while she did so, then scowled harder at the pink helmet left in his hand. Finally, he shrugged and stuffed it over his brown locks. He posed for her and she nodded, playfully encouraging of the girly helmet on his head.

She seriously thought he would go back to exchange for a different helmet, but he didn't. "Don't move," he warned her, and he ran back toward his own kart. "And buckle in."

She obediently located the straps and snapped them into place, although she felt that being buckled into this ungodly contraption was less safe than remaining unbuckled. Benjamin drove his car up beside hers. He shouted, "Go on three, okay? One ... Two ..."

She slammed her foot against the pedal and sped away from him with a laugh.

"Cheater!" he screamed behind her, but she could hear the amusement in his tone. He pursued her down the track.

Emma laughed back at him but sped steadily forward. The kart was not a smooth ride. The numbing feeling crept up her back and down her legs. Yet it only took a couple rounds on the track to get the hang of steering. She smacked into the tires occasionally, but Benjamin only laughed at her and shouted suggestions for getting herself clear. She never let him get ahead of her, though, even when helping her was the reason he stopped his own kart. As soon as she was free of the tires, she sped off again, leaving him shouting after her and declaring she was a cheater.

She rounded the entire track once without hitting the tire line, and adrenaline pushed her onward. She let her speed climb, and she cut off his attempt to maneuver around her. He crashed into the tires with a shout of profanity. Laughing, she started a second lap, gunning the pedal as he tried to disentangle himself from the sideline. Behind her, she heard Benjamin shouting challenging trash talk, but that only made her want to go faster.

A sharp curve in the track brought her in view of the interstate. A sinking feeling in the pit of her stomach cooled her playfulness. She saw a silver BMW parked on the shoulder of the road. She panicked. Leader had somehow tracked her down. Maybe he had been serious that he had a tracking device embedded in her spine.

In her panic, she failed to steer correctly, and her go-kart slammed into the painted white tires lining the track. The safety belt kept her seated but bit painfully into her shoulders as she tested their effectiveness. Her head slammed back against the seat, making her grateful for the helmet after all. Her car rolled backward until it hit the other line of tires across the track, and finally stopped. She attempted to catch her breath and remove her safety belt at the same time. She was frantic to get out of the go-kart.

"Are you all right?" Benjamin asked, braking next to her. He shut his car down and jumped out to her aid.

"My ... my father," she panted. She yanked at the safety straps, but they wouldn't release.

Benjamin looked all around. "What do you mean ... ?"

He squatted beside her and grabbed her hands. "Let me get it, Emma," he demanded, pushing her hands out of the way. "God, you're white as a sheet." He clicked the button to release the straps and grabbed her hands to help her out.

Despite the numbness in her buttocks and legs, Emma ran to the edge of the track. She grasped the chain-link fence, climbed onto the white-painted tires, and stared out of the streaming traffic below. But the car that had been parked on the roadside only a few moments before was now gone. She gulped in a breath as if she had run a marathon, then she bent over to rest her hands on her knees. The fear she felt at seeing what she thought was Leader's car pounded at her chest and fed in the pit of her stomach. She struggled to keep from crying.

"Emma," Benjamin said gently, coming up behind her. He placed his hand on her back in what might have been an attempt at comfort, but Emma was unaccustomed to being gently touched, so she straightened and backed away swiftly. Benjamin responded by backing away, as well. "I did not mean to frighten you. You do not look well. What happened?"

Emma touched the chain-link fence separating her from the interstate and began to cry. She could not hold it in. "I'm sorry," she apologized through her sobs. "I just thought ... I thought I could get away from him, but I can't. I never can ..."

Benjamin tried to approach again and this time she let him come near. He placed his hand over hers on the fence. "You don't have to be afraid," he promised her with steady conviction. "I won't let anything happen while I'm with you, Emma."

She spun around so her back was to the road. She stared Benjamin hard in the eye. "I saw his car right up there, like somehow he followed me here. But how can he know where I am? How can he know I ditched the field trip? It doesn't make any sense! My phone was confiscated at school and then I got on a bus and left. But maybe the buses have surveillance, or maybe my uniforms ..." She grabbed at the white collar of the shirt she wore and stared at it, as if expecting it at any moment to reveal the secret of Leader's influence. "I wouldn't even know if he bugged my clothes. I wouldn't even know."

Benjamin grasped her shoulders. "Emma! There is no one watching us right now, okay?" He opened his hand to the abandoned go-kart track and the accompanying amusement park. "We are completely alone right now, and no one knows you're here except me. It's just us."

She looked around, tears flooding her eyes. But what he said was true. No one was there except the two of them. There was no silver car stopped on the shoulder of the interstate below. There was no one in the amusement park but the two of them. And if Leader knew she had ditched school for the field trip, he would already have picked her up. He would have gotten to her before she ever got on the bus.

She allowed herself to calm down.

CHAPTER TWENTY-SIX

Benjamin studied Emma's face. "I'm worried about you," he finally admitted. There was no playfulness in him now. "And not a little concerned about your family dynamic. I saw your father the night of the party, storming in as if he owned the place and making all kinds of demands. What did he do to you?"

Emma took a deep breath and tried to relax against the fence, to pretend to be at ease, but as soon as she leaned, the metal links of the fence sent pain waves across the bruises on her back. She jerked forward again. "I'm sorry to alarm you," she whispered. She pushed past him and walked back onto the track. He followed.

"It's not alarm, Emma. It's concern!" He sat on the hood of his go-kart. "I am concerned because I know what it is like to have overbearing, even *abusive* parents."

Emma rolled her eyes. "What is it? Share your family sorrow day?" But she could not pull off the indifferent, sarcastic attitude with leftover tears still on her cheeks. She covered the act of wiping her tears by removing her helmet and examining it.

After a long pause, Benjamin said, "We don't have to talk about your family if you don't want. God knows my family is never my favorite topic of discourse." He opened his palms to her and said, "But I do think you should tell me what caused you to crash your go-kart and start crying."

Emma watched him from the corner of her eye. She smoothed her helmet in her hands and finally set it down on the go-kart seat. She settled on the hood of her car and looked at him steadily. "I have never gotten into much trouble, you understand."

He flashed her a grin and said, "I figured that much out on my own, Harris."

She smiled back but it was short-lived. "I got into some trouble the night of the party and had a horrible weekend. I don't know what possessed me to go on the field trip when I knew Lea—my father would disapprove. But I just wanted to get away from him! The field trip seemed like the best way to do it without being directly disobedient. And then I saw you there today and, even though my mother has forbidden me from being friends with you, I agreed to come on this little excursion. I guess my fears were not buried deeply enough because when I saw the car parked on the shoulder up there," she motioned toward the distant interstate. "I thought maybe Lea—my *father* had tracked me down. I guess I was not in a position to handle it."

Benjamin cocked his head to the side and stared at her. "There are so many questions I want to ask, but notice me respecting your privacy?" He glanced toward the freeway. "Was it really him? I mean, it could have been anyone, Emma. Maybe your fear just made you believe you saw him. What can he do to you, anyway, if you ditched school to go to the capitol building? That's not like a co-ed booze-infested party with slutty party guests and handsy morons." He shrugged. "Which you seemed to handle well the other night, I noticed."

She gave a small smile that again quickly faded. "It probably was not him. Maybe I just thought I saw him because I am so afraid of getting caught with you."

He pulled a face. "What do they have against *me*? I'm a nice boy and, despite my school troubles, I get pretty good grades."

Emma flashed a smile again and this time it lasted a little longer. "It has nothing to do with you. It's them. They are crazy protective. It wouldn't matter if you came with a guaranteed list of credentials and the highest GPA in the universe; they would never let you within 50 meters of me."

A dark look of distrust appeared in his eyes. She recognized it because it was a frequent expression around the Guild House. She had seen it in her own expression once or twice over the past few years. Still, seeing the expression in someone outside the Guild made her nervous. She backed away from him.

"I think you should take me home now," she advised.

The distrust left his expression in a flash of confusion. "Harris, it's all right," he exclaimed. "It probably wasn't even your parents. And if it was, you're already out and going to be in trouble. What's a couple more hours? Besides, I haven't even given you anything to eat. What kind of privileged rich kid would I be if I didn't even flash around my daddy's credit card? Come on," he motioned back toward the gate. "I'll take you to lunch and then we'll drive to your school before your mom catches wind of your illegal disappearance."

She studied him a long time, waiting for him to show signs of anger or distrust like at the Guild House, but he just continued to smile encouragingly. Finally, she nodded. "Okay." He opened his hand and she took it.

"Let's go," he said and pulled her away. They crossed the track, abandoning the go-karts as they approached the gate.

"Are you going to wear that pretty pink helmet to lunch?" she asked innocently.

Benjamin startled and scrambled to remove the helmet. He threw it behind him and it crash-landed on the black-top track.

"Are rich privileged kids not expected to clean up after themselves?" Emma asked, looking back to the go-karts and the helmets strewn across the track.

He shrugged. "Not in my family. Oh, my dad will probably throw a fit when he realizes I lifted the keys off his park manager, but there's not a lot he can do to me from Venice."

"Your father's in Venice?" she asked, although she was not really interested in the answer. Leader went out of town all the time. Business men frequently had to travel.

"Or London or Bangkok or any number of places." His tone had a strain of unconcern. He did not care where in the world his father was. He shoved the gate closed behind them and strolled across the sidewalk toward his truck parked on the professionally-manicured lawn. The parking lot was only 20 feet away, but he had not seemed to care when he had parked his truck on the grass. "My father spends as little time at home as he can."

"Lucky for you," Emma said.

Benjamin unlocked the passenger door and opened it for her. "Lucky for *us*," he replied with waggling brows. She climbed in the cab and let him close the door behind her. She leaned across and unlocked his door for him, causing him to smile at her as he approached.

"Mother always said that girls who lean to unlock your door are keepers," Benjamin told her with a wink. He climbed into the truck and put the key in the ignition.

"Glad she'd approve."

"Oh, I wouldn't go that far," answered Benjamin with a laugh. "She'd cut you into little tiny pieces with her glares if she thought you were spending time with me to get into my father's pocketbook."

Emma scoffed. "What the hell kind of good would more money do for me?" she exclaimed. "My father's fortune has kept me well all these years. I want for nothing."

Benjamin's expression of concern hinted that he knew she wanted for things money could not buy. He looked at her for a long moment. Too long. Emma turned away from him and stared out the passenger window. "Where are we eating?"

Benjamin gave her one of his mischievous chuckles and said, "It's going to be epic."

"Like go-karts?" she asked doubtfully and shot him a playfully disdainful look.

He pointed a finger at her and corrected, "GO-KARTS!" in his triumphant superhero voice. He backed the truck out of the grass then peeled away down the road. Emma laughed.

Emma stared at the sign over the fast food counter then turned her doubtful expression on Benjamin grinning at her side.

"Hotdogs?" she asked dryly. She had never actually had hotdogs, since they were not considered by Leader as healthy additions to a balanced diet. And she had never thought she was missing anything.

"On a stick," Benjamin replied as if the stick was a necessary qualification. "It's the best way to eat them."

"Is there a best way to eat something this disgusting?" She looked around at the other fast food fronts in the mall food court.

Benjamin turned her head with one finger under her chin and said, "The best way is on a stick," he promised her, pointing to the colorful menu sign overhead. "Just try it and, if you hate it, you can always have tacos or something. What do you want?"

Emma had never had tacos either, but she agreed. "Okay. Get me one of those disgusting battered hotdogs."

Benjamin scowled at her description, but then approached the counter and ordered two corndogs and two cups of lemonade. When he returned to her, he took her hand and tugged her over to the distribution counter to wait for their food to be served.

"I don't think go-karts and hotdogs are much of an improvement on the Capitol," Emma teased him, staring at her hands held in his gentle grip.

Instead of being insulted, Benjamin laughed. "The company is better, I hope?"

Emma nodded. "I think so." Thoughts of Cara and her snotty posse bounced forward, followed by Brinley's dark family secrets. "I'm really glad you showed up at the Capitol and stole me away, Benjamin. If I'm going to get in trouble for doing something stupid, I'm just glad part of it will be worth it."

"The hotdogs will be worth it," he said, giving her a solemn nod.

She shook her head and rolled her eyes. "*You* are worth it. Thanks for not freaking out about my freak out."

He shrugged. "Freak outs are a natural part of life for the rich and privileged. Don't sweat it, Harris. Sometimes I freak out, too. Only, when I freak out I usually buy a Porsche and drive as far as I can get across country before my father's security tracks me down and drags me back kicking and screaming."

Emma laughed softly. "Has this happened more than once?"

Benjamin placed one finger beside his nose and confided, "I'm always planning my escape."

"Here you go, sir," said the young man on the other side of the counter as he passed a food tray to Benjamin. Benjamin spun around to take the tray.

"Thank you, good sir," he replied in a formal accent. He picked up the tray with one hand, grasped Emma's hand with the other, and maneuvered through the jumble of tables and chairs into the seating area. He selected the table she would have chosen. It had a bench against one wall and it looked out over the mall and the entrance doors leading outside.

He slid the tray on the table and motioned for her to be seated. She slipped onto the bench so her back could be to the wall and was surprised when he sat beside her rather than across from her. She handed him a napkin from the tray and took one herself. She unfolded the napkin and placed it across her lap under his mocking scrutiny.

"Do you think you are at a state luncheon?"

"I have good table manners," she shot back.

He scoffed but he also placed his napkin in his lap. He put a corndog basket beside her and when she just stared at it, he nudged it closer. "Do you trust me?"

She laughed out loud at the idea of trust, but then she sobered immediately. "I do," she said aloud as she realized it. "I do trust you ... sort of." She touched the corndog. "But that doesn't mean I have any idea how to eat this."

He picked up the stick of his own corndog and said, "I will demonstrate." He took a giant bite from the top, and then exclaimed, "Delicious," with his mouth still full.

Emma pulled a face and took a timid bite of her own food. It tasted like clogged arteries and excess fat cells, but she would not disappoint him. "It's acceptable."

Benjamin laughed. "You hate it," he said and attempted to take it away from her.

She pulled the basket out of his reach. "I do not hate it," she lied, and took another timid bite. Then, to wash it down, she tried the lemonade. She blinked in surprise when her face involuntarily turned up from the taste of the lemons. She had never had lemonade before, either, but this she liked, despite its effect on her mouth. She took another swallow.

"It's the best lemonade in the world," he announced. He looked pleased that she appeared to enjoy it.

"It is an abysmal amount of sugar and acidic fruit, but ..." she glanced up at him through her lashes. "I like it."

He shook his fist at the ceiling. "Success!" he declared.

She smiled at him and pushed his corndog basket toward him. "Just eat."

He laughed, but he obeyed.

The truck pulled through her school driveway 14 minutes before the final bell. She could see Monique's car down near the front of the line of cars already parked and ready for pickup. There was no way she could know about Emma ditching the field trip, but Emma's heart pounded nervously. Benjamin clicked the lock on the door when she attempted to open it, caging her in. She looked at him in alarm, but there was only gentleness in his eyes.

"Tell me we can do this again," he urged.

She gave him an exasperated smile. "I don't know how we ever could. I'll be lucky if I ever get to leave the house again after today's little excursion."

Benjamin waggled his brows at her. "Do you imagine I'm the kind of guy who will accept that as an excuse? I can find a way. Give me your number." He tugged a pen from a shelf in the dash and clicked the button to open the pen. He held it over his hand, intending to write her number directly onto his skin.

She shook her head at that. "You can't ever call it. My father traces all my calls."

He stared hard at her for a moment, then he clicked the pen again and tossed it back to its place. Slipping his own phone out of his pocket, he passed it over to her. "He might have a hard time tracing this one."

She held the little phone in her hands and he closed his hand around hers. "I'll go buy myself another one. And I'll call you later. Okay? Take it."

Emma knew this plan had holes, but she tightened her hands around the phone and said, "Okay. But don't call me until after midnight."

He smiled. "I promise," he said, and he clicked the unlock button. "Be safe."

She sat there a moment longer, feeling the phone in her hands, then she leaned up and kissed his cheek quickly. She wasn't sure anymore if her heart was pounding because of the imminent danger of Monique or nerves related to Benjamin.

"Please don't forget to call me," she whispered, and she slipped out the door before he could answer. She landed on the sidewalk running.

"I won't forget," he called after her. She did not look back.

CHAPTER TWENTY-SEVEN

Monique looked up as Emma climbed into the front seat of the family Lexus. With an arched brow, she glanced at her watch, then up at Emma expectantly.

"I got out early," Emma lied and looked away to avoid Monique studying her eyes.

"Where's your backpack?"

The question sent a jolt of fear through her heart. It tried to thunder out her guilt, but she recovered quickly. "I left it in my locker on accident. I forgot it."

Monique grasped her chin, turning her face to meet her stern eyes. "Is that where your phone is?"

Emma sighed and sat back against the seat, extricating herself from Monique's grip. "No, ma'am," she answered with dry accusation in her tone. "Mr. Johnson in homeroom confiscated it when you called this morning. I had forgotten to silence it." She shot a searching glance up at Monique's impassive face. "The school policy is extremely strict."

Monique turned away and sat staring out the windshield for a long time. Then she shut the car off and climbed out. "Let's go," she ordered.

"Where?" Emma asked in alarm, panic striking her heart again.

"They won't give a phone back to a student without a parent present," Monique replied tersely. Her eyes darkened at Emma in threat. "But I do not owe you any explanation, Emma. Get out of the car and come with me right now. Or did I not effectively teach you the value of Obedience this weekend?"

Emma immediately got out of the car and closed the door behind her. "I'm sorry," she said as contritely as she could.

Monique's six-inch heels clicked on the sidewalk and then on the tile floors of the school entryway. "Go get your backpack and meet me in the headmaster's office," she commanded as she stepped up to the glass door at the office suite.

"Yes, Mother," Emma replied. She hurried away from Monique, not daring to look back over her shoulder. She hurried through the commons area, rounded the bend, and entered the east hall as the final bell rang through the school. Within moments, doors burst open all along the hall. In an instant, she was surrounded by other students. This allowed her to relax a little. The hubbub and noise gave her the chance to open her locker and tuck Benjamin's phone into her backpack pocket while the halls were full of students distracting Leader's surveillance eye. She was careful to keep the phone hidden in her palm while transferring it so even if he was watching he would not see it. She slung her backpack over her shoulder and stepped into the crowd heading toward the exits.

Cara reached through the crowd and grabbed her arm. "Emma," she said firmly, hauling her into the middle of Brinley, Megan, Madeline and the others. "So? How was your day out?"

Emma was very aware of the surveillance, and so she only smiled. She did not want to give Leader any information upon which to set up a line of painful questioning.

"She's not going to tell us anything," Brinley snapped coldly. "Look at her, though; she's absolutely glowing. She had a good time."

Cara searched Emma's face for confirmation of that, so Emma smiled again. "See you tomorrow," she greeted the posse and then backed away from them.

"We'll see," Cara answered darkly. "Tomorrow ..."

Emma abruptly turned and walked away to avoid any more questions that could incriminate her in Leader's eyes. She held one strap of her backpack to keep it on her shoulder and maneuvered through the halls, back across the commons area, and into the administrative suite. Monique waited inside. She was pacing, which was never a good sign. Emma approached her cautiously.

"Mr. Johnson has not returned your phone to the office yet," she hissed at Emma. "They are supposed to send it to the office immediately, with a demerit slip." She glared at Emma, leaning toward her. "A *demerit*, Emma! For carelessness."

Emma cocked her head to the side. "I'm sorry, Mother. I have never received any calls during school. I guess I never needed to turn it to silent before."

Monique approached at a dangerous stroll. "That sounded a little bit caustic, Emmalyn Harris," she murmured ferociously. "Maybe a tad disrespectful."

Emma backed down immediately in the face of that anger. "No, Mother. I meant no disrespect." She glanced past her at the school counselor who had just entered the waiting room from her office. The curious woman studied Monique and Emma for a moment, then crossed the waiting room toward them. Emma discretely motioned with her head to give Monique warning of the counselor's imminent approach. Emma said calmly, "I am certain Mr. Johnson only got busy and he will bring the phone to the office shortly."

"Good afternoon," the counselor said when Emma finished speaking. Monique, her back still to the counselor, barely refrained from rolling her eyes. She turned slowly around.

"Good afternoon, Ms. James," she greeted with a smile. She offered her hand to shake, and Ms. James took it in a firm grip.

"Miss Harris, good day," Ms. James said, leaning around Monique to give Emma her patented condescending smile. "How was the field trip?"

Emma winced slightly when Monique turned sharply to give her a questioning look. But under the scrutiny of the school counselor, Emma could not defend herself to Monique. Instead she gave a brief smile and nodded. "It was very educational."

Ms. James smiled in return. "I think that was the design, Miss Harris."

Emma nodded again. "Yes, ma'am."

Ms. James turned back to Monique. "The annual Capitol Building field trip," she explained, as if she knew Monique did not know anything about it. But Monique recovered extremely well.

"Of course," she said lightly. "Speak to local government and see legislature in action. Noble attempts at helping children understand their potential futures."

"Yes," Ms. James smiled warmly. She placed a hand on Emma's shoulder. "Who knows? One day Emma could be our state senator."

Monique gave a chuckle that Emma recognized as menacing. "Emma is not going into state politics."

Ms. James glanced from Emma to Monique, then smiled in the way only professional counselors can. "I hope she will choose to do something for which she is passionate."

Monique and the counselor stood locked in a mutual gaze for a long moment before Monique said, "Could you find my daughter's cellphone, please? Mr. Johnson confiscated it but never turned it into the office."

Emma let out a breath of frustration for Monique's clear disdain of the counselor's responsibilities. She was not an errand runner. Her job was to take care of the emotional health of her students. But the counselor only smiled and said, "Of course, Mrs. Harris." And she strolled away across the office. Monique placed a hand casually across Emma's shoulders, tugging her closer, and quietly suggested, "Well, don't we have some things to talk about?"

"You never said I couldn't go," Emma replied too quickly.

Monique squeezed her neck and whispered, "We'll talk about it later." She waited quietly with her hand still on the Emma's neck until Ms. James returned to them. "Any luck?"

"I'm afraid the phone has already been claimed, Mrs. Harris," the Counselor explained. "It was signed out at noon. I am sorry about any confusion. The receptionist who told you Mr. Johnson had not turned the phone in was not here this morning when he delivered it. She's new."

Monique's hand on Emma's neck came under the counselor's scrutiny. When she noticed it, Monique stepped away and nodded. "Thank you for your help, Counselor. Good day." She turned away as if she had promptly forgotten the hired help; she sauntered toward the exit. "Come along, Emma. Let's get home." Her firmly clacking heels reiterated her firm command.

"Thank you," Emma exhaled at Ms. James. She hurried after the clacking heels.

Once they got out to the car, Monique slashed harsh eyes toward Emma. "Get in," she snapped as she stalked around to the driver side. "Where the hell is Scott?"

Emma threw her backpack into the back seat and opened the front passenger door. As she climbed in, she looked over her shoulder and saw Ms. James standing at the school gates watching her. It unnerved her to see the counselor had followed them out the door. She slipped into the car and settled back in the seat. Monique leaned out to grasp at a parking ticket under her wiper blade. It was against school policy to leave a parked car in the drive through. When Monique slipped back into the car, she crumpled the paper ticket and tossed it into the center cupholder with a stream of curses. She fished her $1,200 phone from her $2,000 purse and dialed with a single button.

"Put me through to Leader," she ordered. She waited for a moment before saying, "Fine, Amos, just tell him I called, and I need him to take care of a parking ticket before it hits the Cortex. No ... Amos, it's fine. I'll tell him, just have him call me. And, Amos? Get a hold of Scott and ... He's home? It would have been nice to have been informed ... No, it's fine; I'm just glad he's safe ... Emma's with me ... Right. Later." She hung up the phone and dropped it beside the ticket in the cupholder.

"Seatbelt," Monique ordered briskly as she put the car into gear. She sped out of the drive through lane, cutting off a Jag and an Escalade as she merged into traffic. When Emma reached for her seatbelt, she looked over her shoulder and saw Ms. James still standing at the gate looking after Monique's car. Monique saw her, too, through the rearview mirror.

"Well, she's nothing if not determined," Monique muttered.

"Determined to do what?" Emma answered, clicking her seatbelt firmly in place.

Monique sighed and glanced at Emma from the corner of her eye. "School counselors are a menace to the Family. They make interference a daily pilgrimage. She'll probably start asking to see you in her office, so she can analyze your quirks and witticisms."

Emma stared straight ahead at the road and felt the weight of anxiety on her breast. "Why? What will I do?"

Monique blinked in surprise and studied her for a moment. "Sometimes I forget how very young you are," she said aloud, but Emma thought it was not meant for her. Monique reached over and patted her knee. "Don't worry about this," she soothed. Her tone became brisk again in an instant as if making up for the physical contact that was so foreign to her. "Julia James will be dealt with, and, in the meantime, you will be trained to handle her nosiness."

"Yes, Mother," she answered. The idea of talking to Ms. James about her troubles was terrifying. She hated people prying into the life she could not talk about.

"You have observed the other students at your school," Monique added. "Haven't you ever noticed how they handle interrogative situations?"

Emma thought about that. She thought about what Brinley had told her today. She had made up a story to explain her bruises. And everything Emma knew about Cara said she told her parents falsehoods to keep out of trouble. It did seem to be a recurring theme of high school.

"They lie," Emma explained, looking up at Monique, who glanced at her before refocusing her attention on the road.

"Of course, they do," Monique said dismissively. "But not skillfully. You will be expected to be a skilled liar."

Emma sank lower in her chair as she heaved a sigh. "I can hardly get realistic practice telling lies, Monique. Leader would never stand for me to lie to him. And I don't think it's a practice that makes people highly reliable."

Monique chuckled, and for a wonder, Emma thought she really was amused. "Well, being frank is its own kind of skill, I suppose. But it won't deliver you from the counselor's clutches. And I don't think transferring you to a new school would make her let up. As soon as your transcripts were requested by another school, James would contact that school's counselor and you would be in the same position; you would still need to be a skillful liar."

Emma stared out the side window. "What am I meant to lie about?"

Monique waited for a moment, then asked, "Are you really serious?"

"Yes," Emma answered truthfully, but she did not look at her. She really did not know what she would have to say to the counselor. What was it counselors wanted to know about that threatened the Guild?

"He was right," Monique murmured, again as if speaking only to herself. "I have neglected you."

Emma turned and looked at Monique, capturing that black gaze in time to see real concern before it vanished into fierceness. "Is there something I should already know that I don't? Leader told me I could ask questions, but his answers only left me more confused than ever. All I have ever wanted was to understand what I'm doing here, and where I came from. Did I have parents before, like the kids at my school? If yes, why have I been put into the Family? What are we even doing here? What significance are we?"

Monique cleared her throat twice before answering, and Emma wondered if she was uncomfortable with the stream of questions. "You were made for the Guild," she said in the formal way Leader had said those exact words. "The Guild is your family. And the Guild mission is—"

"I know," Emma interrupted in frustration. "It's on a need-to-know basis. And I don't need to know. But I think I really do. Do you have any idea how frustrating it is to try and explain my life to people? I can't tell them anything real, and not telling the truth has never come particularly easy to me."

"To your credit," Monique interjected.

"So, I end up keeping to myself all the time and not making any friends because I don't know what I am allowed to say and what is restricted Guild business, so people don't know how to talk to me, and, frankly, I don't know how to talk to them, either."

"Stop," Monique interjected again, and this time Emma paused for a breath. "Do you think the Guild is set up as a 12-step ladder by accident, Emma? It's a process. Of course, I understand how frustrating it is to hide your true identity from others; I did it, too, when I was Twelve. And guess what? So did everyone else. You can't beg to know everything yet, Emma, because you're not ready to know it. When you are, you will be instructed."

Emma's breath exploded from her in exasperation. "Then why do you keep saying you have neglected my education? If it really doesn't matter what I know, why tell me anything?"

Monique pointed a finger and firmly warned, "Careful ..." for Emma's tone. Emma turned away again and stared out the window rather than face Monique. The truth was, Emma did not care so much about Guild business today, but she did worry about Monique asking too many questions about the field trip, seeing as Emma had ditched out only halfway through. Emma was truly an inexperienced liar. Before Cara had entered her life, she never told a single lie to Monique before. She was not equal to creating stories Monique would not immediately see through. Keeping her occupied was the best alternative.

"I have neglected your Guild education, Emma, because you do not know how to handle intruders like Ms. James or bullies like Scott and Adam when they try to get you in trouble for their mistakes. I have failed to teach you some basic human interactions that will help you maneuver your way out of awkward situations. Like that McCormick boy you nearly killed for simply being friendly."

Emma's mouth dropped open and this time when she turned to argue, it was not just trying to keep Monique occupied. "Friendly?!" she shouted. She had never shouted at Monique before. She was unused to the thunderous sound it made coming from her throat.

It reverberated off the car's interior, and for a wonder, Monique's fierce impassivity broke in surprise. "If that jerk was being friendly when he grabbed me and tried to hold me against his body, I don't even want to know what you consider inappropriate. He would not let go of me, and he was drunk and being stupid. I reacted with violence because that was what I was trained to do, and my words were not having much of an effect."

"If I must stop this car to calm you down, you won't like the result," Monique warned in a quiet tone. Quiet like the cock of a gun. "I never did get the full story from Leader."

Emma did not back down. "Leader wasn't even there the whole time! He doesn't know how that prick treated me or why I resorted to violence—" She cut off abruptly as Monique swerved into the far-right lane and put her blinker on. She was going to pull off the road and do whatever it was she had warned Emma to avoid.

"I'm calm," Emma hurriedly said, altering her voice, her heart pounding. "I'm calm now."

"Are you?" Monique demanded.

"Yes!" Emma insisted, frantic to keep Monique from putting the car into park. "I'm sorry. I should not have lost my temper. Please don't stop the car, Monique."

Monique arched both brows at her. "No more outbursts from you," she said, like it was a condition for her to keep driving.

"Yes, ma'am," Emma whispered. She looked out the car window again, determined to lose herself in the silence and her thoughts.

Monique's tone was a little amused when she said, "But I am glad to see you found your backbone. I was beginning to worry."

They rode on without speaking to each other. Monique picked up her phone and made calls to her law office. Emma thought it must be exhausting to be Monique. Having to deal with Leader and the Guild business on top of a full career as a lawyer; it seemed an unreasonable expectation.

Chapter Twenty-Eight

When they approached the Guild House, Monique pressed a button on her steering column to open the garage door, but as it slid slowly upward, it revealed a red Porsche in her parking space. She cursed under her breath and slammed the car into park in the driveway. Without saying a word, Monique climbed out and shut the door behind her. Emma followed her up the front path and along the stone steps leading to the front door of the house.

Leader stood leaning against the open doorframe with a dark look on his face. Emma hung back near the bushes, afraid maybe it really had been him on the side of the road at the go-kart track. It made no sense that he would not have come to collect her if he had found her there, but she did worry.

"Is that your new acquisition in my garage?" Monique demanded. "A lofty expense, even for you, Leader."

Leader's face did not change but for some reason Emma thought he became more menacing. Monique was not shy of him, though. She approached at her normal brisk pace. "I don't answer to you, Monique," he countered. "I never have, and I never will." His eyes gained intensity. "I am supposed to go to South Africa tonight, but I couldn't leave since that—" he jerked his head toward the direction of the garage, "arrived. I hoped *you* made an unwarranted purchase."

Monique blinked in surprise. "I would never make that big of an unwarranted purchase without just cause. You know that, Leader."

He nodded. "I said 'I hoped,' not 'I thought.' All this means is the Guild has been compromised. Why and how?"

Emma pulled a face. How could a red Porsche arriving at the Guild House mean anything had been compromised? Cars were a big part of the Family's cover, but how could one addition to the garage make Leader think anything negative?

Monique stood still and quiet for a long moment while Leader looked at her with dark, expectant eyes. All at once, Monique started and exclaimed, "I will find out." He nodded, as if that had been what he was waiting for all along. Monique side-stepped past him over the threshold and disappeared into the house.

Emma pulled her thumbnail into her mouth, hoping Leader would follow Monique inside. He didn't. He was waiting for Emma to come inside. Emerging from her hiding place in the bushes and tugging her nail out of her mouth, she shifted her backpack on her shoulder and trudged down the path. She closed the distance between them.

"Good afternoon, Father," she murmured as she tried to step past him with Monique's side-step maneuver. He blocked her with a solid arm across the threshold.

"Afternoon, Emma," he greeted, dangerous music in his tone. Moving his opposite hand into his suit jacket, he removed her cell phone. He held it in front of her face without a sound until she reached up and took it. She did not dare glance up at him, but she felt his unwavering gaze on her.

"I am sure you know that school demerits are unacceptable. I am certainly glad for your sake that your teacher has decided to be lenient." He retracted the obstacle barring her path. Emma breathed down at the porch in relief and attempted to move past him again. Too slow. She realized he had only removed his arm so he could use it to encircle her shoulders, to pull her around, to lean in close enough to whisper dangerous musical words in her ear.

"We'll talk later about your little field trip."

Preemptively defensive, she met his dark gaze. "You never said I couldn't go."

"Didn't I?"

Desperate to keep him from asking too many questions, she hardened her tone. She made it more sarcastic than she had dared use with him for a long time. Since the night back in Scotland when she had run away from home. That night, before she ran, before she turned his wrath on her by trying to escape him, she copped an attitude.

"What's the worst thing that could happen if I don't *do the dishes?" She had snarled at him from down the long dining table. "Will you kill me? Will you beat me?" She shrugged defiantly at him. "Will you send me to bed without my supper?"*

Leader's arched expression down the length of the table had not stayed on Emma; it swept up to Monique at his right. The look Monique shot down the table curdled her blood, but Emma didn't stop. Even with them both—and everyone else, too—staring at her in dismay, Emma insisted, "You can't actually make *me do anything. All you can do is threaten me and then punish. If I stop caring about the punishments, you have no power." She'd read through a psychology textbook pilfered from Ilene's bookshelf earlier in the day. It talked about being assertive and understanding that you belong only to yourself.*

"Nope," Amos told the room, anger clouding his blue eyes. He got up from the table then and stood on Leader's left side. "You do not get to behave this way at dinner, Emma." He stalked the length of the table and tugged her chair out. "Go upstairs to your room right now. You are not going to ruin our dinner with this bad attitude." But Emma did not move. Resolutely defiant, she remained in her seat with her arms crossed, glaring down at Leader with every piece of resolve she had. Amos squatted down in front of her, meeting her eyes with his own angry scowl. "Right now, young lady." Emma did not move, except to glare at Amos instead of Leader.

"Amos," Leader called, sternly composed. "Do not let her defy you like that; it's not Refined." Amos picked Emma up and tossed her over one of his broad shoulders. She tried to fight him, but he was too strong. He carried her up to her room, told her in his sternest voice that he was disappointed in her choices, and promised her a comeuppance for it when the Guild finished their meal.

Emma did not wait around for that. As soon as he'd locked her in, she threw open her window and scaled her way across the narrow ledge of brick that served as her toehold. At the drain pipe, she shimmied down and then she ran. She did not know where she planned to go. She just wanted to get away from Amos' disappointment, and Leader's musical authority, and the promise of menace in Monique's eyes. In the falling darkness of the moors, Emma sprinted away.

She was captured near the village by a tattered old man with a deeply-lined face and alcohol on his breath. In the moonlight, the man spotted her, called to her, then grasped her wrist. He refused to let go. When he called her by name, Emma panicked. No one should know her name. She kicked him—form 38—and extricated herself. But the man chased her, directly into the beaming headlights of Leader's car. That was the last time Emma copped an attitude with him because that was the first night she witnessed his ferocity and power with her own eyes.

Leader emerged from the car, a silent shadow that flashed a blade in the darkness, eyes wild with determination. Emma, relieved to see him, called out, "Leader!" He shoved her aside, out of the capturing arms of the tattered old man. Looking up from the dirt road where she had fallen, Emma watched as Leader cut the man's throat. She watched as the man died with a curse still coming from his gaping mouth. She watched as Leader stood over the body, breathing down at him in rage. When he spoke then, it was a musical rebuke, "No one has a right to endanger my Guild."

He had looked over his shoulder at her then, a tempestuous passion gleaming out of his eyes in the dark night. "You do not get to endanger yourself! You do not get to wrap yourself up in sarcasm and snark and then run away from me! You are mine."

She had not fought him when he grasped her arm and hauled her back to the car. Back at the House, Monique administered the punishments for her disobedience and insolence, but her true punishment happened out on the road that night when she watched Leader kill a man without a second thought.

She had not dared cop an attitude with him since that day. Yet, looking into the intensity of his eyes and the challenge in his tone as he demanded, "Didn't I?" Emma could not restrain herself. She jerked away from him, only to find his hand clasping tightly around her wrist to keep her from escaping. Breathing too hard, she glared up at him.

"What harm could it do to see the Capitol Building and meet local government officials?"

"That's the whole point, Number Twelve. You don't *know* what harm it can do, which is why you should be Obedient." He cocked his head to the side and sized her up, dark eyes trying to see her more deeply than she wanted.

Emma fought down the terror rising in her chest. She tried to move away from him, but his vice-grip would not give. There would probably be bruises on her wrist that she would have to hide from Brinley tomorrow. This realization made her angrier. "Leader, you never said I could not go. You never *said* it."

He nodded slowly with pursed lips, and for the briefest moment Emma thought she had convinced him. She thought she had won and that he would relent.

"Did you know my intention was for you *not* to go?" he asked, dreadful cold music sang threats to her ears. "When I told you it was pointless, and refused to sign the permission form, did you understand that you would *not* be attending the field trip?"

Emma wished she did not have to answer that, but his grip on her arm tightened around her silence. He jerked her nearer, staring down at her with no intention of yielding. She flinched both from the pain of his grip and from the threat in his eyes.

"Yes, I knew your intention."

His face loomed close as he whispered, "Then you disobeyed me." He released her from his grip while simultaneously propelling her into the entryway. "People in my Guild do not get *off* on a technicality."

She backed away from him quickly. He let the door glide smoothly shut, then he pursued her until she backed into the stone column. She cried out as her bruised back contacted with the rough stone. The shock of it sent her backpack to the floor with a thud. Thoughts of Benjamin, of his phone tucked securely in her pack, made her more nervous than Leader's hand as it closed on her shoulder. He held her against the stone column.

"I said before, we *will* talk about this later." He stood looking at her for too long. She had to look away. "Do you understand?"

Emma swallowed. "Yes, sir."

As if all he had been waiting for was her compliance, he released her and turned away. Without a backward glance, he glided out of the room. "You will learn to Obey me in your heart, Emma," he called nonchalantly over his shoulder. "I will teach you Obedience if it kills me."

Emma watched him go with her breath coming in gasps. The pain and fear were beginning to overwhelm her. She squatted slowly and retrieved her backpack, desperate to have it back in her possession and power. She tugged it to her breast. The phone hidden in that backpack was the major reason she was frightened. And the only reason she was not terrified.

Chapter Twenty-Nine

Emma went to her room. She placed her own phone on its charger on the desk as she walked past it. Her room, like every other room in the House, was probably filled with surveillance cameras, so she was careful to remove Benjamin's phone under a stack of her notebooks. Her fingertips lifted it and when she set her notebooks on her bed, she slipped the phone under her pillow, again with the tips of her fingers so it could not be detected. She doubted even a person watching over her shoulder could have seen the transfer.

Emma had no homework today due to the field trip and her research paper for Mr. Johnson's class, due tomorrow, had been turned in a week ago. She flipped through her notebooks anyway and reviewed some of the concepts. Her history notes were where she finally landed.

History intrigued her. It was filled with romance and vengeance and passion and justice. She loved stories of the Roman Empire, especially its long-expected fall from power. Also fascinating were the tales of European kings and Chinese dynasties. This semester she journeyed into the world of King Henry VIII and his forceful world changes. He was her favorite historical figure. He was more real to her than anyone else in history because his experiences were conceivable. She could never understand why Thomas Jefferson and John Adams and all the others worked so hard to provide freedom from England. She especially did not understand *how* they had managed it. But King Henry's struggles were well understood. When he did not like his circumstances, he did not fight and sneak and jab in the dark—although Emma's teachers might disagree with her assessment of his values—he forced the world to change. *Won't let me divorce a woman I don't want anymore?* he may have thought. *Fine. I'll make my own rules.* He started multiple wars. He created an entire religion simply from stubbornness, although it was clearly derivative. Emma understood him. He was Leader, only hundreds of years prior. He was so much like Leader, in fact, that she wondered if King Henry's name was in that precious Guild Book Leader had on his shelf.

Emma stretched out on her bed with her History textbook in hand, and for several hours got lost in the reign of Bloody Mary, the king's heir. She, too, was an interesting study.

Emma forgot about the phone under her pillow until it rang and made her jump. Quickly, she looked around to be sure she was alone. Then she grasped the phone in her hand and pulled it out enough to see it, but had it still carefully hidden between her body and her textbook. The phone screen said **Jameson**. Emma considered picking it up simply from curiosity, but Benjamin might not approve of her having conversations with his friends. She declined answering with the touch of a button and it sent the call to voicemail. She turned the phone onto silent mode, not even trusting a vibration not to be overheard by some suspicious Guild superior.

She slid the phone back beneath her pillow just in time; Amos opened the door and looked in.

"Honey, are you hungry?" he asked kindly. He was always kind to her. But his eyes did carry a weariness she was not accustomed to seeing in him. He usually seemed tireless to her. "You never came to get a snack and I was told you did not eat your lunch."

Emma reached for her backpack and looked inside for her lunch sack. She choked when she saw it was gone. When had it been taken? She had not let that bag out of her sight since she had entrusted Benjamin's phone to its safekeeping. Puzzled, she looked up at Amos.

"Leader collected it from your locker when he went to pick up Scott from school at noon," Amos explained. "If you haven't eaten since breakfast then you are probably hungry. I want you to come down and get something."

She gave him a fond smile after glancing quickly at the clock. "I can wait until dinner."

Concern etched Amos's face. "I won't have you going hungry simply because you're stubborn." No one in the Family was permitted to go hungry; their health was closely monitored at all times.

"I really can wait, Amos. I promise I am fine. Dinner is an hour away. I can last."

Again, Amos studied her. Then he finally nodded. "What are you doing?"

"Reading. Studying." She shrugged at him.

Amos shook his head slightly, a playful smile tugging at his lips.

"I am sure not. In the Guild, people study at *desks*. They do not compromise their sleep habits by conditioning themselves to do anything but *sleep* in a bed."

That was the rule he so gently quoted at her. She was not permitted to study in bed because beds were for sleeping and that was all. Under his watchful eye, she hurriedly climbed off. Before she had the chance to move toward the desk across the room, Amos grinned.

"Well, as long as you're up, you may as well come and help prepare the meal."

Emma shot him a wry look. "I see your mischievous ploys, Amos. You distracted me from studying because you didn't want to peel potatoes."

Amos laughed. "You know me well, my dear, but not completely. I do hate peeling potatoes, but Leader ordered Spanish Mushrooms. And I like to think of this as my way of doing *you* a favor rather than the other way around. When Leader emerges from the depths of Guild stress for long enough to deal with your little jaunt to Salt Lake, you had probably better be hard at work on some Diligent task. It might take him down from a boil to a simmer."

The point was taken, but she could not help adding, "I think nothing cools Leader's fire once he's heated up."

Amos sized her up. He nodded somewhat grudgingly. "You're probably right."

He lowered himself onto the desk chair and said, "Emma, I should not be up here when I know Leader is about to singe your hide, but sometimes I can't help but intervene."

She startled at his frankness and sat down on the edge of her bed. "What do you mean?"

He removed a handheld electronic from his pocket and tossed it to her. She nabbed it out of the air and looked at it. It was mostly a screen, like a phone, but with only one button. She pressed the button and the screen flashed a series of numbers before turning into a surveillance image. It took her a moment before she recognized herself passing in the distance down a Capitol Building hall on Benjamin's arm. Benjamin was obscured by shadow and her figure, but she recognized him immediately. She slowly put the device on the bed beside her and folded her hands on her lap. She peered up at him.

"How is it you intend to intervene? I can't imagine you have that image without Leader's knowledge, so ... ?"

Amos nodded. "Of course not. That image is only what I was able to poach from Leader's surveillance file. If he doesn't know yet, he will, and I welcome him to find out because I trust him entirely."

"How?" Emma demanded, jerking her head up to challenge him with her eyes.

Amos spread his hands. "I have known Leader all my life and he has never let me down. But other people have. A *lot* of other people, outsiders, have given me every reason to believe them only to disappoint me again and again. I would like to spare you that pain, if I may."

"How?"

"By deterring you," Amos insisted. He pointed at the device beside her. "Who is he, Emma?"

When she looked away and refused to answer, Amos rose to his feet.

"Leader certainly has everything, even if he hasn't reviewed it yet. When he asks you these questions, he will be considerably less understanding of your hesitance." Amos paced across the room and back again. He opened his hands toward the ceiling as if waiting for something to be dropped into them. "I am trying to help you, you know. You can never be stealthy enough that the Guild won't find out who he is."

Emma rose to her feet. "It won't matter if everyone finds out everything," she lied. "He's nobody. If I have to answer to Leader, I'll say the same thing to him: I was goofing around on a field trip I was never supposed to be on in the first place, and when a nobody guy slipped his arm through mine, I let him. I wanted to mess around because I tasted an ounce of freedom and I liked it. For a minute, I wanted to be the kind of girl who lets some handsome boy slip an arm around her. But, if I have to talk to Leader, I don't want to talk to you, too. Once through that conversation is quite enough for me." She stepped toward the door, trying to move past him.

Amos snapped his hands shut and his brows shot up in surprise. He said, "Well, Leader did warn me that my congeniality would get in the way of others' respect for me." He caught her arm in a firm, though not painful grip. With his other hand, he pointed to her bed. Sternly, he ordered her, "Sit down right now, Emma."

Her knees bent, and she sat down almost before she even realized. Amos shook his head at her, his brown eyes clouded with concern for her. She felt a twinge of regret that he was disappointed. Disappointing him was the pain of her life!

"Do you think I don't know how it feels to be Twelve?" Amos asked insistently as he pulled her desk chair around. He straddled the chair, crossing his arms across the ladder-back. "The boy from the capitol building is a welcome diversion from Guild struggles. But your familiarity with him suggests he's not some random guy who slipped an arm through yours to be goofy. Who is he?"

Emma looked at her lap and fiddled with her hands. "He is nobody, Amos. Really."

Amos used one leg to grip the chair. He half stood and used his other leg to move himself and the chair forward until he was only a couple feet from Emma. He settled himself again. "Emma, since when do you have any friends? Much less a boyfriend?"

Emma shook her head hurriedly. "No, Amos, it's not like that. He was just a guy on the capitol building field trip. He offered his arm to a couple of us girls and I was being silly and took it." It was all true, just not *complete* truth.

Amos studied her face. "I don't think that's true. You can always tell me the truth, honey. I understand better than you think I do."

"There's nothing to tell," Emma insisted, forcing her head up to meet his gaze. She picked up the device and held it in her hands. Pressing the button, she looked again at the image, picking out specific details. She wanted to be certain Benjamin could not be positively identified. If this was the only picture they had, he was safe, but she doubted it would be the only one. "I knew Leader had surveillance at my school, but I have to say it comes as a surprise that he had me followed only to capture images of me disobeying him. Especially since my disobedience was a harmless jaunt into the city."

Amos smiled and he shook his head at her. "Don't flatter yourself, Emma. Leader doesn't have you followed. He has the Capitol bugged, of course."

"Of course," Emma whispered in return. Numbly, she reached out to hand him the device. The import of his news was staggering. If Leader had the Capitol bugged, then this would certainly not be the only image of Benjamin. They would figure it out. Even if they did not have sound—which she could not dare to hope—there was sure to be an image that identified Benjamin as the Stillwell boy Monique had warned her of. Worse, if Leader's surveillance spanned to the exteriors of the building, he would find out she had not returned on her school bus. He might discover she had climbed into the truck of that "random nobody guy."

Hoping to change the subject, to back away from Benjamin as much as she could, Emma asked with some coolness to her tone, "What good does it do him to watch local government foul the democratic waters? Monique has made it very clear that the Guild has no interest in politics."

Amos sighed. "The Guild *is* politics. Assume every encounter in your life is political. You will be better prepared for disappointment that way." He slipped the device into his pocket then reached forward and clasped her hands in a fervent grip. "I don't want you to get hurt, Emma." When she tried to speak, he continued, "Just listen! I respect your desire to keep your own counsel on these matters, but I can assure you that every interaction in your life is political. In the Guild, you always know the angle of attack, so you can always be prepared. Outside the Guild, you should always be expecting anonymous attacks, but you never know how they come. For that reason, you must be on your guard all the time. You *cannot afford* to *trust anyone.* No one. When you are weakest, they will hit you with everything they've got. And soon, you will learn you're just an assignment on someone else's mission."

Emma shook her head, knowing he was right, but in denial. "It was nothing."

Amos' grip on her hands tightened and his eyes gained a fervor she had never seen before. There was pain hidden there. "Will you just do me one favor while you are protecting your secrets, honey? If he says he loves you, run away. Don't let him use your heart to manipulate you; it only brings suffering." He spoke from experience and, despite her intention to pretend she was not interested, her curiosity got the better of her.

"What do you mean?"

Amos eyes darkened as he delved deeper into his memories. "Just trust me. People don't *really* fall in love. They lust or they trust, but love is just the combination of emotions with an added level of hormones for extra kick. It's like Santa Claus: a nice idea but entirely unlikely and a colossal waste of time." His eyes returned to the present, and he gave her a sad smile. "Love is a weakness that clouds judgment. If they say they love you, they are trying to manipulate your sensibilities."

He paused a long time, waiting for her answer. She rolled her eyes but said, "Okay."

He squeezed her hands again, insisting, "Promise me?"

Emma sighed and nodded. "I'll be careful not to let my heart get tangled."

Chapter Thirty

Amos dropped Emma's hands and shot to his feet. He spun around as the door opened to reveal Leader. Leader shot one glance around the room, then fixed Amos with a stern glare. "Have you decided to start rallying for my position, Amos? You'll have to beat out Monique, and you know she'll have her viper fangs in your back long before you usurp her authority."

Amos laughed, a move that Emma thought was dangerous considering the look in Leader's eyes and his current mood. Amos did not seem intimidated by him.

"I am content to let the Guild stand as is, Leader." He used one hand to move Emma's desk chair back into its place under her desk. "I did not realize that talking with a member of the Junior Guild was grounds for suspicion of treason."

"Talking with Emma is not the treason I was referring to," Leader answered blackly. "I don't care who you talk to in the Guild." He narrowed his gaze on the books and backpack scattered across Emma's bed as he stepped into the room fully. Emma hurriedly moved to organize the clutter and shove it out of sight into her backpack.

"What I want to know, Amos, is why you took my car out today. No one but me drives my car. Do you see why I thought you were confused about your relative position?"

An amused surprise washed over Emma. She never would have thought Amos had the guts to steal the BMW for the day. Where was Leader that he hadn't noticed? Why hadn't Amos taken one of the other vehicles?

Her amusement died when Amos removed the device from his pocket and passed it to Leader's outstretched hand. She sank back onto her bed and watched as Leader pulled up the image and studied it. He continued the conversation as though his eyes were not transfixed by the image. "I don't know what this has to do with stealing my car."

"I did not *steal* your car, Leader," Amos answered skeptically. Forcefully. "When everything went to hell today and you got trapped in a meeting, I went for a drive to clear my head. I knew you would come out ranting, and I wanted to be prepared to answer your ungenerous accusations. Your car was parked in the first garage and I took it out for an hour. It's not a big deal."

Leader finally looked up from his intense study of the image and said crossly, "It is a very big deal to me. You accessed Stone Satellite from my car's mainframe and adjusted its target. That sounds like more than a head-clearing drive, Amos; it sounds like treason."

Amos blinked at him. "Are you kidding me?" His sarcastic tone overwhelmed any remorse. "I did not betray you. The car is the only place I knew I would not have to hack your system too extensively to get what I needed. A sharp image. A *real* image. I did that, Leader. Did you not study the images I sent to your email? I expected you to be pleased."

Leader's fingers tightened on the device in his hand. He said, "You were following a kitten when you should have been catching a tiger. Do you think it is an accident that we were hit during the hour you had rerouted my satellite? They knew, and they exploited our moment of weakness. You have manipulated us into a defending position when we had been solidly standing on the offense for months. Your incompetence is going to destroy us."

"Better their car in our garage than our property in theirs," Amos replied, not the least bit concerned at Leader's blame. "I was acting in the best interest of the Guild, Leader. I can admit when my actions are a blunder."

"But not today?" Leader asked in the dangerous tone Emma trained herself to avoid.

"Not today," Amos Confidently replied.

Leader looked down at the device in his hand again for a moment before he said, "Very well. I will give you an hour to come up with a convincing argument to put you back into my good graces. If you did this, and it was not treason, you'll have a good explanation in an hour and I can move onto more important matters." He tossed the device up and caught it again. "If not, you have a one-hour head-start on outrunning my wrath."

Amos laughed, but Emma did not think Leader was joking. "I can be ready in twenty minutes or less." He gave Emma a nod and then left the room.

Emma hated the choking feeling that automatically came with being alone with Leader, but she couldn't control it. Her body went into hyper-fear at the thought of his anger. As it had for over a year, his anger caused her to see a glinting blade in the darkness, passion in his eyes.

Leader did not look at her. Instead, he stood silently, staring into the middle distance for a long time. His fingers caressed the device in his hand, but his mind was clearly far away. Emma sat perfectly still, afraid to break the spell and unleash a monster. Yet, if she could have run out without attracting his eye, she would have.

Finally, his head turned, and his dark eyes found hers. He held up the spy toy in his hand. "I am certain when you give me a full account of today's proceedings, you won't forget to mention the names of any new friends you have made." He said it like it was a simple suggestion, but it was an order as clear as if he had been wearing a drill sergeant uniform.

He glanced at her backpack, still open after her hurried attempt to clean up her mess. "And if I want you to disrupt your sleeping habits, I will have you sleep on the floor."

"It won't happen again," she assured him, picking up her backpack and tossing it toward the desk. A couple books dislodged, scattering papers across the floor, and the backpack itself landed short by several feet. Emma did not care that it was out of her control any longer. The phone was safe under her pillow, so Leader's eyes roving over the mess did not cause her concern.

"I want a written account of your day," he announced, raising a dangerous brow at her. "That way I can read it in depth to see if you're leaving out any details. I have a fact checker, of course, so I will know if there's anything awry. Be sure there isn't. After disobeying my intentions, you are already skating thin today."

"Yes, Leader," she promised. She was relieved because in an interview with him, she would have a much harder time thinking up lies he might accept. This way, she would have time to figure out what she could say about her day. While lying was coming a little more easily every time, she was still no professional.

"We won't hold dinner for you," he added as he moved toward the door. After that threat, he walked out, pushing the door open all the way as he went. Emma sighed in relief once she was sure he was gone, even though she knew she was not out of trouble yet. She was not permitted to miss dinner, because Monique would kill her for not taking care of her body. Like Amos, Emma had one hour to come up with her defense and write it out for Leader's casual perusal. Unlike Amos, she had a lot to hide. She sat at her desk and set to work.

Emma sank down into her bed as the clocks in the house all rang 10 p.m. She was exhausted from her day of gallivanting, and her dishonest accounting of it all. She rolled onto her stomach and stretched her arms under the pillow as she always did when preparing for sleep. Her hand knocked Benjamin's phone toward the edge of the bed and she barely caught it before it could fall. She gave a pained sigh of relief.

Benjamin was supposed to call her in a couple of hours. She could not go to sleep or she would miss it. She did not dare alter the silent setting on the phone, so her only option was to stay awake. Emma slipped her head under the pillow and pulled the phone near her face, so she would see it when it lit up. She waited.

She dozed off a couple of times over the next two hours, but she came awake fully when the phone lit up and a number flashed on the screen. **Incoming Call**, the screen told her. She listened carefully for any signs of Leader or Monique walking through the House, then clicked answer.

"Hi," Benjamin said from the other side. "You don't have to talk. Okay? That way no one can hear you. Just listen. I am coming up to Utah County tomorrow during school hours. If you can meet me in your school's track field, I should be able to be there about noon. Press any button for yes. Press twice for no."

Emma hesitated, but finally pressed once. Then she whispered, "See you at noon." She hung up the phone.

She had no idea how she would escape Leader's surveillance long enough to meet Benjamin on the track field. She didn't care. She wanted to see Benjamin and she fully intended to do so, even if it risked Leader's wrath, which it most certainly did.

She sat caressing his phone for a long time, thinking about the day she had had with him. There was not another day in her history that compared to it. And she wanted more. Like a drug, a good time seemed to summon her back for more.

Chapter Thirty-One

"Happy Birthday, Miss Harris," Mr. Johnson said the next morning after rollcall. It startled her. She forgot today was her birthday. Maybe because no one at home had mentioned it. Not that she ever would have expected them to. Birthdays were of no consequence in the Harris home. She could not even be certain it was the real day of her birth. At the House, her birthday was merely the day she went from being one age to being the next, with little to no fanfare.

"Thank you," Emma replied politely, quietly. He nodded then turned to gather some papers from his desk. When he started his lesson, Brinley leaned over and hissed, "Were you going to tell any of us it's your birthday?" She sounded accusatory.

"I forgot," Emma whispered back, shrugging at the girl.

Brinley rolled her eyes. "You're such a colossal annoyance." Under her desk she began texting, all the while watching the teacher to keep from being caught. "How can you forget your own birthday?"

Emma was intrigued Brinley could text without looking, talk to a friend, and watch the teacher all at the same time. It was more than Emma was able to do. Just watching the teacher and listening to Brinley was taking every bit of her concentration. And she was Guild-Trained.

"I don't know why I forgot it," she replied in as hushed a tone as she could manage. "No one at home mentioned it, and I suppose it slipped my mind."

"Miss Harris?" Mr. Johnson asked, turning from the board at the front of the room to pin her with a stern look. "If you have something to share with the class that is of more importance to our educational wellbeing than my lesson, by all means raise your voice so you can be heard by everyone." He waited while Emma withered in her chair. "No? Then I trust you and Miss Taylor will allow me to do my job now?"

It was not really a question, but Emma murmured, "Sorry."

Brinley did not bat an eye, and she was still texting.

Emma had trouble concentrating on the lesson. Her mind was caught up in Brinley's question. *How can you forget your own birthday?* Emma knew why. Birthdays meant nothing in the Guild. They were a meaningless passing of time with no significant accomplishments attached. Today, Emma was finally 14 years old. Next year she would be 15. And then, after an interminably long time, she would at last be 16 and eligible for a driving license.

Most girls in this school could not wait for their sweet 16, because it meant they were of dating age. Emma did not think turning 16 would be any more eventful than turning 15, 14, or any other age. She would only be allowed to date if it served the Guild or kept up significant cover.

Yet Emma was surprised no one had mentioned it. Usually Leader said something. On her 13th birthday, he captured her face in his hand at breakfast and stared deeply into her eyes.

"A teenager," he had said, musically surprised. "My little Em is growing up."

On her 10th birthday, he found out about some mischief she had caused and used her age as a weapon: "You're in the double-digits now, Emmalyn. Ten-year-olds have enough experience to know that I will not tolerate disobedience." But even if Leader missed the day, Amos always remembered.

However, Emma recalled with a sudden curious realization, no one in the Senior Guild had been around this morning. Only yesterday Monique claimed she would drive them to school until the end of time, then today Waylon had taken them in the family Escalade. Both Leader's and Monique's cars were missing, as was the red Porsche and the Jeep Amos and Thomas usually drove. Piper had made breakfast. Emma could not remember the last time someone other than Amos ran the kitchen.

It had not occurred to her to question it in her hurry to escape the House before Leader found her and asked questions about the holes in her written account. But Emma now wondered where everyone in the Senior Guild had gone to so early in the morning. Did it have something to do with the arrival of the red Porsche? Or maybe it had to do with Leader's abrupt departure from Monique's business dinner last week? Was is all connected?

A wonderful idea came to her amid her curious concern. It was her birthday! And the Senior Guild—the ones responsible for surveillance and discipline—were all absent. Maybe sneaking away to the track field to meet Benjamin would not be altogether impossible. With Leader distracted, and Amos caught up in yesterday's drama, and Monique gone, maybe Emma could get the best birthday present she could imagine: a few more minutes alone with Benjamin Stillwell.

Shortly before the first dismissal bell, a student stepped into the room with a note in his hand. Mr. Johnson said, "Contemplate the meaning of the word *magnanimous* as it is presented in the context of the previous sentence whilst I deal with the minor interruption at the door." Emma did not follow his instructions. No one did. They watched him.

A note in the middle of class usually meant a student was being summoned to the office. That meant either the student was in trouble or a parent was picking them up early. Emma watched as Mr. Johnson scanned the page, then looked up directly into her eyes. Somehow, she was not surprised. She had felt the note was about her.

"Miss Harris, take your things and go to the office please," Mr. Johnson instructed. "Did you copy the homework from the board?"

She hadn't. Usually it was what she did very first when she sat down, but today she had forgotten. Hurriedly, she copied the reading assignment and made note of the draft that was due tomorrow. Mr. Johnson waited impatiently for her to retrieve the note from his outstretched hands and head toward the door.

"Have a good day, Miss Harris," he said once she stepped upon the threshold of his classroom door. Avanair Preparatory School was insistent that its students be respectful and polite. Emma paused and turned back long enough to acknowledge the teacher's kind greeting.

"Good day, Mr. Johnson." Then, as she and her peers had said every day on their way out his door, she added, "Thank you for enlightening my mind."

That was clearly all he had been waiting for. He said, "You are most welcome," and then he returned to teaching as if there had been no interruption at all.

Emma hurried into the deserted hall. She shoved her planner and her textbook into her backpack before she read the note. It was to Mr. Johnson, asking him to excuse Miss Emmalyn Harris for the remainder of class, and requesting he send her directly to the Counselor's office in the Dean's Suite. Emma stared hard at the paper.

Only a moment ago she's been thanking the lucky stars that had taken the Senior Guild away from the surveillance cameras, and already she was wishing they were back. Hopefully, she reached for her phone, but found only a text from Brinley to practically everyone in the school announcing **Emma's Birthday Today!** Emma rolled her eyes. Who could possibly care about that?

She put her phone away, and resisted the urge to check Benjamin's phone, which was hidden safely away in her bra. She slipped her backpack onto her shoulders, ignoring the slight pain of pressure on the healing welts on her back. Emma trudged toward the Dean's Suite.

She tried to imagine what her conference with Ms. James could be, but she had no frame of reference. She had never been called to see a counselor before and she had no idea what Ms. James might want to talk about. The counselor had good timing, though, because with the Senior Guild preoccupied with Guild business, Ms. James was free to interrogate her as she pleased. It would not be the only interrogation she had ever suffered; her every conversation was an interrogation at home. In fact, even Brinley and Cara spoke like interrogators. The only person who spoke to her any differently was Benjamin. He spoke as if he cared about her.

The Dean's suite was directly off of the commons. It housed the main office, the Dean's office, and the Vice Dean, as well as the board room for the Board of Directors, Ms. James' office, and several other rooms Emma could not identify. She walked into it with as much pleasure as she would being called into Leader's office. She approached the reception desk.

"Good morning, Miss Harris," the receptionist greeted after glancing first at a list in front of her. The woman spoke like they were old friends when in fact Emma would not have been able to pick her out of a line up. She doubted the woman had ever even seen her before. "How can I help you this morning?"

Emma was almost positive that the clipboard also provided the reason for her visit. Annoyed, but unwilling to admit it, Emma softly said, "The Counselor sent for me."

"Of course," the receptionist answered, and there was no surprise in her eyes at Emma's announcement; she had already known why she was there. "I will let her know you're here. You can sit and wait, if you'd like."

Emma did not care to sit or to wait, but the waiting did not seem like much of an option. She chose to stand. She was annoyed when it took Ms. James nearly five minutes to come out. By then, the bell had rung. Emma could have stayed in her first class the whole time rather than missing the end of Mr. Johnson's lesson only to stand alone waiting in the office.

"Good morning, Emma," Ms. James greeted as she crossed the room. "How are you?"

"I am well," Emma lied, not bothering to keep the annoyance from her tone. "Am I in trouble or something? Why was I pulled out of class?"

Ms. James gave her famous hiding-something smile. "Of course, you are not in any trouble. I just wanted a chance to talk to you for a few minutes. Why don't you come back to my office and we'll get started?"

"My second period is starting," Emma argued, gesturing with her head toward the office door and the educational experiences beyond.

Ms. James' smile did not slip in the slightest. She placed a hand on Emma's shoulder and gently directed her toward the hall to her office. "I'll write you an excuse," she promised cheerfully. If it was meant to reassure her, it failed. But Emma said nothing more as they walked through the Dean's Suite to the Counseling office.

CHAPTER THIRTY-TWO

Ms. James' office reeked of her. It was pristine and fake like she was. Every surface looked recently cleaned and dusted. A bookshelf on one wall held hard leather-cover copies of classics like Jane Eyre and Moby Dick. They did not look as if they had ever been opened. One of the lower shelves, which was mostly hidden by her desk, held a collection of counseling and self-help books. These probably had been read. Funny she chose to keep them more or less out of sight. There were a few picture frames on her desk, and some trinkets and decorative items on the shelves. A clock on one wall showed precise atomic time. A couch and some chairs took up one part of the room that was lit by a standing lamp.

"Have a seat," the counselor said. Emma ignored the cozy corner with the lamp and the side table holding tissues. She went straight to the seat across the desk from the counselor's chair. She and Ms. James weren't close friends who could snuggle up in the corner and talk about all Emma's woes. This was a business meeting, as far as Emma was concerned. She would keep it professional.

Emma was certain the counselor analyzed her seat choice. She slowly took the chair behind the desk and crossed her arms on top of the pristine oak surface.

"How are you doing, Emma?" she asked politely.

Emma stared back at the woman before carefully answering. "I am quite well, thank you. How are you?" Emma had thought they already established they were well back out in the reception area.

Ms. James smiled. "I am well, thank you." If she had paused, Emma would have gotten up, thanked her, and left. She didn't give Emma a window, though. "I thought it was time you and I had a chat and got to know one another a little better."

Emma removed her backpack from her shoulder and slid it onto the floor at her feet. With a resigned sigh, she settled herself carefully against the back of the chair and placed her arms on the arm rests. It was all to buy her time, and both she and the counselor knew it.

"Why?" she finally asked and looked directly into the woman's eyes.

Ms. James smiled like the direct stare did not intimidate her. "I just thought it was time," she answered in a benign tone of voice. "You have been at this school several weeks now and I wanted to know how you are adjusting."

Emma blinked. "I'm fine. I'm a good student. I'm not a troublemaker. I work hard, and I mind my own business. Why do you want to talk to me?"

Ms. James' plastered-on smile was beginning to grate on Emma's nerves.

She tapped a folder on her desk. "I have read your transcripts and I can see you are a very driven student indeed. You have maintained a perfect grade point average and you test off the charts. Do you get much help from your parents?"

Emma glanced at the clock, but it had been less than two minutes since she walked into the room. "Not really," she answered truthfully. Her tone slipped into contemptuous boredom. "I don't need help. At an early age, I developed good study habits. I know my learning style, and I am driven, so I am pretty self-sufficient as a student. Is that all?" She made as if to rise, but she knew the meeting wasn't over. Ms. James shook her head.

"Sit down, Emma," she prompted gently. "Have you managed to make any friends at Avanair?"

Emma resettled in the chair, giving up on the idea of a quick escape. "Yes, ma'am," she answered, clipping her words short. When the counselor only continued to stare at her, Emma expounded, "I have recently made the acquaintance of Cara Winters and we have become fast friends." It wasn't completely true, but it was a claim she could back up if need be. Cara was sort of her friend now, and Brinley certainly was. Emma had no idea what it meant to be friends, except they didn't tell on her when she skipped out on the field trip, and they walked with her in the halls.

"Cara Winters is a nice girl," the counselor said with a smile. Emma wondered if she knew how much what she said was not true. There was nothing nice or kind-spirited about Cara. She was mean, cliquey, and self-centered. So was everyone in her group of friends. Emma did not even know how to *act* like them.

"Yes," she agreed with the counselor. But in her head, she said, *You're an idiot*.

"What kind of goals do you have for your future?" Ms. James suddenly diverted to something Emma was completely unprepared for. When she did not answer, Ms. James specified, "You said you're driven. Have you thought about universities?"

Emma nodded, but she did not know what to say. Should she tell the truth? Should she give the same story Leader had told Henshaw last week?

"Do you know where you will apply?"

Emma nodded again. "Yes. I will apply to Harvard, Princeton, and Yale. I suppose I should also apply to Stanford, Columbia, and Brown, although those are not my father's first choice."

"Where would *you* like to go?" Ms. James asked, settling sideways in her chair to cross her legs at the knee.

Emma thought about the question, really thought about it. Instead of giving the answer she thought Leader expected her to give, she said, "Notre Dame." It didn't really matter to her. Notre Dame appealed to her only because it was so far away from the Guild. Leader's threats and Monique's punishments would be a lot easier to avoid at Notre Dame.

"That's a very good school," Ms. James complimented with a nod.

"Yes," Emma replied. Of course, it was. It was an Ivy League school, and Avanair disputed no students' ambition toward the Ivy League.

"Schools like that are looking for more than just a good GPA, Emma," the counselor went on, and her tone took on a more interested note. "What kind of extracurricular activities have engaged your interest?"

Emma wished she had an answer to this, but she didn't. "I have studied martial arts for years," she answered truthfully. Nothing else she did in her real life was something she could mention at school.

Ms. James gave her painted smile. "Good to hear. Is there anything we offer here at the school that seems to appeal to you?"

No, Emma wanted to say. But that would alarm the counselor. Would these counseling sessions become a permanent thing if Emma's answers did not satisfy the woman?

"I considered the basketball team, but my father would like me to do something more ..." she clenched her teeth on the memory of Leader's flat denial of all her extracurricular choices. "... *academic*. I haven't settled on anything yet."

"The paper is always looking for talented writers," Ms. James suggested. "Your English teacher insists you write excellent papers."

Emma could not help but give the woman a condescending smile. "I am a 4.2 student, Ms. James. Of course, I turn in good papers."

Ms. James chose to laugh and be amused rather than offended, although Emma had meant to be offensive. "If you have no interest in writing, you might consider debate or even student government."

Emma wanted to laugh at those options. Leader would never in a million years let her enter student government, and debate seemed like a clever way to create an argumentative monster. Monique would never allow that. She shook her head. "I think it will be in my best interest if, for now, I simply focus on my studies. I'm still very young." She was advanced in school a full year; the deflection of her youth was not a lie. "Maybe next year I can consider the newspaper."

"I think you would be very good at it," Ms. James complimented with a determined nod. She meant it as a compliment, surely, but Emma did not take it as one.

"I'm good at everything I do," she replied, at once losing her patience with the counselor. "You said it yourself, I test off the charts. I could probably *take over* the paper and do it all myself with better success than the entire current newspaper staff." As soon as the words were out of her mouth, she regretted them; it made her sound like a pretentious snob without any idea of her own weaknesses. With those words loosed on the world, Emma sounded like a perfect addition to Cara's group of snotty friends. This did not set well in Emma's stomach.

Surprisingly, Ms. James did not seem alarmed or taken aback.

"Maybe you could apply to be the editor and make some changes." She suggested with the lift of one beautifully manicured finger. "The paper does seem to be struggling this year."

Emma stared at the woman in disgust, wanting to rail at her about the ridiculousness of a newspaper in a generation that received all its news from social media and messaging. But she nodded and lied, "I'll consider it." She did not want to be the editor of the Avanair Review. Besides the fact that no one ever read the school paper and it was therefore a waste of her time, she had no interest in running a paper or writing for one, for that matter. She wanted to go to school, play her part, and go home. Period.

"So, you have considered universities," Ms. James segued. "Have you selected an area of study?"

"No," Emma answered shortly. It was true. She would not be the one selecting it, anyway. Leader would tell her which program she would enter, and she would study it diligently. It was who she was: Obedient and subservient.

"Is there anything of particular interest to you?"

"No," Emma replied. She slipped into simple rudeness now. She was tired of this conversation and ready to be finished.

"I see," Ms. James said, settling back in her chair. And for a wonder, Emma thought she did see. Emma did not want to talk and now Ms. James only looked at her, like a specimen in a Petri dish.

"Are you uncomfortable talking with me, Emma?" she asked in a tone of gentle coaxing.

"Why would you think that?"

"Because you seem reticent to share your thoughts."

"So?" Emma replied, blinking at the woman in challenge. That was all. It wasn't her most intelligent reply, but it served her purposes. So what if she was reticent? Reticence was not a crime. Being uncommunicative was not a punishable offense at school.

"You're safe here with me," Ms. James said gently with a tap of one finger onto her desktop. "The things you say to me here are only for the two of us to hear and discuss. You are free to share whatever you like."

Emma scoffed. She was so innocent, this counselor. She did not live in Emma's world, where nothing was private. No conversation went unmonitored, and no place was safe. Emma was envious of the counselor's world. It must have been a lovely experience growing up with parents who care about you—*for* you—and not for your mission. It must have been lovely to choose a career based on interest and not just aptitude and necessity. Ms. James' world seemed like a fairy tale where evil witches are defeated and knights on horseback slay dragons to rescue princesses from tall towers. People in Ms. James' world had the possibility for happily ever after. Emma hated her. Emma hated all of them; all the people in Ms. James' world of possibilities.

"No place is safe," Emma snapped at the woman's benign words. Snatching her bag from her feet, Emma shoved out of the chair. When she got to the door, she heard Ms. James call, but she did not look back.

"I hate you," Emma said, quietly enough that Ms. James could not hear. It was not meant for her, though. It was meant for the surveillance cameras. It was meant for Leader.

Chapter Thirty-Three

Emma hid in the bathroom for the rest of the period. She sat on the floor in the corner of the room with her backpack between her knees. At first, she felt the anger trying to make tears form, but she resisted the urge to cry. After that, she only felt numbness. She thought that if Leader had really been watching the cameras this morning, he might have called her by now, but her phone lay still and silent on the floor beside her.

Now Emma assumed that if he was unhappy with her, she would hear about it later at the Guild House where she would suffer for her disrespect to the counselor. And for ditching class. But she didn't care. She could not bring herself to care.

Between classes, the bathroom became a busy place, and Emma escaped. She snatched her phone from the black and white tiles, pulled on her backpack, and walked into the crowded halls. She went straight to the exit, dropping her Guild phone in the trash can on the way out.

There was nowhere to go from Avanair. It was in the canyon, a couple miles from a gas station even, but Emma didn't care. She had to get away from the cameras, and the prying eyes of the school faculty. She had to get away from the students shouting, "Happy Birthday!" at her back. Not because they knew her or cared about her, but because she was one of Cara's people now and they were terrified of Cara.

Emma slipped past the gate monitor, ignoring his shouts at her back, and walked out onto the canyon road. Once she was certain she could no longer be seen by Leader's cameras, she fished Benjamin's phone from her bra and turned it up from silent. She held it in her hand like it was the object of her salvation. And she marched down the side of the road.

Happy Birthday, she told herself. It was silly. She had never cared about her birthday before. It was an insignificant passing of time that aged her. That was all. But this year it was personal. This year she had seen how Cara, who was in general a horrible person, had been treated by her friends and family on her birthday. This year she had heard "Happy Birthday!" first from a *teacher*. This year she wanted to have more. She felt she *deserved* more.

A driver in a car on the canyon slowed as if to stop, but she flipped him off and he drove on. He was probably just a nice guy concerned for the wellbeing of a young woman, clearly in a high school uniform, walking alone on the side of a canyon road. But any driver with bad intentions would get a surprise if they tried to jump her. What she did to the perv the night of the party was nothing like what she could do if she thought she was in actual danger.

Where am I going? she asked herself. She did not know. There was nowhere to go. The canyon fed out into a valley of religious lunatics. If she called home, she would get picked up and taken to a houseful of dangerous lunatics.

She could keep walking, but how long would it be before Leader decided to have her tracked by the sinister microchip in her spine? How long would it be before she was returned to him for safe keeping? Even if she had told the counselor the truth about her life, who was to say she wasn't just another creepy drone under Leader's thumb? What if all of this was part of the test he promised he would give her to see if she had learned the value of Obedience? Ignore her on her birthday, set her up to be interrogated by a woman who knows nothing, and see how she reacts? It sounded like a plot Leader would create.

She kicked a stone out into traffic. It smacked against a car and ricocheted back into the canyon. The driver swore at her but did not slow the car.

The phone rang. Emma startled. She stopped walking and turned it over in her hand. Even though she had discarded her Guild-issued phone, she still half expected the call to be from Leader. She was relieved to see it was the same number that had called in the middle of the night last night. It was Benjamin.

She picked up.

"Hi," she said quietly.

"What are you doing?" he asked, but not in a way that meant he was interested. He was amused and perhaps a little chiding. He could see her. She looked around frantically, spun in a circle, and spotted his truck. He made an illegal U-turn through a police turnaround and headed her direction.

"Walking," she answered his question. But she felt sheepish now.

He pulled up next to her. "Climb in," he ordered. He hung up the phone at the same time. She ran to the truck, which was blinking its hazards. As she reached the door, Benjamin leaned across to open it for her. She slid into the seat and jerked the door closed. She sat there against the seat, not looking at him even though she felt his unwavering gaze.

"What are you doing?" he asked again, not as amused this time. "I have no doubt you can take care of yourself, but this is not exactly safe hiking, Quicksilver."

Emma turned and finally looked at him. He smiled.

She crumpled into tears.

He calmed her down. It took a couple minutes on the side of the road, with him apologizing for teasing her, before she could pull herself together enough to laugh.

"It's not you, I swear," she exclaimed, laughing and trying to wipe her tears away. "I'm just having a bad day."

"So, you cried from relief?" he asked, still in a teasing voice.

"Yes," she answered with a mock glare. "Will you please drive? I can't just sit here. For all I know, my father could be on his way to get me right now." She looked over her shoulder toward the school, but it was not visible beyond the trees and the stone walls surrounding it. "Let's get out of here before they call my family. If she hasn't already." Visions of demerits and Leader's fury danced through her mind, but she smashed the fear. She crumpled it and hid it away in the place in her mind that held her other unused emotions.

She pulled the seatbelt around herself and as she clicked it stifled all regrets. She was not going to care what Monique thought or what Leader would do. Today she was going to be free.

Benjamin returned to canyon traffic with a quick jerk of his wheel and a couple of other drivers' horns. He watched the road, but he also watched Emma.

"So, we're not just talking on the track field today," he finally said. "We're ditching school."

Emma kicked at her backpack under her feet. She shot him another teasing glare. "Weren't you already ditching school to come talk to me? It's not like I'm a bad influence on you."

He laughed out loud. "I never thought that! We both know the truth: *I'm* the bad influence. I'll never argue with my parents again when they say it. Because look what I did, I took a nice, bright, well-behaved young woman and turned her into a school-ditching, rule-breaking, badass ..." He shook his head in mock shame. Then he smiled darkly and winked at her. "I kind of like it."

She smiled in return. "You can't take all the credit. Part of it goes to the family that doesn't care it's my birthday, and the counselor at school who decided it's her life mission to solve all my problems. And the fact that everywhere I go I feel like I'm being watched and manipulated."

Benjamin reached across the cab and placed a hand on her knee, just above her stocking. "Happy birthday," he said, latching onto the one part of the rant that he could do something about.

"I turned 14 today," she told him. "Way too young to be hanging out with a senior in his truck."

He squeezed her leg gently, but he teasingly replied, "*Way* too young."

They sat in silence a few minutes, his hand never leaving her leg. Emma relaxed. She shrugged off her anger at the counselor for being completely useless and the pain of being ignored on her birthday, Guild business or no. She drew steady breaths and watched the road. The further she got from Leader's surveillance, the better she felt.

"Where are we going?" she finally asked when they reached the freeway.

Benjamin chuckled. "I have some places in mind, but you did not like my choices yesterday, so perhaps you had better choose today."

She shook her head and answered on a sigh, "No, I will accept your choices another day. But this is your last chance to impress me." She waggled her brows at him.

His mouth dropped open. "Go-karts and hotdogs aren't impressive?" he asked like it was brand-new information. "Well, I guess today I had better knock your socks off." He glanced down at her uniform. "Maybe literally. We have to get you something serious to wear. This screams, 'I'm ditching school, truancy officer! Come pick me up!'"

She rolled her eyes at him. "I have never even seen a truancy officer."

Benjamin tapped her on the nose. "You have never ditched school before." He returned to watching the road, cruising through traffic at ungodly speeds, completely ignoring the speed limit signs, even as he reached road construction and the giant blinking signs that said **Your speed: 83! Speed Limit: 55**.

"I don't think it matters what clothes I'm wearing," Emma told him suddenly. "If any truancy officer in the state sees me with you, they will know I am ditching school."

"That's true," he answered with a little laugh. "They stop by my house every day just to check. My truancy officer is on a first-name basis with my parents." He looked her up and down again. "I still say we need to pick you up some real clothes. You can't really skip school if you carry it around with you all day."

"Well, I can't exactly go home," she challenged.

"Of course not." He opened his hand as if presenting her with a new idea. "I was thinking more along the lines of the mall."

She opened her hands to show him her empty palms. "I don't have any money, Benjamin. Unless you're taking me horseback riding, I can do anything in a skirt."

Benjamin cut through three lanes of traffic to the exit, leaving swerving, honking cars behind. It was as if he didn't even notice.

"Do you remember how I'm rich and privileged," he teased, reaching into his back pocket. He slammed his wallet down on the storage column between them. "Daddy's credit card! And while my dad may say 'No, No, No!' his credit card is a world of 'Yes!'"

She glowered at him again and said only "Hm!"

He glared right back. "Besides, what if I decide I do want to take you horseback riding?"

She ignored all of her feelings of doubt and laughed. "Fine! The mall it is."

He bought her an entire outfit to wear out of the store, which included tight-cut jeans, tall brown boots, a baby tee and a slim sweater, a collared brown jacket, a lace scarf, fitted gloves, and a brown loose-knit hat. The hat was simply for fashion, because it would never have succeeded in keeping her warm. The ladies in the store cut off all the tags, folded her uniform and put it in a shopping bag, and gushed about her beauty the entire time she was in the store. Any time the gushing stopped, all Benjamin had to do was point out another item for her to try on. He had the money, they knew, and he wanted to see Emma smile.

And Emma did smile. She smiled at herself in the mirror. She smiled at Benjamin across the changing room. She smiled at the ladies, enslaved by Benjamin's credit card.

"Thank you," Emma told Benjamin as they walked out of the store. He held her shopping bag with her school uniform, and with his free hand reached out and clasped her hand, entwining his fingers in hers.

"Happy birthday," he told her gently. "You look beautiful."

And she felt beautiful. She had lovely clothes at home; so many, in fact, that she wouldn't be surprised if what she wore today were duplicates of something already in her closet. But everything at home was to help her play a part, not to make her feel beautiful and well cared for. Benjamin made her feel that way and more.

He opened the passenger door and helped her up. He crammed her bag of school clothes and her backpack behind the seats. When he climbed in, he rested his hand on the storage column between the seats, opening his palm for her hand again. She felt her pulse rush a little then placed her hand into his.

Chapter Thirty-Four

Benjamin drove through the Kneaders drive-thru to pick up a couple of lunches to go, then he stopped at a cupcake store to get a couple of those. His last stop was at a refueling station, where he sent her in with some cash to get a couple of hot chocolates.

"It's not all that cold, Benjamin," she scolded him. She gestured to her boots and her hat. "Are you trying to roast me?"

"Yes," he said, giving a playful maniacal laugh and dry-washing his hands together. "You have figured out my evil plan. I am going to dress you in warm clothes and feed you hot chocolate until you roast to death." He grabbed her hand and pulled her close to him with a smile. "Just go get the hot chocolate, and trust me, will you?"

She did not want him to let go of her. But as soon as she said, "Okay," about trusting him, he relinquished her. He selected premium fuel and began pumping.

Emma used the machine inside the station to fill two cups with hot chocolate. In hers, she added every kind of unhealthy creamer. Into his, she only added the French vanilla, doubting he was feeling the need to rebel today like she was. She placed a lid on each of them, dropped in a stirrer as a straw, and paid for the drinks at the counter. When she got back outside, she saw that Benjamin was on the phone. It was his new cell, black but with a bright orange protective cover. He finished pumping gas, but had not yet replaced the nozzle. His phone conversation seemed heated.

She approached slowly, wanting to give him plenty of opportunity to see her so he wouldn't think she was trying to eavesdrop. He saw her and smiled, beckoning her with a nod of his head.

"Everything okay?" she mouthed at him as she climbed up to get into the truck.

He rolled his eyes and pointed at the phone, mouthing back, "My father."

He finished putting the nozzle away, printed a receipt that he tucked into his wallet, but he did not climb into the cab with her. She barely heard him say in exasperation, "I will be home when I get home!"

She tasted her hot chocolate, nearly gagging on the sweetness, then placed it beside his in the drink holders of the storage column.

"Dad, I don't want to talk about this now!" he snapped. That she could hear clearly. "I'm with Emma. It's her birthday, and I am taking her to have a good day. Please don't bother us again." He snapped the phone shut.

Emma stared at him in surprise as he climbed in. He buckled, turned on the engine, and swerved out onto the road before he acknowledged her.

"Sorry," he said with a shake of his head. "He just came home from Vienna and wanted to know where I was."

"And you told him," Emma said in surprise.

"Of course, I did," he answered simply, matter-of-fact. "I mean, I am sure the school already told him I never showed up today, and what good would it do to lie to him when he can just have me tracked and followed? Remember the Porsche stories? I can never run fast enough he can't find me."

She was surprised by his honesty, but that wasn't what she meant. "I mean, you told him about me. You said, 'I'm with Emma.' Like he already knows about me. You have been talking about me to your dad."

His smile was a little sheepish. "He called last night, and I told him." He gave her a little shrug. "Does that bother you?"

It didn't, Emma realized. It only surprised her. She imagined from everything Benjamin said that he was not close with his parents, and that he would never in a million years tell them about a girl he helped skip school. It was surprising to find that her first impression of him was all wrong.

"No, it doesn't bother me," Emma answered, she looked forward through the windshield and shook her head at herself, at her snap judgment of him that turned out to be all wrong. "I was just a little impressed with your honesty." She turned abruptly to face him again. "What did you tell him about me?"

Benjamin shrugged once more. His smile was self-conscious. "First of all, I told him you were a Harris of the River Bottoms Harrises, so he would be immediately impressed like I was." She rolled her eyes. "Then I told him we danced at the party last week and that's how we met, and I discovered you were a goody-good girl. At this point in the story my father warned me not to corrupt you, but I assured him it was far too late for that." She found herself blushing and had to look away again. She never heard of anyone talking about her before, except Leader and Monique when they argued about the right way to discipline her. It made her feel special and embarrassed all at once to hear Benjamin speak kindly of her.

"He wanted to be sure I was being a gentleman, so he told me I ought to ask you out on a real date and pick you up at your house and everything, but I told him you weren't necessarily *in* to gentlemen and that, despite what you say, you enjoyed the hotdogs and go-karts yesterday. I told him impromptu dates seemed more your style."

"Did you tell him I was supposed to meet you in secret on the track field today, but that for some reason you came early, and I had run away from school in the opposite direction of our rendezvous?"

He scowled a little. "No, and I probably won't. Why did you run the opposite direction, now that you mention it?"

She shook her head. "Nothing to do with you, honestly. I just wanted to leave, and it seemed easiest through the front gates rather than over the stone walls."

"It had nothing at all to do with my bad influence, I'm sure," he added with a pious nod.

"Don't be so sure of yourself," she retorted. "Before I *met* you I had never told a lie, never went to a kegger, never skipped school, and never held hands."

He seemed surprised by that. He twined his fingers through hers. "Never?" he asked. She nodded. He squeezed her hand a little tighter. "And, FYI, Cara's party was not a kegger. There has to be a keg for it to be a kegger, and preferably no parents around to monitor the situation." She shrugged because the distinction did not much matter to her.

They drove up the canyon and then down several winding roads, for which he needed both hands on the wheel. She reluctantly released his hand. She cried out slightly when he suddenly veered off the road and his truck crashed through bushes on its way through a wild patch of grass.

"What are you doing?" she demanded. He chuckled.

"It's an off-road vehicle," he explained innocently.

"You're crazy," she snapped, but she wasn't angry. Her heart beat normally again, and she glared at him. "You could have given some kind of warning."

"What? And miss scaring you half to death?" He shook his head. "You know, Quicksilver, I'm starting to get the idea that you're sort of ... sheltered."

She scoffed. "Where would you get an idea like that?" she answered sarcastically. "Private school? Never been to a party? Crazy lunatic of a father comes in a rage to collect me from said party? Enticed away from a field trip by a boy I barely know who drives a big truck?"

Benjamin spared her a glance before returning his eyes to study the path through the wilderness. He smiled. "So, it's the truck that does it for you, is it?"

Emma blushed slightly and sat back against the seat. "Does what?"

"You like me because of my truck," he stated, and glanced at her again. Finding her scrunched up to the seat, he laughed.

She sat forward abruptly. "First of all," she lectured, "if I wanted a boy with a truck, I could stand in the middle of my school parking lot, close my eyes, spin, and point. There are that many wannabe cowboys. Second, who said I even like you?"

"So, me and my truck are merely for convenience purposes," he answered but he still smiled.

Emma glared at him and sipped her chocolate. "Yeah, I'm *that* girl."

He laughed at her grumbling tone. It was a ridiculous idea that Emma could be the kind of girl to use Benjamin merely because he was convenient. No one could be convenient enough for Emma to risk Leader's anger over it. Cara and Brinley were the kinds of girls who could have a "convenience" boyfriend, and no matter how much time Emma spent with those girls, she never could be one of them.

"Well, now I know the truth of it," Benjamin continued to tease. "I'm a good time on the side, hidden away from your family and friends because you're ashamed I have a truck and might be mistaken for a cowboy." He laughed again when she refused to answer. "Come on, now! If I was the respectable boy you generally date, I would have picked you up at your house nice and proper like my father suggested, brought you flowers, got interrogated by your overly-protective daddy ... You're hiding me."

Emma put her drink in the cup holder and turned to face him. "You know I'm hiding you," she answered, serious now. "You gave me your phone because I'm hiding you from my family."

"Because I'm a bad influence?"

He punched the gas as they reached the top of a small hill, so they were airborne for a few moments before the front end of the truck smashed down and they continued over an empty field.

Emma clutched at the handle over her head. She did not know why fancy trucks had these handles, but today she was grateful.

"Slow down!" she ordered. "And it has nothing to do with your bad influence at all. If my family was worried about bad influences, they would encourage me away from being friends with Cara Winters."

He did slow down, not in obedience to her, but because they were approaching a copse of trees. "Cara is not so bad. She's conniving, but she'll probably marry some new money in a few years and spend her life getting plastic surgery and harassing her maids. She's harmless. You're the dangerous one, Emma. Everyone is still talking about how you kicked the crap out of that obnoxious kid at the party."

He drove his truck slowly through the trees. A few times some branches scraped along the sides of the truck and Emma cringed with thoughts of his pristine paint job. But he didn't seem to notice.

"So, tell me why," he said, but his focus was on safely maneuvering his vehicle through trees.

"Tell you why I almost killed that boy? I thought it was obvious."

"No," he said, voice dripping with scorn. "Anyone watching could see that kid had it coming." His tone softened. "Why are you hiding me?"

Emma squirmed. "They don't allow me to date."

"So, we're dating? That was fast."

She blushed to her hairline. She felt the heat in her face and looked out the window to avoid him seeing her out of sorts.

"That's not what I meant," she mumbled, but she couldn't say anything more.

He slowed the truck and finally stopped it altogether. "Emma," he said, reaching to touch her shoulder. "I was only teasing you." When she refused to look at him he said again, "Emma, come on. I was teasing. I did not mean to embarrass you."

She looked at him. His eyes focused on her and had no hint of teasing left in them. "Monique—my mother—told me to stay away from you." She told him that before. "I don't know why."

He sighed in frustration and his eyes darkened slightly like they had the last time they talked about this. "Maybe they heard about my reputation. It often precedes me and does me little credit."

"I don't care about that," she said, studying his eyes for any reaction to her words. "And I don't care that Monique warned me against you. I have never disobeyed her intentionally, but I think this time I don't care what happens."

He let out a breath almost like a snort, but his voice was still soft. "I'm going to skip right over the weirdness of you calling your mother by her name and say 'Wow!' You have never disobeyed your parents, Quicksilver? I'm starting to think I really am a bad influence on you."

Emma agreed with him, actually. But it wasn't his fault. She *wanted* to do what she was doing. "Bad Influence" seemed like a kid who had no brain and just went along with a crowd because she had no moral conscience.

"Does that change it?" she asked him, staring into his eyes, waiting for him to recoil. "If I am 'badly influenced' by you, does that mean you want to take me back home and never see me again?"

For too long he stared at her. For too long his eyes were clouded in thought. Then he leaned forward, and his lips pressed against hers. She kept her hands in her lap and let herself be kissed. She let herself forget about Leader and the Guild, and the nosy counselor at the school. She gave in to the sensation of warmth spreading everywhere at once. Even her scalp and her toes seemed to tingle.

It was not long. He pulled back and said, "It changes nothing." And continued driving. Emma sat staring at him for a moment. The color in her cheeks was no longer from embarrassment. It was a new feeling that she could not describe, even in her own head. It was warm and exciting at the same time. Exhilarating like a rollercoaster and at the same time comforting like a warm quilt.

After a few minutes, she recollected they were in the mountains in the middle of the woods. "Where are we going?"

He smiled. "Quicksilver, you're going to have to trust me now that we're dating."

"So, we're dating now?" she asked, saucily. "That was fast."

He rolled his eyes.

Chapter Thirty-Five

It was cold in the mountains. Emma was suddenly grateful for the gloves, the jacket and hat, and even the sickeningly sweet lukewarm chocolate. Benjamin had driven through the copse of trees and across another patch of wilderness to a cliff edge. He parked so the bed of the truck faced the valley and they could see for miles out over the land. There was snow here already. She was grateful he had blankets in the backseat. He laid one out on the bed of the truck, and the two of them huddled beneath the other to eat the food he had ordered in the drive-thru. She could ignore the cold because of his arms around her. It was enough of a reason never to leave this spot.

"Where will your father think you are?" Benjamin asked her as they ate their picnic.

Emma shrugged. "I don't know, and honestly, I can't care about that now. What's done is done. If he was telling me the truth before, he'll be able to track me down wherever I go."

Benjamin smiled. "Well, it's as unlikely a place as ever I've seen. It will take some voodoo magic or military satellites for him to find us here." Emma did not want to think about those possibilities.

"You bring all your girlfriends here?" she teased him.

"No," he answered, pretending to be offended. He scoffed. "Just the ones I like."

"So, you like me?" she asked, bumping her shoulder against his playfully.

He shrugged. "Jury's still out," he answered and took a bite of his sandwich. She rolled her eyes at him.

After she finished eating, she lay down and looked up at the mid-afternoon sky. It was a little overcast in the mountains, but she enjoyed it. The tops of the mountains had a ring of clouds independent of the other clouds in the sky. She was overwhelmed with the idea that the mountains were living, and those clouds were the mists of their breath. It was a silly comparison, but she wanted to share it with Benjamin, so she did. She half expected him to laugh, but he lay down beside her and looked upward toward the mountaintop.

"That's a beautiful idea, Emma," he said in a soft voice. "It sounds like poetry."

She gave a short laugh, almost a scoff. "Well, I'm not a poet."

He rolled onto his side and looked at her. There was only seriousness in his face now. "I think you are, Emma. If you let yourself be. Your mind just does this; it makes pictures and comparisons that other people don't think about. Poetry is not all love and mushy like Shakespeare."

Emma laughed at him a little. "Shakespeare was a playwright more than a poet, and anyone who has read Shakespeare knows that his stuff is not all mushy and love. It's revenge, and passion, and irony, and violence."

"Listen to all those words, Quicksilver! You're a poet for sure. Did you hear what I said? 'Mushy.' Game point."

She cocked a brow at him. "Game point?"

He shrugged slightly. "Yeah. From tennis. It's the point in a match when one point gained ensures a player's win."

She tried to stifle her smile, unsuccessfully. "I know what a game point is. I do not know what it has to do with Shakespeare."

"Oh!" He settled back down on the blanket. "It has nothing to do with Shakespeare. I was informing you that I had just won the game point in our argument. That means I made a point that beat you and so I win the argument." He placed his hands behind his head and looked at the sky, but Emma thought he was watching her in his peripheral vision.

"I'm sorry, I was not aware we were arguing or that an argument was a sport to be won," she exclaimed. "So, I claim technical foul and ... What's that?" she cupped her hand to her ear. "Yes, yes, the referee just confirmed it, argument is still going."

He shrugged in apparent unconcern. "Argument's over, Quicksilver. I got the game point. If you want to start another match, well, I could go again."

She clenched her fists in minor frustration. "What point did you make exactly?"

"I said you were a poet because other people don't use words as artfully as you do. And then I used the word mushy and it made my point. Game point. Because mushy is not a real word."

"It has a dictionary definition," she answered, sitting up.

He grabbed her arm and pulled her down into his embrace. "Settle down. It's not your fault. I'm a pro at this sport."

She obediently snuggled against him. "What sport? Arguing?"

"Been doing it almost since birth. I argued with my parents, my teachers, and my friends. The police. My dad's security personnel."

"A juvenile officer," she added playfully.

He shook his head. "No, not that. But I argued with the lawyers both times I was almost turned over to juvie. They won those arguments, fortunately, and I did what they said so I got free. I don't fault myself for those losses. Lawyers hold championship titles in arguing."

She laughed. Then she rested her head against him and closed her eyes. Being this close to another person filled a piece of her she did not know had been vacant. It made her feel that, at least in this moment, she was complete. She was whole and nothing else in the world mattered.

"Quicksilver, wake up!" Benjamin said urgently.

Emma came awake, certain she would see Leader's scowl of displeasure looming over her. He wasn't there. Only Benjamin was, but he seemed worried. Then she noticed the sleepy look to his eyes and the twilight all around them.

"What time is it?" she demanded, sitting up and pushing the blankets off her. It was very cold now that the sun was going down. "How long was I asleep?"

"I don't know," he confessed miserably. "My phone's in the truck."

At that idea, she fished his other phone, the one he had given to her, out of her pocket and clicked the button on the side to light it up. The time and date flashed on a blue background.

"Ten after seven," she breathed out in shock. "We slept for four *hours*." She looked up at him, pained at the idea of Leader's anger. If the school hadn't called him, he would certainly have noticed she was missing when someone came to get her from school. He and Monique must be frantic by now.

"Half a night's sleep," he agreed with a shake of his head. "Why did you let me sleep that long, Quicksilver? You're the responsible one."

She mock-glared at him. "I don't know what you're talking about. As far as I'm concerned, you kidnapped me and carried me away into the mountains to keep me out of sight while the search parties try to locate me."

"Right!" he snorted. "They'll have a real hard time finding the giant trail my truck left through the bushes and fields. God, my dad's going to kill me." He stood up and jumped off the side of the truck. She followed him and helped him collect the picnic basket and the blankets. He didn't bother folding them, he just shoved them into the backseat with her backpack and the shopping bag filled with her school clothes. He climbed in the truck and turned the key while she was still climbing in.

"Will you be in big trouble?" She did not really know what 'big trouble' was in a normal family, but she wanted to show some empathy. Especially since she would probably never see him again once Leader got his hands on her.

He turned on his high beams as he drove back into the copse of trees and carefully maneuvered back the way they had come.

"Yeah," he admitted after a pained moment. "He warned me to be on time to dinner. He's expecting some guests. The mayor, probably, and the mayor's wife and bratty kids." He grabbed his phone from its resting place on the dash and checked for missed calls. "Yeah, I'm in trouble. He's called twice and sent four messages." He was silent for a moment as he tried to drive and read his texts. "He sent his guys after me an hour ago. He's pissed."

"I'm so sorry," she whispered. "I was so busy feeling angry at Leader and the school counselor, and so determined to be rebellious, that it never even occurred to me you might have other obligations, too. I feel so bad, Benjamin. I should never have fallen asleep."

He shot a glance her way. "Hey," he said in a soothing tone. "Don't you be sorry at all. I would rather spend any time with you over time with my family. It just so happens that tonight was important to my dad and I blew it. It's fine. He'll throw a tantrum for a few days and make a bunch of empty threats and then life will be back to normal."

She thought about that scenario in order to keep from imagining what her own family scenario would be. Unfortunately, he brought it up.

"What about you, Emma? Is it safe for me to drop you off at home? How mad is your dad going to be? Because I caught a sight of the guy the night of the party and he seemed pretty pissed about a couple hours at a well-lit, supervised party. How is he going to take a quiet, romantic afternoon date with a boy?"

Emma decided to be honest. "Not well. I can almost feel his anger. The thing is, the school probably contacted him as soon as I didn't show up to third period. Maybe sooner, if I know that annoying counselor ..."

"I'm getting the sense that you and the counselor had a rough day. What did she do?"

"She pried," Emma answered sharply. The sharpness was not directed at him, but he clearly thought it was because he did not ask any more questions. That softened her.

"She thinks I'm being abused and she is looking for a way to prove it."

Benjamin watched the field where he was driving and said nothing for a long time. Then he glanced at her.

"Are you?"

There was a lot of concern in his eyes and for a moment she considered telling him the truth. But what could he do? It would worry him needlessly and he would be even more helpless than she was. At least she could control her decisions. She knew what to do to keep Leader at bay: Obey him.

"No," she lied.

"Are you sure?" he asked. He knew. He knew she was lying just like Ms. James suspected and Brinley assumed.

"I'm sure. Leader will be angry and I'm sure he'll restrict me as much as he can, but he's not abusive."

"Okay," Benjamin answered, and returned full concentration to driving.

Before they reached the canyon road, he said, "Can I ask you another question?"

She wanted to say no because if he felt the need to ask permission to ask it, it was probably a question she would not be able to answer. And she did not want to tell him any more lies. But she said yes.

"Who's Leader? Is that your father? You've said it twice."

She was glad for the dark of the cab hiding her cringe over her slip. *Twice?* "It's a nickname. My brothers and I often call our parents by their names. When we started it a few years ago, my father was not fond of the change and we somehow started referring to him as 'Leader,' instead, to tease him for being old-fashioned. I guess it stuck."

It wasn't a great lie and she knew it, but what else could she say? Explaining his title would create the need to explain the Guild, and her place in it and that was a whole mess of problems she did not need to heap on Benjamin. Especially not in the light of his own troubles, and the fact that she would probably never be permitted to see him again.

"It's weird," he answered, but he dropped it, to Emma's immense relief.

"Yeah," she agreed. They rode on in silence for a little longer.

"Listen," he said as they pulled onto the canyon road. "If I can drop you off at a friend's house, I'm willing. Maybe he'll believe you if you tell him that you were there all afternoon, and you lost track of the time."

She considered it, but it would never work. By now Leader would know she ditched school and he would be searching for her. Her "friends" would be some of the first contacts. Besides, Amos knew there was a boy in her life, and he had shown the surveillance image to Leader. They had to be assuming she was with the boy.

"Unless you're offering to drive me across state lines, I don't think subterfuge will be effective," she said with a smile.

He chuckled. "Oh, my father's men will be at the state lines by now. No way can we escape them all. But did you just ask me to run away with you? It's sudden, Emma, but I'll think about it."

She scoffed. "I'm not going to dignify that with an answer."

He laughed. "To the river bottoms."

"No, Benjamin," she corrected. "Like this: 'To the *River Bottoms!*'" she said it in a booming voice, much like he had announced go-karts to her. She even went so far as to lift her fist into the air for effect.

He repeated her exactly, "The *River Bottoms!*"

Chapter Thirty-Six

They reached the gate leading into her neighborhood.

"What's the gate code?" Benjamin asked as he pulled up to the key panel.

Emma shook her head. "Just drop me here. I'll go through the walk-in gate."

Benjamin snorted. "No, Emma. I'm taking you to your door. I'm not afraid of your father. And he should see me, so he can tell me to my face why you're not allowed to see me anymore."

Emma drew a long breath and turned to look at him, images of glinting blades and dead bodies swimming up in her memory.

"No."

He seemed ready to argue, but she went on, "Listen, Benjamin, my father is a dangerous man. He's bound to be furious at me and I will not risk that fury ricocheting off onto you simply because you want to walk me to my door. My house is only a few blocks from here in a gated community; I'll be fine." She reached for the door handle, but he clicked the child-lock button to keep her from getting away.

"He's dangerous?" Benjamin asked sternly. There was no playfulness in him now. It was not like the last time he locked her in the truck, when he was teasing her and not wanting her to go without promising to call him. He was deadly serious now. "What kind of dangerous?"

Emma expelled a breath in exasperation. "I will be fine."

Benjamin looked at her, anger and frustration all over his face. "Emma, I am not going to leave you here if that man is going to hurt you. I'm taking you all the way in or you can come back to my place where I know you will be safe."

Emma could not imagine which scenario sounded worse to her. She wanted to spend more time with Benjamin, but he was already in serious trouble without bringing a girl home. And what would Leader and Monique do if she did not come home? What could they do when they found her?

Emma looked out the window at the now fully darkened sky and shook her head. By now, Leader knew about her interview with the counselor. He was bound to be searching for her. She had to go home. It's not like she could stay at Benjamin's forever. And if Benjamin's family thought Leader was abusing her, they would contact Social Services and have her placed into foster care. No matter how difficult her life was sometimes, it was her life.

"Four, nine, one, three," she finally said. When he continued to stare blankly at her, she said, "The gate code is four-nine-one-three. You can drop me off at my house, but you can't get out of the truck. Okay? You drop me off and turn and leave."

Benjamin turned to punch the code in the key panel, but she grabbed his arm and waited for him to look at her.

"You have to promise me, Benjamin," she said earnestly. "I really like you. I want you to live through the night." He scoffed but she hurriedly insisted, "Promise me you will turn and drive away."

He narrowed his eyes at her, but then he leaned and kissed her gently. "Fine. I will take you to your house and I'll stay in the truck. But if he hurts you, I'll kill him."

Emma did not say that Benjamin would never stand a chance against Leader in any combat style. She smiled softly and settled against the seat. Benjamin punched in the code and waited as the gate opened smoothly. He pulled through.

"I'm glad you like me," he said smugly. When she did not answer, he chuckled and said, "I like you, too."

"I figured that out when you wouldn't leave me alone," she said, but there was no heat in it. She smiled at him. "Take the first left."

They wound their way through the streets of the neighborhood. Before they reached her street, she placed a hand gently on his arm. He glanced at her, then slowed and finally stopped the vehicle to give her his attention.

"Thank you for my birthday, Benjamin," she said. She was completely sincere in these thanks. It was the best birthday she had ever had. She never wanted to forget it.

"You're welcome," he said decisively with a small smile. "Sorry we fell asleep and had to cut everything short."

"No," she replied, placing a finger against his lips, quickly rejecting that anything was less than perfect. "It was the best birthday I could have asked for." She reached for his hand and squeezed it softly. "I don't know when I'll be able to see you again. But I had a great time."

He would have kissed her, but she looked away before he could. "It's just ahead. Next right."

He sat silently for a moment, but after giving a slight sigh, he moved his foot from the brake onto the gas and turned the corner. Any thought of romance or sadness left Emma's mind when she saw her street teeming with people and vehicles. Several news vans complete with camera crews and reporters stood at the edge of this side of a police blockade of the street. Beyond them red and blue lights flashed from half a dozen cop cars, an ambulance, and two fire trucks. The trucks blocked Emma's view of her own house. Her heart pounded heavily. Was this because she had gone missing? Had Leader really contacted the cops and alerted the media? It was very unlike him.

Benjamin and Emma were stopped before they reached the police blockade. An officer approached the driver window. Benjamin slowly rolled it down, but he did not look away from the flashing lights and the ominous scene before them.

"What's your business here?" the officer asked, not unkindly. He sounded bored more than anything.

"I ... ah ..." Benjamin swallowed. "I was just a friend of the Harris family." He finally looked intently at the officer. "Is everything okay? What happened?"

"I can't give any information," the cop answered, still bored. "There was a fire. Now it's out. That's all I have for you."

Emma jumped out of the truck without so much as a word to Benjamin. All she could hear were the officer's bored words: *There was a fire.* At the Harris house? Was anyone hurt? She felt a seize of panic in her heart and she slipped past the media and the bystanders, hitting the sidewalk at a run.

"You! Stop there!" called another officer.

"I'm Emma Harris!" she called in answer. "That's my House!"

The reporters heard her better than the officers did. They whipped their cameras to get her face, but by then she had slipped in between the cop cars and out of their sight. She had assumed the vehicles were there because she was missing, not because of some other emergency. The idea of an emergency never crossed her mind. She was surprised at how much fear she had over the thought.

She was stopped by other officers and officials in suits and uniforms before they let her within a house lot of her home. She stood in shock, staring at it from across the street. The half of the mansion that housed most of the bedrooms and the office was a black ruin. The garage was sagging and black as night. She swallowed. There were no cars that she could see. Where was everyone? A panicked thought came: *What if they had been caught in the fire and she was now alone in the world?*

She drew shaky hands to her face. Until this moment, she had no concept of how much she cared about the rest of the people in the Guild. Until the idea of losing them occurred, she had assumed she hated them.

"It's not as bad as it seems," a kindly fireman said beside her. She glanced at him, finding him sweat-covered and exhausted looking. "We put it out pretty quick, before it could spread to the majority of the house."

"Where is everyone?" she asked, trying to control her voice and maintain outward calm.

"Emma?" Leader's voice penetrated their conversation. She spun to find him in the sea of officials around her. He crossed through the men. They moved aside for him without even noticing they did it. Everyone always did that for Leader. He wore a suit, but the tie was loose and his shirt half-tucked. This was as distraught as she'd ever seen him.

"Emma!" he said again, and this time his pace became a jog. Upon reaching her, his hands seized her face and he peered into her eyes intently. He let out a long breath, as if he had been holding it for a lifetime. "Are you okay? Where the hell have you been?"

Emma had never heard Leader use profanity before. It was a measure of his distress. "What happened? Is everyone okay?" She hoped he would overlook the fact that she ignored his question in light of the unusual circumstances.

His eyes narrowed, and she knew she had no such luck. But he answered. "Monique is at the hospital with Julianne and Adam. They were both caught in the fire, but they got out with little more than minor burns on the feet. Scott was the only other person home, but he had sense enough to get out as soon as he smelled smoke. He called 911 when he saw the fire on the roof."

Emma felt a sweeping relief. But Leader's grip on her face tightened. "Are you okay?" he asked again and with some urgency. He had been worried about her, she realized. He still was.

"I'm fine," she answered, managing to cut herself off before giving him a title. There were people all around. "I'm really okay."

He continued to look into her eyes, searching intently as if he knew she was lying. Then he pulled his hands away. One of his hands grasped her wrist and pulled her along behind him toward the edge of the street. Amos waited there with his arms crossed, watching the activity across the street in front of the mansion. The cops and firemen crawled all over the Harris property, but no one else was allowed nearer than the sidewalk across the street.

When Amos turned and saw her, he crossed himself like a Catholic. "Thank God!" he exclaimed, but it was more like a curse than a prayer. "I was so afraid you were inside hiding somewhere!"

"I told you she wasn't," Leader answered, but it lacked his usual snap. He did not relinquish his hold on Emma. "Stay here, Amos, in case they need you to answer any more questions, or they have any more information for us. I'm going to take Emma to the hotel."

Amos shot Emma a quick glance. "If you want, I will take her, Leader."

Darkness entered Leader's eyes and the pressure on Emma's arm increased slightly. "Just Obey me, Amos! Call Monique and tell her we can stand down; I have Emma."

Amos's eyes jerked forward at Leader's rebuke, and he continued to watch the activity around the house. "She'll be relieved."

Leader scoffed slightly. "Yes," he agreed, but his tone was off. It was ironic. "I'm going. Don't let them hassle you too much."

Amos glanced at Leader with a slight smile. "I won't. One more question about insurance providers and I might snap." He focused on Emma for a moment. "Honey, I'm so glad you weren't here." There was such sincerity that Emma thought there was more to all of this than she could perceive.

"Come on," Leader ordered. He let go of her arm now and strode away toward the end of the street. There were police barricades up here, too, but thankfully no press. Leader's car was parked just beyond the barricade. Emma followed him and waited patiently while he spoke to the officers. He told them to direct further questions to his brother and pointed to Amos. Then he walked away from them. He glanced back once to be sure Emma was following, which of course she was. Not out of fear, her usual response, but because she was so relieved he was okay.

He opened her door for her and held it while she climbed in. It closed with a smack. Leader walked around the back of the car and climbed in on the driver side. He turned the car on and put it into drive. In silence, they drove down a back road and through an exit gate out of the neighborhood.

Finally, Leader addressed her, "Where's your backpack?"

The question surprised her for the few seconds it took to analyze. This was Leader's way of telling her he knew how long she'd been gone.

"It's in my boyfriend's truck," she answered, deciding to be truthful, "with my school uniform."

He nodded as if it was not at all a surprise that she had a boyfriend, and it was perfectly okay that she had left her things with him.

"Where were you?" Cool as ever, but not as focused. His mind was engaged in other occupations besides this conversation. But Emma thought he was relieved to be having it.

"In the mountains."

His head jerked around at that revelation. He seemed alarmed and a little angry. "What?"

"I was in the mountains, sir."

"Doing what?" he demanded. His car sped out into traffic. His driving began to resemble his sour mood.

"Having a picnic." She was surprised by his sudden fury until she realized the direction. "It was just a picnic, Leader, and that's all. We fell asleep in the bed of the truck, but all we did was *sleep*."

Leader shook his head. "If you get pregnant ..."

"Leader, it was a picnic and that's all! That's all!"

He looked at her and for a moment she thought he seemed amused, but if it was true, none of it showed on his face. He continued to drive in relative silence.

"Who is he?"

"His name is Benjamin."

"Stillwell?" Leader asked, evidently as acquainted with Benjamin's reputation as Monique seemed to be.

"Yes." She did not give him time to snap threats or make barbed comments. She admitted up front that she knew she had been disobedient. "Monique warned me away from him, but I kept being thrown into his path, and finally I stopped trying to keep him at a distance." Truthfully, she had never tried hard, but Leader knew that. Leader knew her.

"He seems like a good enough boy," he replied, emotionless. Emma thought she must be hallucinating. He seemed very unconcerned. "Well, Emma, you may as well ask me."

"Ask you what, Leader?" she shot back, uncertain, and afraid of what he might have to say on the matter.

Leader raised both brows at her as they pulled up to a stoplight. "You know perfectly well that Monique is to be Obeyed when she commands you. You ignored her, as you seem to have developed a habit of doing in the face of authority lately. She will be responsible for distributing due punishment for that crime." He turned to watch the light; it glowed an angry red at them. "If you will not ask me for my forgiveness and for permission to have a boyfriend, Monique may break you once and for all." He hit the gas as soon as the light turned green, slamming Emma into his leather passenger seat. "So, do you plan to at least ask me?"

Emma pulled herself up straight. "I never thought for one second you would allow it. Seems to me you have always discouraged boldness in me."

He snorted with a shake of his head. "Only because boldness was the one value you did not lack in any form from infancy." He shook his head at her, or perhaps at himself, before saying. "I encourage—nay—I *demand* honesty. What are your chances otherwise? If you ask me, and I say no, you're no worse off than before. But if I say yes, you can drag your mischief out of the darkness and not keep trying to hide from me." He shot a dangerous glance at her. "It will never work, you know: hiding. Lying. Disobedience."

She blinked. It was okay to *ask* to have a boyfriend? What if he said no? Then she would have to continue on in her deceit. Except then she would be deliberately disobeying him, and that had negative connotations attached. Was there a glimmer of possibility that he would say yes? She would have a boyfriend and maybe even be able to spend time with him without risking Leader's wrath. Emma felt a strange seed of hope grow in her heart. What was the worst thing that could happen if she did ask?

Leader turned onto a busy street and his concentration seemed to be all on his driving. She almost lost her nerve and blamed it on the idea that Leader was too busy to listen. She considered that he was only taunting her with her hopes, dangling the idea of his approval so she would jump through hoops for him even if he had no intention of yielding. But then she thought about Benjamin, and the picnic, and the go-karts. And the kisses.

"Leader, would you permit me ..." she started. He looked at her and again she almost lost her nerve. His eyes were pools of superiority and sternness. *What if he said no?* Her every hope would be dashed because, if he said no, he would not give her the chance to be disobedient. "May I maintain Benjamin Stillwell as my boyfriend?"

Leader looked at the road, moved into the turn lane. He adjusted his lights, checked his gauges, and focused on driving. For a confused moment, Emma imagined she had not spoken out loud. Even though her words filled her ears, she worried that she had not really gathered the courage to ask him.

"Yes, I think," Leader said at last.

Emma let out a long breath. It felt like she had been holding it in all her life.

"On a few conditions."

Chapter Thirty-Seven

"Conditions, sir?"

The weight Emma thought had been lifted weighed down on her again.

"Yes, and you must accept them all or I will not permit you to date until after you graduate." That was a very real and abiding threat. She had no doubt he and Monique would enforce it strictly with her. "First, I will need to meet him very soon, so I can look him over again and make certain I can condone him spending time with you. Second, you may never, ever again skip school to spend time with him. School must come first. Is that clear?"

Emma stared hard at nothing. These were reasonable expectations. "Yes, Leader, that is very clear."

He went on. "Third, under no circumstances is your relationship permitted to become physical. I will not condone any kind of—" he cut off. He probably saw the shift of her shoulders and the blank expression on her face. "What?"

"He kissed me already," Emma admitted, hardly able to believe that she was telling him this. "It just happened, and I don't know if that goes against your conditions."

He swerved the car out of traffic onto the side of the road. They moved so quickly in the BMW that he was parked with his hazards on before she had time to fully comprehend what had happened.

"What kind of kiss?" She had expected him to be angry, but he was not. He seemed very interested, but there was no anger.

"It was very chaste, Leader."

He sat waiting, one eye raised expectantly, so she went through an awkward and very uncomfortable description of the kiss. He listened intently. Finally, he nodded.

"Acceptable," he pronounced. He held up a finger in her face. "You are never for any reason to kiss him lying down. He may not touch your body anywhere between your neck and your knees. I don't so much as want his hand resting on your back! You may not touch him, either, and if he asks you to do so, you must tell me at once. I do not want you spending excessive time alone with him."

"Yes, Leader," she answered, embarrassed but grateful. "Are those all of your conditions?"

"No," he rejected with a musical sternness that swept through the car. He crossed his arms thoughtfully. "I will also expect daily reports from you including your conversations and every detail of your every interaction. We are the Guild, after all, Emma, and that means no relationship stands alone. You have a boyfriend, then so does the Guild."

That was a daunting idea. She had always expected this was the way it would be, but she also only supposed she would be allowed to date if it served Guild purposes. Since that was proving to be untrue, she had to figure she may have misunderstood some things.

"You may see him one school night each week and any weekend days or evenings where your Guild duties do not call you away, but never more than four hours at one time. If you are at the Guild House, he may stay until I send him home." He held up a hand. "If you leave the House, you will take Piper or Ilene as escort. You are far too young to spend time all alone with a young man." The idea that masculine, fiery Piper or icy, winter-cold Ilene would have to come along if Benjamin took her anywhere was daunting, but Emma continued to listen. She still was not entirely sure she could believe this was happening.

Leader squeezed her knee with a strong hand. "I will permit you to continue your relationship with this boy as long as your Guild responsibilities do not slip. And what are your responsibilities?"

"To learn, grow, and Obey," she answered immediately.

"Yes," he said. "Perfect Obedience is how you will demonstrate your desire to keep your boyfriend." It was not said unkindly, but it made Emma uneasy. Benjamin was a tool Leader could now use to keep her in line; a much more effective tool than hurting or humiliating her had been. But she had to agree to his conditions. She had no doubt he could end her relationship with Benjamin very thoroughly if she refused.

"As you say, Leader."

He studied her a long moment, then nodded.

"If I think of any additional conditions, I will let you know." It was simple; he was reserving the right to be stricter as he pleased.

Emma nodded at that, because he needn't have reserved the right. He already had the right because he was Leader.

"Thank you, Leader," Emma answered, truly grateful for his permission in this, however restricted her time with Benjamin would be. He nodded at her, and then turned back to his steering column. He reached for the hazard lights, but he did not touch it.

"Did you decide to brave Monique's anger, then?"

"Sir?" Emma answered, confused at his question and the intense stare he was giving her.

"I will give you over to her completely, you know. She has a right to expect your Obedience nearly as much as I do."

Emma sighed in frustration. "After you have said I can have a boyfriend, why will you give me over to her?" It was a regular routine with them. Whenever Leader decided he did not want to deal with Emma's recalcitrance, he passed her over to Monique without a backward glance. He was terrifying in his quiet, musical way, but Monique was exacting. She was demanding and precise and would never let Emma slide on anything. She never had. When Emma got back into Monique's power tonight, the woman would be fueled by worry and anger, and that combination would make her unbearable.

He raised a dangerous brow at her tone. "You know, little girl, I'm not completely unreasonable. You can ask me to forgive you. You will have caught me on a good day for it; I am exhausted with Guild disasters left and right and tired with mischief and misbehavior. If I believe your sorrow to be sincere, I may wish to forgive you rather than take the time and energy to punish. Especially once I know all you have to tell me on why you ran away today. I can be compassionate when I put my mind to it."

The idea that she might escape punishment for this was impossible, but it made her hope. If he forgave her, Monique would have no right to contradict him, no matter how angry she was.

"Leader, how do I obtain your forgiveness?" She had no idea on her own. She had never asked his forgiveness before.

"*Ask* for it," he replied tersely, because he had already told her that twice. "If I give it, I give it. If not, then not." He shook his head and looked away into the darkness of the night. On a sigh, he said, "You have a lot to learn yet, Number Twelve." He returned his gaze to her with sharp interest.

They waited a moment in the silence on the side of the road until Emma peeked at him. One brow shot up as he watched her.

"Leader, will you …" she swallowed when his eyes seemed to grow colder, when the words sounded ridiculous in her mouth. "Will you forgive me?"

His eyes narrowed further and his voice cooled, "For what?"

She found she could not look away from his icy gaze. "For disrespect to the school counselor and then for skipping school," she listed. "Also throwing away my phone so you could not contact me …" Her heart thumped in her chest at that admission, and she cut off in distress. There was no way he would forgive her. The list was too long. He was going to use his cold, musical voice to condemn her, and then turn her over to Monique, anyway.

In the quiet while she battled her nerves, he reached into his jacket pocket and retrieved her phone. Without breaking the silence, he placed it on her lap. The daunting idea that he had tracked her phone to the trash and retrieved it to return to her was one more reminder of his power. She slowly clasped her hand around it but did not remove it before his hand engulfed her own. She looked up into the dark compassionless pits of his eyes and drew a sharp breath at the sudden anger there.

"Is that all?" he asked, cold, calculating.

She wanted to say yes and be done but there was blackness to his gaze that made her think he knew more than she had told him. Could she afford to leave anything out? Could she afford to tell all the truth?

"No," she whispered, almost hoarse from the pain of his unrelenting grip on her hand. "I disobeyed Monique when she told me to steer clear of Benjamin. I talked to him the night of the party and saw him again on the field trip. I left the field trip with him and we went to his father's go-kart track and then to lunch at the mall. He dropped me off at school when Monique was planning to pick me up. And you told me to write a full account to update you on any new friends I might have made. I left Benjamin out completely, of course, and made up most of what I 'saw' on the field trip from information I got online." She paused long enough to draw a breath.

She had to tell him all. She knew she had to tell him everything, because if he really would forgive her, she wanted all of it out in the open where she could be safe from later retaliation.

She drew Benjamin's phone from her pocket and held it up for him to see. "And Benjamin contacted me on this phone, so you couldn't have a transcript."

There was a strange look in Leader's eyes as he released his grip on her hand. "Emma," he said, almost softly, in contrast to the hard look in his eyes. "Emma," he said again, but almost as if he could not find the right words, he reached forward and pressed some buttons on the control panel in his car. She wasn't sure what it controlled, as it certainly did not come standard in every BMW sold. He punched a final button.

The dark screen came alight, and she watched as it blinked several numbers and letters before it settled to a written transcript like the one she had seen the day he took all her comforts away.

Stillwell: *Hi. You don't have to talk. Okay? That way no one can hear you. Just listen. I am coming up to Utah County tomorrow during school hours. If you can meet me in your school's track field I should be there about noon. Press any button for yes. Press twice for no.*

Emma: *See you at noon*

"Audio," Leader stated. Benjamin's voice came through the speakers of the car, saying the things he had said on the phone last night, the words boldly filling the screen in front of her eyes.

She had thought she was safe with Benjamin's phone. She had thought the phone could not be tracked, traced or transcribed. After Benjamin's voice finished his instructions, there was a pause before Emma's voice whispered, clearly and solidly, *"See you at noon."*

"End," Leader commanded. The screen went blank.

Leader took Benjamin's phone from her hand and deposited it in the drink holder compartment between them. She did not try to resist him, as small as she felt. He had known. He told her he would remove all her comforts, and all the new comforts she found continued to fall into his hands.

"I hold *all* the cards, Emma." Again, his voice was almost gentle. He turned on his blinker and in a matter of moments was back in traffic, allowing her to deal with the emotions that threatened to overwhelm her.

It was true, that he held all the cards, even the ones she did not know he had. She had certainly never suspected he knew anything of Benjamin's phone. Her brain was racked with all the possible ways he could have obtained that information, but she could not make any sense of it with his words repeating in her mind. *I hold* all *the cards ... All* the cards ... ALL *the cards ...*

She resisted crying. What good did it ever do? She even resisted her urge to look away out the window as she often did, and pretend his words had no effect on her. Instead, she turned her face and looked at his profile.

She drew a long, cleansing breath, and said, "Leader, I believe you." And she did. She did not know how he knew everything he knew, but she would not be surprised at this moment for him to pull up a transcript of her conversations with Benjamin in his truck today or even a video of their picnic. She would not be surprised to find that she had accidentally referred to him as "Leader" in front of Benjamin. In fact, at this very moment, if he said he could read her thoughts, she would accept it. She accepted him, fully and completely, as her master and superior.

"And I forgive you," he replied quietly. She thought his forgiveness must have been contingent on her willingness to be straightforward or her acceptance of his authority. Whatever it had taken, she welled with relief that this day of disaster did not have to be finished off by Monique's blistering tongue and rough handling.

"What happens now?" he asked her, glancing her direction momentarily. He was testing her, but she had no idea what he was talking about.

"What do you mean, Leader?"

"I think I have all your comforts now," he said, eyes on the road. "And I have given you several opportunities to prove yourself to me. What next?"

She knew the answer to that, of course. He had drilled her on the five stages he would use to help her learn to serve the Guild willingly instead of out of fear. The first step had been to establish his authority. He'd done that all her life, but today she thought maybe he finally succeeded. The second step was to remove her comforts. Again, that was fully achieved only today. The third step was to give her as many opportunities as it took to prove herself.

"I do not think I can ever prove myself to you," she answered honestly, feeling a little sad when she thought about it. But she had been standing up to this man all her life. She'd looked up into his beautiful dark eyes, studying him, learning from him. He was thorough, but she was not a wallflower. Even when she wanted to control it, sometimes the snarkiness slipped out of her mouth. Sometimes the rebellion grasped her heart. He preached Obedience at her for as long as she could remember, and it was still not her first response in most situations.

He shot a glance her way and then laughed. She had not meant to amuse him, but he laughed out loud!

"You're probably right," he said when it was within his power again to speak.

Emma smiled wanly at him. "So, I guess you'll continue to test me." And she realized every moment of her life might be part of his tests.

"I will," he promised her with a decisive nod. "And what's next?"

"Instruction," she answered, surging with hope. "You said you will instruct me in all I need to know to succeed."

He nodded again as he turned into a hotel parking lot. "Soon," he promised her. He drove up to the front of the hotel, under the entry porch, and put his car into park. He didn't shut off the engine.

Leader hit the unlock button and looked at Emma, pointedly waiting for her to exit.

"Tell Monique I went back to the House and I'm working," he instructed, his tone of command returned completely, former gentleness gone. "She's in the penthouse." Of course, she was. Emma was surprised to find that any Orem hotels *had* penthouses, but where else would the Guild hole up after a fire?

Emma opened the door and climbed out, carrying her personal phone with her. She looked once at Benjamin's sitting in Leader's cupholder, but she did not dare touch it when he had pointedly removed it from her.

"What do I say when she inevitably tries to beat delinquency out of me?" Emma asked, a bit afraid that he would leave her to herself in dealing with Monique's anger.

Leader lifted one brow in thought. "Tell her I have forgiven you," he replied, as if it was the simplest answer in the world. She nodded, hopeful, and shut the door. She walked toward the hotel doors, amused to find they had a doorman as well as a penthouse.

"Emma!"

She turned at Leader's call before she could enter the hotel. His window was open and he watched her with those dark, intelligent eyes.

"Yes, Father?" she asked, remembering to call him "father" in front of the doorman.

"Happy Birthday," he said, with the slightest of smiles. Then the BMW raced away and he was gone. She smiled after him. It *had* been a happy birthday, she decided.

Chapter Thirty-Eight

Emma knew the kick would hit true. She had only enough time to turn her shoulder into it, since it was stronger and could afford the hit better than her chest. She had no way to avoid the hit completely.

She was swept from her feet and fell heavily to the padded flooring. Her head bounced against the protective mats they'd brought in to construct a temporary training arena in their hotel suite. When she opened her eyes, she found she was sensitive suddenly to the light overhead and the sound of Monique's voice shouting from across the room. *Concussion?* she wondered. Could it happen so quickly?

"Emma, Emma!" Scott was saying frantically from beside her. "Are you okay? Can you breathe?"

She thought she was breathing. She had no way of knowing if she was okay, because he was over the top of her, keeping her from sitting up to assess the damage.

"Get out of the way!" Monique snapped, shoving Scott to the side. "Don't sit up, Emma," she ordered, putting a hand on her shoulder to keep her on her back. Emma wasn't trying to sit up; she was trying to figure out why Monique had to talk so loudly.

"Is she okay?" Amos asked, crossing into the room, drying his hand on a cloth that he then threw on the floor. Now Monique was on one side and Amos on the other, looking her over, speaking in too-loud voices, and in general concerned for her.

It was amusing, Emma thought, though for some reason she could not laugh about it. They, who had been so angry at her yesterday for disappearing all day with Benjamin, were now as concerned as could be. She thought it was funny, but she could not have said why.

"I'm not sure she's hearing me," Amos' voice broke into her thoughts. Of course, she could hear him! He was talking like there was a crowd. "Emma? Can you move your hands?"

Her hands? Why shouldn't she be able to? The only reason she did not try was because she was too tired. She had just gotten up before she went to the practice mats, but she was suddenly very tired again. Yesterday had been a long day and she had not slept herself out. She had gotten up for training on time, even though it had been early for such a late night.

"She's not even hearing me!" Amos cried.

"I'm sorry!" Scott shouted from a short distance. "It was an accident. I didn't mean to. Monique, I swear I didn't mean to!"

"Scott, I don't know how many times I have warned you to spot before you attack!" Monique snarled. "If she's hospitalized, I swear on the Peace that you'll be in the bed beside her."

"It was an accident! An accident!" Scott screamed. He sounded scared. Emma thought that was funny, too. When she had walked into the penthouse yesterday, Scott had been as contemptuous as ever. He hated her and everyone else. He was big and bad and not afraid of anything. But he sounded afraid right now. He sounded terrified.

"Where's Julianne?" Amos said. Emma felt his hands on her face, warm against her sweat-cooled skin. There was such concern on his face that she wanted to reassure him, but Monique's hands on her shoulders kept her from moving, and Amos' hands on her face kept her from speaking. She closed her eyes, allowing herself to sleep.

"Emma!" Leader's voice penetrated through all the others. Her eyes opened and there he was, standing over her. He hadn't slept, she decided. He still wore yesterday's clothes. They smelled like smoke from the mansion fire.

"Emma," he called again, his voice cutting clearly through the commotion in the room. "Keep your eyes open. You are not to go to sleep."

She had no idea why he would restrict her from sleep when that's all she wanted to do, but she Obeyed him. Indeed, how could she do anything but Obey? He had proved his dominance yesterday. Obedience was what he required for her to keep Benjamin.

"Test," she said aloud. But it did not come out loud. It came out as a whisper, and only one word. She had meant to snap at him that she knew this was another one of his elaborate tests for her, to prove herself to him. Well, if he thought she would fail, she'd prove him wrong.

"What did you say, Emma?" Amos asked her. "She spoke, I think! *Shut up, Scott!* We know it was an accident."

Suddenly, there was much less sound in the room. Either Scott and the others had stopped speaking or they had gone away. She didn't care if he went away forever. His kick had been delivered with an excessive amount of Aggression, and she had not been in a position to defend it. He knew the rules: spot and modify. It was the only way the Family kept from killing each other on the mats. Is that what had happened? Had Scott killed her?

That was a hilarious idea and she laughed, or tried to. It came out more as a whispered croak.

"Be still, Emma," Leader ordered, and suddenly, he was the only one in her vision. "Watch me with your eyes." And he moved from one edge of her vision to the other. Her eyes followed him, because she did not dare disobey him. "Move your toes." She did so. "Now your fingers." She did so, amused that he thought this was a worthy test for her. How to move her body was one of the first lessons she had learned in the Guild. "Lift your head," he told her.

She did, but immediately the world spun around her and she vomited, all over him. Leader's arms held her, so she did not choke, and then he placed her gently back down on the mats, on her side, and called for Julianne. Emma, weakened from sickness and thoroughly dizzy, no longer found any of this amusing. She felt small.

"I think it's serious," Leader told Julianne as she came into Emma's vision.

"I doubt it," Julianne answered confidently. Strange that Julianne had no fear of contradicting him. Emma would not contradict Leader for anything! At least, not to his face.

"Let me look her over and dose her and she'll probably be fine in a few hours," Julianne went on. "If it's more serious, I'll let you know."

"All right," Leader said, tame as Emma had ever seen him. He looked worried, she thought. There was a strain of worry in his black eyes.

"I'm okay," she croaked, but Julianne hushed her.

"I'll call the school," Monique said from somewhere across the room.

"Do," Leader ordered. "And take care of Scott while you're at it. Who was refereeing the match anyhow? Piper? I want her hide, too. Where the hell was she when this happened?" His voice got further away, if not softer.

"Emma," Julianne said, placing a hand on her head. "Lay still for me, okay? I'm going to look you over and see if I can ease your pain."

Emma did not know about any pain except the pain of staying awake when all she wanted was to sleep. She couldn't sleep, though, not when Leader had forbidden her. Time may have passed or stood still. Emma didn't know. All she was aware of was a dull ache behind her eyes and the desire to sleep. A cup was forced against her lips.

"Drink this, okay, Emma?" Julianne encouraged her. Emma tried, but found it was harder than she remembered, and eventually had to let Julianne pour it down her throat.

"Sleep now," Julianne told her.

Emma wanted to, but she resisted. Every time her eyes slid shut, she forced them open. Something had been in that drink, she realized, something to force her to sleep. She had to resist its powers, no matter how unfair it was. Drugging her to see if she would break her promise of Obedience was cruel, but she would not let him win that way.

"What's wrong with her?" Leader asked, coming back into her vision all too suddenly. "Shouldn't she be sleeping by now?"

"Yes," Julianne announced in her clear alto, a little frustrated. "I have never met a patient immune to this juice."

Emma could not fully understand their words, but she knew what she had to do. She forced her eyes to stay open. He could never say she was disobedient.

Leader squatted beside her. "Emma? Are you in pain? What's wrong?"

"Test," she said, and this time her voice was strong enough for the word to carry. "No sleeping."

He stared at her for a long moment, studying her with dark eyes, and then he smiled. Shaking his head, he stroked her face and sighed at her. "You passed, Emmalyn. Now close your eyes and sleep."

She Obeyed him.

Emma awoke in bed. She was naked, she realized, and there was a bandage across her chest. Breathing was by no means easy, but at least her head was clear. She sat up, and the pain of that torturous activity nearly made her lie down again. She forced herself to work through the pain, removing the blankets that impeded her so she could look down and see for herself what was causing the pain. She gasped, an action that caused her more pain. She was bandaged well for what she could only assume was a broken rib or two. The gasp had come when she saw the blackened bruise across her breast and up to her collar. Then she remembered: Scott had kicked when she wasn't ready to defend.

She struggled to her feet, stumbling over the hotel slippers beside her bed to find a light switch. She found one that illuminated the three lamps in the room. A clock on the wall said it was only 2 in the afternoon, but the shades had been drawn across the window, making it semi-dark in there. Emma moved to the mirror across the room to see the extent of the damage to her person. The bruise was limited to her breast, her arm, shoulder, and collar. Perhaps there were no broken ribs at all, only bruised ones. Her neck ached, and she wondered how hard he had hit her. Hard enough to drop her to the mat, certainly, and padded though it was, it was never meant to protect someone who wasn't defending herself.

She worked the dresser drawer with her left hand, since moving the right one was more painful than it was worth. She pulled out a pair of sweat pants and a light t-shirt. They were her size, but still had the tags on them. When she saw them marked with BYU swag, she rolled her eyes, but clothing was clothing.

It took her a lot longer to get into the shirt than the pants. Every miniscule move of her right arm pulled the muscles in her chest and made her want to cry out. When she finally had it settled over her slim body, she slipped her feet into the slippers and walked out the door. The light in the hallway was an assault. It took her a moment to adjust.

The sound of voices led her down the hallway to the main living space. The kitchen was empty, but she got herself a drink from the water container in the fridge and eyed the food thoughtfully. She was hungry, but everything seemed like more work than it was worth. She continued her quest to find the voices.

They were in the large room that must once have been a TV lounge but remodeled into a boardroom. The black wood table and 12 chairs had probably been taken from a boardroom right here in the hotel. To where had the TV and lounging furniture been moved? She wondered idly as she peeked in.

Chapter Thirty-Nine

Leader and the rest of the Senior Guild were in the room, seated in the chairs with computers and stacks of papers all around them. Monique, beside Leader, stared at the screen of her computer with an exhausted expression on her face. To her left, beyond an empty seat was Ilene. Ilene had a stack of papers in her hands and was evidently comparing them to an image on her screen. Across from Ilene, Amos was the only one not concerned with the computer. He lounged with his arms above his head, leaning back as far as the chair would allow. If it was not on rollers, he would probably have been balanced to two chair legs, Emma thought amusedly.

Julianne sat serenely, as always, watching Leader, while beside her Thomas' fingers worked on his keyboard at an impossible pace. His eyes kept flashing up at Leader, who was speaking while Thomas typed.

"It's feeling a little more confining every day," Leader said. "I have submitted a location change, but God knows that could take months to organize. And I don't think we have months."

Thomas' hands paused long enough for him to say, "Every way I look at it, we are at their mercy. Their messages have been inane, but they have been clear."

"That's what I think, too," Leader replied with a respectful nod. He lifted a hand as if holding a round object. "On the one hand, I think … let them try. And I probably would if circumstances were different. They have played their strongest hands against our weakest. It's no wonder they seem to be coming out ahead."

"I have been over and over this record, Leader," Amos suddenly put in, motioning toward his computer. "It's clean. They have us over the fire."

"I refuse to believe that," Leader answered sternly. Amos shrugged and went back to his indolent leaning.

"Your refusal doesn't make their position appear any less intimidating."

"I will not be intimidated into yielding my position or showing my hand," Leader snapped back. "Now sit up and pay attention or find me another alternative."

Amos sat forward, but his expression shouted that he was of his own opinion still.

Emma was fiercely curious. She had never seen a Senior Summit before. They usually met before dawn to go over daily business. That Leader was meeting with them in the day clearly meant trouble in the Guild, but she had no idea what kind of trouble.

"Maybe we aren't giving Emma enough credit," Monique offered, shrugging once at Leader. Emma drew a sharp breath. They were meeting about *her*? Why? She held completely still, afraid even to breathe for fear she would be noticed.

"I agree," Julianne put in. "Emma is strong and smart. I think she's perfectly capable of thwarting disaster in this case."

Thwarting disaster? That had an ominous ring to it.

"She's a foolish child," Ilene countered, and Emma felt herself flush at the complete disregard Ilene apparently had for her. To think Emma had ever thought she was beautiful!

"She's not been acting particularly clever, but I hardly think she's foolish, Ilene," countered Monique with a bite in her tone. She would have gone on; indeed, Emma could see with some satisfaction the spark of anger in Monique's face, but Leader interrupted.

"She's extremely clever—she's brilliant—which is why we are in this predicament in the first place."

"She cannot be trusted," Ilene argued, her sniping tone filled with scorn. Emma felt her face flush with unexpected anger. What led Ilene to believe she could not be trusted? Hadn't she proved herself? Or had her failure to defend Scott's illegal kick lowered her in their estimation?

"You are not the judge of that!" Leader barked, silencing the room. "I am Emma's entire judge and jury right now."

Amos was not intimidated. "And what's your judgment, Leader?"

Leader lifted a challenging brow at Amos then glanced around at the others, who were all watching him expectantly.

"I still have to teach her about her duty," he said after a long moment of silence broken only by Thomas' unceasing typing. "Emma must learn that she is beholden to the Guild. There is no escaping the Guild. She's so very young. But I need to teach her."

Monique drew a tired breath. "It's my responsibility."

"You failed," he interrupted, slicing through her words as easily as mud. "Now I must teach her about her duty, so I can be sure she learns it. I think you'll have your hands full with Scott at the moment. And Piper."

Monique appeared ready to argue, but she lowered her gaze and said simply, "Yes, Leader." Emma felt sorry for her. It wasn't Monique's fault that Emma made as many mistakes as she did. Emma knew she was willful and defiant. She had been trying for years to find a way out from under Leader's authority.

"So, if you've taken charge of her, when will you correct her outlandish behaviors?" Ilene demanded. Emma realized now that everything she had ever known about Ilene was a lie. She thought Ilene was soft hearted and sweet tempered, but clearly, she was angry, bitter, and fiercely unfriendly about the Junior Guild. "Take that ridiculous trek through the wilderness yesterday! Conveniently absent when the fire spread through the mansion ... Do you really buy that, Leader? And what about skipping school and turning the counselor on us?"

"I forgave her for that," Leader replied, but more gently than Emma would have thought or hoped.

"Right," Ilene snorted. "Forgiveness for all of her mischief? Look what she's done! She's nearly brought ruin upon us and there you sit, as unconcerned as ever."

Monique nearly came out of her seat, but Leader grabbed her arm and pulled her back down. He lifted his voice and said, "Come here, Emma." That effectively silenced all, even the typing.

When Emma stepped sheepishly over the threshold, everyone snapped the covers closed on their computers and turned hostile gazes on her. All except Leader. He watched her enter and then cross the room without so much as blinking an eye. Emma ignored the others. She moved steadily toward him.

When she passed Monique's chair, the Second let out a long sigh of frustration. But then Emma was in front of Leader, who had turned his chair to face her as she approached.

"How do you feel?" This was the last question she had expected to hear from him.

"Fine," she answered, and then when his eyes darkened slightly, she amended, "I mean, I'm in pain but I'm okay. My arm hurts."

"It took the brunt of the hit," he informed her. "How's your head? Any pain?"

"Not really," she replied, shaking it a little because of the fog. "I'm a little surprised, because I thought maybe I had a concussion, but there's no trace of a headache now. My eyes are still a little sensitive to the light."

He nodded as if he had expected nothing less.

"Did I break a rib?"

"No. No fractures, fortunately. You're pretty bruised up, though."

She nodded. That she knew. But the lack of any fractures surprised her, considering how hard Scott had kicked her.

"Teach you to duck, I guess," Monique muttered. Leader shot her a severe look.

"If I had ducked, he would have gotten my head," she told Monique coldly, her eyes never leaving Leader. "And I hardly think I would have avoided harm then."

"No," he agreed, tone cooling a bit over that idea. "Scott admitted that he didn't modify or pull back. He would have killed you if he'd been even inches higher."

"I wasn't ready to defend," she admitted, remembering the lightning speed at which Scott had attacked her. "He's a lot faster than I am."

Leader nodded. "He's always been exceptionally talented." There was something strange about his tone, almost as if it lacked tone at all. He tilted his head to the side, peering at her. "What do you think?"

For a moment, she was sure he would turn to direct that question at someone else, but his gaze never moved away from her.

"Leader? What do I think about what?"

He lifted a brow but did not say a word. She sighed at that warning brow. She could not get away with pretending she did not understand him. She nodded. "I think Ilene is probably justified in thinking I'm a nuisance, but I'm really not trying to be one." Someone scoffed, Amos or Thomas, and she insisted, "I'm not!" She glared at their side of the table.

Leader slapped the tabletop with an open palm, though what that meant, Emma had no idea. "Who are you?"

They all answered, "We are the Guild," although not in perfect union. Monique took a little longer to respond and Leader shot her a stern look.

"Do you think you're trustworthy?" Leader asked. Emma glanced around, waiting for them to answer, but when her eyes returned to Leader, he was watching her intently. The question, she realized, was meant for her.

Emma did not know how to answer that. She dared take a moment to look away from him, into the middle distance where she could contemplate his question and the various possibilities of an answer.

Trustworthiness was such a strange value to assess. Emma knew she could be trusted. She had spent her life in the Guild, keeping its bizarre secrets even though she did not understand them, changing her cover every time they moved to a new location. She had been Obedient far more often than she had wanted to be. Not *always* Obedient, and never *perfectly* Obedient, but she tried.

"Yes," she finally announced, meeting his gaze once more. "I think, in general, I always have been. I do not know what kind of disaster I may have caused or be able to thwart ..." Someone inhaled sharply at that. "... but I certainly never wanted to lose your trust, Leader."

"What is it you wanted?" he asked, still with that deadened tone.

"A place to belong," she said decidedly. "That's all I ever wanted. But no amount of you telling me I belonged here made me feel like you believed it. Any of you." That last was a jab at Ilene, but it was apparently Monique who felt it, because she let out a pained breath.

Leader nodded. "We're talking about you because we think the Guild events that have happened over the past few days have been directed at you," he said, suddenly his regular animated self.

He snatched a page from the table and handed it to her. It was a still image of the Porsche that had shown up at the mansion the other day. The Porsche that had evidently thrown the Guild into a flurry, had caused Amos to steal Leader's car, and was a secret message Emma did not understand.

"This was sent to the mansion for *me*?"

"As a threat, actually, but, yes, we think for you."

Emma studied the car thoughtfully. It was an obnoxious color, and she wondered again why something this giant and expensive could be an insult or a threat to the Guild. It was a pretty nice car.

"Can I keep it?"

Amos laughed out loud. "You can't even drive."

"Not yet." She shrugged.

"No," Leader said but even he sounded a little amused. "It's already gone."

"What did you do with it?" Emma demanded, looking up at him. An eerie silence fell, and Emma wondered if she had inadvertently stepped into a center for discord.

"I sent it back home, with a few minor modifications."

That sounded ominous and Emma did not press him. "I do not understand how that could have anything to do with me, but I'll take your word for it."

Leader leaned back slightly to look her over. "It wasn't their first strike and it most certainly won't be their last." He glanced aside at the others before jerking his gaze back to hers. "I think Benjamin may be working for our enemies."

Emma stepped back so abruptly that she hit Monique's chair and jostled her arm painfully. "No," she denied, shaking her head. "No way."

"It's awfully convenient," Amos said in a quiet, concerned tone. "He suddenly showed up in your life everywhere you go, with a strong interest in you despite the rather marked age difference. He has the resources to whisk you away."

Emma shook her head in denial. "No. He likes me. He is interested in me because he *likes* me."

"He may very well be responsible for the attack on the mansion," Julianne offered, trying to be gentle but not willing to sugarcoat it for her.

"NO!" Emma shouted, silencing the room. "It doesn't even make sense. If he was the one who started the fire, how could he have done it when he was with me the whole time?"

"I don't think anyone believes he started the fire, Emma," Leader reassured her. "But the people he is working for may have arranged it."

She shook her head. "That doesn't make sense, either. What good would it do to have me be away from the mansion when it went up in flame? The rest of you would be out looking for me and it would all come to nothing." She shook her head, completely denying the possibility. "You have his old phone," she told Leader, turning an entreating hand toward him. "Do your voodoo and make it cough up its old conversations. I am sure you'll find that he's innocent. I'm sure of it."

"It came up clean," Leader said. He would have gone on but she interrupted him.

"See? That was the phone he had when he met me and when we talked as long as we did at the party. If there was anything incriminating, it would have come up."

"It was a plant," Leader replied, not gently, but attempting to break the news to her without shattering her. "If not, then his father would have shut the phone off the instant he'd gotten a new one."

"No," Emma replied in denial. She could not believe it. It made a lot of sense, but she would not believe it. Benjamin was sincere. He liked her. He was her first real friend and confidante. "You have proof? Where's your proof?"

"No, we don't have proof," Leader answered with a dark glance toward Thomas, who hurriedly returned to his typing. "But we have had our eyes on the

Stillwells for a while now. They have been involved in some very incriminating circumstances. Their political agenda is pockmarked with dark deeds."

Emma stared at him, incredulous. "They are a rich and politically minded family," she shot back, although she knew very little of their politics. "Of course, they are wrapped up in sketchy projects. So are you!"

Leader let out a breath almost like a scoff. "Indeed," he agreed, as if that was the strongest evidence against Benjamin.

Emma backed away again, this time carefully avoiding Monique's chair. "This is just a ploy to separate us," she realized as she spoke aloud. "You told me I could keep him and now you want to renege, so you decided he's a threat. That's all this—"

Leader was to her in two steps and had seized her chin in his fearsome grip. "I did tell you that you could keep him," he agreed, but his tone was ice. "But I would not need any reason to separate you. I could quite easily separate you for no good reason at all." That was true. She believed him. Her eyes stung with unshed tears. "I never said I was separating you from him. In fact, I would like you to invite him over so I can meet him."

He released her, and she fell, banging her arm as she did so that she cried out in pain. Monique came to her, glaring fiercely at Leader as she assisted Emma back onto her feet. She snapped something at Leader in a language Emma had not yet learned. It had Scandinavian tones, but she spoke it too quickly for Emma to hear any cognates or Latin roots.

Leader replied in the same language, colder than Monique's voice, but with as much authority as he ever managed in English and Mandarin—the two languages most frequently spoken in the House.

He seated himself in his chair again, holding Benjamin's phone aloft in one hand. With a short answer that Emma thought sounded like acquiescence, Monique plucked it from his hand and placed it gently into Emma's palms.

Chapter Forty

"One of the conditions I set you was that I get to meet Benjamin," Leader said to the air in front of him. Then his gaze contacted Emma almost forcefully. "That will be true of any man you date, but in this case I set it because I believe he may be a threat to the Guild."

"What will you do?" Emma asked. What if something Benjamin said made Leader believe he was a threat? Would he slit his throat and abandon him on some lonely highway? When Leader did not immediately answer, Emma went on, "Will you hurt him?"

Leader seemed about to say something explosive but at the last moment, after a shared glance with Monique, he said only, "No. That would only cause avoidable problems. If he is the threat I think he is, he will have a noticeable mark on his person. My meeting him could well be the only way his name could be cleared, if he's innocent." His tone displayed how likely he believed that was. "Call him. Invite him to dine with us."

Emma did not want to. She did not want him to see her bruised up and surrounded by her crazy family. But her Obedience was one of the conditions she had agreed to. She turned the phone in her hand and dialed his number. With one last pained look at Leader, which he did not acknowledge, she lifted the phone to her ear.

"Speaker," Leader ordered, and she complied with a sigh, pulling the phone down.

It rang. Once ... twice ... three times. She almost wished he would not answer. Then it picked up. "Quicksilver, is that you?" Benjamin asked on the other line.

"Yes," she answered with a small smile. Very aware of the scrutiny of the entire Senior Guild, she turned her back and paced a few feet away. She did not dare go any farther since Leader wanted to hear the conversation.

Benjamin laughed. "I thought you might be calling me soon. You're probably in need of your backpack."

Emma had forgotten about that. She let out a small laugh of her own. "Yes, actually! I'm sure I will. I did not go to school today."

"Because I stole your backpack?" he asked, laughingly apologetic.

"No."

He sobered. "Because of the fire? Was it your house? They wouldn't let me onto the street."

She glanced back over her shoulder at the table and the eyes on her. The air in the room turned tense the moment he mentioned the fire. She gave Leader a look pleading for help, and he gave a slight nod.

"It *was* my house, actually," she told Benjamin.

"Oh, Emma, I'm so sorry. Was the damage pretty extensive?" The entire Senior Guild tried to get her attention, either nodding or shaking heads, but she ignored them.

"I don't know." It was the truth. The house had looked fairly destroyed but the fireman said it wasn't so bad, so she didn't know. "I'm glad I wasn't in."

"Was anyone hurt?" It sounded like a genuine question, but the Guild again tried to get her attention. Leader waved them down like swatting pesky mosquitos.

"Not really," Emma said, letting her relief sound through. "My father and mother were out looking for me, and my sister was on a date. My brothers were God knows where, so we were all safe."

"They were looking for you?" he asked, concern tingeing his voice. "Were they pissed? Are you in a lot of trouble?"

Emma turned her back on the Guild again. "No," she answered honestly. "I actually think they were so relieved I didn't get hurt that they were pretty forgiving. I wasn't sure my father would be but once I told him where I was and assured him I was still a virgin, and let him know you would be happy to meet him, he relented."

"Whoa! Wait just a minute," Benjamin said with a laugh. "What was all that about me meeting him? I thought you said he was dangerous and would eat me or something."

"He *is* dangerous," Emma replied without looking back to see how Leader would take that. "Especially with boys dating his baby girl. But he was willing not to harm you if you will come to dinner."

Benjamin laughed again, good-natured about it all. "I would love to come to dinner, Quicksilver. When would be convenient?"

She had to look back at Leader for the answer to this question and was somewhat horrified when Leader mouthed, "Tonight."

"I would like to see you tonight," she said, playing for casualness even though her heart hammered in her chest. "Unless you're in real big trouble with your father?"

"Nah," Benjamin said. She could just picture his nonchalant shrug. "He yelled a lot and Mother assured me that she was highly disappointed in my skipping school again. He was more upset over my missing dinner with the Congressman."

The Guild reaction to that was almost verbal, so she stepped away a few more feet. "So, not the mayor, after all," she answered him. "Does the Congressman have snotty kids, too?"

"I don't know," Benjamin answered with a chuckle. "But if he had, I would have missed them, since I drove around for a couple more hours before I went home."

"What?" she demanded in mock severity. "And after your hurry to get home?"

Benjamin laughed at her tone. "Well, once I dropped you off, I thought better of my hurry." His tone changed to severe for a moment when he said, "And, by the way, don't you jump out of my truck without saying something to me ever again. I thought you fell out or something."

"I'm sorry," she said, truly contrite. "I was only overcome with worry for my family."

"I'm glad they're safe. When that cop told me I couldn't follow you, I almost hit him."

"Yikes. I'm glad you didn't. Picking you up from jail would probably not have improved your father's temperament."

"Don't I know it?"

Behind her, Leader cleared his throat, so Emma hurried on. "So, can you come tonight or are you grounded or something?"

"Grounded?" he laughed at the very idea. "My father would be hard-pressed to enforce a grounding. I can come, but I'm worried it might be a hard time on your family and I don't want to intrude."

Emma would have reassured him, but Leader spoke, "What did he say, Emma? I'm not letting you have free talking time with a boy I haven't met."

Emma blushed, afraid Benjamin would detect that he was on speaker. "Yes, Father," she said away from the phone. "I have to go, Benjamin. What do you say? Will tonight work?"

"Yes, yes, Quicksilver," Benjamin told her. "Reassure *Leader* for me. I'll be there."

"Seven o'clock at the hotel Beaumont on 8th. Penthouse," she instructed before quickly clicking the end button. The Guild reacted to his use of Leader's title. She could not let Benjamin hear that.

She spun toward them and lifted a pacifying hand at their myriad of reasons why he should "know to call him that."

"I told him," she said, and that had its own response.

"I told you! I told you she was a fool. She'll ruin us!"

"What could you have been thinking? This is an unparalleled disaster!"

"I can't believe this! You were warned! You were warned to keep certain things quiet."

"What do we expect from Twelve?"

"*Silence!*" Leader demanded and got an instant response. "Emma, explain."

Emma drew a pained breath and looked into Leader's eyes. They were by no means friendly, but compared to everyone else, he seemed warm.

"It was an accident," she admitted, and then quickly explained how she had become careless while talking to Benjamin and the word leapt out. She also told how she had accounted for it, which caused Monique to roll her eyes and mutter, "Amateur."

Leader nodded when Emma finished speaking. "It's workable. We'll explain it to Scott and Adam, and let Lara in as an annoyed sister. It's fine. Kids nickname their parents all the time ... probably. I'm just glad I was graced with something respectful, rather than what you called Leader during your tenure as Twelve, Julianne." She blushed but seemed smug, as well. Emma desperately wanted to ask about it but she didn't dare pry now.

"I think we're done here, for now," Leader announced, standing up. "Monique, see about dinner arrangements. Amos, get something for Emma to eat. I need her as healthy looking as possible. It will be hard enough to mask her injury as it is without her falling faint with malnourishment. Julianne, be sure to do a quick look before you leave today. Take Waylon and Piper with you to the job site. No mistakes.

"Thomas, pick up the boys and Lara and brief them on tonight's situation. I'll send you specific orders for each of them, but make sure they understand the immensity of this dinner. And be sure Scott understands that this changes nothing about his current status, and that if he displeases me, he and I will take a walk."

Everyone responded to their orders with quick nods then gathered up their papers and computers and left the room. Ilene and Emma were the only ones left. Leader turned toward Emma.

"Come here," he ordered, and waited until she was directly in front of him to say in a deathly cool tone, "I do not renege on my word, ever." He might as well have slapped her, for the force of his cool words rocked her to her core as easily. "Is that clear?"

"Yes, sir," she replied promptly.

"One day you're going to trust me," Leader said firmly. "I hope by then it is not too late."

The ominous sound of that was on a level with the idea of taking a walk with Leader. She had no desire to experience the meaning of either.

"Yes, Leader."

"You're lucky I forgave you yesterday for everything or I might be tempted to show you how I feel about you nearly blowing your cover."

She knew what that meant. She had a part to play and no boyfriend could stand in the way of that. If she could not effectively play her part while maintaining a relationship with Benjamin, Leader would bring the relationship to a swift conclusion.

"I will not slip again," she assured him. She meant it. Leader held *all the cards*.

"I know," Leader replied, completely secure in his hold over her. "Go get something to eat and let Julianne look you over."

"Yes, Leader," she said, and turned immediately to walk away from him. She heard him say a grim, "Come here," to Ilene then. Emma wondered if he would have severe or loverly words, but she did not stay to hear. Either would have been unpleasant, and Emma did not dare risk disobeying Leader by delaying to listen in on his private conversation.

She got an answer to her wonderment, though, when she was seated up to the table in the kitchen eating stew. Ilene came in. She had the slightest impression of a handprint on her face from an obvious slap. Her eyes were reddened from tears. Amos would have spoken, but Ilene shook her head, gathered a feast of fruit and a couple of sandwiches, and walked out again without a word. Amos shook his head after her retreating figure. *Yes*, thought Emma, *being Leader's lover must be trying indeed*.

Emma had doubts about this dinner. She was sure they could never make Benjamin believe they were a regular family.

When Thomas came through the door with Adam and Scott, he was swearing like a sailor and demanded Amos' immediate attention to some problem with Lara, who was not in attendance. Adam scowled mightily at Emma and skulked away. Scott slowly approached the giant chair she was sitting in. His face faded into a snarl, which suggested he had not come to apologize for harming her. He did not get any chance to do anything because Monique called to him from the next room.

"Scott, get in here!" she ordered, and Scott sprang away from Emma immediately.

"BYU, indeed," he snorted as he went. She glanced down at the college swag and quickly up at Scott's retreating figure. She vowed not to find herself alone with Scott any time soon. Whatever his antipathy toward her, she was not likely to change his mind, and quiet moments with him could mean serious injuries. Not for the first time today, she wondered if this morning's event had indeed been an accident.

But reminder of her outfit pushed away her worry over how her family would be perceived; she had to worry about herself. The room she had been allotted and was having to share with Lara was sadly lacking in appropriate attire. She searched both dressers, both closets, and even looked inside Lara's bedside table, but there was nothing. And little wonder: her clothing from yesterday had not been returned from the cleaner yet, and her room at home was charcoal. Yet she couldn't very well entertain Benjamin in pink BYU sweats and t-shirts.

"Monique?" she asked, peering carefully around the door to the room Monique and Julianne were sharing. She peeked first to be sure Scott wasn't in there receiving a punishment she would not want to see. He wasn't. He was sitting up to a table writing in a black leather-bound book.

Monique was seated on the bed flipping through a similar book. She looked up at Emma's call. Scott did not.

"Yes, Emma?" she asked, briskly as ever.

"Are we going to be able to salvage any of our clothing from the mansion? I don't exactly have anything suitable to wear to dinner tonight."

Monique shook her head. "No, the mansion is a wasteland, and we won't risk anything from there even if it's in good condition. I'll run by the store today."

"Thank you," Emma said.

She would have turned to leave but Monique said, "Scott failed to pick up any assignments from your teachers, but I assume you have the numbers of some of the students in your classes. Call them and find out what homework and reading you need to do tonight."

"Yes, ma'am," Emma answered. She hadn't even thought of that. She had Cara's number, and Cara would have access to every kid in school.

"Right now," Monique ordered.

Emma said, "Yes, ma'am," again and set off to do her bidding. With Cara's help it was fairly easy to track down the assignments she needed to complete. She avoided calling Brinley, in case Brinley thought she had skipped school due to abuse. Ms. James probably thought so since it was only the day after she skipped out of her meeting with the counselor.

When she was at the table in her room, in the middle of her reading assignment for literature, Monique came in and dropped a bundle of parcels on her bed, including five school uniforms in plastic garment bags.

"This should do for you," Monique said. "For a couple weeks, at least. I'll wait on any more wardrobe purchases until we know our next move."

"Thank you, Monique."

"You had better get dressed," Monique added. "Will you need help showering?"

"No, thank you," Emma replied quickly. "I can manage." Shower time was one of the few times of the day she could be assured of her privacy. She would not give it up easily.

It did cause some problems, since every move hurt and washing her hair was nearly impossible. Then Julianne was there to look her over and make sure she was okay, so her privacy was ruined, anyhow. Julianne washed and conditioned her hair for her, and then blow-dried and styled it down.

"I don't think you should wear a bra," Julianne cautioned her as she examined the injury. "It wouldn't hurt anything, but getting it on would be very painful. And besides, you should celebrate your youth as long as those things are still pointing up." Then in a soft aside, "You should probably still be resting, anyway."

Chapter Forty-One

When 6:30 rolled around, Julianne and most of the Guild was gone. Only Monique, Leader, Adam, Scott, and Emma remained. And Amos, who would evidently be acting as the chef. She had no idea why Lara was not present, but she didn't ask any questions about it since Leader and Monique both seemed strained around the eyes when her name was mentioned.

"This seems like a bad idea," Scott muttered as they assembled in the sitting room to welcome their guest. One threatening look from Monique silenced Scott.

The front desk rang up at ten to 7. "Send him up," Leader told the person on the other end of the phone. He allowed Emma to precede him to the door but bade the others to remain in the sitting room.

"Do you really think you will be able to ascertain his innocence tonight, Leader?" Emma asked while they waited.

"If he is who I think he is, there is no mistaking it."

The elevator gave a chime as it approached behind the doors. Leader punched in a code to allow them to open. He was fully on his guard, as if he expected an army to plunge out. But the only person there was Benjamin. He wore slacks and a jacket, and suddenly Emma was glad she had chosen the soft pink dress over the leggings she was considering. She was at least as dressed up as he was. In his hands he had a bouquet of paper-wrapped lilies and a bottle of wine.

"Good evening," he said cheerfully. Emma hurriedly took the wine from him hands so she could be close enough to widen her eyes at him. She briefly kissed his cheek and whispered, "Thank you." She was not just playing her part tonight. She was really very grateful that he had come. If he was the miscreant Leader thought he was... no! She wouldn't think that way. He wasn't.

"Father," she said as she turned. "This is Benjamin Stillwell. Benjamin, my father, Eric Harris."

"We met at the Lansing party," Leader said gruffly, and for a moment Emma held her breath, afraid he would be the man Leader thought. But then Leader offered his hand. Benjamin shook it and smiled.

"A pleasure to meet you again, sir."

"Yes," Leader replied, though not at all welcoming and with no pleasure. "Through here." He turned to lead the way into the parlor.

"Wow," Benjamin whispered and pretended to wipe his forehead. "I had forgotten I'd met him. He's intimidating as hell."

Emma nodded her agreement and hurried after Leader. In the parlor, Monique and the boys were seated on the couches, but they all rose to acknowledge Emma's guest. Monique put on her company smile and came forward.

"Benjamin Stillwell," she said, offering her hand. He leaned in and kissed both her cheeks.

"Mrs. Harris, how are you?"

"I am well. I am well. How is that sweet mother of yours? Well, I hope."

"Quite well," he replied with a nod. "She and my father both send their warmest regards. And condolences, too. When I told them that you were out of your house, they were most distressed." He then offered her the lilies. "I brought these for you, Mrs. Harris."

Monique smiled as she took them. "What a thoughtful boy! I'll put them in water right away."

She carried the flowers out and smiled over her shoulder as she went. Her ruse was alarmingly well played. For a moment, Emma stared at her in surprise that she could be so warm and inviting. Monique was generally the harsh and violent one. Emma felt as though she didn't recognize her as this sweet tempered housewife. A sharp glance from Leader, though, reminded Emma to maintain their cover.

Leader presented the boys. "These are my sons, Adam and Scott." Benjamin took both of their hands in turn and shook them, making polite chitchat.

Finally, Benjamin took the wine from Emma's hands and offered it to Leader. "I thought you might enjoy some of my father's first vintage," he said as he offered it.

Leader scowled as mightily as she had ever seen and did not take the bottle. "How old are you? Aren't you still in high school?"

"Yes, sir, I am. I'm a senior."

Leader gave a single abrupt nod. "You're too young to bring wine to dinner," he accused. "How did you buy it, fake ID?"

Emma wanted to cry out against the unfair treatment, but she dared not. And Benjamin was well capable of handling his own affairs. He smiled and said, "No, sir. I only use my fake ID to get into clubs." When Leader wasn't amused, he said, "I'm just kidding. I don't have a fake ID. The wine is from my house."

"Raid your father's liquor cabinet?" Leader asked, cold as ever.

"Ah, no, sir," Benjamin said, amusement leaving his tone completely. "I asked my mother to pick it up for me this afternoon."

"You said it was your father's vintage," Leader accused.

Benjamin glanced at Emma, but he said, "Yes, sir, it is. It was from a shipment sent from his vineyards overseas. I asked my mom to pick it up at the warehouse this afternoon, when she told me it was polite to bring wine to dinner."

"You're too young to bring wine," Leader repeated.

"I'll remember that for future reference," Benjamin promised. Only then did Leader take the wine and walk away toward the kitchen.

"Leave him alone, Leader," Adam said with an eyeroll at Benjamin. "Don't mind him. He's just touchy that little Em has a boyfriend. Come sit down."

"Little Em, huh?" Benjamin said, not a bit worse for Leader's wear. He nudged Emma in the side as they moved toward the available loveseat.

"We never thought it would happen, you know," Scott added, with a pointed look at Emma. A mean look.

"Stop it," Emma said, trying to be playful, but meaning what she said.

But Scott could defy her; he was higher in the Guild. "She's very ... Adam, what's that nicer word for annoying and selfish?"

Benjamin chuckled when Adam said, "Independent?"

"Yes," Scott agreed, looking back at Benjamin with a nasty smile. "Our sister is very *independent*."

Monique entered by then and shook her head playfully at Adam and Scott. "Don't tease your sister, boys," she chided. She flashed their guest a beaming smile. "Do you have sisters, Benjamin?" She sat down on the loveseat across from Emma and Benjamin.

When she sat like that, with her legs crossed, all brusqueness gone, she was the most beautiful woman in the world, Emma thought. It was a wonder Benjamin managed to look away and give Emma's hand a squeeze. He held onto her hand, to her delight.

"No. No siblings. It's just me and my parents."

"Tell me about your school. Do you like it at Mountain Park?" Monique probed, just exactly like an interested mother might question her daughter's boyfriend.

"It's an excellent school," he replied. He jerked his head to one side, moving the hair from in front of his eyes. "It's better than the last school I was at. West Hill."

"The military school?" Monique asked, managing to sound scandalized. "I should think so! Mountain Park is supposed to be one of the finest schools in the country."

"That's what I hear," Benjamin replied. He nodded politely as Leader returned to the room. He still looked as sour as before.

"Come here, lover," Monique said, patting the seat beside her. "Benjamin was just telling us about his school." Leader sat beside her and in that amazing way they had, they instantly appeared to be the devoted couple they portrayed at the Lansing party. Obnoxiously affectionate. Both her hands twined around the arm he rested almost inappropriately high on her thigh. "I bet you're a good student, aren't you, Benjamin?"

"Are you? Do you get good grades?" Leader demanded.

"Yes, sir," Benjamin answered without hesitation. "I wouldn't be welcome home with anything but perfect grades. My father is a task master."

"Grades are important in this world, boy, and should never be underestimated," Leader pronounced. "Emma has a 4.2 grade point average. Did you know that?"

Benjamin turned to grin at Emma and squeeze her hand again. "I'm not surprised, sir. She's smart."

"She's *very* smart," Leader said, but it sounded more like arguing than agreeing.

"Yes, sir," Benjamin answered, because what else could he say?

"Daddy," Emma said, desperately wanting to turn the conversation. "Benjamin said his dad travels a lot for business. Just like you."

Benjamin nodded. "He's an international legal consultant," he added. "His father's company, Stillwell Law, is a major firm now represented in more than 15 countries."

"Helping illegals into the states?" Scott asked. He was only teasing, but Benjamin responded vigorously.

"No, no! He generally works in conjunction with the United Nations. It's all very political and idealistic."

Leader said, "Hmm. Does that mean you're headed to law school?"

"If my father has anything to say about it," Benjamin said with a laugh.

"It seems like law school might only be the beginning," Adam guessed.

"Yes," Benjamin said with a deliberate nod. "It's a heavy workload, but I think I'll be up for the challenge."

"What college are you going to?" Monique asked. "Have you already started the application process?"

"Oh, yes, ma'am," Benjamin replied. "I have to apply to three US schools to satisfy Mountain Park's requirements, but I also elected to apply to two foreign schools. Harvard is my father's choice, of course, since it's his alma mater. And it undoubtedly has the best reputation in the way of law schools. But I think at least for my undergraduate I would like Cambridge."

"Prestigious," Leader asserted.

"Have you heard yet?" Monique put in with a scolding pat to Leader's arm.

"Oh, no, not yet," Benjamin answered with a laugh. "The deadline for most schools is January 1st, so there's time. And I won't hear from any of the schools until April, at the very earliest."

"Well, I sincerely wish you luck. Cambridge and Harvard are both excellent schools."

"Yes, ma'am," Benjamin said. He shifted slightly to look at Emma, who stared up at him with an encouraging smile.

"Emma's going to an eastern school," Scott added, cutting his eyes at Emma as if he was annoyed by her. His tone mirrored his expression. "Yale, probably, if she's smart enough."

Emma rolled her eyes. "Sarah Lawrence."

Monique let out a grunt of disbelief. "Princeton, Harvard, or Yale, Em. Every other school is inferior."

"Cambridge is the number one school in the world," Adam said. "I read that online the other day. It beat out Harvard."

"And where was Sarah Lawrence on that ranking list?" Monique asked with an innocent blink at Emma. Adam did not try to answer. It was not on the list.

"How do you maintain good grades when you skip school in the middle of the day to whisk my daughter away?" Leader demanded. His voice cooled the room. Adam and Scott glanced nervously at each other. Monique let out a small sigh.

Benjamin drew a sharp breath. "Wow," he whispered at Emma again and then smiled politely at Leader. "You're mad. I get it. I would be mad, too. But I assure you it only happened the once and will never occur again."

"Twice," Leader contradicted, holding up two fingers of the hand not occupied on Monique's thigh.

"Sir?" Benjamin asked, confused.

"I'm trying to determine your honesty, and it seems to me that you can't get your story straight. Did you or did you not take my daughter away from a perfectly educational field trip a few days ago?"

Benjamin looked toward the ceiling at the same time giving Emma's hand a particularly hard squeeze. She squeezed it back, wishing she could apologize for this ambush. She tried to interfere.

"Daddy, please!" But he cut her off with a wave of his hand.

"Well, Benjamin, what is it? Once or twice?"

"It is twice," Benjamin amended. "You're right, sir. I had forgotten."

"Will you conveniently forget tomorrow that you gave your word today not to whisk my daughter away from school anymore?" Leader pushed on. "How can I know she's safe with you if you can't even remember something as big as a day spent with my daughter?"

"Father ..." Adam began but he was silenced as well.

"What's next? You *say* you'll have her home by 10 but *forget* and keep her out 'til 1? You *say* your mother and father will be going with you to a play but *forget* and take my daughter to a rock concert, or an orgy?"

Scott and Adam laughed at that, earning them a severe glare from Leader.

"Daddy, stop it! Mother, please!" Emma pleaded. And there was no acting in it, her gaze sought Monique's and silently begged her to stop the interrogation.

"Eric," Monique put in gently. "I think that's enough."

"But if you hear of any 'orgies,' be sure to let me know," Adam said with a giant smile.

"Adam, go check on dinner," Leader ordered, cutting his eyes across at the young man.

"Yes, Father." Adam was prompt to rise and exit, chuckling as he went.

"Mr. Harris," Benjamin said with firm resolve. The tone pulled Leader's gaze back to him in astonishment. Emma pleadingly squeezed his hand but Benjamin plowed on. "Sir, I know you don't know me well and you don't like me dating your daughter, but I like her a lot and I am going to be careful with her. I assure you, Mr. Harris, if the curfew is 10, she will be in the door by 10. There's no chance in the world I would ever agree to a double date with my parents, but if you need to know where Emma is going and what she will be doing at all times, I will submit an itinerary to you. I do not smoke and the only drink I have ever had was wine at my father's foreign launch party, and only because my father insisted that I partake. I do not have a fake ID, have never had one, and in fact never had a need for one because I do not break the law. I wear my seatbelt. I have never had a traffic ticket. I believe in chivalry and will always show your daughter utmost respect. And I apologize for interfering with her schoolwork. I swear to you, *swear* to you that I will never do so again. I do wholeheartedly support the pursuit of education and I will not interfere."

Leader narrowed his eyes at the young man, dark pools measuring and weighing him. "Don't think I won't check up on you."

Benjamin only nodded as if he expected nothing less. Leader said, "I will accept your word, Benjamin Stillwell. And if you never, ever break it, I think we'll get along just fine."

"Yes, sir, I agree."

"Dinner is ready," Adam announced from the doorway.

Leader rose smoothly and offered his hand to Monique. "Shall we, my dear?" he asked, all traces of the interrogative monster were gone. He was as charming and delightful as Monique pretended to be.

Scott offered Emma a snarling smile as he left the room behind Leader and Monique. She shot him a scowl, but stayed behind with Benjamin to take up the rear.

"I am so sorry," she insisted, turning to face him and grabbing his hands. "You must believe me; I had no idea he would behave this way. When he asked me to invite you, I sincerely thought he wanted to meet you. If I had known—"

"Emma," Benjamin cut in with a gentle smile. "It's fine. I promise. I do not scare off that easily. He's just protective. It's fine."

"He didn't scare you?" Emma asked, relieved and surprised.

Benjamin let out a little laugh. "No, he terrified me. He's the scariest man I have ever had to impress. But I'm an impressive guy. He'll come around. And in the meantime, I get to see you, and that's worth it."

"Are you sure?" She was certain he would bolt as soon as he had a chance.

Benjamin very bravely leaned forward and kissed her quickly. "I am sure," he announced. They moved, hand-in-hand, toward the dining room. Before they reached it, he leaned toward her again and added, "Your mother's nice. Your brothers are jackasses."

She smiled at his daring. "Yes, they are," she agreed, and did she ever truly agree! Adam had at least been tolerable, but Scott was a jackass, plain and simple.

Chapter Forty-Two

The table was decorated with taper candles and crystal centerpieces in a semi-formal setting that Emma recognized very well. Scott and Adam sat at either end of the table and Leader and Monique were on one side together, leaving the other side for Benjamin and Emma.

Benjamin pulled Emma's chair for her and then sat beside her. Emma tried not to seem surprised when a maid, perhaps employed by the hotel, brought in their salad course. So, this is what Leader had meant when he sent Monique on "dinner preparation." Emma forced herself to eat the salad, even though it was fancier than she liked and had a strange flavor. Benjamin did not seem to notice.

"This is a delightful meal, Mrs. Harris," he complimented, every bit like he meant it. Emma did not know why she was certain he was lying, but she said nothing. Monique accepted his compliments with as little sincerity, and again Emma said nothing about it.

After a few awkward minutes of silence, Leader said, "Emma tells me your father owns go-karts."

Benjamin was caught with a mouthful of food and had to swallow and take a sip of his water before saying, "Yes. But that's nothing, really. Father owns half of Utah."

"And vineyards overseas?"

"Yes, sir, in Italy itself. He owns enough real estate to house a small country." Benjamin smiled. "And you, sir? Are you in real estate?"

"No," Leader answered, but did not elaborate.

"That's a very fine jacket you're wearing, Benjamin," Monique said as she patted Leader's arm gently, as if to tell him to settle down. Emma was relieved by her interference.

"I have no eye for clothing myself," Benjamin admitted with a rueful smile. "I still let my mother select my clothes, and she has never failed me." Emma found it hard to believe considering he had selected her clothes for their forbidden outing yesterday; she had looked beautiful. She had *felt* beautiful.

"Well, she has done you a good service. Did I understand from Eric that you were at Cara Winter's birthday party the night Emma went?" Her tone was the same lightheartedness she had been faking all evening, but something about her words caught Emma's attention. Monique's eyes, still smiling, took on a sharper cast as she waited for his answer.

Benjamin swallowed quickly again. "Yes. My family has been friends with the Winters as long as I can remember."

"They're really good people, the Winters," Monique said with a nod. "Cara attends school with Emma and Scott at Avanair. She seems to be well liked."

"She has an uncanny knack for making friends," Benjamin said with a short laugh. "She's like a sister to me, really."

"Not likely," Scott muttered. Benjamin ignored him.

"As close to a sister as I'm likely to get. She always invites me to her little gatherings. I was lucky to be able to go because my father was supposed to be in town and we were going to the Smith Symposium. He canceled at the last minute and left me free for the evening. I'm glad I went to the party, after all, since it gave me and Emma a chance to get to know one another."

Monique's hand on her glass seemed clenched until Leader placed his over the top and soothed her. Emma wondered what could be making her so angry.

"Well, our little Em had a great time at that party," Adam said in mocking, pinning Emma with a feisty grin. "Didn't you, Em?"

"Leave her alone, Adam," Leader cautioned.

"I saw you there that night, sir," Benjamin went on, ignoring Adam completely. "You stopped the fight, and incidentally salvaged what was left of Bryan Mc-Cormick's pride."

Leader studied him silently for a moment then said, "Strange. *You* managed to evade my notice that evening."

"Well, you were preoccupied," Benjamin allowed but something about this conversation was alarming for Emma. They seemed almost as if they were speaking in codes to one another. Codes Emma did not comprehend and had no part in. There seemed to be something in Benjamin's eyes that challenged Leader, although his tone was deferential in the extreme.

"I was attempting to salvage my daughter's modesty and reputation," Leader responded, the challenge in his voice clear to any Guild member. It was a musical challenge, though, and Emma wondered if there was the slightest possibility Benjamin had picked up on the danger of the situation.

"By embarrassing her in front of her friends?" Benjamin's voice was light and almost playful, but this was not a game Emma wanted him to be playing. She grabbed his hand under the table and he squeezed it reassuringly.

Benjamin did not stop, though. He hammered on, relentlessly challenging Leader. Emma feared that at any moment this would crash down around them all. Her breath froze in her mouth, and she wondered if Leader was armed.

"Mr. Harris, you have a very roundabout way of salvaging your daughter's reputation if you thought you achieved that by humiliating her in front of half the school and making them wonder about her safety in her own home." His smile was as dashing as Leader's could be, and as viperous.

"Teenaged wisdom never ceases to amaze me," Leader replied caustically, his eyes hard.

"Let's have the duck," Monique said suddenly, breaking into the conversation and rising to her feet. "I hope you like duck, Benjamin. It's a family recipe."

"I love duck," he answered, giving Emma's hand another reassuring squeeze. "Thank you, Mrs. Harris."

Emma found out very quickly that she did not like duck. She had rarely ever eaten meat anyway, since in general the Guild found other sources of protein to satisfy them. She could not force herself to eat more than a third of her meal before abandoning it. She wanted more than anything to have a regular salad or vegetables, or at least some of the highly nutritious concoction Amos made for dinner.

The conversation turned to local college sports and eventually hit the weather. Emma was pleased it had steered far away from her.

When dessert was served in fancy crystal dishes, Benjamin watched her to see if she would eat it. He knew well that she leaned toward nutritious eating, and the dessert did not resemble fruit or vegetables. She daringly lifted her spoon, gave him a pointed look, and took a bite. And almost gagged on the sweetness. Benjamin continued to watch her, amusement all over his face as she forced herself to swallow the spoonful with a straight face.

"It's no hotdog," he murmured for her ears only. She put down her spoon without looking at him and he laughed at her.

Amos came into the room before anyone had had more than two bites. His eyes were serious as he leaned down to whisper to Leader, who immediately sprang from his chair. His alarm silenced the room and drew every eye to him.

"Excuse me," he said as he dropped his napkin on his chair. "It was nice meeting you, Benjamin." He followed Amos from the room. Emma watched him go, concerned and not a little surprised by the abruptness of it all.

"What's that about?" Adam asked, watching Leader's retreat.

"I'm sure it's nothing," Monique answered, but her gaze was locked, as Adam's was, on the place where Leader had left them.

"Well," Benjamin said, drawing all eyes to him. "I should probably be going, anyway. My parents are expecting me home by 9."

It was nearly 8:30 and if it was true he was supposed to be home by 9, he was not likely to make it all the way back to Draper in time. Monique politely asked if he'd had enough to eat, and offered to package his dessert to go, which he declined. They all made polite chitchat again as they led Benjamin to the door. Emma followed him into the elevator, though Monique almost grabbed her and pulled her back into the penthouse.

"I'm going to walk him out," Emma said, eyes staring at the hand Monique placed on her arm. "I'll be right back." Monique pulled her hand back and smiled, keeping up appearances.

"Of course," she said with her plastered on company smile. "Not too long, though, Emma." Her eyes flashed a warning.

"Yes, Mother." She hit the button to close the elevator door and was relieved when it whirred immediately into motion, taking her and Benjamin away from the prying eyes of her family.

It was silent for two floors before Emma could get up the courage to say, "I'm so sorry they were so ..."

"It's fine," Benjamin said but he didn't sound as confident as he had before dinner. He stared straight ahead at the elevator doors, hands in the pockets of his slacks.

"They were awful to you," Emma whispered, trying her hardest to get him to look at her. She turned so she could touch his arm. "I'm sorry they were so ..." Again, she could not find a bad enough word.

"Emma," he said firmly, finally looking her in the eye. "It was fine. I already told you, your father is terrifying and your mother's a gem."

"But you're mad," she said, pretty sure she was right about that.

"I'm not mad," he argued with a slight shake of his head. "Not exactly. I just ... You're so *different* around your family, Emma. You're so quiet and reserved, as if you're afraid to speak up. When it's just you and me you have a really daring personality. I don't like that you hide who you are when your parents are around."

"But I'm not hiding, Benjamin. I was just nervous."

He sighed and said, "It's just that I'm not sure who you are, because when you're with your family you're kind of robotic, but when you're alone with me you can be playful and sassy. Which one of those girls is the real you?"

She stepped back from him and said, "Both," in a serious, hurt tone. "You don't get to dictate who you want me to be, Benjamin. I am who I am."

"That's not what I'm trying to do," he argued, tone fraying into annoyance. "You were just so passive." He shook his head and made a frustrated sound in his throat. "Until today, you never exactly struck me as a passive person. I was surprised." The expression he shot at her was disappointed. It reminded her of the way Leader usually looked at her. "I'm not trying to make you into anything."

His disappointment cut her. She flamed into anger. "When I'm around my family, I tend to wash into the background. There are a lot of them, and, I'm sure you noticed that they require a lot of energy. Also, I can never do or say anything right with my parents, no matter what they wanted you to believe." She crossed her arms beneath her chest and looked away from him. "So what if I am a little more daring when I'm one-on-one with someone? It's not like I just transform my personality when I'm with *you*."

Benjamin scoffed at the tone. "Don't get self-righteous—"

"Don't tell me what to do!" she snapped back. The elevator doors slid open to the main lobby and she bit off the rest of her words. He stood in the elevator a few moments, just breathing. When the door tried to slide shut, he put out a hand to stop it. He glared over at her once before he stalked out. She followed him.

"You're just leaving like that?" she demanded in a hushed whisper, not wanting the hotel workers and doormen to hear their argument.

"You're not listening to me, anyway," he answered, not bothering to lower his voice. She followed him from the hotel and out to where his truck was illegally parked in a handicapped space. She caught his arm and pulled him to a stop just before he reached for his door.

"I'm listening," she insisted, feeling a rising panic. "Don't leave mad. I'm listening."

He turned with a sigh and leaned back against his car door. "I'm worried about you, Emma," he said, tone softer than before. He shook his head at her in frustration, insisting, "When your father speaks to you, you clam up. I watched it that night at Cara's party. You stood there, white as a sheet, and let him speak cruel words to you in front of half the kids at your school. And then, as if he had not just humiliated you, you hopped to obey him when he crooked a finger. And then tonight? He was unconscionably rude to me, and I pretended not to notice and laughed it all off, but you just sat there, like he can do whatever he wants, and you'll let him."

He was right. However painful his words were in general, he interpreted her correctly. But he did not understand the reality of her life. She always let everyone do whatever they wanted because she was so far beneath them all.

"I know."

"Are you *that* afraid of him?" Benjamin asked, concern all over his face and dripping from his voice.

Emma shook her head but the answer was yes. She was afraid of Leader. She had felt his anger and his warped form of justice too many times to simply shrug it off and face him boldly. She saw him pull a knife on someone for far less than arguing or challenging his authority. Emma *was* afraid of him, but not the way Brinley was afraid of her abusive father or the way a teenage girl with strict parents fears retribution. There was no easy explanation for the way she behaved around Leader. She could not tell Benjamin why she faded to the background and let people walk all over her. The truth was scarier than fiction. Besides, Guild business was not permitted to be shared with him. His concern, though, was genuine.

"If you're that afraid of him, I have to wonder how he treats you," Benjamin said quietly with a shake of his head.

Leader's forgiveness yesterday had done its duty, Emma realized with self-loathing that it had soothed her into thinking Leader cared about her. It made her think he had her best interests at heart. But, looking into the true concern in Benjamin's eyes, Emma had to face the truth: Leader's forgiveness was just another move in the chess game that was her life. He used his forgiveness as a pawn to placate and manipulate her into feeling grateful. Her gratitude made her forget that Leader was the reason the others in the Guild treated her so carelessly. His example and the way he treated others was the standard by which everyone else lived. His anger fell through the chain, being taken out again and again—superior to subordinate—until it inevitably fell on Emma's head, whether it was meant for her or not.

"I'm sorry I didn't stand up for you," she whispered. And she meant it. She really was sorry, but she did not know how she could change it.

Benjamin pulled her into his embrace. "That's not what this is about," he shot back in exasperation. "It's not about *me* at all. I can take care of myself. I'm just worried about *you*."

She allowed herself to be hugged until his tightening arms made her wince and she extricated herself carefully.

"You have been favoring that arm all night," Benjamin said, eyes narrowed toward her right arm. "What's wrong?"

"I'm okay. It was an accident on the mats today. I'm pretty bruised up."

His eyes narrowed as if he did not quite believe her, which rankled because this time she was really telling the truth.

"How did it happen?" he asked, darkness taking over his tone.

Emma shook her head. "Not my father, Benjamin. My brother. He kicked before I was ready to defend and knocked me to the ground. I swear to you that's what happened. My father was really angry with him for being careless."

Benjamin carefully pulled her closer and kissed her softly. "Sorry I was mad."

"It's okay. You had a right to be. I should not let my fear guide me."

He kissed her again until it took her breath away and she had to back away. She smiled up at him. "I think you passed the test, though. I don't think he'll try to get rid of you."

He chuckled. "That's a relief. But I guess I better live up to my word and not interfere with your education again. That seemed to be the biggest offense in his eyes."

She nodded. "I actually think it was less about school and more about deception. He likes to be informed and in control, so when you show up and whisk me away, he can't control it. That pisses him off."

"When can I see you again?" He winked, adding, "Preferably alone."

"This weekend," she promised, running her hand gently across his back. "Bring your itinerary and you can take me away all evening." She smiled at his eyeroll. "I'll tell you all of his insane rules then." She tried to pull away.

"Tell me now," he insisted, keeping her pinned against him.

"No way," she denied with a toss of her head. "If I tell you tonight, I might never see you again. If I wait until this weekend, I at least get to see you one more time."

"If tonight did not scare me off, I don't think any rules can," he scolded her, sliding his hands down her back. She stepped immediately out of his arms, remembering Leader's insistence that their physical relationship remain chaste. "Fine. Keep your rules. I'll see you this weekend."

She scoffed playfully. "We'll see. Maybe I'm washing my hair."

"Good," he answered, opening his passenger back door. "I like clean hair." He reached in and retrieved her backpack, handing it to her good arm. Then he climbed into his driver seat.

She smiled at him as he started his obnoxiously loud engine and put his truck into reverse.

He rolled the window down and called, "I forgot to tell you that you look beautiful tonight. Your father was staring me down, so I lost my nerve."

She blushed. "Thank you."

"Call you tomorrow, Quicksilver," he promised and drove away.

Chapter Forty-Three

Emma startled awake. Something pulled her out of sleep, but in the darkness of her room, she could not detect anyone or anything. She pushed the covers away, at the last moment remembering to use only her left arm since her right arm was still throbbing from Scott's spectacularly illegal kick yesterday. She sat up and grappled with the lamp and her textbooks on the nightstand before she found her phone. One touch of the button showed her it was only three in the morning. Why was she awake?

"What does that mean?!" Leader shouted from another room, startling her again. She lay back down with a frustrated sigh. She missed the mansion. The hotel was too small to keep her in her state of ignorance. Ignorance, she discovered, was a commodity in the House.

She heard another speaker, probably Amos, speaking quick, urgent words. Emma gave another frustrated sigh and tried to bury her head in the pillow. She did not know if Monique was sending her to school tomorrow, but if she was, Emma would need to sleep. Even if she wasn't, Emma would need her full eight hours to be able to train and then deal with the Guild all day.

She closed her eyes and tried to imagine sheep and balloons and other soothing ideas that might allow her to fall back into precious slumber. When sleep did not immediately come, she rolled carefully onto her side to look at Lara's bed. It was too dark to see very well, but Emma thought it was empty. Sitting up, she used her phone flashlight, shining it toward the other bed. It *was* empty. Where had Lara slept? Unless she was the one talking with Leader. She missed dinner; maybe she was sharing her excuses even though everyone in the Family knew Leader did not allow excuses.

A loud bang accompanied by an assault of light burst over her as the door to her room was thrown open. Emma could not help but cry out in alarm. It was only Ilene, but she looked frantic and called abruptly, "Get up, Emma. Throw some shoes on. We need to leave." And then she was gone. Emma heard her repeat the orders to the boys in the next room.

Emma Obeyed, smashing her feet into the new sneakers Monique had bought her yesterday. Emma took the time to grab a jacket and her backpack. She was all the way to the door before she remembered to go back for her phone, and Benjamin's.

"Emma!" shouted Ilene from somewhere else in the suite.

"Coming!" she called, hurrying out.

"Festino!" Ilene answered in Latin. Emma followed the icy voice into the elevator entryway. Scott, Adam, Waylon, and Piper were with her. Emma was pleased to note that Adam and Scott had also grabbed up some personal items, so she was probably not being silly to bring her backpack along.

"Hurry!" Ilene said but this time it seemed to be directed at the elevator.

Leader came around the corner. "What, are you an idiot?" he accused her, ferocious with his criticism. He pointed a finger beyond them to a locked wooden door. "Use the stairs!"

Ilene did not answer him, only moved immediately to unlock the wooden door with the swipe of a card. She led her little exit party down the steps. Waylon held the door for them all to pass through. Emma looked back once at the last moment, but Leader had already moved away. This appeared to be the second night in a row he would not sleep.

"Where are we going?" Emma asked Waylon, who was behind her and urging quickness on the steps. It was hard, because her backpack was heavy, and she couldn't adjust it very well because of her injury.

"I don't know," Waylon answered. When he saw her struggling, he grabbed her backpack and slung it on his own shoulder. "Hurry," he urged in his quiet way.

By the time they got downstairs and through the lobby, three Guild vehicles were parked under the portico. Waylon motioned his head toward the black SUV and Emma hurried into the backseat. Waylon tossed her backpack in at her as he climbed in beside her. Piper jumped into the passenger seat. Amos was in the driver seat already, and as soon as Piper's door shut, he jerked the vehicle into drive. One of the other cars, the one with Scott, Adam, and Ilene, followed right behind him.

"What's going on?" Piper asked as she tried to buckle her seatbelt in the moving vehicle. Emma was glad Piper had asked because Emma was curious and didn't know what to say. Besides, she was having twice the struggle with her seatbelt as Piper was. Once his own seatbelt was secure, Waylon leaned over and clasped the safety belt for Emma. She gave him a wide-eyed expression of thanks and settled back against the leather upholstery.

"We're going underground," Amos replied. His concentration was all on the road, as if at any moment he expected to see it disappear.

"Underground? Like caves?" Emma had a chill thinking about being in a cold, clammy cave all night.

Amos gave a bark of laughter, but his eyes never left the road. "No," he answered with gentle teasing in his voice. "Underground, like incognito."

"Why?" Piper asked, an edge of irritation in her tone.

"Have we been compromised?" Waylon asked gently from the backseat beside Emma. His face was crumpled in concern. Emma saw his chest rise and fall with nervousness. Since he was over ten years older than Emma, seeing his worry made her own heart pound nervously.

"Courage," Amos replied, shooting a glance at Waylon through the rearview. It seemed to be a glance of warning. Yet, Amos' next words were not reassuring, nor did they promote courage. "We *have* been compromised." A grim silence answered that. Waylon drew a long, heavy breath, and then his emotions faded from his face. Somehow, he had been able to deal with his fear in a way Emma did not yet know how.

Emma did not know what "compromised" meant but she had a sinking feeling. What if Leader had been right about Benjamin? What if he had only been a plant to destroy the Guild? She had a tough time imagining how a teenaged boy with no connection to them could accomplish such a feat, but she feared it. What if Benjamin did not like her at all, but only wanted to use her to find out about Guild business? If that was true, he would have a long wait because Emma did not *know* anything about the Guild. Not really. Not anything valuable, like what they were doing or why. All she knew was what *she* was supposed to do: learn, grow, and Obey.

"Is it … Was it Benjamin?" she asked, terrified of the answer.

"No," Amos replied. Then he chuckled again. "Listen to you, terrified back there! No, Emma, you will be happy to know that Benjamin is as clean as anyone I have ever investigated. Cleaner, actually. Almost alarmingly clean. But he was not why we were compromised."

"Why, then?" Piper shot back, eyes glowing with intensity in the darkness.

"Lara," Amos said. He did not elaborate.

"Where is she?" Waylon was Lara's direct superior in the Guild. His tone was lightly tinged with concern and frustration.

"Hopefully with Monique by now," Amos answered confidently. "And if I know Monique, nothing will stand in her way. We might be doing some of our own 'compromising' tonight." The smugness of his tone suggested someone would not appreciate what the Guild might do. Emma sat back against the seat and watched the lights of the city whiz past her head, trying not to worry about what might be waiting out there in the dark.

"Sometimes," Waylon said in his most philosophical voice, "I think the Guild spends more time in its vehicles than all other places combined; as if we can't bear to stand still."

Emma smiled at that idea, and silently agreed.

Waylon woke her when they reached their destination. They were in a large parking garage like the ones at airports, except this was cleaner and brighter with giant fluorescent lights in the ceiling. The wall in front of their parking stall was marked with a giant numeral **III**. Ilene's car was parked several spaces down in **VI**. Across from them on the other side were six stalls all marked with the numeral **I**. Five of them had cars she had never seen before, but all extremely expensive. *Did these all belong to Leader?* she wondered. She saw other cars parked deeper in the cement-walled garage. Most were concealed with canvas covers. There was a stark unfamiliarity about the place. Emma felt goosebumps climb up her arms as she looked around in the eerie quiet. The piece of this that was causing her unease was the quiet, she realized. Parking garages were notoriously noisy places—of coming and going, car horns, and human chatter and hubbub. No garage Emma had ever seen was as quiet as this one.

Amos slid a hand to her shoulder, pushing her toward the end of the garage, away from the quiet and the old tarp-covered vehicles. There was an elevator at the cement wall nearest the empty stalls marked **I**. As Emma came abreast of Scott and Adam, she saw they were both looking around curiously. Like her, they seemed to be trying to figure out where they were or what this place could be.

The elevator required a key to enter. Amos extracted his key ring from his jeans pocket and slid it into the lock. He turned it but nothing happened. For a moment, he only stared at the door then he smiled almost ruefully. Covering a key panel with his hand to block it from the view of the others, Amos keyed in a code. Emma watched his shoulders in the silence. She figured out the code despite his attempt to shield it. If it was a standard 10-key panel, anyway.

Five-five-seven-four-two-zero-three-seven-five-one. She heard it in the tones that sounded with his movements. Emma could not keep herself from hearing and remembering useless information like this. She would never need it, because she had never been permitted to leave the Guild House alone in her life, and she doubted that regime would be changed under the current circumstances. Additionally, if she did not have access to the key, she could never get in on her own, anyhow.

A tired, silent group climbed into the oversized elevator once the doors slid away—one vertically into the ceiling, two horizontally into the walls. The elevator car was big enough that they could have probably driven right into it with room to spare. Emma looked around at the slightly mirrored chrome interior. She caught Adam's gaze in the surface of one wall. He pulled a face at her. She turned her head to watch Amos hit a series of unmarked buttons on the inner panel. Amos crossed to the other side of the elevator and turned to face the back wall. Ilene joined him and, after giving them curious looks, so did Piper and Waylon. Emma followed, squeezing past her superiors to stand beside Amos. He reached out a hand and placed it gently on her shoulder while they rode.

The elevator moved smoothly. The only reason Emma even knew they were moving at all was a soft chime for every floor. After five dings, the back wall opened onto a lighted room. The floor was carpeted in green and the walls had been painted a soft cream. The only adornments were several framed mirrors on the opposite wall.

"What is this place?" Adam asked as Amos led them out of the elevator.

"It's a safe house," Ilene informed them in a cool voice. She glanced around, taking in the cream-colored walls and the stillness in the air. "We call it the Bunker."

"So, we *are* underground," Emma stated unhappily. Scott rolled his eyes at her.

Amos shoved Scott's shoulder, but he smiled at Emma as he answered, "Kind of." Emma scowled in confusion, trying to decide how something could be "kind of" underground. Wasn't the nature of prepositional phrases decisive where "underground" was concerned? Did not something have to be under the ground to be considered underground? Emma let it go, though, too tired to argue semantics.

A large archway in the left wall led out into a giant living area. There were couches and large lounging chairs on one side of the room, and shelves housing a vast number of books in another section. The kitchen area was in a corner next to a long table with exactly twelve chairs. It had been a long time since Emma had seen a table in the Guild House that could seat the entire Guild. These chairs had the vaguely familiar embossed numbers on them, too. They were etched in silver paint on the wooden back of each chair.

Another archway led to a long hallway across the room. The hallway L-turned right at the end and became stairs going up. A shorter hallway off to the right of the living room had several doors on either side before becoming stairs going up half a flight. The stairs ended in familiar black mats. Emma assumed that must be the training rooms, although she had never seen a set of training rooms placed so near the family living space before. Although, Emma realized, thinking back to the key and the code to access the elevator, it was not likely civilians would wander in looking for the mall.

From what she could see from her quick glance around the Bunker, with its vaulted ceilings and large open floorplan, it could probably swallow the mansion whole.

Emma examined the couches and looked at the framed art on the walls in the library section. The floors were concrete and covered in large, decorative rugs. Only the kitchen had tile, black and white in checkerboard fashion. Emma amusedly thought it was a big enough space that they could play live chess if they had more people to be pawns. It was beautiful, Emma thought, lacking only windows to bring in a softer light than the overhead fluorescents.

"Okay," Amos said, turning to face them. "I do not know when Leader will be joining us, so I'll run you through everything briefly. He will probably give you a more elaborate run-through eventually.

"Through there," he motioned toward the short hallway to their right, "is Leader's office and the Office Suite. If you continue through the second door and down the stairs, you'll get to the infirmary, storage, and the pool." He gestured upward toward the mats Emma could see. "Up the stairs is Training. We have the privilege of having a complete Training Suite in the Bunker. Expect to make use of it all."

Amos pointed toward the other hall, across the vast room from them. "Sleeping quarters. In the safe house, everything comes in 12, so there are 12 rooms. Your room is marked with your Guild number. In your room, you should find everything you need, such as toilet paper, hairbrushes, and all that. Each room is equipped with its own shower and toilet." Emma's eyes widened at the unexpected luxury of privacy. Amos winked at her. "I know; it's an amenity we are going to enjoy as long as we're here. There won't be any clothing yet, but Ilene and I will get to the warehouses downstairs soon. I'm sure they will have anything we need, including toothpaste and deodorant." He waggled his brows playfully at Adam and Scott. "Because we are going to want to locate *that* as soon as possible." Adam rolled his eyes, smiling at Amos. Scott only scowled.

"If you continue down the sleeping quarters to the stairway headed up, you'll reach Leader's room. I don't think I need to remind you that, without an invitation, you are not permitted inside his room. He's possessive of his privacy, so don't tempt him to punish you.

"Here is the library," he motioned toward the shelves. "Three thousand volumes last I did inventory, so no one will get bored. Over here is the living room. Don't get too excited about the television; it's closed-circuit. Leader does have several hundred old movies in his office that he might be persuaded to let you watch, if it pleases him.

"The kitchen, of course, is over here," he went on, motioning to the tiled section of the room. "Two ovens, ranges, dishwashers, and microwaves, although Leader's feelings about microwaving food has not changed. If you're hungry, there is always food, however not until I get the load brought up. Set meal times will be arranged, as is usually the case when we're locked in together." That had an ominous feel to it. Emma was not the only one to pull a face.

"No one may enter the elevator without permission. Don't even try because it requires a code and will lock you in if you input any characters out of sequence. The lights are all on a timer. They change on their own, even your bedroom lights, so don't touch the lighting panels. If for some reason you want your room fully dark in the middle of the day, I can reprogram for you. And, let's see … Leader will probably post a schedule after he discusses our situation with us tomorrow. Senior Guild will still meet for Summit unless Leader says otherwise."

Amos looked into the glossy, sleepy eyes of his audience and softened. "I think that's all you need for now. You can go to bed."

"How long are we going to be here?" Emma dared to ask, thinking suddenly of Benjamin and their tentative date for the weekend.

Amos studied her face for a long moment. Then he looked at each of the others. "I don't know," he admitted. "But Leader usually doesn't send us to the Bunker unless he plans for us to be here awhile."

Emma's heart sank. She pulled out Benjamin's phone, but it was no use. There was no service in this cement tomb.

Amos' eyes caught sight of the phone and announced, "I need your phones!" to the people retreating toward the sleeping quarters. "All the phones need to be turned over to me for reprogramming."

He accepted Emma's phone and then waited expectantly until she also turned over Benjamin's. As she watched him slip the phone away into his pocket, her heart sunk even further. She had no idea where she was, but it was far away from Benjamin. The worst part was that he had no way of even knowing what happened to her.

After handing over his phone, Adam motioned toward an old-fashioned telephone hanging on the wall. "Is that a payphone?" He sounded skeptical.

Amos glanced at it. He cut his eyes back to the others. "It doesn't call out," he announced gruffly. Then, when they only stood there staring, he said. "It's just decorative. Go to bed." He motioned toward the sleeping quarters with his head.

Emma's room was the first door on the left in the hall. It was decorated with dark pictures of rocks and waterfalls. The bed linens were a dark blue, as were the towels in the restroom. It was not what she would have chosen, if she had ever been given a choice, but it would serve very well as her prison. After investigating the contents of the closets and dresser drawers, Emma found her only delight: the lock on the bedroom door. She experimented, locking the door and trying the handle to feel that it was secure. She never had a door that locked the rest of the Guild out. In the mansion, and in the condo in New York, there was no such thing as privacy.

Emma locked the door again, then, leaving it that way. She went to her bed, slipped out of her shoes, and fell asleep thinking of Benjamin.

Chapter Forty-Four

Emma awoke to Scott pounding on her locked door.

"Get *out* here!" he was shouting, more annoyed than angry.

Emma had to Obey him, no matter how he phrased his commands. She scurried to unlock the door before he caused an even bigger scene. He looked tired and not just a little frustrated. He presented her door in a way that meant "What the hell?" without having to say the words.

"What do you want?" she asked, not nearly as politely as she ought to have spoken to her direct superior.

"Leader is calling the Guild to breakfast," Scott snarled back. He reached for her but she backed away. "Get out here."

"I need to get dressed," she countered, backing away faster. He would brook no delays, though. He followed her and snatched her arm at the elbow. Ignoring Emma's protests, he dragged her into the hall and the several steps toward the kitchen before she wrenched herself free.

"I'm coming," she snapped, attempting to regain some composure. It was not easy to do with mussed hair, sleepy eyes, and Cougar pajamas. She preceded him to the dining room, where the rest of the Guild was mostly assembled. Lara was still missing, and Monique was not in her place, but Leader was standing at the head of the table, impatience in his eyes, and mouth turned down. She hurried to her seat and sat down, aware of every eye in the room. How long had they been waiting?

"Now," Leader said once Scott and Emma both were seated, "we had some security glitches this week that endangered the Guild and put us at risk. I have known for several weeks that we were being targeted. At first, I thought maybe it was CIA just starting to catch up to us in our new location. I was unable to substantiate that, and after talking to the Director, I have been assured that the

Agency has backed off its claims against me. I have fairly strong suspicions we are being targeted by a rival guild trying to shift the balance of power."

Those words startled Emma. *Rival Guild?* She had no idea there was such a thing. It never occurred to her all this time that the Guild did not stand alone. There was no reason why there shouldn't be others, she realized in awe. Her Guild could not be the only one in all the world. Except, until this moment, Emma had really thought it was.

"It's annoying," Leader went on in his darkly musical voice. "But it's as well you get used to it. In any place when we're under cover, if at once we are discovered, it's only a matter of days before Arrow Guild locates us. They are almost as sophisticated, with many resources. Of course, they are undertrained and not as well-developed. Fortunately for us, they are not well-organized, either. We can counter because we have well-honed systematic responses to attack.

"I was pleased with our response time last night, especially as it has been many years since we had a drill. Ilene, you did well in opening the Bunker and getting the Junior Guild secure. Amos, I have been over and over your security routine and found nothing wanting. We're safe here because of you, and for that I am immensely gratified."

"Is Lara okay?" Piper asked from her seat down the table from Emma. Her green eyes pierced Leader, daring him to answer truthfully.

Leader's congenial mood evaporated in the face of Piper's question. "She's alive and well enough. She was foolish; she trusted when she should not have, and for that she almost lost her life." Piper shook her head slightly but, at a dark look from Leader, cleared her face of emotion.

"Then, is it definite that the threats sent to the Guild were because of Lara?" Thomas asked with a quick glance down the table at the Junior Guild. "The Porsche, the letters, the attack ..." He met Emma's eye. She raised her brows at him for his scrutiny. "All of it?"

Leader looked to Amos, who said, "As far as I can tell. They all smack of the same crude mind, and it would be incredible to believe that we would be attacked from multiple parties all at the same time."

"Although, there is a precedent," Leader toned in. "It has happened at least twice that I know of, according to the Guild Book. I'm not borrowing trouble, though. The Bunker will keep us safe while we track and respond to the attacks."

"How do we respond from inside the Bunker?" Scott asked. For a wonder, he did not look angry or disinterested. This was a fascinating topic for him to discuss. It was all disturbing for Emma, though. She liked things to run smoothly.

"I have my methods," Leader replied enigmatically. He looked up suddenly as Monique entered the room from the sleeping quarters hallway. She looked tired. Her eyes were bloodshot and ringed with dark circles. She took her place at the table with her usual deadly grace, ignoring the silence that fell around her and all the searching gazes.

"Everything set?" Leader asked, capturing Monique's eye.

"Yes, Leader," she breathed at him. She then leaned back in her chair marked with a silver **II** and glanced around the table in the silence.

"Where's Lara?" Adam asked bravely, though he winced when Leader's hard eyes fell on him, and then again when Monique narrowed her black eyes. Adam had a right to ask, Emma thought. He knew Lara best, as he was her direct subordinate. Also, to Emma's sure knowledge, they often shared a bed, despite the part they played as brother and sister. He had reason to be concerned.

"She's in the hospital wing," Leader replied, with no intention of elaborating.

"She's stable," Julianne assured the room, ignoring the glare Leader shot her way. "She'll recover with not much worse than bruises."

"And, I hope," Monique retorted, "a more cautious attitude." She looked at Leader. "She said she trusted her professor. Trusted him! I could strangle that girl."

"I think she's been through quite enough," Julianne answered back archly.

"Stop it," Leader ordered, lifting a hand to silence them. "Lara was extremely foolish to trust anyone outside the Guild." He waved a warning finger around the table. "Her professor sold her out and for that she was kidnapped and grossly mistreated. They probably hoped to keep her for ransom but did not anticipate my ability to track my minions. But tracking did not save Lara from harm last night.

"*We do not share Guild information outside of the Guild.* Can I be plainer? Out there, with them—with everyone—we play a part. It is only inside the Guild with your fellows that you can truly be *you*. Make friends out there, by all means, but only to serve the Guild. Your entire existence is to serve the Guild. And if that doesn't suit you ..." He drew a knife, some kind of scary-looking switchblade, from his back pocket and lay it down in front of him on the table. "... I can take care of you quickly and cleanly."

His threat hung in the air for too long while every one of his subordinates digested the idea that Leader threatened to kill them if they failed to serve. Fear fluttered in Emma's stomach, reminding her that her relationship with Benjamin was not in service to the Guild; it was for her own pleasure. Would Leader *now* renege on his offer to let her keep her boyfriend?

He left the blade on the table as he spoke into the now uneasy stillness. "A tragedy like last night's serves to remind me that I have obligations to my Guild, to your protection and education. Lara's defection was my fault as much as anyone else's. Had she been instructed more thoroughly, watched more closely, something like this would never have happened."

Emma was dubious. How could Leader possibly watch *more* closely? He already saw and detected more than should have been possible for one man.

"It was this oversight, more than anything, which made me realize we could benefit from some time away from the World."

He finally sat down, suddenly all businesslike. "Ilene will be making up schedules for everyone. These schedules will include study time, workouts, meal preparation and other chores, personal hygiene schedules, mat times, and privilege periods. You are to adhere to her schedule strictly. I should not have to remind you—but I will—that you are to sleep in your own rooms, in your own beds, unless you have clearance from me to do something different." He looked pointedly at Waylon and then over at Thomas. "Is that clear?"

Everyone answered affirmatively, although Waylon and Thomas did not reply with much haste. Emma had no idea why anyone in the Guild would want to sleep with anyone else. They all hated each other or seemed to. Emma relished her time on her own and would never give it up if she didn't have to. She did not understand the appeal of sex, as it seemed to her just another excuse to give away pieces of herself for use by others.

"I will most often be in the office," Leader continued. "But if I am not, go to Monique. I may have reason to be in some of the other wings. I assure you, until our safety can be determined, I will not leave the Bunker. I do not leave my Guild to fend for itself, even under the best of circumstances."

"And these are *not* the best circumstances," Monique added in a dark undertone. Leader appeared amused at her comment, and even smiled. But he often smiled at Monique for reasons Emma could never comprehend. Perhaps Leader was not as displeased with her as he was with Emma and the others.

"Piper and Waylon on breakfast," Monique announced suddenly. "Adam, Scott, and Emma, get cleaned up so that you're ready for Training as soon as you have had some nourishment. And, school or no school, you will have a full academic workload."

Leader nodded, either in approval or support of Monique, and he rose, snatching up his ugly knife as he did. "Ilene, get on the wire and see if you can get a temporary transfer of their records from Avanair."

"To … ?" Ilene asked, sassy tone diminishing when his dark gaze contacted hers.

"France," he said but his tone suggested he did not care.

"I'll do it," Amos suggested. His voice changed dramatically into a French accent. "After all, it eez— 'ow do you say—my native 'ome, no?"

"Fine," Leader agreed, shooting one last stern glance Ilene's way before he sauntered off.

If Amos was French, Emma was a lily pad. She did not share her doubts or her concerns over her transcripts being requested, although that seemed like a very permanent change. She got up to do Monique's bidding.

Leader turned before he got many steps toward his office. Thoughtfully, he said, "Emma, come with me."

As always, the feeling of dread swept over her at the prospect of being alone with Leader. She tried to force it down and walk naturally after him, but her mind immediately conjured up ideas to explain why he would want to speak with her alone. What had she done? She made a list in her mind of possible infractions, such as resisting Scott when he tried to bring her to the dining room this morning. Nothing seemed to be a particularly dreadful violation of Leader's rules, but one never could be sure with Leader.

Chapter Forty-Five

Leader crossed through the lounging area and led Emma down the hall to the first door on the left, his office. It was much larger than his mansion office, with an entire board-room style table and six chairs, a large glass top desk, shelves along three walls covered in black or brown leather-bound books. An entire wall near the boardroom table had monitors and screens, but only one showed a recognizable image of the Bunker garage. The rest were blank. An open door across the room gave her a glimpse into what appeared to be an inner office, with another desk, more shelves, filing cabinets, and two large utility cabinets with padlocks on them.

Leader leaned, as he often did, against his desk. She approached him at a leisurely pace, unsure what to do. When she came to stand in front of him, he only watched her for a long moment before he motioned her to a chair in front of him. She took it gratefully, though still not relaxed.

A large clock on the wall ticked off the seconds loudly. Several clocks, Emma realized, and shot them a glance. Each clock showed a different time zone, like clocks in train stations or airports.

"They attacked me," Leader suddenly said. Emma startled at both his voice and the content of his words.

"Who did?" she asked, shocked that anyone would have the nerve, and a little surprised by her anger at the unknown culprit.

"Arrow Guild." He shrugged. "*Probably* Arrow. It could have just been a local gang of misfits who only wished they were organized enough to play on the World Market. Hard to know. It was dark and I was off my guard, thinking about impressing Henshaw into giving away information. I was a fool and went alone on business that should always be a group project."

Why was he telling her this? He had never shared any information with her freely before. He only ever insisted on her Obedience. She sat very still, waiting for something. Something else had to be coming. He couldn't just be sharing to share. Could he? He had Ilene for that sort of thing.

"When I realized what was happening, I was able to counter, a move that saved my life. And ended theirs." He sat on the desk now, pulling himself back until his feet dangled. He put his knife down on the keyboard of his computer. "It was a terrifying moment, and for a man with a life of terror, that is saying something."

"When?" Emma asked into the quiet that followed his eerie words. She did not know if it was wise to ask questions or even what questions to ask, but the silence was penetrating.

"When?" he repeated. She nodded. "The night of the Lansing party."

"When you came home with a black eye," she said, surprised she had forgotten it.

"Right." There was amusement in his dark eyes. "A true testament that even the best of us can't avoid a direct hit now and again." She dared answer that with a wan smile, very aware of her throbbing right arm.

"That wasn't the first attack," he said, back to serious music in his tone. "There had been a couple other attempts on me, Monique, several others. The reason I chose to leave Brooklyn was because we were no longer safe there. Our cover had been blown."

"And now it's blown here?" she asked, afraid that he was trying to break it to her gently that they were never leaving the Bunker.

But he said no. "It's not so bad. If it is Arrow, they're down a few trained men and that means they're weak. If I can get to the rest of them, their records will be an invaluable addition to my growing library." He did not motion toward the shelves all around them, but she glanced around, anyway. Would Leader kill men simply for their books?

"Are they employed by the same people who employ you?" she asked, watching his eyes for any hint, since she was sure he would not answer.

He surprised her. "I am not employed, Emma. The Guild is sacrosanct. It cannot be purchased or hired. The Guild is self-sufficient. It does not need employment. The Guild is superlative. It cannot be diminished." His words had a cadence to them of overuse as if he were quoting. He likely was, she thought and glanced around the room at the shelves of old books.

"I thought you told me you had to put in for a transfer," she replied. "I just assumed that meant you answer to a higher authority."

"You *overheard* me say that to the Senior Guild," he corrected. That was no answer at all. He smiled. "We all answer to a higher authority," he said, motioning lazily toward his chest as if to say she answered to him.

"So, who's your higher authority?" she asked. "God?"

He scoffed, and that was all the answer she was likely to get. He shifted, swinging one leg up to rest on the knee of the other.

"Sometimes, knowing information can prove to be dangerous." She knew that. Lara had had God knows what done to her for information. "The night I was attacked, they wanted information in my head I would die to protect. It's that Passion, more than anything else, that the Guild is protecting. It is the one very powerful distinction between the Guild and organized crime."

Emma scowled, doubtful. "And we're not just another organized crime base?" It seemed as if they were.

He blinked at that. "No."

She tried to fold her arms, but her right arm resisted the movement. She gave up trying to look nonchalant. "What are we, then?"

"We are the Guild." As if that was the whole answer.

"But you said that other group, that 'Arrow Guild' was your rival. How can we be '*The* Guild' if there are rivals?"

He barked a laugh. "As well ask a king how he can be 'the king' when he has enemies." He shook his head, dismissing her question as if it was nonsense.

"They always want me to give away my information as if it was a schoolyard secret," he told her, very serious now. "It's not. The Guild is very serious business. From your vantage point, I know it looks mystifying and dark. It is. And it's convoluted. It is complex. It is complicated. You're not crazy; you just don't have all the answers. And you cannot have them. Yet."

Emma nodded, accepting that. She knew that. He already told her that Guild business was need-to-know. If she did not need to know, why was he taunting her with it?

"The Porsche they delivered was just one of many taunts," he went on. "They infiltrated my Guild and they wanted to harass me into overreacting. I am not easily goaded, but they succeeded in distracting me long enough for me to allow Amos to divert my satellite from watching them."

"In your car," she said, remembering the fuss. "He had to prove to you that he was loyal."

Leader batted that idea away with a hand. "His Loyalty was tested when he was Seven. He had to give me an explanation, and a true and just cause."

"He must have done well because you appear to have forgiven him," Emma boldly offered, staring at Leader with challenge in her eyes.

He nodded. "Tracking you was a noble cause." His words startled her out of her challenging expression. Amos had been tracking her?

"He found you at the go-kart track," Leader pushed on, and Emma became increasingly uncomfortable with every word. "And followed you to the mall. He tracked you back to the school and watched you engage in your lover's farewell with the Stillwell boy."

Leader stretched his legs back out and crossed them again, this time with his other leg on top. "It was important that he do so," Leader went on, darkly musical. "That way, I could get the information quicker than I would have otherwise."

"I thought I saw your car ..." she whispered, remembering the horror she felt on seeing it there on the side of the road. As it had then, her heart beat painfully. Anxiety bubbled up inside her, but she could not look away from him, from his casual manner that she thought could not be truly casual at all.

"Yes," he answered, lifting one disapproving brow. "That was a little sloppy of him."

"Why are you telling me this?" she suddenly asked, climbing to her feet, bold in her fear of him. Hadn't he forgiven her? Wasn't this already all out in the open?

Leader gave the barest motion of his head toward her chair, and said only, "Sit down." She watched him for a moment, long enough for his brow to cock dangerously at her disobedience, and then she sat down again.

"I am telling you because you need to know why we suspected Benjamin," he went on once she was seated before him again. "No one outside the Guild is ever innocent enough, but Benjamin is almost annoyingly guilty-seeming. He went out of his way to dance with you at the Lansing party, then happened to show up at Cara's birthday party, and then was miraculously at your field trip only days later. Now he has ensconced himself in your heart. It appears to be so decisive that it could not be anything else."

"But Amos said Benjamin was innocent," Emma whispered, stunned by the accusations that, upon close inspection, did not appear empty.

"The breach in information was not flowing through you, yes," Leader answered back in what might have been a magnanimous voice if not for the vulture-like coldness in his eyes. "We had thought it must be through you, young and inexperienced as you are, and so sloppy with the part I gave you to play."

"But I don't have any information!" Emma argued, feeling a bitter panic rising inside her, terrified of how this conversation might end. Terrified that Leader might be right about Benjamin. "What could I possibly give away?"

"Oh, you have plenty," he replied dismissively, shaking his head at her. "You know every Guild member, their rank, their strengths and weaknesses. You know where we meet, what our covers are, what parties we attend, and Guild members' jobs at those parties. You have a very thorough understanding of my security layout, where I go on business trips, and who I bed. You are a student of my martial arts and you have seen the Guild Book."

"But ..." she sputtered. "But ... that's nothing! Drips and dribbles!"

"And from drips and dribbles, Amos tracked your entire relationship." That silenced her. "What more could an experienced nemesis do with drips and dribbles about my Guild?"

Emma sat in stunned silence until she realized his question had not been rhetorical. She gave a little shrug. "A lot, I guess."

"A whole lot."

"This is a warning," she realized even as she spoke aloud. "You're warning me to keep my cover."

He blinked. "You wouldn't like what I have to do with outsiders who learn too much," he replied, affirming her fears and suspicions.

"Kill them?" she demanded, furious and frightened all at once, remembering the man on the dark road who died in the glinting steel moonlight.

Leader only lifted one eyebrow in answer, and she shook her head. "All to protect the Guild?" This time she was more angry than reverent about the idea of his "sacrosanct" Guild.

His feet hit the floor with a hollow thud and he leaned toward her. "'All for the Guild,'" he said, and this time it was distinctly a quote. "'Live for the Guild; work in its honor. Fight for the Guild; shoulder its weight. Die for the Guild, if the Guild should demand it. All ... All for the Guild.'" He cocked his head to the side. "Is that clear enough for you?"

"It's neurotic," she answered, furious. She had a feeling she knew where this conversation was headed now, and she was desperate to avoid getting to the end. She was desperate to divert him, even if that meant risking his anger.

He nodded, allowing her words to be truth. "It's amazing what almost fifty years in this neurosis can do to a man."

Fifty years! She was appalled by the number. How old must he have been when he came to the Guild? He didn't look much past 35, so he must age well.

"My caution for you is this: do not get waylaid by youthful silliness." He narrowed his eyes at her. "Benjamin appears to be clean. He has no obvious connection to Lara's professor, who has been the source of our biggest problems, but there is never any guarantee. He seems like a nice young man, but rare is there a teenager who puts up with my horrible treatment without an ulterior motive. It could be simple. It could be hormonal. He could simply want to get you comfortable enough to rob the Guild of your virginity. But it could just as easily be that he is a pawn in the wild and untamable game we play."

"Or he could *like* me," she snapped, color rising in her cheeks. Benjamin did like her! She knew he did.

Leader's eyes narrowed dangerously. "He's a senior, Emmalyn. You're only 13 years old."

"I'm 14," she replied, pain stabbing through her at what he said. At the possible truth that Benjamin was too old to be interested in her at all. "And I don't want to be a part of your 'wild and untamable game.'"

Leader clicked his tongue and shook his head back and forth. "You don't have a choice." He gave no sign of concern for her predicament.

"If you don't want me to date him, why aren't you just commanding it?"

"Calm yourself down," he suggested, but his undertone hinted at a threat. "I *don't* want you dating him. That's partly because, in my mind, you're still a four-year-old stumbling clumsily into my arms and sitting on my knee."

She had a hard time imagining herself ever being that comfortable with him, but she took his word for it. She thought she even remembered climbing up into his lap at the dinner table to steal the broccoli off his plate. It was a dim memory, but she recalled his scandalized cry, and Monique's throaty chuckle. Emma had slid out of his arms, ducking under the table, and scurrying out on Amos's side for his protection, while she devoured Leader's broccoli. Staring at Leader in this Bunker Office, though, Emma felt there was an impassible gulf between them. She did not want anything from him—not his broccoli or his orders or his meager explanations. She did not want his information, told in cold words that beat at her heart and made her question Benjamin's interest.

"I have not restricted this yet," Leader went on firmly, almost as if he could read the rebellion in her heart, "but I want to be very clear: You may date Benjamin, pretend with him, play 'high school sweethearts' as long as you can. But not for any moment may you slip out of the character I created for you. You, my blonde-haired, blue-eyed, little misunderstood genius, are his girlfriend. The dark, intelligent, fierce Guild creature you are may never be displayed. It's worth my life to protect that creature."

And she suddenly knew why he had wanted to talk to her. He was warning her, but not to be on her guard, not to Obey the Guild rules. There was something deeper, beyond the sinister cast to his dark eyes. There was pain, she thought. Like Amos, Leader was speaking to her in earnest, warning her—not to protect the Guild, since that was always a given—but to protect her heart.

"Is it possible to be in a relationship if you never show your true colors?" she demanded, but not really for him as much as for herself.

He shrugged dismissively. "High school is full of that kind of romance."

That didn't reassure her. But so much made sense to her now. Leader and Monique were excellent at pretending to be lovers, because it could be only a part they were playing. If they were truly in love, it would be dangerous to be seen to be so, if indeed there were factions trying to pry the Guild members apart. No wonder Leader kept his relationship with Ilene on the down-low. She would be in danger if anyone outside the Guild suspected he had feelings for her. Love could very well be the undoing of the Guild. Although, honestly, Emma did not know that what they were protecting was worth all this hassle and heartache.

"It is worth it," he told her, thoroughly startling her. She must have betrayed her surprise, because he smiled knowingly. "I could recognize the look of doubt anywhere, Number Twelve." He stood up and stretched his arms over his head. "You're lucky, you know. Being here in the Bunker will allow us the time to give you the instruction we have neglected."

She gave a mirthless laugh. "That doesn't sound lucky."

He looked down at her for a long time, studying her with a speculative gaze. "What is it?"

She narrowed her eyes thoughtfully at him. "We're not going to spend any time relaxing while we're here, are we?"

He sauntered around his desk, lowering himself into his tall-back desk chair. Once situated, he watched her intently. "No," he finally said, almost apologetically. "Not much."

"We train at least as hard as the military."

A bark of laughter escaped from his lips. "Hardened military career men might find our regime grueling. But we must train that hard; we must be better, harder, and faster. Constant training is how we maintain our stamina." He smiled at her, an eerie contrast to the power in his gaze. "And it keeps us young."

Emma stared into his eyes, searching for a hint of compassion or humanity behind the intensity. Sometimes, she wondered who he would be if he was not the Guild Leader. Would he be like Cara's dad, full of happiness and pride in his daughter? Would he be a business titan with a little family at home, a devoted Ilene as his wife? Would he love?

But his affection was for the Guild. He lived for the Guild. He had given his entire life to it. How could it not consume him?

And, she realized hopelessly, he expected it to consume her, too.

Chapter Forty-Six

Emma stopped thinking and launched herself at Scott, striking with a quick jab that he was too surprised to counter. He spun low and came back up, a determined cast to his snarling features. He would not be caught unawares again. The vengeance in his face was nothing short of malevolent. Scott was not striking to wound this time, but to kill. Emma had had nearly as much training as Scott. He had been only six when she had entered the Guild. This was almost a fair fight. He was faster and more agile, but she had good instincts.

"What the … ?" Amos said, suddenly there in the kitchen with them. He could easily see Scott moving in on Emma and Emma poised to defend. The look in her eyes was probably haunting, since Amos knew her as mostly timid when she got around Scott.

"Hold!" Amos bellowed, propelling himself toward them before they could set a catastrophe into action. "Stand down!"

But Emma was not about to let this slide. She stood by and let Scott torment her for too long. He endlessly needled her. He never showed her an ounce of kindness and, for no reason at all, he went out of his way to make her life miserable. For years, she toadied to him, been cowed into submission by his bullying, and for what? His constant, nagging hatred and cruelty? And now, being cooped up with him for over a month in the Bunker, she'd reached her limit of his vicious handling. She would not allow it even one more second.

She neatly sidestepped Amos' approach and attacked with fervor. Her sidekick was knocked aside and countered, but she was too smart to get caught in Scott's strangle hold. When she saw it coming, she used his momentum against him, feinting at the last second so she could drop and use her shoulder to knock him over. He anticipated her, swinging around and managing to barely avoid her maneuver.

Amos made it between them. He screamed orders at them, attempting to use his body to shield them from one another. Emma heard him shout about

"Aggression" but she was too furious to worry about the rules of order. There was no space in her brain right now to worry about the consequences for off-mats aggression.

Scott rushed her, barely managing to slip past the arm Amos threw out to stop him. Scott tried to kick her, but he overestimated his distance slightly. Emma moved in on him, managing another solid fist strike to his body before he tackled her. They grappled as deftly as they had on the mats, although with more passion than ever. Unlike matches that were refereed by their superiors, this match would have one clear winner and one clear loser. Emma intended to be the winner.

Amos tried first to grab Emma, but she was too slippery, and an attempt at Scott only earned Amos a kick to the groin. Emma could not think about Amos or Guild rules when she was fighting for her life. She could not think about the implications of having a deep loathing for her direct superior in the Guild where she was destined to spend her life. She could only think of one thing: kill or be killed. Her anger had never been this cold before. Not even when the boy at the party tried to grope her. Not even when the school counselor tried to pry into her life. Nothing compared with this moment; the moment she would destroy Scott's hold over her for good.

Emma did not allow herself to feel fear of defeat when Scott seemed to be winning. Anger, cool and controlled, would win over the white-hot rage burning in Scott's eyes. She grappled, twisting out of his grip, too liquid to be held by him. And then she realized she wasn't losing. He was overconfident, certain that he would defeat her. His cockiness was his undoing. She suddenly pinned him in a position to break his neck. What she wouldn't give to see the look in his eyes before she landed her final blow.

A slam caught her alongside her body, knocking her toward Amos as easily as a doll. Amos caught her before the toss could cause her any severe damage, but he could not protect her from Leader's wrath. Leader cuffed Scott when the stupid boy attempted to attack him, and Scott went down flaccidly. Emma tensed as Leader approached her, and for good reason. His backhanded smack jolted her more thoroughly than any damage Scott had managed to inflict. The Guild ring on Leader's middle finger cut her lip. Blood tricked down her chin almost immediately, and her ears would probably ring for days. She could not focus on the pain, though. Leader grasped her by the hair at the base of the neck, hauling her to her feet. And she went because she had no power to fight him. He was stronger, scarier, and more determined than she had ever seen him before.

Bending her over the counter, Leader forced her head into the sink. He turned the industrial faucet on her. The frigid water attacked her, drenching her face and neck sufficient enough to freeze away any residing anger at Scott. Perhaps she had not been as cool and controlled as she thought.

Leader hauled her out of the sink, took one look at her, and shoved her back in. She could not resist him. He was too strong. She cried out when she thought she might drown and he jerked her back out of the powerful stream.

"Are you done?" he snarled at her, the blackness in his eyes reminiscent of the night he'd pulled his belt from its loops.

Emma did not trust herself to speak, but his grip tightened on her hair, and she nodded as far as his rigid hold would allow. He shoved her away, and she fell heavily to the floor beside Scott's unconscious form. She pushed herself onto her hands and knees, whipping her sopping hair out of her face in time to see Leader round on Amos.

His hit to Amos' ear was by no means gentle, but was a love tap in comparison to how hard he had slapped Emma. It still rocked Amos back. He kept his face turned away while Leader boiled rage at him.

"What were you going to do? Stand there and let them annihilate each other? What in the name of Hell is the matter with you?"

"I ..." Amos said, shaking his head. "They ..."

"You are Number Three, Amos. Number *Three*! Have some balls!"

"I tried to stop it," Amos argued but that only incensed Leader further.

"They're children, Amos!" Leader shouted, gesturing toward Emma and Scott with a rigid finger. "Do your job!"

Amos would have said more but Leader stabbed his rigid finger at Emma. "Beat her!"

Amos recoiled. "Leader, I think she—"

Leader was back in Amos' face instantly, his malignant finger jabbing Amos' chest. "Insubordination? Really? On top of everything else? She *disobeyed* you, Amos! She attacked another member of the Guild. She brought Aggression into the House and used the gifts we have given her to harm someone else. Beat her or I swear to *Lucifer*, I will do so to *you*!"

Amos sucked in a long and wary breath, and on his exhale acceded, "Okay."

"What was that?" Leader said, voice dropping to a menacing whisper.

"Yes, Leader," Amos answered, his voice slightly stronger. He met Leader's eye.

"I *am* your Leader," Leader snapped, and strode away before Emma could even comprehend his words. "I am your Leader, Amos," he shouted over his shoulder. "And God help the Guild when you Ascend."

Emma stared up at Amos' back. He stood watching Leader walk away, and even from behind, Emma sensed his dejection and humiliation. That's what it was all about, she realized. Leader wanted to humiliate Amos, just as Scott wanted to humiliate Emma. The cycle of humiliation in the Guild must have been for some important reason. Although, for the life of her, Emma could not imagine what it could be. Yet Leader humiliated them all, not even sparing Monique, who was his Second.

Emma shifted, climbing to her feet so she could approach him. Perhaps she could comfort him in some way? Amos was not cut out for Leader's criticism. He was too tenderhearted.

Amos spun around, and Emma froze in the act of rising to her feet. The furious expression on his face made her rethink her earlier analysis of him as tenderhearted. She fell back onto her bottom, very afraid of the rage in his brown eyes. He stalked the two strides toward her and hauled her to her feet by her arm. She shuddered in his hands, deeply punished by his manner long before his actual punishment began.

Emma buried her head in her pillow but couldn't get comfortable. In her mind, she rehearsed the disaster that had led to her bruised hide and wounded pride. Scott. What was it about what he had said today that offended her so thoroughly? He was always obnoxious and condescending. What triggered her violent reaction?

She shifted her body again, wincing when she felt the pain across her shoulders and back. Amos was by no means as severe as Leader, but he had done a thorough enough job to keep her in pain for a couple of days.

Thinking of Amos dried her mouth. He was the tender soul who always tried to be understanding. He always showed mercy and compassion. Emma had broken him! There had been not one ounce of compassion in him today. He had not even offered her a painkiller.

Desperate to avoid thinking of him, she turned her mind back to her problem. What about Scott set her off? Could it have been his constant teasing about Benjamin in the last few weeks? Or was it the orders he gave her to keep her from completing her scheduled tasks on time? Monique had been furious enough with Emma to supply him endless amounts of pleasure in her pain. No. He was no worse since coming to the Bunker than ever before, it was just that there was nowhere to get away from him. At least out in the world there was school, and the diversion of Guild activities, and Benjamin. Here, Emma had nothing. In the Bunker, she was at his constant mercy, and he took full advantage of the meager power he had over her by his minimally higher rank.

If she was looking for some romantic or justified reason for attacking him, she would never find it. Attacking him was not justified, because what Leader said was true: Emma used the Training they gave her to turn on one of their own number. It was a gigantic crime in the Guild, and disobedient to boot. Yet, if she had Obeyed Amos' command to "stand down," she would never have felt the strap. But it still would not have excused her physical attack on Scott.

I hate him, her mind said automatically. She forcefully had to eject the thought from her brain. She could not hate him. He was too important to her happiness in the Guild long-term. He would be with her in the Guild forever, as his Second. She could not imagine a worse situation, but she had to become resigned to it. Hating Scott would not make either of their lives any easier.

She slid her feet around to the edge of the bed and pushed herself out of it and onto the floor. The lights in the Bunker were all out, so she navigated slowly and carefully through the total dark to the door. The hall had safety lights on, so she could see Scott's closed door across the hall. She stared at it a long time, and then gave a cautious glance up the hall toward the rest of the sleeping quarters. Amos was up there somewhere. When he sent her to her room after the punishment, he had not stipulated a time when she could return. Was it disobedient to come out?

She took the chance. Crossing the hall on quick feet, she grasped Scott's door handle and pushed his door open, relieved to find it was not locked. She left his door open, so she had the meager glow of the safety lights behind her to guide her to Scott's bedside. She heard him breathing. It would be so easy to hurt him like this, she realized with a gross fascination. He would never have a chance to defend himself while he slept peacefully, chest rising and falling with his unsuspecting innocence.

Chapter Forty-Seven

E mma shook her head to dispel the treacherous thought. Hurting Scott was not what had gotten her out of bed.

Emma reached out a hand to wake him but startled when his eyes were suddenly open and staring at her in the darkness. She sprang back in nervous surprise.

"What?" Scott asked, as angry and calculated as ever.

Emma did not allow herself to back down now, although she was sorely tempted just to run away.

"Earlier today, before I ... *hit* you," she began.

"Before you sucker-punched me," he corrected forcefully. He sat up and continued to glare up at her. "Say it right."

She nodded, determined to Obey, as Leader required her to. "Fine. Before I sucker-punched you today, you said something. You were mocking me about Benjamin, and then you said I was lucky to be ignorant."

"What I said was that you are crack-ass lucky to be the ignorant little bitch you are," he corrected again. Emma managed not to wince at a repeat of the words that had earlier today provoked her to violence. She restrained another urge to throttle him.

"Yes," she acceded, clenching her fists to keep them busy and under her control. She relaxed them and let out a slow, calming breath. She asked what she came in here to ask. "I was wondering what you meant."

He seemed uncomfortable for a moment, eyes narrowing at her in the darkness. He cleared his throat and looked away. "You better forget about that." He cleared his throat again. "I need water."

He would have gotten up to get some, but she forestalled him by handing him the glass water bottle from the nightstand. "I can't forget about it, Scott. What did you mean?"

He bought himself time by drinking long from the bottle. When he pulled it away from his mouth, he said coldly, "You have had a long time to be Twelve. That's all I meant." But that did not seem to be all he wanted to say, so she waited.

Scott tossed the bottle back into her hands and shook his head a little disgustedly. "You still think this is *your* life and you have to contest with the Guild to have any control. It's ignorant," he snapped, scornful as always. But there was something behind it today. His tone betrayed a longing she had never heard before. As if he envied her ignorance.

"In what way is it ignorant?"

"In every way!" He tossed a hand, gesturing toward the door. "Get out of here!"

"I will," she replied firmly, "in a minute. Just tell me why it's ignorant."

Scott looked past her toward the door and, just when she thought he was about to order her out again, he whispered, "You think there's a place out there for you somewhere, like a regular kid who has to find her place in the world? You think you can have relationships and go to school functions, like a normal person, like a normal teenager. You think there's something about you that makes you unique and special? All that tripe they try to piss off onto us at school, about 'going somewhere' and 'being the important person you are.' You think that actually applies to you! And it doesn't. You are *not* special. You're *not* important. Do you know what you are?"

She winced, afraid he would tell her what she was, in his normal colorful, explicit detail.

"You're expendable."

Emma blinked. It hadn't been a curse word, but it was somehow worse. Her response came out as a whisper, "What do you mean?"

"I mean you are *not special*," he replied, tone tinged with hardness that she thought might betray pain deep down inside. "You're like a worker ant. There's always another one coming up behind you. So, if you drop dead, it doesn't even matter. We can push you off into a ditch somewhere and carry on like you never even existed."

Emma stared at him, surprised by how much his coldness affected her. Is that what he thought of her? She was just someone who could die tomorrow, and it would be like she had never existed at all? It was so much darker than she thought even he was capable of. Her chest rose and fell in deep, pained breaths. She begged herself not to cry, not to let him see that he affected her. She forced herself to speak, to push away her hatred for him.

"We have a long time to serve in the Guild together. I think we should try to get along."

He scoffed and shook his head at her. "There's no guarantee we *will* have to serve together. You could die today. Or next week. You could trip in the hall and bash your head against the doorframe."

He wanted her to die. He *wished* it! Emma blinked and took a step back. "I'm not trying to annoy you."

Scott rolled his eyes and tossed himself back down on his pillows. "You don't annoy me. Get out of here."

"I must," she countered, heart aching on his hatred. "Or I must have done something terrible. If you think so ill of me that you want me to bash my head against the doorframe, I must have somehow, at some point, annoyed you so much that you think I'm—"

"You didn't do anything!" he shouted, his voice reverberating off the walls, bouncing into the corridor. *"Get out of here!"*

"Scott," she gasped out, backing away from him. "I wish you would tell me why you hate me so much. If you tell me, maybe I can make it right."

He shoved his covers aside and climbed out of his bed, feet slapping to the floor. There was real menace in his eyes as he approached her. Frightened for her life, Emma bolted. And ran straight into Leader standing in the doorway. He spun her around somewhat forcefully to face Scott's attack, holding his hands on her shoulders firmly.

"Leader," Scott said, surprise overtaking his voice. And Scott dropped to his knees like a parishioner, keeping his head bowed low. Emma was thoroughly confused by that reaction to Leader's presence. She had never seen it before and she was not certain why anyone would fall to their knees in Leader's presence.

"He doesn't hate you," Leader said. Emma was surprised to hear that his voice sounded only conversational, not angry as she supposed it would be. "He hates *me*."

"No, Leader," Scott hissed, but Emma did not think he was denying Leader's words.

"He hates me because of Lela-Cate," Leader went on. His hands tightened slightly on Emma's shoulders as he spoke the girl's name, but the pressure eased again right away.

"No, Leader," Scott pleaded, reaching out as if to stop the words with his hands.

"She was supposed to be you, Emma," Leader went on, apparently unconcerned by Scott's pleading and his humble form. "The year I took Leadership of the Guild, I filled the Number Twelve spot with the bright and beautiful Lela-Cate."

"No," Scott moaned. He slid down onto his side and now tried to press his arms over his ears, in agony at Leader's story. But Leader seemed to take no notice of him.

"She was only five but was perhaps the most engaging youngster I had ever seen. I hoped she was going to be a powerful addition to my little family. She learned quickly and was eager to please." His grip tightened a little more on Emma's shoulders. "A good quality for a Twelve to possess." Emma looked up at him but found that his gaze was invariably fixed on Scott on the floor. Scott, crushing his skull between his own hands, moaned as if he was being tortured. "Monique was smitten with Lela-Cate from the moment the girl completed her first form. She was poised and attentive. She was, in short, the perfect student."

Scott moaned aloud, "No. Don't, Leader! Don't!" But Leader ruthlessly continued. And it *was* ruthless, Emma thought, when the telling caused Scott so much agony.

"She and Scott were the same age when she came, and they became close friends the instant she walked in the door. They were cute, actually, in a kind of annoying sort of way. They would sneak into each other's rooms in the middle of the night. I would catch them there giggling together under the covers while they played imaginary games. She would be a princess and he a knight. They would be wild wolves howling at the moon. He would be 'Leader' and she his Second. Oh, the amount of spankings I gave for being out of bed!" His voice sounded amused.

Emma could not imagine what it would be like to know the Scott who pretended to be a knight for Princess Lela-Cate. She could not imagine play; she did not remember ever engaging in something so normal. Especially not with Scott.

Emma thought Scott was weeping. Though if he was, it was soft. She could not remember ever seeing him cry. She did not remember him ever seeming vulnerable.

"One day on the mats, Monique walked away to take a call," Leader's voice hardened slightly. Emma felt a tingle of fear for what was coming. "Scott and Lela-Cate *loved* training! They were told to stand in formation, but they were very small, and unaccustomed to Obedience. After Monique had been gone a little while, they began to play at martial arts." Emma held her breath. She had been instructed by Monique severely that martial arts was *not* play and should always, always be treated as a highly dangerous training activity.

Scott drew his knees up against his chest, wrapped around himself in a convoluted knot. He was openly weeping now, and Emma watched him in horror as Leader continued with his story.

"Within minutes, they had weapons down off the wall, and were mimicking movements they had seen others make. Rough approximations, really; they were only six-years-old. Scott spun around with a bō-staff swinging and caught Lela-Cate aside the head. He hit her several more times, thinking she was playing, but by then she was lying unconscious on the mats. When he saw a cut above her eye, he started screaming. It was a minor cut, because her real damage was internal. He had no way of knowing.

"Monique rushed back into the room and tried to revive Lela-Cate. It was obvious to her immediately that the girl was in danger. She called me and I called an ambulance." He paused long enough to nudge Scott in the side with his shoe. "It wasn't your fault, Scott," he said, firmly. "If anyone can be blamed, it's Monique, for leaving little children alone in a room full of dangerous weapons." He said this coldly enough that Emma wondered if that was when Leader had beaten Monique within in an inch of life, as he claimed to have done.

"There was nothing anyone could do," Leader went on, squeezing Emma's shoulders in his strong hands. "Lela-Cate went on life support that morning. I pulled the plug in the afternoon when she showed no improvement." He said it so callously, Emma wondered if he felt any sorrow at all for ending the girl's life.

"That's why Scott hates me," Leader concluded.

Scott murmured something Emma could not quite understand. Leader apparently did because he said, "She would *not* have made any improvement, Scott. She was already dead. It was an empty shell I unplugged that day, and if I had it to do over again, I would make the exact same choice." If that was meant to give comfort, it missed, because Scott's weeping continued and, if possible, became stronger.

Emma turned away. She was not able to look any longer at the dark silhouette weeping in a fetal position on the floor. She looked up at Leader instead.

"That doesn't explain why he hates me," she whispered, wishing that Scott's weeping would keep her words from his ears. It seemed so cold to refocus the conversation on herself when Scott was so obviously affected. But she had not known Lela-Cate, and though she could imagine a bright-eyed and vibrant child, Emma felt no real connection to her.

"It does," Leader countered firmly. "Because on my way back from the hospital, I picked you up and brought you home with me."

His words jogged a memory. She could remember him picking her up in his arms and placing her in a booster seat in the back of a blue car. He had touched her face softly, buckled her securely in the seat, and closed the door. She remembered him turning on the music to a children's station and singing along with "I've Been Working on the Railroad." But where had she come from? She did not bother asking; he would never tell her.

"He doesn't hate you," Leader went on. "He resents that I killed Lela-Cate and had no compunction against replacing her that very day. We did not have a funeral, so he never did properly grieve for her loss."

He spoke up slightly as he went on, wanting to be sure Scott heard him. "There was no time for a funeral because we were moving to New York the next morning. And honestly, I wanted to leave Lela-Cate behind us when we moved on. I was fairly arrogant at the time, and I thought she was a black mark against my short reign."

Emma's heart hurt. She could not make herself focus on anything but the memory of "I've Been Working on the Railroad." It played in her brain, sounding over and over as she tried to bring vibrancy to the memory. She tried to flesh it out, searching backward. *Where had she come from?* She did not remember coming to the Guild; it had simply always been her life, for as long as she could remember.

"He doesn't hate you," Leader insisted again, bringing her back into the present, though she resisted. "He hates that you're not Lela-Cate."

Emma backed away from Leader, looking at him in consternation. She studied his face, hoping to see in his eyes some compassion or humanity. Something to tie him to the man in the car playing "I've Been Working on the Railroad." But Leader's gaze was unvaryingly fixed by Scott's fetal form.

Emma looked at the boy on the ground and felt a rush of pity for him. She knelt at Scott's side. Looking up at Leader with a scowl for his callousness, she shook her head. Scott had been a little tiny boy, and everything that happened was an accident. She reached out a hand and placed it on Scott's arm. He jerked away from her, but when she persisted, he allowed himself to be comforted. In short order, Emma had his head in her lap and was stroking fingers through his hair.

"I'm so sorry," she whispered. It was an apology he needed years ago, although it ought to have come from Leader. Who, however, remained in the doorway like a cold-hearted statue. "I'm so sorry she never came home, Scott. I would have hated me, too, for replacing her so heartlessly."

It all made sense now. He could not show Emma any kindness because she could be gone tomorrow. He told her she was expendable because everyone must be if Leader could replace Lela-Cate in one afternoon simply because she was an inconvenience and he had a deadline to keep. It was so cruel! And it frightened Emma, because Leader could do it again if he became annoyed enough with any of them. He had even threatened Amos' life today. They all really were expendable.

"I'm not her," Emma admitted sadly. "But I am your Second, Scott, and I will never raise my hand to you again."

He pulled out of her hands, his weeping slowed now. He gathered himself enough to come up to his knees, trying to gain distance from her. Over his shoulder, he glared hard at her, as hateful as ever. "I'm not weak."

"I know," she answered truthfully. He had to hate her. How else could he show his loyalty for Lela-Cate?

"Get out of here," he hissed, and turned away from her to rest against the side of the bed.

Emma Obeyed, climbing to her feet. She meant what she said. As his Second, she would never try to hurt him again. She owed him that much just for being born in time to replace his best friend. As she slid past Leader in the doorway, she looked up into his eyes, searching for pain or regret, but there was only stone. Even as he reached out a hand to stroke the side of her face in a seemingly gentle way, he was completely impenetrable.

Chapter Forty-Eight

"Emma!" Monique snapped, getting her attention. "Did you hear me?"

She blushed. She had done it again. "No, ma'am, I'm sorry." She focused her attention on Monique, who was standing near her at the kitchen sink.

"The water has clouded," Monique repeated, annoyed to have to repeat herself. "You cannot wash dishes in cloudy water. Empty and refill."

Emma nodded. "Yes, Monique," she said humbly as she pulled the plug.

Days were passing slowly in the Bunker. Since the night of Leader's horrible tale of Lela-Cate, Scott did not treat Emma with much less animosity, but he no longer went out of his way to make trouble for her. And he never called her dirty names. She thought that was as good a truce as they would ever get. Amos was another matter; he rarely looked her in the eye, and when he did, he turned away again immediately. It might take a long time before Emma obtained his forgiveness for the disobedience that caused Leader to humiliate him.

Emma kept herself busy to distract herself from thoughts of Benjamin. He came to her mind at the most inopportune times. Often questions launched her direction would remind her of him and she would daydream before she had a chance to respond to an increasingly impatient superior. She missed Benjamin more than she thought she should for such a short acquaintance. She could still feel his lips against hers and hear his words in her mind, *"Call you tomorrow, Quicksilver."* What must he think about her sudden disappearance? Or had he already forgotten about her?

"Where is your head these days?" Monique launched the rhetorical question at her before marching away.

Tempers were getting high. At dinner yesterday, Ilene made an innocent comment about the asparagus, which sent Thomas into an uproar. It was fascinating for Emma, who had never seen Thomas so angry. Leader came out of his study to see why they were shouting and ended up joining the argument. Before it was over, Ilene slapped Leader in the face and dumped the dish of steamed asparagus in Thomas' lap. Julianne waved the Junior Guild away to hide in their rooms, but the safety of her locked door had not saved Emma from hearing most of the ensuing argument.

Being enclosed was not good for a group of highly active, energetic people. They were used to the busy schedules and endless routines of the outside world. Rest was not in their vocabulary, much less their regime. And while Adam and Scott seemed to think the flaring tempers and sniping comments were funny, Emma was concerned. How much longer could they be at this before someone got really hurt?

"I'm going out of my mind," Amos said from the library. Emma looked up, saw that he was talking to Leader who had just entered the room, and went back to washing the dishes. She wasn't permitted to use the dishwasher because Leader thought it was important to keep the Junior Guild busy, to keep them out of trouble.

Scott's muttered answer to that had been, "We're not the ones shouting insults and throwing vegetables." It was the first joke Emma ever heard him make that she thought was funny. When she smiled, he acknowledged it with a slight nod. It saved neither one of them from the pile of extra, useless chores Leader heaped on them for disrespect. Washing the never-used Russian Tea Service was one of those chores. Scott was drying.

"You'll manage," Leader responded with no compassion to Amos' complaint.

"I have to *do* something!" Amos retorted. "Maybe I'll go to the surface again and check on the—" He rose to leave, but Leader stepped in his way.

"Stay out of the surface," Leader ordered.

"Oh my god, you have got to be kidding me!" Amos snapped. "I can't read one more book! I have to *do* something. Let's go for a drive, just you and me. We can check on the outpost."

Leader shook his head. "No, but you can contact the broker and see if we can sell today. The stocks are going to drop, and I don't want to be angry on top of bored."

Amos made a comment that Emma did not understand and chose not to remember for its coarse language. He stalked away toward the elevator. Emma envied him his access to a keycard. She would give anything to see something other than the inside of the Bunker walls.

Julianne came from the elevator room, followed by Amos, who had an interested look on his face.

"Leader!" Julianne said, but instead of going toward him, she went to the hall where the office was. Monique, who had also been sitting in the library trying to read, hopped up and followed the group away.

Scott shook his head. "They're whiners. Seven weeks in captivity and they're making toilet paper installation into an issue."

She turned a perplexed look on him.

"Didn't you hear about that?" he asked, his scornful voice reminding her that they were not friends just because they were sharing the same punishment.

"No, sir," she answered with every ounce of respect she could muster.

"Yesterday, Adam crashed their Senior Guild meeting and the biggest issue on the table was which direction toilet paper should face when it's on the roll." He shook his head and chuckled. "Toilet paper!"

Emma smiled as she washed another dish. "What did they decide?"

Scott scoffed. "Hell if I know! Apparently, Leader was determined that it should always face out, end coming from the top, while Julianne insisted it come from under. Monique kept shouting that it was a ridiculous fight, but everyone took sides eventually. It was girls against boys. I suppose boys won, since Leader is a man."

Emma shook her head. "I don't pay close enough attention to notice the toilet paper."

"It's a frugality thing," Scott added with a slight shake of his head. "They are certain that one way is more economical than the other. I think a few pennies doesn't make that big of a difference."

Emma did not agree, but she didn't share her thoughts with him. She thought that if Leader and the Senior Guild had to decide where every Guild cent was spent, they had better pay attention to little things, like toilet paper installation. There couldn't really be an endless supply of money, although it often appeared to be that way.

She shrugged. "They could have been talking in code," she suggested. Scott turned his head slowly to analyze her.

"Code," he tried out the idea. He grinned and then laughed. "Of course! They were talking in code! Adam will be so relieved!"

They stopped talking and bent to their work as Leader, Monique, Julianne, and Amos came through the room and walked toward the elevator. Emma watched them leave. She turned a questioning look on Scott, who only shrugged to indicate that he had no idea what the excitement was. It could be as simple as someone had changed the part in their hair; nothing of much interest had happened in almost two months.

"Keep on, Twelve," Scott encouraged, calling her back to her work. "We still have to dust the library and wipe the baseboards."

Emma Obeyed, but after a few more dishes, she looked at him and sighed. "Why are we still here? Leader indicated to me only the first day that he knew we were not in any danger. If that was true, why are we still here? He's almost as obnoxious as the others, storming around with a chip on his shoulder like he does. He wants out of here as much as any of us. So, why?"

Scott studied her thoughtfully. "I don't know. Maybe he was only trying to reassure you that first day. Or maybe he has an agenda."

Emma shrugged at that. "He always has an agenda." She returned to the few remaining dishes, but the train of thought would not go away. "He must have a reason. If they caught Lara's professor—the leak—and they have her safely ensconced in this fortress somewhere, and there are no other immediate threats, why are we still here?"

Scott packaged a few of the dishes carefully and returned them to the box. For a while he said nothing, so Emma returned to her work. She washed the final dish, emptied the water, and wiped the sink as she had been taught to do.

"You're right," Scott finally agreed. He flipped her with his towel, but not trying to hurt her, just getting her attention. "He must have a reason. They must know something we don't know. I mean, obviously they know stuff we don't, but I mean Leader must have an important reason for staying here." He looked wistfully toward the direction of the elevator. "I would give almost anything to get outside in the fresh air again."

He shook himself back to his work, pointed a commanding hand at the pile of dry dishes that needed repackaging, and returned to drying the final dishes. Emma picked up a saucer and wrapped it carefully in bubble wrap and cardboard.

"Did you notice Monique lost her flawless tan?" he asked in a voice barely above a whisper.

She *had* noticed but would never have mentioned it to anyone. It was an observation one did not make lightly. She nodded, though, and shared a smile with Scott.

"No tanning facilities in the Bunker, and no sunshine," he said smugly.

"Isn't it harmful for us to be indoors all the time?" Emma asked. "I thought I heard that somewhere."

He rolled his eyes. "What are you going to do? Grow up and become an environmentalist?"

Emma smiled at the idea. "What if the environment is what the Guild is fighting for? What if knowledge of the environment is the entire reason we were formed, Scott? What would you do if you were called on to be in charge?"

He pulled a face. "Kill myself."

Scott carried the dishes back to the storage room while Emma started dusting the bookshelves. She did it the right way, removing rows of books so she could gloss each shelf. Scott joined her a few minutes later. He started on the other end of the room.

"Do you wonder, then, what the Guild is all about?"

She looked up in surprise at his honest query. "Yes, all the time."

His work never slowed but he mused aloud. "Sometimes I think we must be some kind of top-secret government agency; the kind with a license to kill and the wherewithal to do so."

She shook her head. "I have it on fairly good authority that the Guild was formed before the government was."

That caught him by surprise. "What authority?"

"Leader. He read me a passage from the Guild Book and said it was from around the time the United States was founded. The section he read was midway through the book, so I assumed there had been passages from before America's founding."

He seemed impressed by her knowledge. "What did the passage say?"

Emma shrugged. "I don't remember exactly. Something about Guild members being subject to weakness if left to themselves."

He pulled a face Emma did not think she was meant to see so she went back to dusting each shelf carefully.

"It's kind of intimidating, isn't it?" Scott asked, his thoughts distracting him from his work. "Back at the time the United States was founded, Leaders were having the same problem with their subordinates as he has today. Maybe people don't really change throughout time. All problems are still the same problems."

Emma nodded once in agreement, but she really thought about his words. She wondered if somewhere, in some Guild Book, a Number Twelve had fallen in love with an outsider. Would Leader get inspiration on how to deal with Emma from ancient Leaders who had the same problems? Or might some future Leader, like Scott or Adam, read about the experience and use it to guide their own Guild?

Leader returned suddenly from the elevator room, ushering a quiet and sickly-thin Lara ahead of him. Monique, Amos, and Julianne followed a short distance behind them as if worried they would encroach on Leader's time with Lara. Emma watched them across the room, comforted by the fact that Scott was also watching instead of working.

"This is the Bunker," Lara said, blinking around in surprise. She still sounded like herself. Emma expected her to sound as frail as she looked. She appeared to have returned from the grave. Dark, sunken shadows were under her eyes and her hair hung in a stringy mess around her shoulders. Its usual vibrant, auburn shine was gone, replaced by a dull brownish hue. Leader's hand on her shoulder pressed her clothing down, making her bony shoulder blades and collar show through the t-shirt. Lara always seemed like a beauty queen to Emma, flawless and poised. Now she looked like a recovering drug addict. Emma wondered idly if drug rehab had been the recovery she underwent these past weeks.

Leader directed Lara toward the sleeping quarter and said, "Yes, we are in the Bunker for the duration. I did not want my enemies to have any confusion about my intentions. When we come out, we come out strong and powerful. All of us."

Lara tilted her head to look up at him and said, "I'm sorry, Leader. I'm so sorry."

He nodded at that. "Good. We'll learn from this and be better than ever."

"Yes, sir." Her wan smile was a pale imitation of the power of her full, real smile. "And I will never doubt you again."

He gave a wry chuckle. "I expect not." And by then they were in the sleeping hall. Monique, Amos, and Julianne hung back.

"She's looks terrible," Monique said, sparing no feelings.

Julianne shook her head sadly. "She's actually recovered a lot, Monique. I swear. She's looking much better than she was."

"She looks terrible," Monique replied, unmoved by Julianne's assurances. "I know the ghastly state she was in, remember? I delivered her to you. But I thought she would heal up better than this."

Julianne chose not to get ruffled. "I think a few more weeks will return her to the beauty she has always enjoyed."

Monique did not appear to be satisfied, so when her eyes scanned the rest of the room, Emma quickly busied herself in the work. Monique might just choose the first shirker to take out her frustration on, and it would not be Emma. Luckily, Monique grabbed Amos by the arm.

"Spot me," she ordered, and walked away toward the workout room. Amos obediently followed. Julianne watched them leave, and then hurried after Leader and her patient.

After a few silent minutes, Scott said, "Monique's right about Lara. She looks ghastly."

Emma sighed. "Yes."

"Are we waiting for her to get well?" Scott asked. "I kind of thought that's what Leader was saying about returning in full strength or whatever."

Emma did not know. "I hope not," she fervently prayed. It could well be a very long wait, as bad as Lara looked.

A phone rang. It startled both Emma and Scott. The ring was unlike the ringtone of her mobile phone. It had a baser tone and came off a little wobbly in the large, open room. The two of them scanned the room for the source of the sound. Scott pointed it out: the pay phone on the wall near the entrance.

"So much for 'just decorative,'" he mumbled. He put down his cleaning rags and moved toward the phone. Emma followed him cautiously.

"Should we answer it?" she tempted him, staring hungrily at the phone. She was desperate for outside contact. For anything outside these cement walls.

Scott rolled his eyes. "No," he said like it was obvious. "Amos said to leave it alone. For someone who is studying Obedience, you sure have a tough time remembering your orders." She ignored his scorn and moved closer to the phone.

"Should we call for someone?"

"Leader's with Lara," Scott said doubtfully, shrugging.

A normal phone would have gone to voicemail by now, but the phone on the wall kept ringing. Emma was sorely tempted just to answer it. Who could know this number? Who could possibly be calling them? For a moment, she fantasized that Benjamin somehow tracked her down, but if that was true, it would be hard to trust that he was a normal guy interested in dating her because he found her fascinating and pretty.

Emma stepped forward and reached for the red phone.

Chapter Forty-Nine

"Don't touch it!" Thomas shouted, running in from the pool. Still slightly damp, and wrapped in a towel, he raced toward the sleeping quarter hall. He shouted, "Leader! Leader!" at the top of his lungs as he went. Scott and Emma scooted away from the phone quickly, lest it appear they intended to disobey.

"I guess we should have called for Leader," Scott told her under his breath. He shrugged and smiled sheepishly at their mistake. They managed to make it back to their dusting before Leader burst into the room. He snatched the phone from its hook and said, "Alpha, alpha, two-oh-four," into the receiver. After a pause, he said, "This is Leader."

Emma was transfixed. Perhaps this was the "higher authority" Leader answered to, if indeed he answered to anyone.

"What does that mean?" Leader asked, annoyance tingeing his tone. Thomas, Waylon, Ilene, and Julianne emerged from the sleeping quarter, watching Leader in concern. A word from Thomas sent Waylon off to the workout hall, presumably to collect Amos and Monique.

"No," Leader snapped. "That's unacceptable ..." He rolled his eyes over at Julianne, as if she knew what was being said on the other end of the line. She made no movement at all, so Emma wasn't sure if she did.

"Twelve million?" Leader asked, almost scoffing. "That's completely inadequate. What do you expect me to do with twelve million?"

Adam joined them now. He was not in the know, like the others seemed to be, because he appeared at least surprised to see Leader using the decorative phone. He sidled up to Scott and whispered, "What's going on?"

Scott filled him in quickly and quietly.

Leader smiled slightly but dropped it when he said, "I guess I'll make do with whatever pittance you can deign to offer at this time. Give him my sincerest regards and don't forget to tell him I'm looking forward to seeing him again."

Monique and Amos came in then and crossed directly to Leader, whispering and signaling for information until Leader made a cutting motion at them.

"No, no," Leader said into the phone. "Be assured if I was threatening him, I would speak to him directly. I don't threaten by proxy." Amos' eyes widened in surprise but Monique gave a dark smile. "It's no trouble," Leader went on, waving at Monique unnecessarily for quiet, and she likewise unnecessarily shushed the Guild. "Absolutely. Put him right through." He slipped his hand over the receiver and gave Monique a smug look. "I thought he'd want to talk to me," he whispered at her and gave a conspiratorial wink.

Then next instant he smiled and said into the phone, "Good morning, Mr. President! So good of you to give me a moment ..." He paused. Emma thought she could hear the angry voice on the other line. "Is that so? Thirty? Is that as high as you can go ... ?" He cocked a brow at Monique who made a motion at him that he seemed to understand. He nodded. "Fine. For you I will make a rare exception." He waggled his brows at Monique and said into the phone. "It will not be allowed to happen again."

Scott nudged Adam and whispered, "What do you think?" Monique shot them such a quelling look that Adam did not dare to answer.

Leader pulled the receiver away and drew a long breath, obviously to expel the anger that had suddenly blossomed in his eyes at whatever was being said on the phone. "I suspected as much," he said coldly when he pulled the phone back into place. "He will be dead by Friday."

Those words shocked Emma so much that she sat with a heavy thud in the arm chair behind her. *Dead?* He was promising to *kill* someone by Friday? He told her they were not organized crime, but this sounded like crime to her.

Leader hung the phone up without another word and stood looking at it. He shook his head once, and then laughed. He laughed so heartily and with such enthusiasm that several others smiled. Emma only stared at him in horror. How could he so callously laugh when some man's life was on the line? Didn't he have any common decency at all? It was all she could do not to throw her bottle of wood gloss at him.

His laugh ended in a smile when he looked around at the rest of them. Piper and even Lara slipped in when Emma wasn't watching, so now the entire Guild was present. Leader looked them over with a kind of intense scrutiny and nodded.

"Happy Christmas, Family."

Emma wondered if it really was Christmas. She did not understand the holiday at all. They never celebrated anything in the Guild. Most of what she knew came from conversations she overheard in school all her life, and from elementary school plays. She had heard people in Utah talk about the true meaning of Christmas. She did not understand how anyone could glean true meaning from a myth about a red-suited fat man sneaking into the house at night to drop off gifts. It had been a source of great contention between her and a couple of students when she was in second grade. She had gotten into a fight with a fifth-grade boy because Emma told his little sister that Christmas was an elaborate fairy tale. Everything the little girl told her about the North Pole and magical reindeer and overworked elf slaves seemed macabre. And what any of it had to do with the birth of a God, Emma never could understand.

She wondered idly at Leader's choice to wish them a Happy Christmas when no one in the Guild had probably ever celebrated Christmas.

Leader motioned vaguely toward the ceiling and announced, "We will proceed with normal operations!"

They hooted and in general seemed very excited about the whole thing. Emma watched them quietly. She would be just as grateful to get out of the Bunker and get back to normal life as the rest of them. Two months was much too long in any one place. But Emma wondered about the abrupt change. Was it, as Scott had suggested, because Lara had recovered? Or was the imminent death of the man Leader had threatened the real reason for their sudden deliverance? If it was, it was worse than overworked slave elves.

Leader left his BMW in the Bunker garage next to several other expensive cars. He selected a Lexus GX sedan instead. It was black with fancy interior features and lots of storage and comfortable seating. It did not seem to suit him at all, Emma thought. While a Lexus seemed completely in his nature, a sedan was not. He was a sporty-little-car kind of man. She allowed that her opinion could simply have been based on her previous observations, when all she had ever seen him drive were sporty little cars.

Emma was relegated to a back seat that unfolded from the floor when Lara, Scott, and Adam took the middle seats. She sat next to a small mountain of mostly empty luggage. It seemed silly to her to drive around with empty luggage in the car as it took up space and was completely useless. She supposed Leader wanted to be sure anyone who saw them exit the vehicle would see they had been on vacation in France.

Outside the car, Leader and Monique seemed to be arguing. Emma watched them with interest, noting the slight changes in them over the past few hours. Monique, wearing an extravagant mink coat she must have extracted from Bunker storage, wore eyeliner and lipstick again. For the last few weeks, she gave up on everything except mascara, and even that had not been every day. Her hair, which was in dire need of professional attention, was pulled into a fancy up-do. She wore supple gloves on her hands, probably to hide the fact that she had not had a manicure in two months. She was never unattractive, but today she was already back to being stunning. It was a vital component of the part she played so beautifully for Leader.

Leader, on the other hand, never lost one jot of his regular charm. He was as well-groomed as always, and had been during their entire sabbatical. He wore suits every day, but today he kicked the wealth factor up a notch. He wore a dark gray suit with a deep purple shirt that made his eyes seem fiercer than usual. His light gray tie probably cost more than most people's entire wardrobe. His watch cost more than most people's cars. It was such a silly ruse: throwing riches into the faces of the people around them when the Guild did not really enjoy their wealth. Lots of wealthy families traveled frequently and bought every new gadget invented. Their children not only attended private school but were in every kind of extracurricular program and activity. It seemed silly to dress up for the role and then not play the part to its fullest.

Leader made one final comment or command and Monique let out an annoyed breath. She tucked her handbag under her arm and walked around the back of the car to the passenger side. Leader went around the front to the passenger side in time to open it for her with a blank expression. In a likewise uninterested way, Monique nodded thanks to him and climbed in. It was comical to watch their interactions. Leader had no real sense of chivalry, Emma was sure about that. He only ever did anything to prove a point. Monique's argument with him must have been about who was going to drive, because he seemed almost smug when he climbed into the driver seat.

"Buckle," he ordered needlessly. They always fastened safety belts in the Guild. It was a rule they learned along with their first training forms and their first expectations of Obedience.

Leader snapped his fingers at Monique, who reached into her handbag to retrieve the ignition key. Without even looking his direction, she passed it to his outstretched hand. He started the engine but did not move from park. He held out his hand again in Monique's direction. Monique's breathing changed, and

Emma was sure she was annoyed as she reached in again and pulled out a handful of phones. *This* is what they had argued about, Emma realized. For some reason, Monique did not want to surrender the phones. Leader plucked them easily from her hand and tossed them into the backseat. Adam and Scott caught them.

"The black is Adam's and the gray is Scott's. The other is for Emma."

Leader's words caught Emma's attention. As Scott tossed a pink phone back to her, she was filled with a gnawing hunger to hear Benjamin's voice again. Had he forgotten her? But when she touched the button to turn it on, she saw she had no service. Also, she would not want her first conversation with Benjamin after her disappearance to be in front of her family. Especially not Scott, who had finally stopped teasing her about him.

"Lara," Leader said, holding up a phone in a bright purple case. "I'll just be hanging onto yours for a while."

"Yes, Leader," Lara said, without even a hint of the guilt in her voice Emma might have felt in similar circumstances.

Leader tucked the phone into a pocket inside his jacket. He adjusted the mirrors and seat positions then reversed the car and pulled out of its designated spot.

Through the side window, Emma saw Amos and Julianne standing at the door to the elevator. They were just watching Leader drive away, with expressions of doubt in their eyes. They had that look in their faces all afternoon, ever since the impromptu meeting of the Senior Guild this morning, after the mysterious payphone call. Emma did not waste time wondering what they were all worried about that apparently did not concern Leader. Emma did wonder why Amos, who had been chomping at the bit this morning to get out and do something, stood idly on the steps watching them drive away. Didn't he want to get out as soon as he could?

Emma was not the only curious person. Adam asked, "Isn't the entire Guild returning with us?"

"No."

Leader's answer was abrupt. Emma thought they weren't likely to get more from him. She would not have pushed. Adam was not of her mind.

"What? They get to stay here and rest on their laurels while we do all the important work? That doesn't seem very fair."

Leader glanced over a shoulder at Adam and said, "Stop it." Adam shrugged, completely unconcerned. His Guild responsibility was Confidence. Perhaps that was why he got away with saying exactly what he was thinking. Emma did not try that trick, not in front of Leader. With Monique, she tended to be more open and sarcastic. But not to Leader.

"The entire Guild shares the workload," Lara said softly, almost as if she were quoting. Leader gave a smiling glance and a wink through the rearview mirror at Lara. When he saw Emma watching, he winked at her, too. Emma turned away, never sure what to make of his affection.

The garage seemed to go on a long time, winding down deeper and deeper into what Emma could only assume was a mountain. It was very like an airport parking garage, after all. Floors upon floors of garage levels. Emma started to feel claustrophobic when Leader finally took a ramp-like exit almost straight up and came out in a giant white-painted room. It was five times the space of the Bunker rooms where Emma had spent the past two months. It lit up progressively as they drove along. When they came to the end of the room, a door large enough to allow in an aircraft rose slowly and let in real, actual daylight. It burned Emma's eyes.

Leader and Monique had pairs of sunglasses handy; the rest of them had to make do with shading their faces until they adjusted to the brightness. Part of the problem, Emma realized when she could see again, was the sunlight reflected off miles of untouched snow. Emma looked back over her shoulder in time to see the giant building behind her. All this time she had thought they were literally underground they had only been in a giant building! *Why no windows?* she wondered, a little grumpily.

The phones beeped in unison a few miles down the deserted country road. Monique looked to Leader in surprise.

"Upgrade?"

He smiled in amusement. "Big one. I think it will even impress you, Monique, and I know so little can." She shot him an arched look. "I thought it was time for a few minor changes. We just passed the Division boundary. Our phones chirp at us to let us know, but other people might get a kind of nasty surprise from their electronics."

Monique's arched look faded into a menacing smile. "You're right, I am impressed."

Emma stared at her new phone in alarm. Her old phone had been tracked, hacked, and transcribed. It had never really been her phone at all, which meant it was dangerous enough exactly as it was. Uncomfortably, Emma wondered what changes Leader had deemed necessary. She wondered what new disturbing features it could include to steal her comforts and test her Obedience. The phone lit up as she tapped the screen experimentally. The date and time shone out at her, but she saw she still had no signal.

"It *is* Christmas," Emma announced, confirming the date on her phone as December 25.

"Of course, it is," Leader said, glancing over his shoulder to give her a quizzical look. "I said as much." Emma did not answer his disparaging tone. She looked out the window and away across the snow-covered mountains.

"I think my criticisms have finally forced Emma into the box I have been building for her," Leader said to Monique, but loudly enough to be heard by the entire car. Monique shook her head, but her expression was hidden, so Emma had no way of knowing how she felt about Leader's sarcastic comment. Emma looked at her hands and would not meet Leader's eyes in the rearview mirror. She would not acknowledge his nastiness. And she *was* in a box. Leader had them all in boxes made of fear, hatred, and self-loathing.

"About time," Adam murmured, glancing over his shoulder at her and waggling his eyebrows. "Maybe she'll learn to be Obedient now. That is her *only* responsibility."

Leader might have responded, if Scott was not quicker to words. "What the hell do you know? You were only seven years old when you advanced to Eleven. It's probably hell to stay at Twelve for ten years, and you have no concept of it." Scott did not even back down when Leader turned an arched look on him. "Putting up with everything in the Guild without knowing why, without ever complaining, is pretty freaking hard without the extra scorn and insults." Leader seemed amused as he returned his attention to his driving.

Adam scoffed, and Scott answered it with a harsh, "Leave her alone."

It was silent for a few moments while Emma processed the idea that Scott was sticking up for her. Maybe they were becoming friends, after all. There had been no reason for him to think he needed to step in on her behalf, since he and Adam both could say practically anything they wanted to her without retribution. In fact, they frequently did. However, Emma felt a soft burning in her heart that he had come to her aid.

"I think Scott is saying it's time for you to move on," Monique mentioned with a chuckle for Leader, who snorted in derision. "It's out of compassion for you, I'm sure. I mean, ten years is quite a long time to be Guild Leader. You must surely be getting tired of carrying the world on your shoulders."

"I'm fine," Leader answered drily. He shot another wink at Lara through the rearview. "As long as the entire Guild shares the workload. Perhaps the problem is not my prolonged stay, Monique, but your lack of Diligence. If you worked harder, I might not be as tired." At a scoff from Monique, he added, "If it pleases you, I'll Ascend in January and leave the world squarely on your shoulders."

"No," Monique answered emphatically. She held up a stalling hand. "You would leave me this disaster you created? No, thank you! You clean up your own messes, Leader!"

Leader glared at her, a look that made Emma's stomach tingle with chills. It was reminiscent of the expression he had worn when he slaughtered the old man on the road in front of Emma's eyes.

"I will have all the messes cleaned up very soon."

Monique shrugged in unconcern. "We'll see, then. Maybe I *would* like to be Leader."

Leader rolled his eyes.

Emma drowned out the rest of their conversation with thoughts of going home. It would be strange to return to the Guild House without the rest of the Guild. Emma was not even sure if they were going home at all or if the House was even habitable. The last time she saw it, it had been blackened from the fire and did not seem very promising. Mind racing, Emma wondered if they would move or return to a hotel. She bit her thumbnail as she considered whether she would go back to Avanair at the end of the Christmas holiday. Thoughts of pretending to be friends with Cara and overly concerned Brinley filled Emma with confusion. The duplicity of her life created layers of stress. The Bunker had been dreadful for a lot of reasons, but Emma enjoyed being more herself than she ever could at school. And if that meant earning the sharp edge of Monique's tongue occasionally, and the stern arch of Leader's brow, it was what it was.

Emma slouched back into her seat and closed her eyes, trying to stifle her fears of the future and the annoyances of the present. She dreamed of Benjamin.

Chapter Fifty

Emma awoke because her phone rang. Her eyes popped open and she searched around for her phone. It had fallen from her hands while she slept. Retrieving it from the floorboards, Emma scanned the screen. She did not recognize the number. She looked up to see Leader watching through the rearview. Monique had turned in her seat, staring, as well.

"Who is it?" Monique asked with a guarded expression in her eyes.

"I don't recognize the number," Emma admitted. "It might be Benjamin."

Monique looked at Leader, eyes darkening, but Leader ignored her. "Answer it," he ordered before his eyes flashed back to the road.

Very aware of Monique's and Leader's scrutiny, and Lara—who, unlike the boys, was still awake—Emma clicked the receive button and placed the phone at her ear.

"Hello?"

"Hello?!" Cara said over the phone. "OMG! Is that all you have to say to me after all this time? 'Merry Christmas' at least would be appropriate!"

"Who is it, Emma?" Monique demanded, eyes watching with fiery intensity.

"It's Cara," Emma answered with pacifying hand. No one dangerous.

"Of course, it's Cara. Who were you expecting?" Cara asked through the receiver. "That was a pretty nasty trick you played, Emma! Disappearing on your birthday before at least throwing a party. And not even bothering to call! Or to answer my calls or messages!"

Emma sighed at the girl's pouty fury. "Merry Christmas, Cara. I'm back now. I'm sorry I left without saying anything."

"In the middle of the day!" Cara snapped back, not yet ready to be forgiving. "When you didn't show for lunch, I thought, 'She ditched school? Emma?' It didn't seem very like you. But then I heard about the fire, and I guessed your parents got you out early or something."

Emma was annoyed that Cara in any way thought she knew Emma well enough to know she would not skip school. But she let it pass.

"I went out of town after the fire," Emma explained. "I lost my phone, so I never received any of your calls or messages. My dad just got me a new phone today. I suppose he was trying to teach me a lesson about taking care of my stuff. It has been really strange to be without one." The lies came more easily to Emma than she would have expected after only truths in the Bunker.

"Sucks!" Cara exclaimed. "Did he know your friends were worried about you? Did he know we were about two days away from calling the police and saying you had been kidnapped?"

That was a little melodramatic but Emma only said, "I'm sorry to cause you so much concern. I did not realize our friendship constituted a need to let you know I was going out of town. If I had told my father, he might have let me use his phone to contact you and tell you I was safe. I am safe." As safe as anyone could be in the Guild.

"You didn't think ...? What do you take us for, Emma? Heartless? Of course, you should have let us know you were going out of town. Oh my god! Brinley was beside herself."

Emma was sure that was true, knowing what Brinley thought was going on at Emma's house. "Please tell Brinley I am really fine."

There was a short pause as Cara spoke away from the phone to someone in the background. Then, "She wants to see you. Can you come to my party next Friday?" Another party? This girl was more spoiled than Emma ever imagined.

"What kind of party?" Emma asked, and when Leader jerked his head around to shoot her a stern glare, she continued, "My father is opposed to your kinds of parties, Cara."

"He's annoying," Cara snapped back. "It's a New Year's Party, of course. There will be music and streamers." Sure, Emma thought, like her birthday party was going to be cake and movies.

"I probably can't come," Emma said, and Leader shot her another look, this time with a firm nod to confirm her assumption that he would not allow it.

"You have to come," Brinley's voice was suddenly in place of Cara's, as she had obviously taken the phone from Cara's hands. "Just don't tell him where you're going."

Emma scoffed. "Because that worked out so well last time? No way, Brinley. It's not like I can tell him I'm in a study group again."

Leader snorted at that.

"I thought you said it was Cara on the phone," Monique said. Her gaze never left Emma.

Emma covered the receiver and said, "It's both Cara and Brinley together. I didn't know Brinley was there."

"Aren't these girls expected to spend Christmas with their families? Why are they calling you right now?"

Emma shrugged expressively. She had no idea why they called. She had no idea why they were not with their families. Well, she could imagine Brinley's reasons for being away from home, with an abusive father and all that, but she chose not to share her thoughts with Monique.

"I'll ask him," Cara was back, and now her voice sounded a little more distant, as though they had switched to speaker mode. "He won't say no to *me*."

Emma laughed mirthlessly. "No, Cara, I don't think that would be a very good idea. First of all, he would most emphatically tell you 'no' as quickly as he would me. And also, I'm not bothering him with this. We can see each other at school."

"Just ask him," Cara prompted. "I'll wait."

Emma looked skyward for a moment. Then, without bothering to pull the phone away from her mouth, she raised her voice slightly and said, "Father, Cara invited me to her New Year's Party next week. Can I go?"

Leader eyed her through the rearview. "I think not. I don't approve of Cara's parties, and I won't send my fourteen-year-old to a place with alcohol and a lack of supervision. I think it's best if I keep you close to home for a while, Emma."

She did not like the sound of that, but she said into the phone, "He said no."

"He's extremely annoying," Cara answered with an exaggerated sigh. "Well, don't lose hope. Maybe we can sneak you out."

"I'm not sneaking out," Emma snapped back. "I am content to Obey my father. Let's just plan something else after school starts, something that doesn't involve alcohol or loud music and boys."

"We could go shopping," Brinley suggested. "Tomorrow."

"I *just* got back into town," Emma explained, trying hard to be patient with the girls who for some reason had decided to be her friends against her will. "I am sure my parents don't want to chauffer me around the mall the day after Christmas."

"*They* are not invited, obviously," replied Cara at her most haughty. "I'll drive."

"What could you possibly need to buy the day after Christmas?" Emma asked, perplexed. One of the things she understood about Christmas was giving presents to each other was a big part of the celebration. If Cara and Brinley both received a bounteous Christmas, as she was sure they had, why would they need to go shopping the very next day?

"You sound like a poor person, Emma, honestly!" Cara's acerbic reply grated on Emma's nerves. "We don't shop because we need something. We shop because it's an excuse to get out of the house. And, because we have nothing better to do during the break, we get together. You're like a Martian, you know that?"

Emma had no idea what little green aliens had to do with anything, so she said aloud, "Cara and Brinley invited me to go shopping tomorrow. Can I go?"

Leader's look was very dry, but his tone was sharp. "Get off the phone, Emma."

"I have to go," Emma told the girls. "We'll talk later, okay?"

"Wait!" Cara exclaimed. "What did he say? Can you come? If you don't come, you won't get to see my fancy new car."

Emma let out a soft breath. Her parents gave their 15-year-old a new car for Christmas? That girl was so spoiled!

"He said, 'Get off the phone!' and I had better," Emma replied. "I'll see your car later."

"Fine!" Cara said. "Later. I'll call tomorrow and see if he's changed his mind."

Brinley added. "We could come get you tonight. Cara's mom made Christmas dinner and it's going to be divine!"

Emma shook her head in exasperation. "I can't! I have to have Christmas dinner with my own family."

Leader's eyes began to darken. "Get off the phone," he said slowly, in the dark pitch she had recognized as one of his more dangerous tones.

"I have to go," she announced to Brinley and Cara, and quickly ended the call. "Sorry," she said to Leader. He turned back to concentrate on his driving. They reached a freeway and were zooming along on mostly deserted roads.

Monique readjusted herself to face forward. The car quieted for a few moments. Then Scott, who Emma thought had been sleeping in the seat in front of her, said, "Did they say they were going shopping tomorrow? That's weird, isn't it, the day after Christmas?"

Emma sighed. "Apparently not. It's an excuse to get out of the house and spend more money after the ridiculous amount spent in their honor already. Her family bought her a car for Christmas."

Scott whistled. "God, she's spoiled."

"That's what I thought," Emma answered.

"Did she say what kind?" Leader wanted to know. Emma was amused he was interested. But then it didn't seem so incredible. He did love fashion cars, and Cara was sure to have gotten one of the best.

"No, sir," she answered. "But I didn't ask."

He nodded, as if he had expected as much, and took an exit onto another freeway.

"It seems kind of impeccable timing," Monique murmured toward Leader. "I was afraid this was going to happen. Emma's too inexperienced to deal with this sort of thing."

"Don't," Leader answered in the tired way of someone exhausted with an argument.

"You have to admit that the timing was peculiar," Monique snapped back.

"Don't," Leader said, in a little heavier tone.

Emma did not understand Monique's alarm. Cara was so self-absorbed; it would never have occurred to her that calling on Christmas was rude or would be inconvenient for other people. And, knowing Brinley's concerns about abuse, it was likely that one or another of them had called her every day since she had unceremoniously walked out of the counselor's office on her birthday.

"I just think ..." Monique began.

Leader leaned over and did something Emma had rarely seen him do: he flipped on the radio. An eerie Christmas carol about a talking lamb blared into the speakers, startling Adam from his slumber with a ravaging string of curses.

Emma leaned back and listened to the song as it progressed toward its conclusion about prayers for peace. She had rarely listened to the radio. She intended to enjoy it as long as Leader needed a distraction from Monique's arguments.

It was fully dark when they arrived in the River Bottoms, allowing the professional lighting on every house to shine into the night. Unlike some of the other neighborhoods in Provo, the houses in the River Bottoms were restricted to moderate displays by the Homeowners Association. There were no giant inflatable snow globes or tacky projected images of the nativity on their garages. Most houses had only white lights strung from every eave, illuminating the house in a way that was aesthetically pleasing, and not overdone.

When they turned onto her street, Emma noted with some amusement that even their own house was decorated in such a way. The fire may have destroyed the garage and the upper stories of the house, but now there was no evidence of the destruction. The house had been rebuilt with a few slight variations and repainted. New landscaping replaced some of the damaged trees and bushes near the garage, which had been rebuilt to face the opposite direction. Emma thought it looked nicer not facing the street, but she was sure Leader had other reasons for reconstructing it this way.

The first garage opened as Leader drove up. He parked in his customary spot and turned off the ignition. As soon as he opened his door, the Christmas carols stopped. Adam demonstrated his relief from such deliverance with a very noisy sigh.

"The changes are nice," Monique said, not looking at Leader.

"It will do," he answered, not looking at her but not exiting either.

Silence.

Emma shifted slightly. She considered asking if it was okay to get out. She had been riding in this position for several hours and was tired of sitting.

"Do you really think this is a good idea?" Monique's sharp voice broke the silence.

Leader shook his head but in exasperation, not in answer. "I gave my orders. I shared my opinions. My decision is made, Monique. Why are you still fighting me?"

Monique looked at him and, even as far away from them as Emma was, she felt the cold of that gaze. "Because I think you're wrong and I am willing to go to the mattresses for it."

Emma had no idea what mattresses had to do with anything, but Leader seemed to understand the reference. He said, "Noted" in that icy tone that meant he would allow no other arguments. Monique nodded her acquiescence.

They got out of the car. Their move apparently gave the signal for mass exodus, as the others in the car also got out, leaving Emma to figure out how to exit the back of the vehicle. She finally climbed over the seat, an option that surely Leader would not have approved of, but she couldn't figure out if there was a latch to fold the seats down for a more convenient escape. She looked once through the window at the pile of useless luggage that was now left in the car, further demonstrating its uselessness.

Chapter Fifty-One

The entrance to the house had changed a great deal. Where the lockers once stood there was now an open entry way. The lockers had been relocated to a cloakroom where Emma went to hang up her coat on an empty hook and leave her boots on a shelf for that purpose. The entry had two halls leading from it. One went toward the kitchen and living spaces; she could recognize it by the sound of Monique banging around in the kitchen. Emma chose to avoid that route lest she be pulled into an activity she would regret. Monique was not any kind of homemaker. That unpleasant task always fell to Amos, who was not here. If Monique was responsible for the feeding and care of the Guild, they might be eating soup from a can. But not even that unpleasant thought made Emma want to volunteer to assist in preparation. Monique's lack of skill in the kitchen made her a disagreeable taskmaster.

Emma took the other hall. She imagined it led toward the front of the house and, she hoped, the stairs.

"Emma!" Leader called when she had gone the length of the hall. He stood in the dark next to the stairwell that would have been her escape. She resisted sighing.

"Yes, Leader?" she asked, hoping he would sentence her to the kitchen rather than want to talk alone with her.

He seemed to know what she was thinking, because he slightly smiled as he reached behind him and pushed open a door under the stairwell. A jerk of his head was all the invitation she would receive. She trudged through the door into his new office. It was a vast improvement on his old one, she saw. It was three times the size and had infinitely better furnishings. His desk could have been the same, for all she knew, but his chair was definitely different, and the equipment along the back wall looked more high-tech than anything he had in there before. It was a hidden office, she realized. It had windows at the back, but from outside in the hall, no one would know it was here if they weren't looking for it. Perhaps that was why his high-tech equipment could be out in the open. His old office had been ready to receive guests at any time. This was clearly a Guild-Eyes-Only place.

"I guess everything is getting an upgrade," she noted.

Leader answered that with a dark chuckle and pointed to a chair. She sat down, and he sat on the couch across from her. He crossed his legs as he often did and leaned back at his ease. At least someone was comfortable. Emma was not. All she had wanted was to evade notice long enough to go upstairs and call Benjamin. Sure, Leader would have had access to her conversation via his creepy network of surveillance and spies, but for a few minutes she would have felt like she had some time alone with her boyfriend.

"Emma," Leader said and then paused.

When he didn't go on, she said, "Leader," in a tone closely resembling his. He responded by cocking an eyebrow at her and she put up her hands to gesture surrender. She would stop playing when he clearly had something serious to say.

"You'll be returning to school next week," Leader announced. Emma stared at him and nodded. He went on. "Monique has some concerns about it. She said that over the past couple months your academics have improved immensely and that you have a knack for science. I mean, obviously I knew you had potential. Science was part of your genetic profile. However, Amos' profile had him on a level with astrophysicists, and we barely got him through computer science. The specs are by no means foolproof."

Emma looked away from Leader, thinking about poor Amos who had probably not had a moment's peace in the Guild when he failed to show the aptitude in science that had been foretold by the specs. However, he did seem to be an adequate computer engineer, if indeed all the surveillance was his creation.

"I hate science," Emma admitted. There was nothing she really loved in school, but of all her classes, only civics was less enjoyable than science. Of course, she was doing well in it. She did well in all her classes. Leader had not been lying when he condescendingly told Benjamin that she was very smart. She didn't have a choice but to do well. It was unacceptable in the Guild to be less than excellent in everything.

Leader drew a breath slowly as he studied her. "You hate science," he said, but it wasn't really a question, so she didn't reply. He lifted a hand in a dismissive gesture. "Irrelevant." His voice took on an annoyed expression. "You have strong aptitude and I can't just ignore that. I had my fingers crossed that you would prove to be smarter than Lara, Adam, and Scott, and it turns out your intelligence could actually challenge them collectively."

That was harsh. "Everyone in the Family is smart," she said judiciously.

Leader uncrossed his legs and leaned across the distance separating them. "I know that," he allowed. He held up one finger to point at his chest. "But *I*," and his finger stabbed her direction, "selected *you* for the Guild."

Ah. She understood his investment. Especially since he had lost Lela-Cate so quickly into his tenure as Leader, he needed Emma to prove herself worthy to hold her place. And evidently science was the mountain he intended her to climb to obtain that proof. Fortunately, she did find it easy, even though she didn't care for it.

"So, you're saying Monique wants to keep me out of school because I'm smart," Emma asked, carefully schooling her tone not to hint at the ridicule she felt.

He caught it anyhow. "Careful," he warned her. "No, she's worried that sending you to school takes you back to the unimportant aspects of the part you're playing and distracts you from your education."

Emma's throat constricted slightly, anticipating the direction of this conversation and not caring for it. "I can study well at school," she assured him. "I will apply myself diligently to prove to you both that I can be trusted."

Leader shook his head dismissively. "You'll never obtain my trust. You won't have the time."

Emma clenched her fists on her knees. "Very well," she said slowly. "I will prove my Obedience, then. You said you would test it eventually. This can be part of that test. I'll go back to school and show you that nothing will distract me from my education. I will be a model student and a model scientist, if that's what you wish." It wasn't going to be enough. She saw that his decision was already made. "Please don't restrict me from school, Leader. It's the way I keep my sanity. Stuck in the Bunker all day every day proved to me how unfit I am for captivity."

That notion seemed to amuse him, though Emma had no idea why. "I don't actually concur with Monique's opinion that you should be kept from school," he informed her. She breathed out a sigh of relief. "I agree that your education needs to be your priority. Your education will be the vessel through which you will serve the Guild." Emma figured that out. Julianne's medical training had certainly come in handy, and Amos' computer science and engineering was responsible for most of the technology they enjoyed. She was fairly certain Ilene had a psychological background, and she was sure Thomas studied business. Watching Leader, she wondered what he had studied back when he was in college. And Monique? She could have been anything from a surgeon to an assassin, for all Emma knew.

"I will apply myself diligently," Emma promised.

"I know," Leader said, and his tone suggested that had never been a concern. "Monique is afraid you're not ready for the realities of Guild life, and that returning to school will return you to the illusion that you are a regular girl living a regular life."

Emma interrupted him. "There's never any chance of that. If anything, school is a reminder of just how different I am from the rest of the world."

He watched her silently for a moment. That was the only reprimand she got for interrupting him.

"I know," he said again, more slowly this time. "I said these were *Monique's* concerns. She wants you here where she can watch you and coddle you until you are ready for the responsibilities of Guild life. She does not think you are ready to commit to those obligations. I do not agree. I think I can thoroughly test your dedication long before school even begins next week." He crossed his legs again, but he didn't take his eyes off her.

Emma was nervous about the idea of being tested by him. He could do anything he wanted to her. The day she attacked Scott, he had tossed her like a rag. When she had run away from the field trip, it was Amos' ingenuity that tracked her, but it was Leader's satellite. She was not naïve enough to believe that Leader did not know about everything that happened in his Guild. Even with half the Guild across the state, Leader probably knew everything that was happening. What more proof did he need from her? She would Obey him. In the Bunker she worked very hard to prove that she would Obey him in everything. She Obeyed them all.

"I have tried to be the person you require me to be," Emma began, desperately trying to hide her frustrations and her fear. "That's not going to change simply because people like Cara and Brinley are back in my life."

Leader's left brow shot up. "It's not them I'm worried about. I know you have no real connections with either of them."

Emma shot to her feet. "Benjamin. You're worried about Benjamin. We already talked about this, Leader, the first day in the Bunker. I will remain in character when I am with him. I will follow all your rules, even the fussy ones. You said I could maintain my relationship with him."

Leader rose to his feet and she regretted standing because he now towered over her. "I changed my mind."

Emma's stomach plummeted. Panic rose inside of her. "What? But I have done nothing but follow your rules and Obey your commands. I proved myself while we were in the Bunker! You can't just change your mind!"

"I can," Leader replied, crossing his arms on his chest, staring down at her like she was a specimen in a jar. "And I have. It's my privilege as Leader of the Guild to change my mind as much as I choose. And you did not prove anything in the Bunker. There was nothing to test yourself against, so nothing could be proven. Don't be silly. You're not a silly girl."

Emma could not stand to look at him. Her hands clenched, and she stomped away as far as the edge of the couch. She did not dare actually walk out on him. If he chose to follow her to her destination, she might not like his reward for disrespect. Her heart pounded in her chest. Fury rose in her ears and in her throat.

"I can't believe this," she snarled at him, not bothering to keep the incredulity from her tone. "Why? You tell me why!" She shouted her demand and even turned to face him. It had been many years since she felt brave enough in his presence to make demands. The fact that it seemed to amuse him made her angrier. "Tell me!"

Leader's brows rose at her tone, but he answered, "He was a threat. He was dangerous and possibly an enemy of the Guild."

Emma stepped toward him, hands outstretched, reaching for him, wanting to strangle him or shake him or plead with him. "But he was proved innocent! You said he was no longer considered a threat to the Guild."

"Exactly," Leader said, swiping at her hands as if they were fruit flies.

Emma shook her head. "Exactly? What do you mean?!"

Leader pursed his lips. "Lower your voice."

She hissed at him, in as low a tone as possible, "What do you mean?!"

"He's no longer considered a threat," Leader went on in a conversational tone. "When it was definitely a possibility that he could harm the Guild, it was prudent to allow you to date him. It was sensible to keep him as close as possible. While he was dating you, I knew there was little harm he could inflict that I wouldn't know about, and I knew from your side I would be able to control the information he was fed. Now that he no longer seems to be a viable source of information, he's really … just a distraction." Leader raised his brows at her again, waiting for her reaction to his words.

"So, because he's no longer a threat to the Guild, I can't associate with him?"

"That's as good a reason as any."

Emma wanted to be violent. She wanted to attack him, but she knew that would result in him wrapping her up like a pretzel. Instead, she took her anger out on his fancy glass coffee table. All it took was one swift, well-timed stomp, and it shattered. Leader did not even react to her meager display of violence.

"So, we understand one another?"

Emma shook from the rage she could not contain. She vibrated with the need to do something more, something that would push him to show his humanity. She wanted him to feel pain, because she felt pain that she could not control. "No! I don't understand you at all!"

Leader's expression suddenly showed zero compassion and even less tolerance. "I believe I have made myself perfectly clear, Emmalyn. Benjamin is a needless distraction from your education and your Guild responsibilities."

"My only responsibility is to Obey!" she shouted back, not letting her fear of Leader's icy tone bring her out of her own rage.

He leaned toward her, closer to her eyes, but she did not back down. She glared at him as he spoke slowly, clearly, enunciating every musical word, "Then what better test to assess your dedication to Obedience?"

A fist of helplessness grasped Emma's words, tangled them up, stole them away. Without words, all she could do was scream out in frustration. She screamed at him in exhaustion, and betrayal, and injustice. She had no other recourse.

In response, Leader gave a heavy nod. "It seems you do indeed understand."

Words spilled out of her mouth, pouring out in an uncontrollable mass of tangled frustrations. "You are completely psychotic! Benjamin was the only reason I didn't go completely insane in the Bunker. I knew I would be able to see him again, and that made everything okay. You can't just do this. You can't just play with me like I'm a pawn in your evil, sadistic games! I won't let you! You don't get to do this to me!"

Leader did not seem perturbed by her outburst. "All for the Guild. You can't prove to me that your relationship serves the Guild, so it's irrelevant."

"Not everything can be for the Guild," she screamed back at him. "That night! That night you chased me down and killed that guy! You just ... you killed him like ... You *killed him!* How can that be for the Guild? It's not! And I should have told the police about it!" When he tried to speak, she screamed, "Not everything is for the Guild!"

Leader snorted and looked away from her. "You have a long time for the Guild to prove you wrong about that. And it will, little girl! Believe me when I say it will prove that you and everything about you is for the Guild. When I killed the man who wanted to kill you, it was in service of the Guild, because it saved your life. And because *you* are for the Guild. But I won't wait anymore for you to get that figured out on your own. Before I am done with you, you will know the Guild's true worth." Leader held up a hand when she tried to argue, so close to her face that she squeaked into silence in the fear of him striking her. "If you thought my killing a man for grabbing a hold of you was startling, you will not like to see what I do with a young man who has even darker designs on you. But let me be perfectly clear about this, as it involves your safety, which is my personal responsibility: I forbid you from seeing or speaking to Benjamin ever again."

The cold words clenched Emma's stomach. His command was so final, so complete. It left no wiggle room for her. If he had worded it differently, she could have feigned misunderstanding. She could have fought him over wording and slid by on a technicality. Emma felt her insides caving, and she grabbed Leader's arms as much to steady herself as to plead with him. He never gave her the chance.

"Benjamin has probably moved on by now, anyway."

At the verbal expression of her deepest fears, Emma shoved away from him. He did not move an inch with her shove, but she did not stay to hear any rebuke. She ran from the room, certain she could not handle another moment in his presence. "I hate you!" she screamed behind her. "I *hate* the Guild!"

She did not know if he responded, because she stormed up the steps with thunderous footfalls to drown him out. She did hear Monique shout at her from the kitchen, but she ignored her, too. Monique was unlikely to say anything comforting now that Leader had again robbed her of her every comfort.

The upstairs had been transformed, so Emma didn't know which room to hide in. And she did feel desperate to hide, lest Leader or Monique come after her. She opened the first door she got to, saw that it was a bathroom, and went in. Slamming the door shut behind her, Emma locked it. Alone, when she did not hear Leader or Monique pounding up the stairs after her, she slid to her bottom on the tile floor. Soon, when her fear of punishment washed away, it was replaced by the intense pain of loss.

Benjamin's face, his kiss, his smile washed over her and carried with it a wave of grief. A cry erupted from her, breaking the silence of her hiding place. It was followed shortly by another, and then another. Emma could not stop them. She wept onto the fresh white tile, racking sobs that exhausted her strength and stole away the gall that had given her the power to argue with her leader. She cried until the dullness of Guild life swept over her and she could not handle one more moment of it.

Chapter Fifty-Two

He had planned it all along! Emma realized later when she retrieved her phone from her pocket. She scanned her phone log and found the only number programmed, besides the Guild numbers, was Benjamin's. He deliberately planted it in her phone log to tempt her to disobey. She hated him! She hated the Guild and its tests! She hated his dark, cold, deceitful eyes, and his musical, flowing, quiet voice. She wanted to claw at him, cause him to bleed just so she could see if he was actually human.

Emma deleted the number. When she called Benjamin, it couldn't be from her Guild phone. She had his number memorized already, so any phone away from the Guild would work.

That was when Emma realized she planned to call Benjamin somehow, and see if he was still interested in helping her. She would tell him some story about abuse or something, and let him take her far away, where Leader couldn't find her.

There were holes in her plan. She knew that. Leader's tracking and surveillance would be one hurdle. Getting away from the Guild house was another. But she would find a way. She had escaped the House before. She could do it again. Emma was done pleasing the Guild only to watch it crush her every hope and happiness. She left the bathroom.

And immediately ran into another hurdle. Scott waited outside the door for her. She had no idea how long he had been sitting against the opposite wall, with his arms resting against his knees, but he rose when she came out.

"What?"

"I heard you yell," he replied, as if that was all the explanation that was necessary.

She needed more. "So? That was an invitation for you to come find me, so I could pour out my soul to you?" She was more scornful than he deserved, but she did not care. He was Guild, so he was just an extension of Leader as far as she was concerned.

He rolled his eyes. "Of course not! I just ..." he studied her with narrowed eyes. "I know the feeling, is all. He's testing you. Don't fail just because he hit your hot button. Failing would be much worse than anything he's holding over your head right now."

How could he possibly know that? she wondered angrily. He had been a little boy when his Obedience was tested. How hard could it have been to eat his vegetables on command or go to bed on time? What could a five-year-old have been tested on that in any way could be on a level with this? She said nothing, because she could see he wanted to help. But she wasn't in the mood to listen to Leader be defended in any forum.

Scott looked toward the ceiling and drew a long breath. "Don't do this, Emma. If you disobey him, it's you who loses. He is only given more ammunition to throw at you the next time. And you *must* pass while you're at Twelve, because it gets infinitely harder to impress him as you Ascend."

"Don't defend him," Emma snapped.

Scott's hand flew into the air to bat away that accusation. "Never," he promised. "He's a bastard, pure and simple. But he is in power here, and it's a power you cannot defeat, especially not on your own."

Emma heard a volunteer in his words, and she said so. "Help me! Perhaps the two of us together ..." But he was already shaking his head.

"No, Emma. No way! I am a scholar of Obedience already and nothing would induce me to go through it again. I will not fight him. Even both of us together would lose."

killed Lela-Cate. He *killed* her because he did not want to waste time waiting for her to recover. He did not want her accident marring his Leadership." She may as well have slapped Scott's face; he jerked back in shock and stared at her with wide, haunted blue eyes. "I'm sorry! I know this seems cruel to bring it up, but I can't get it out of my mind. She was only a child, and how was it even possible to have gotten definitive answers from doctors on whether she could recover after so few hours in the hospital? It doesn't add up. There is no doctor in the States who would agree to unplug life support in less than twelve hours. He just killed her and walked out like he had done nothing wrong."

"Stop," Scott urged her. Pleaded with her was more like it. "You don't know—"

"But *you* know, Scott. Tell me you haven't googled the rules and laws! There is just no way what he did was legal! And people who go off life support can sometimes live for a long time. Was she really dead? You tell me if you think she was really dead!"

Scott shook his head emphatically. "Don't do this, Emma; don't turn it into a moral debate. Life support is controversial enough as it is. I had to accept his ruling."

"Why?" Emma snapped back, raging at him for his complacency. "Because he *told* you to accept it? He probably slit that girl's throat, and he'll do it again. This week, probably, since he promised the president that someone would be dead by Friday. Happy Freaking New Year!" She tossed her hands into the air.

Scott grabbed her shoulders and shook her once, hard. "Emma, don't be an idiot! He can probably hear you!"

"Yeah, he probably can," she replied, without bothering to lower her voice. "And tomorrow he'll have it all nice and transcribed onto a piece of clean white paper. He'll probably give it to me at breakfast along with my protein. Here: eat, drink, and be miserable for tomorrow I may decide to unplug your life support."

"God!" Scott swore, shaking her again. "You're hysterical. What the hell did he do?"

That question silenced her. She was so selfish! Here she was, dredging up his past pain and battering him with it, when all Leader had done to her was deny her a boyfriend. She really believed everything she said about the strange circumstances revolving around Lela-Cate's death, but it was mean to attack Scott with it. He spent his entire life racked with guilt over sending Lela-Cate to the hospital in the first place. How dare she, Emma, do this to him? Her pain was in no way comparable.

"I'm sorry," she said, honestly contrite. "I was being stupid."

"Tell me what he did," Scott ordered.

She had been trying so hard to be Obedient! She really wanted Scott to know she respected him, and she had no other way to demonstrate her loyalty than by Obeying him. And so, though it pained her to display her weaknesses, she said, "He told me I can't see Benjamin." And she waited for his scorn.

None came. "Of course," he said, like it was both unsurprising and a revelation. "What else would he do, Emma? He knows how much you care for Benjamin. He knows you'll do just about anything for him; that's first love! I would almost be more surprised if Leader did not exploit this opportunity to show his authority. Come on, Emma! It's such an obvious tactic! He was always obligated to test your Obedience. This is the most likely test."

"I'm going to fail," Emma promised him with a heavy shake of her head. She would wear that failure like a badge of honor. She was not going to let herself get manipulated by Leader's sadistic rules and expectations.

Scott shoved her against the wall, holding her there, pleading in hisses, "Don't be a little fool, Emma! If you fail this, he'll just exploit the next opportunity. Or the next! As many as it takes! He is tireless." Scott's grip on her shoulders tightened painfully. "Don't let him do that to you."

Emma swallowed against the tears that sprang to her eyes. Scott really cared. "He's a bad, bad man," she whispered, choking on her hatred and her devastation.

Scott's explosion of breath had all its normal contempt, but she thought it was not actually directed at her this time.

"Of course, he is! He was made to be, just as you are being made to be. How could he get on the phone and tamely promise to kill someone off unless he was a bad man? He was trained to become that person, one nasty little test at a time. Were you under some illusion we were the good guys, Emma? We're not. We're not the good guys."

She always wanted to believe they were good at the root. She wanted to believe that there was some high, noble purpose to their organization. But maybe Scott was right. Maybe they *were* the bad guys.

"I don't want to be a killer, Scott."

He shook his head, eyes wide. "Of course, you don't. No one *wants* to be a killer."

She relaxed against his hold, not wanting to fight, not wanting to be strong. His hold strengthened to support her.

"Are they trying to turn us into sociopaths?"

He gave a little laugh. "I don't know. But if they are, they are making an art form of it." The laugh she offered him in return lacked any joy. He tightened his arms around her. It was almost like a hug. And it was the closest thing to comfort she had received in a long, long time in the Guild.

They parted several minutes later, staring into one another's eyes. After a moment, he broke their gaze and pointed across the hall at a closed door. "That's your room," he volunteered. "I took the liberty of checking to make sure you had sheets and towels. Everything was ready to go. And I put a dinner tray on your desk. Don't eat in bed, though, because Monique will flay you if you ruin your sleeping patterns."

She nodded. She would never dream of eating in bed. Besides the fact it was strictly forbidden, it wasn't hygienic.

"I'm not going to just let this go," she announced suddenly as she backed away from him. "I can't."

Scott shook his head in frustration. "You have to! You cannot beat him. But even if you could, the Guild is bigger than Leader. It's bigger than you. You will lose if you try to fight it."

"But I have to try," she answered, too quietly for him to hear.

"Go to sleep," he ordered. "And put this out of your mind. Trust me, you'll feel better about it in the morning."

Emma knew there was nothing she could do for now. She had no way out of the Guild tonight. But she could conceive of a way tomorrow. She just had to make it to tomorrow. She chose to Obey Scott, because she thought he really cared.

"Merry Christmas, Scott," she snapped sarcastically as she turned her back on him and stepped over the threshold into her dark room.

He drew a deep breath behind her. "Merry Christmas."

Chapter Fifty-Three

Emma couldn't sleep. No matter how she tried, her eyes just would not stay closed. She ate all of the food on the tray. She paced the room for several hours. But every time she closed her eyes, thoughts of Leader's restrictions came back to her. Her eyes popped open and she glared into the middle distance at an image of him in her mind. In her mind she said all the right things, hurtful things that caused him to flinch. In her imagination, Leader had weaknesses she could reach. He had vulnerabilities she could exploit. In her mind, she used her words to decimate him and bring him to his knees.

Then she would remember where she was, and it would all shatter. All her carefully created fantasies would melt away when reality intruded. Leader had no vulnerabilities. Leader had no weaknesses. Leader had no humanity. Remembering made her angry. Her anger helped her overcome one of the many hurdles in her way.

She got dressed before she heard anyone else in the House stir. She was ready for Training before Monique even knocked on her door.

"Let's go, Emma," Monique said. Emma was pleased to see her startle when Emma suddenly jerked the door open. Monique looked her up and down, spending an especially long time studying her eyes, and then nodded. "Let's go."

In the kitchen, their protein was waiting. Scott passed it over and followed them to the mats downstairs. Where most people in this neighborhood might have put an indoor theatre or a pool, the Guild placed their Training center. The black mats stretched from the weaponry wall on one side of the room to the boxing bags on the other. Through a door to one side was the Still—a training tool Emma had never used—and the private Training rooms.

Emma trained hard. If Monique was waiting for her to make a mistake because she was obviously angry, she was disappointed. Emma completed form after form with flawless execution, and then beat Scott in simulated combat three times in a row before Monique called a halt.

"You can go, Scott," Monique allowed, though her calculating eyes never left Emma's face. "But you need to come back tonight before bed and work some of those forms."

"Yes, Monique," Scott said, but his voice was cool as he watched Emma in his peripheral vision.

She stood in a holding pattern, waiting for Monique to release her. Monique went instead to the weaponry wall and took down a pair of quarterstaffs. She carried them back to the center mat where Emma stood at ready. She proffered one of the pair.

"Arm yourself," she ordered. Emma immediately grabbed the weapon and moved into a weapon-stance with it.

"I find that the use of a weapon can help," Monique informed her quietly. "There is something about the smash of the wood and the force of a staff that eases my mind when I'm angry. It's active and aggressive, whereas silent sulking is passive and not at all helpful."

If Monique had meant to rebuke her or to instruct her, the lesson was lost on Emma. She held onto her anger, focused it, and honed it into a weapon deadlier than the staff in her hands. When Monique gave the start signal, her attack had more ferocity than Monique had ever seen in her before.

Strike! The staff hit and was blocked up high and then immediately opposite on the low. She swiveled in time to avoid Monique's return attack. Monique was going easy on her because she was still training, but Emma was not going to be easy in return. *Strike-strike-strike!* Three hits in succession made Monique sit up and pay attention. That was fortunate for Monique because Emma lunged then and Monique was forced to block or suffer a severe hit to her chest with the butt of the staff.

Now it was Emma's turn to block and parry. There was no denying that Monique was better at this. Emma was only glad that she was forcing Monique to show her true skill rather than the training yield she usually displayed. Emma was able to step out of the attack line and swing her staff almost fast enough to crack Monique in the side of the head. But Monique was faster and blocked just in time.

"If you want to hurt me, you're going to have to move faster," Monique instructed her. It easily could have been a taunt, but Emma thought Monique was trying to teach her.

"I don't want to hurt *you*," Emma answered and struck, once, twice, three times, four times, but was blocked every strike.

Monique shook hair out of her face that had fallen from her meticulous training ponytail and narrowed her eyes at Emma. "Hatred will not make you into a better fighter," she warned. She struck twice and got Emma into a strength war, with both quarterstaffs pushed against one another when Emma refused to allow herself to be pushed farther across the mat. "Hatred will cripple you. Your anger will only stand in your way. It makes you careless. It makes you vulnerable."

Emma was not able to speak and hold at the same time. It amazed her that Monique did not even sound winded. Emma dropped to the mat and spun away, coming up only fast enough to block a downward strike. She rolled onto her feet as fast as she could and had to jump out of the way of a strike meant to knock her down. Dancing back, she blocked as fast and as hard as she could when Monique advanced. She ducked away but took a ringing blow to the hip.

"Don't turn your back on your opponent," Monique sternly instructed. "Be aware. Watch the body. Anticipate where your opponent will go." The attack that followed was a blur of instincts on Emma's part as she defended herself against maneuvers she could not even see. She began to feel a terrible fear of losing. She did not want to lose anything else today!

She blocked high, low, then high again, but Monique backed her into a corner. Emma knew she was going to lose this fight. She could not win against Monique. In a last desperate attempt not to be slaughtered by Monique's ongoing attack, Emma lifted her leg and gave a spectacularly illegal kick to Monique's pelvis that sent her hurtling backward on the mat. Most people would have crumpled and been defeated by that blow, but Monique rolled back to her feet as if she did not feel the throbbing pain that she most certainly was feeling. She was back in attack stance.

"Hold!" snapped Leader from the doorway. Despite herself, Emma Obeyed. And so did Monique. "Stand down!" They each lowered their weapons into a resting stance and eyed each other across the room like two strange cats. Emma thought she could detect new respect behind the anger in Monique's eyes.

Leader crossed the mats and stood between them in his suit and street shoes. "I think it's safe to say you're at your most dangerous when cornered," he said to Emma in a calculated, dangerous tone. She could not bring herself to meet his eyes. She hated him!

"Are you all right?" he asked Monique.

"I'll be fine," Monique answered. "It was a well-timed kick, well-aimed, and strong."

"And illegal!" Leader snapped back. "She ought to have used the staff to discourage your advance."

"There is no illegal move in a real fight, Leader," Monique answered. "I support Emma learning to use all her resources. I think it proves how dangerous she can be when pressed."

Leader's eyes swept past Emma. "Very dangerous, indeed."

"The Aggression rules are only to keep us from killing each other," Monique reminded him. "If she felt her life was in danger, she had every right to fight for it."

"I don't think it was her life she was fighting for," Leader argued. And Emma's gaze shifted so she could look him directly in the eye and confirm his suspicions. She never thought Monique was going to harm her. She might have taken a few hurtful blows if Monique's attacks hit true, but nothing life-threatening. She had never been in any danger. Leader was right. She kicked Monique to unbalance her, so she could get the upper hand. And if she took a beating for it, she didn't care. She might have won that fight if Leader had not interrupted them.

"I want to let it go," Monique instructed Leader firmly.

Leader's gaze was locked with Emma's. He could see there was no remorse in her. She did not even try to hide her guilt. Her look was a challenge.

"Very well," Leader allowed without removing his gaze. "It's your decision."

"I choose to let it go," Monique answered him. She leaned around him to look at Emma. "We will work these weapons again tomorrow, so I can show you how to avoid getting cornered."

Emma did not so much as glance her way. Her gaze was locked with Leader's. "Yes, Monique."

One of Leader's expressive brows shifted slightly upward. He recognized the challenge in Emma's face. Monique ignored their shared challenge and snatched the weapon from Emma's hands to try to break their contact. "Go get cleaned up for breakfast."

Emma lifted both of her brows at Leader. She would not move before he did. She might as well have been trapped in that corner again even though Leader was halfway across the room. His head motioned ever so slightly toward the exit.

"Yes, Monique," Emma responded appropriately and still in appropriate time. She pivoted and stalked away, pretending to forget Leader completely. She tried to ignore his gaze on her back as she walked out of the room. At the last moment, against her better judgment, she looked back and met his gaze again. His eyes were black pits of intensity. Monique might have been willing to forgive her, but

Leader certainly hadn't. The violence of his expression should have made her tremble, but she rejected all fear of him. She lifted her chin slightly, challenging him to do his worst. His eyes glittered dangerously and her answer to that was one last defiant look. She twirled away then and walked upstairs, but slowly so he would not imagine she was afraid of him. And she wasn't, she realized. Her fear had been swallowed by her hatred. There was no more room in her for fear.

Emma saw her phone on the desk in her room and picked it up. She was ready to attempt her escape. Her first text was a simple: **I'm in the River Bottoms. Come get me.** Her second text, to Leader, was: **How long does it take for information about me to get into your hands?** It was a taunt, and she fully expected it to backfire, but she didn't care.

Her first text got a response first. **When? It's kind of early.**

Right now, she answered. **I'll meet you at the southwest gate.**

Emma did not shower as she was used to doing after Training. She washed her face and brushed her teeth and then immediately got dressed in a pair of new jeans hanging in her closet. All her clothing still had tags on it, since her old wardrobe had to be replaced. The red shirt she selected was probably lighter weight than she wanted in the cold of mid-winter, but she didn't think too long about her choices. She tucked it in carefully and then pulled a glittery belt through the loops on her pants. She snatched a fleece vest from the closet and pulled it on. It would keep her warm. Her coat was the one Benjamin had purchased for her on her birthday, and she pulled on the boots he had gotten, as well.

At the last second, she snatched her phone and shoved it into her pocket. If Leader answered her text, she wanted to get it right away. Her house key she left on the desk. She wouldn't be needing it because if she came back here it would be under force, not voluntarily. She slipped out of the room.

Scott was in his doorway and Emma had the eerie feeling he was waiting for her. He scanned her once and shook his head. He need not have said anything because she could read it all in his expression. He said, "This is a mistake."

She nodded. "Probably. But I haven't disobeyed him yet."

"You did in your heart already," Scott replied caustically. "When you chose Benjamin over your Guild responsibilities, you disobeyed."

Emma lifted one shoulder. "So, what you're saying is I have already committed the crime. Then what point is there in your trying to change my mind?"

"I'm not. I'm not an idiot. I'm just *hoping* you will to save yourself this pain."

"I can handle the pain," she snapped back.

He watched her for a silent moment. Then he said, "I'm going back into my room now to pretend I didn't see you. I won't help you in any other way."

She nodded and understood. She waited for him to close his door before she escaped down the stairs. Emma was quiet on the steps, aware that Leader could very well be in his office below her at that very minute. He would not be as forgiving as Scott. She managed to get all the way to the front door without an incident. She had never technically been told to stay in the House, but she still felt like she was committing a huge Guild violation by stepping through the door.

Chapter Fifty-Four

Emma walked neither too slowly nor too quickly across the lawn, leaving boot tracks in the unturned snow.

Emma had to resist the urge to look back when she reached the edge of the property. If Leader or anyone else was watching, she might lose her nerve and she was running out of time.

The sidewalks and roads had all been cleared of snow, so her path was easy once she reached the street. She began to jog. The southwest gate was only a few streets away, but her heart pounded heavily from fear. She was afraid at any moment that Leader's hand would clamp down on her shoulder and drag her back to the Guild House.

She ducked carefully into the bushes of a neighbor's house as a car sped down the neighborhood street. She caught a glimpse of the driver and her heart beat more painfully than before. It was Julianne driving, headed toward the Guild House. How long did she have now? Would Emma arrive at the gate in time to see the other Guild members coming home? She could not think of that now. She ran to the crossing street.

Never had Emma felt so grateful for rigorous training; it taught her how to control her nerves and how to move quietly and efficiently. She ran up the short hill toward the gate, not looking back, not getting winded. She hid behind the giant landscaped boulders as she saw another car coming through the gate. She did not dare to look and see if she recognized the driver. If it was a Guild Member who recognized her, she would be sunk.

Peeking up over the boulders after the car drove around a corner, Emma tried to see beyond the gate. She ducked down again when another car turned to approach the gate. She turned so her back rested against the boulder and took deep, calming breaths. Once the car was gone, Emma would bolt through the pedestrian gate and leave the community behind.

Her phone buzzed.

Emma jumped at the unexpected noise. When her heart began beating normally again, she reached into her pocket and pulled it out. She half-expected the message to be from Leader, but it was from Cara.

Where are you?

Emma peeked around the boulder and saw the side of a red vehicle parked on the opposite side of the gate. She leaned further, looking for the driver, and when she saw it was Cara, she breathed out a sigh of relief. Coming out from behind the boulder, she dashed through the pedestrian gate to the passenger side.

There was something wrong with the car, Emma thought idly as she jerked the door open and tumbled in next to Brinley and Cara. Emma could not quite put a finger on it, because her mind was occupied with fear of her escape. Something about the car nagged at her, but she pushed it away.

"Hi," Brinley greeted. She slipped backward between the two seats and let herself fall into the backseat to make room for Emma in the Porsche. Cara was already pulling out into the street.

Emma buckled her seatbelt before she returned Brinley's greeting. "Hi."

Cara glanced aside at her. "Well, aren't you bright-eyed and bushy-tailed this morning," she said with a smirk. That was when Emma saw that Cara and Brinley were both in their pajamas. Cara had at least pulled on a coat over hers, but Brinley in the backseat did not even have on shoes.

"I got you out of bed," Emma said, horrified to have put them through any inconvenience.

Brinley shrugged and Cara said, "Where else would we be at 7 o'clock in the morning on winter vacation?" She laughed. "Don't look so worried, Emma. We can go back to my house and get ready, and then we can go shopping."

Her phone buzzed again before she could respond to Cara. She reached for her phone while saying to Brinley, "You slept over at Cara's on Christmas?"

Brinley rolled her eyes. "My parents went to Vermont for the holidays and did not want me to come along."

Emma opened her phone. **You are in very real danger.** The text from Leader read. **Get out of the car.**

Emma looked up at Cara and Brinley. Danger? These girls from school were the least scary people in her life. They were selfish and spoiled, and she could take them both in a fight and it would still be unfairly matched on their part. Could Leader simply be trying to frighten her into coming home?

"What's the matter?" Cara asked, glancing at the phone in her hands. "Not out with Daddy's permission?"

Emma looked back and forth between the two girls and said, "Can I use your phone?"

Brinley seemed confused but passed hers forward. "Here! Are you okay, Emma? What's wrong?"

Cara would have turned into a neighborhood but Emma said, "No! Keep driving! Please." Cara shot her a puzzled look but turned obediently back into traffic.

"What's wrong?" she asked now, tone changing to concerned annoyance. "Are you in trouble?"

Emma dialed Brinley's phone by then and ignored the question. "Just keep driving, okay?" The muscles across her back tensed as she dialed the numbers, uncomfortably aware that she was deliberately disobeying Leader's direct orders to stay away from Benjamin and never speak to him again. She closed her eyes, drew a breath, and pressed the send button to complete the call.

Her own phone buzzed again in her lap at the same time Brinley's phone began ringing in her ear. She read Leader's newest text. **Get out of the car, Emmalyn!**

Then it hit her, what was alarming about Cara's car: it was the same color and style as the Porsche that had been sent as a taunt to Leader before they had gone underground. Her mind churned. Leader told her that car had been sent by Arrow Guild. Emma stared hard at Cara. Could Cara have been deceiving her all this time? The birthday party she said her mom had forced her to invite Emma to? Cara's sudden interest in being friendly? Was it all just a part, like Emma's? And what did that mean about Brinley? Wasn't it convenient that the two girls just happened to be staying at the same house? Emma wasn't really friends with either of them, so why had they rushed out of bed to come to her rescue? She had a very bad feeling about all this. What if Leader was not just trying to scare her?

"Hello?" asked Benjamin's voice through Brinley's phone. Emma let out a sigh of immense relief.

"Benjamin?"

There was a pause. "Quicksilver? As I live and breathe! Is that you?"

"Yes," Emma answered, letting out an immense breath of relief. She had never really trusted Cara, even before the appearance of the red Porsche, but she did trust Benjamin.

"Are you okay? What the hell happened to you?" Benjamin demanded.

"I'll tell you," she promised him, trying to breathe down her panic. "Just, please, come and get me first."

Another pause. "Okay, Emma. Where are you?"

Emma looked at the other girls. "I'm in Cara's car with Cara and Brinley. I'm scared." Brinley seemed highly alarmed by that confession, but Cara only seemed annoyed by it.

"Tell Cara to take you to the gas station at the American Fork Main exit. I'll meet you there," Benjamin promised. "Are you hurt?"

"No," she assured him, shaking her head. "Maybe I should leave Cara and Brinley out of this, though." The red Porsche nagged at her mind, clawed at her fears.

"It's fine, Emma. Cara knows me. Just tell her to meet me in American Fork and I'll be there by the time you get there."

"Okay," she agreed, too scared and panicky to argue with him. She trusted Benjamin. And Cara couldn't very well do anything to her while she was driving. And Emma was well-enough trained to take her if she did.

"Emma?" Benjamin added. "I'm so glad you're okay. See you soon."

"Okay," she replied, and hesitantly hung up the phone. She looked at it mournfully for a moment then said, "Can you take me to AF to meet Benjamin Stillwell at the gas station on main?"

Cara glanced at her with a confused expression on her face. "Sure," she agreed somewhat hesitantly. "*You* are at least ready to see people." She motioned with a free hand toward her pajamas. "But me and Brinley are at a slight disadvantage in this situation."

"I'm sorry," Emma replied. But she wasn't. If Cara was Arrow Guild, then going into her house was the worst thing she could do. It did seem awfully convenient that neither of them had bothered to put on clothes, and that would force them to have to return home to change.

Stop it! She shouted in her mind. Not everything in the world could be a conspiracy! Wasn't it possible Cara's parents had gotten her a car similar to the taunt left to the Guild? And hadn't Leader said he sent that back with some nasty surprises? She wished that could comfort her, but his warning that she was in real danger came back to her mind. Was she about to discover firsthand what nastiness Leader had concocted for his enemies? She could not relax. Benjamin was her hope at this point. He, at least, was not a threat to the Guild.

"It's okay," Brinley agreed, all businesslike suddenly. "Turn up here and we'll catch the freeway, Cara." She reached a hand up to touch Emma's shoulder in what was probably meant as a reassuring squeeze. Emma moved deftly away from her hand.

"It's okay," Brinley repeated, settling back against the backseat.

After several minutes in quiet while Cara moved steadily toward the freeway, Emma said, "I appreciate this."

Brinley gave a little laugh. "Look, I know a runaway when I see one. You don't have to talk about it."

Cara expelled an annoyed breath. "I can't believe you're dating Benjamin Stillwell," she replied, coldly disdainful. "You are dating him, right? That's why you called him?"

Emma thought fast but could think of no reason not to answer the question. "Yes, I'm dating him. I think. I was dating him before I left town."

Cara snorted. "Then you're still dating. He's annoyingly monogamous. He would not have gotten another girlfriend without a guarantee you were never coming back."

That served to calm Emma a little. It was comforting to hear that Benjamin had waited for her. "We had only been dating a few hours when the house caught fire."

Brinley's eyes widened. "Your house caught fire?"

Emma nodded, but did not answer. She was tired of lying, but she did not know if she could trust these girls, so she kept to as few words as possible.

"Is that why you left town?" Brinley pressed. Emma thought about it and finally nodded. It was kind of the reason they had left town, so she wasn't exactly lying.

They took a freeway entrance and Emma felt a little calmer as American Fork came closer and closer.

"Okay," Cara suddenly announced after studying the rearview for a couple miles. "Don't freak out, but I think we are being followed."

Emma craned her body around to see out the back window. In the distance there was a small vehicle that changed lanes as Cara did.

"It could be my father," Emma said fearfully, panic squeezing her voice until it squeaked. "Can you lose him?"

Cara looked at her with a skeptical expression and said, "I drive a Porsche, Emma. That's from 60 to 130 in less than ten seconds. Of course, I can lose him. But the construction makes it hard and the damned cops might not be very understanding."

However, she did accelerate and weave through the other cars in an effort to leave their follower behind. Several other cars honked at her, but Cara was a steady driver, if not a safe one at these speeds. Emma continued to watch the road behind them, waiting for the car to reappear. If it was Leader, he would not have been offset so easily.

"What did you do?" Cara demanded after a moment, glaring aside at her before returning her attention to the road. "Why are you running?"

Emma swallowed. "I didn't *do* anything, Cara. I'm just running to run."

Brinley spoke up in a voice that was probably meant to be reassuring. "Well, we won't let him catch you."

Emma snorted. "He's *going* to catch me." There was never any doubt about that in her mind. It wasn't ever a matter of if, but when and where, and would she have enough time to see Benjamin again before Leader caught up to her?

"I'm driving pretty fast," Cara defended.

"You would have to go lightspeed to evade him," Emma answered. Then, thinking of the personal satellite he owned, she added, "That might not even be fast enough."

Her phone buzzed again, and this time, when she expected it to be Leader, she was surprised to see it was Amos' name that flashed on the screen. He was calling. She ignored his call. If he had something to say, he could just say it to her voicemail.

"So, I guess this means we're not shopping today," Cara announced suddenly as she cut off a semi to get into the exit lane.

Emma turned an amazed look on her, at last running out of patience with the spoiled party girl. "No, Cara! I don't think I'm going to be able to make it!"

Cara shrugged. "No need to cop an attitude. I was just checking." She wove through the exiting vehicles in a highly dangerous way. Emma held her breath until they were on the main road in American Fork.

"Be careful, Cara," Brinley cautioned from the backseat. "You're going to get us killed."

Cara rolled her eyes. "Relax, both of you." She hardly braked at all before she made a sharp turn into the gas station parking lot. She glided like a professional racecar driver into an empty spot near the door and slammed on her brakes. Emma let out her breath in an angry explosion. Brinley cried out.

"God! You *are* trying to kill us."

Emma did not wait another second; she jumped from the car and backed away. *There, Leader,* she thought back to him. *I'm out of the car.*

Chapter Fifty-Five

Cara climbed out of the driver side window only far enough that she was sitting on the window frame. Her breath came as a slight mist in air in front of her. Brinley climbed back over the seats into the front and watched Emma through the closed window.

"You can go," Emma prompted them. "Thanks for the ride."

Cara rolled her eyes again. "Right," she said sarcastically. "Like there's any chance in the world I am going to abandon you here! What if Mr. Hotshot doesn't show up, huh? I'm not leaving until I know you're safe."

Emma wanted to believe that was true, but she feared that Cara was just stalling for reinforcements. Unbidden, her mind flew to Lara, and what Arrow Guild had done to extract information from her. Her stomach clenched and she backed away from the car, preparing to run if she saw any kind of threat in Cara's or Brinley's eyes.

Benjamin's truck cruised into the spot behind her before she was able to back two steps.

He opened his door and shouted at Cara, "How the hell did you beat me here, Cara? How fast were you going?" He was as handsome as ever, although his hair was perhaps too long.

Cara shot him an innocent shrug and a challenging expression.

He jumped out of his truck with a nasty glare for Cara then turned all his attention on Emma. He embraced her, holding her against his chest. Then he backed away and held her by the shoulders. She broke his grip, twined her arms around his neck and kissed him soundly. She did not know how much time she had, but she wanted to take advantage of every moment.

"You okay?" he asked when they parted.

She nodded, but she wasn't.

"Let's get out of here," he suggested. She nodded again.

"You okay now, Emma?" Cara shouted from her perch on the menacing red car.

As Benjamin helped Emma into the truck, he shouted back, "She'll be fine. I've got this."

"Now, Stillwell, as confident as I am in your assurances, I think I would rather Emma answered for herself, if you don't mind. Emma? I'm going to go if you're okay."

Emma climbed over the driver seat and was sitting now on the passenger side. She leaned across the seat and waved at Cara.

"Thanks!" she cried, truly grateful. She avoided looking at the car that had caused her so much doubt about Cara's character.

Benjamin jerked his car into drive and was on the road before he bothered to fasten his seatbelt. Emma stared at him, feeling immense relief that he was there. The smell of him and the concern on his face brought forward all the reasons she liked and trusted him.

He glanced at her once before abruptly returning his eyes to the road. "What happened to you, Emma? Are you all right?"

She nodded. "I'm all right. I was only scared. I'm feeling better now."

Benjamin reached across the distance between them and took Emma's hand gently in his. "I don't suppose your father is okay with this? I did promise him an itinerary."

Emma's face flushed when she realized she might be compromising Benjamin's word. "He's not okay with it," she replied apologetically. "He told me yesterday that I can't see you anymore. I ran away."

Benjamin let out a slow breath through slightly pursed lips. Then he gave a mirthless chuckle. "So, he's going to kill me."

Emma blinked at that before she realized he was being ironic. Pained, feeling a sudden urge to cry, she squeezed her eyes shut. She owed him the truth.

"He likely will try."

When she opened her eyes, she found him looking at her with a smile that twisted away when he realized she wasn't joking. "What?" he asked sharply for clarification.

"He's killed before," Emma said, pushing beyond the point of no return. This was the information Leader protected with his life; Guild secrets of which she only knew drips and dribbles. By telling Benjamin, she implicated him, and he could not go back. She pushed on. "He'll do it again. To protect his secrets, to protect his Family, he will do anything he thinks he must."

Benjamin stared at her, eyes pleading for her to be joking. "What do you ... You're serious? God!" He accelerated. "You're serious. You're really ... He'll *kill* to protect you?"

She felt so much shame at endangering him, but it was too late to go back now. She tapped the side of her head. "To protect what's up here, he will do what he thinks he must."

Benjamin's left hand clenched and unclenched on the steering wheel. "I knew you would be trouble," he murmured. That stung but then he looked at her and his eyes were full of concern and gentility. "Do you think we should call the cops?"

Emma panicked at that idea and emphatically shook her head. If Leader had the Capitol Building bugged, what was to stop him from bugging the police stations? And if he was killing for the *President*, how could local cops keep her safe?

"Okay," Benjamin assured her, squeezing her hand again. "We'll keep driving."

Emma shook her head. "He knows your truck," she murmured, desperately thinking of how to get away. She had not left this morning believing she would make it this far. Now that she was with Benjamin again, she began to entertain a hope that they could outrun or outsmart Leader together. But how? "He's probably tracking your truck right now."

Benjamin glanced at her. "Who the hell is this guy, Emma? Your father is the scariest freaking guy in the world."

Emma plunged. "He's not really my father, Benjamin. That's just one of the roles he plays." A tickling fear climbed her spine as she remembered Leader's warning about not permitting her to drop out of character. But she owed it to Benjamin not to force him to walk into this blindly.

"Emma ..." He looked at her, studied her in the moment he could spare with his eyes off the road. "What the hell ... ? What do you mean?"

If not for the still firm grip he had on her hand, Emma might have laughed and pretended like she was joking. But there was earnestness to his features and a real concern in his eyes. She could not go back on her words now that he was emotionally invested.

"He's the Leader of a group of twelve followers," Emma explained. "He selected me to fill the twelfth role when I was only four years old. He raised me and so, for all intents and purposes, he is my father. But he's *not* my blood relation."

Benjamin appeared to be stunned. "And your mother?"

"She's his Second," Emma explained. She choked on thoughts of Monique. Beautiful, furious, brisk Monique. What would she say when she realized Emma had run away from her? "Not my mother any more than he is my father. But she raised me as well, so ... It's complicated. No one else is related to me, either. Not my brothers or uncles or any of them. When we moved to Utah, we took on the characters we have been playing so we could attempt to blend into society here."

Benjamin scoffed a little. "What, you're supposed to be a Mormon?"

She nodded. "Preferably."

He shook his head. "No one in Utah would believe you were a Mormon, Emma." He looked at her too long and had to slam on his brakes to avoid hitting the car in front of him. "This is all a joke, right? This sounds like a conspiracy movie. And not a very good one."

Emma looked at him, pained that he wanted it to be fake. Because all she had to do was laugh and say she was joking and she could give him his peace of mind. She had spent so long alone, dealing with everything on her own. Until recently, she had not even Scott to talk to. She wanted Benjamin to *want* to believe her.

"It's true," she assured him.

He looked at her in surprise, scoffing at her answer. "Of course, it's true, Emma! Why would you lie? What is this creepy organization for? Where did he get you to bring you into it?"

Emma unbuckled and scooted closer to him, relieved that he believed her. "I don't know where I came from. But he had all kinds of genetic information about me. I was probably orphaned or something."

Benjamin looked at her. "But maybe not. You could have been kidnapped. There are all kinds of sick weirdos who kidnap kids to sell into human trafficking rings. We might be able to find out who you are if we can find out where you he got you from."

It was an idea Emma had never dared conceived of. Maybe she did have real parents somewhere who loved her and missed her. She had no idea how to find out, but it seemed important to do so. She nodded. "I would like to know."

He smiled at her. "You're safe with me."

Her phone buzzed, startling her again. "It's probably Leader," she informed Benjamin and she reached into her pocket for the phone. "Or Amos."

Benjamin scowled. "Amos is ... ?"

"Number Three. He's Monique's Second."

Benjamin nodded as if he understood perfectly, and that made her like him even more. "Do you have a Second?"

She shook her head. "No. I'm Twelve. No one is lower in the Guild than me." She managed to open her phone, but Benjamin's question pulled her attention before she could read the message.

"Is that what you call yourselves? The Guild?"

Emma shrugged. "I think so. We say Family most of the time, like the mob. But I believe our official name is Stone Guild."

Benjamin shook his head slightly. "That's weird."

She read the message. **Emma! Cara and her family are definitely implicated. The VIN number on her car matches.** It was from Amos. **There is no reason in the world she would have let you out of her sights unless Benjamin is a part of their organization. They will KILL you.**

Her head shot up and she looked at him carefully. "Amos says you're a Guild enemy."

Benjamin startled. "What? What does that mean? Because I picked you up when you were in distress?"

Emma shook her head, trying to clear it. She had to think clearly. "No," she answered slowly. "Cara and her family were identified as a rival guild. And she let me get into your car without a fight. He seems to think that incriminates you."

That seemed to take him by complete surprise. "What does that even mean?" He shot her a serious look. "I have known Cara practically all my life, Emma, and she's harmless. I swear it to you. She's annoying as hell, but she's not dangerous. And *I'm* not dangerous! I picked you up because you *asked* me to."

Emma tried to relax. "So did Cara," she said on her exhale. "I texted her and asked her to come get me from my neighborhood. She did not come all on her own."

Benjamin shook his head, anger exploding all over his face. "They are just trying to scare you, Emma, and make you believe there are conspiracies everywhere. They are probably not even who they portray themselves to be to you. They're probably just a bunch of warped weirdoes who played too many conspiracy videogames when they were younger and couldn't stand the idea of a regular life."

She wanted to believe he was telling the truth. She had thrown her lot in with him and she wanted to believe he was who he said he was.

"You did enter my life with startling swiftness. It looks sneaky."

He shook his head, getting really angry now. "Emma, I will pull over at the nearest exit and let you out, if that's what you want. You have no reason not to trust me. I am not holding you captive. Are *they*?"

Yes. They were. She had been Leader's slave all her life. She jumped whenever anyone in the Guild told her to. Benjamin was trying to help her.

"No," she said, reaching for his hand again so she could squeeze it. "I trust you, Benjamin. They just get into my head. That's all. They want me to be suspicious of you."

He pressed the button on his steering wheel that opened the passenger window. "Chuck it," he ordered forcefully. "Don't let them control you."

She slid back into her seat. Giving a mighty heave, she threw her phone out the window just as it began buzzing again. It bounced once and smashed on the road behind them and was run over immediately by the next car in their lane. She pulled herself back into the car and Benjamin rolled up the window.

He looked at her. "It's going to be okay now."

"He can track your truck," she answered, wishing she could relax but not managing it.

"I'll stop in Sandy and we can take Trax," he suggested suddenly. "There are cabs and rental cars in Salt Lake. Or if you want, there's a train that goes to Denver and one that goes to California."

She wanted to believe they could get away. "Okay. How long would it take us to take Trax?"

He shrugged. "Slower than driving straight, but I don't want you to worry the whole time. We can take any mode you want."

"What's your dad going to say?" she asked, smirking at him. "Won't he stop you at the state line?"

Benjamin grinned. "Emma, that was kind of a joke when I said it!" He shook his head at her in amusement. "He's in Hong Kong right now. He's a little preoccupied."

"I had no reason to think you were joking when you said it."

"I can believe that," he replied with a heavy sigh. "My father did have a couple of his lackeys follow me to the state line one time. But my father's call ahead to the first police checkpoint had already doomed me. They caught me before his lackeys ever even showed up. It's an anecdote I usually shorten to make my life seem more heartbreaking than it really is. It wins me the sympathy of pretty girls."

Emma rolled her eyes. "So, you were seducing me."

He winced. "I thought you were beautiful. I wanted you to like me."

Emma arched her brows. "So, you lied to me?"

He scoffed. "I *exaggerated* the truth. But, Quicksilver, I think, under the circumstances, we can call it even."

She blushed. She had lied to him far more often and with greater margins from the truth than he ever had. "Agreed," she whispered, not daring to look his way.

He laughed. "There you are," he said as he pointed toward her playfully. "I was wondering if the fear of your crazy guild had stolen away the personality I knew was down in there somewhere."

She looked at him askance and buckled her seatbelt again.

He crowed at her obvious intent to keep her distance from him. "Oh, dear!" he declared. "I tried to seduce you, and now you're going to make me work for it."

She shook her head even though that was exactly what she intended. "It's just safer to sit way over here," she told him innocently.

His infectious laughter bubbled up. He grabbed the buckle for the middle seat. "There is a seatbelt right here."

She pointed at the dashboard. "Airbags," she said sweetly.

By the time they made it to the Trax depot in Sandy, Emma was by his side again and exchanging dangerous kisses at the stoplights. They were honked at several times. He parked his truck in the open lot next to the depot and left his keys on the seat. When she seemed puzzled by that, he explained, "I'll have one of my father's guys come pick it up. If your 'father' can track it, he can just track it back to my house."

She decided not to tell him that Leader was probably using his crazy implant to track her movements right now. They did not have to wait long for the miniature train to arrive, for which Emma was grateful. Every moment they waited was a torturous interval Leader could use to close the gap.

They climbed aboard and took seats near the back. Benjamin held her close to him. It was the safest she had ever felt in her life. There were lots of people riding today. Most of them were carrying parcels they probably meant to return to stores downtown. Emma scanned every person in the crowd around them, looking for faces she recognized. Any darting eyes or lingering glances were noted. She was not going to let Leader sneak up on her this time.

They got off the Trax in downtown Salt Lake where they could blend into the crowd. Benjamin had her hand in a rigid grip with no intention of parting from her.

"What now?" She wanted to know, her anxiousness returning.

He shook his head. "I don't know," he replied. "We can take a cab to the train. Or the airport."

She felt a profound sense of relief at the idea of the airport. For some reason she believed that flying would put her out of Leader's reach, at least for a while.

"Let's go to the airport!"

He nodded. "We'll have to fly commercial," he said apologetically. "My father has the family jet out."

She gave a slight laugh. "You only have *one* family jet? How parsimonious of you." He smiled and pulled her close enough to kiss her. She jerked back suddenly. "Oh, no!" she cried out. "I can't fly! I don't have an ID. Can we take the train?"

Benjamin squeezed her hand. "If you want to, but I can get around the problem of no ID, Emma. I know a guy right here in the city."

Her eyes narrowed. "You told Leader you did not have a fake ID."

He shrugged. "He told me he was your father," he shot back. He pulled his phone from his pocket and made a brief call while they walked the street. He spoke to a guy named "Skiff."

Once he hung up, he announced, "He can get us in right away!"

"You're a shadier character than I thought, Benjamin Stillwell."

His smile was both innocent and apologetic at the same time. They hurried down the street with the rest of the crowds.

Chapter Fifty-Six

Emma held tightly to Benjamin's hand as they darted down a one-way street next to a giant building with no windows that reminded her of the Bunker. She was so wrapped up in staring at the building that she did not notice Benjamin's spasmodic grip on her hand until too late.

Amos pulled up beside them in one of the sporty cars from the Bunker garage. His window was down, despite the frigid temperature, and he leaned so he could see Emma's face.

"What are you doing, Emma?" he asked in the tone she knew him best for: caring, concerned, and slightly exasperated.

"You don't have to answer him," Benjamin assured her. She was mostly aware of her heart beating painfully in her chest. If Amos was here, where was Leader? Could she be expecting him at any moment, flying down on top of her to punish her for deliberate disobedience?

Amos grasped the ledge of the window and leaned further out. "We need to talk, Emma." Despite her fear, she looked at his eyes. He looked so serious, intent on his mission to get her away from Benjamin. Doing Leader's bidding. "Get over here."

"No, Amos," she answered, turning her face away from his caring eyes and firm tone. She backed against Benjamin's chest, and Benjamin wrapped an arm about her waist.

"You need to leave now," Benjamin said, pointing vaguely toward the road, firm in his demands.

The engine shut down and Amos left the car in the road to climb out. He stuffed the key into his pocket and stalked around the sidewalk toward Emma and Benjamin. Benjamin pulled Emma around behind him so he was between her and Amos.

Amos shook his head disgustedly. "You can't *get* in my way, boy. I will go *through* you to get to her if I need to." The dark tone of voice was more frightening to her than the words. He was completely sincere in his intentions.

Benjamin's shoulders squared. "I'm not afraid of you."

Amos scoffed, and tried to step around him to look at Emma. "What are you doing, sweetheart? You can't run anywhere where we can't find you."

Benjamin stepped in front of him again. "She's not your 'sweetheart!' She's going to stay with me where I can keep her safe. You need to leave before you cause a scene."

There were people watching them up and down the street. Even people who couldn't hear their words could feel the tension.

Amos spread his hands. "Is there some reason you think I want to engage with you in the street, Arrow? You need to stay out of this, so you don't get hurt." He looked at Emma. "You need to come home, Emma. This is getting out of hand. If you come home willingly things are going to be hard enough. If I have to drag you back kicking and screaming, your father is not likely to be highly forgiving."

Benjamin backed up and pushed Emma with him. "He's not her father, you bastard! I'm not going to let *Leader* hurt her anymore."

Amos seemed to be startled by the words. He looked at Benjamin like he had never seen him before. "Are you kidding me with this?" he whispered but he didn't seem to be saying it to either one of them. His gaze captured Emma's again. "What did you tell him?"

"Enough," Benjamin answered for her, forceful and dark. "Enough to know I'm never letting her get back in a car with any of you. You need to leave." Amos tried to get around him but Benjamin sidestepped. Amos' fierce look was more frightening than anything else he could have done. Emma took a step around Benjamin so she could attempt to calm Amos before he did something dangerous.

"Don't give in to them, Emma," Benjamin insisted when he saw her trying to meet Amos' eye. "They do not have your best interests at heart."

"God, Emma!" Amos snarled, glancing skyward. "He is lying to you! We might be angry, and we might be scary, but we have never lied to you."

"Don't listen to him," Benjamin insisted in an urgent whisper. "He is trying to control you. They are all trying to control you."

"He's *not* who he says he is," Amos snapped back. "He wants you to believe he's just an innocent bystander, but he's not, Emma. Think about it logically. Do you think it's even a little bit possible he could have shown up at your field trip for legitimate reasons? He's a pawn in Arrow Guild's game. They have been playing you against us all along. But we didn't know, Emma. We were diverted by their attack on Lara and so we did not realize how ensconced they had gotten with you." He jabbed a finger at Emma, rigid and serious. "Listen to your heart. What is it telling you?"

"I don't want to be one of the bad guys," she said softly, shaking her head at Amos. Benjamin grasped her by the hand again. He pulled her along with him down the street. Amos followed with magnetic persistence.

He spread his hands in desperation. "We may not be 'good guys' in the movie-sense of the words, Emma, but we are *yours*. You belong with *us*."

"Don't listen to him," Benjamin ordered back, furiously. "He's trying to confuse you. You don't belong with people who kidnap you and make you call them 'Leader.'"

"Really?" Amos snapped in return, but not at him. He was speaking in earnest at Emma. "Have I ever tried to confuse you, Emmalyn? Me? Ever?"

Emma felt a wave of grief and fear flow over her. Even if Amos was lying, he was still casting doubts. And even if everything he said about Benjamin was true, she would still have a hard time trusting him. Trust was not in her nature. It was not what she had been raised for.

"I can't," she said, breaking her grip from Benjamin and backing away from them both. She shook her head at them, tears clawing at her face. "I can't."

Benjamin pursued her. "It's okay, Emma. I won't let anyone harm you. I won't let any of them get close to you."

She shook her head at him. Then she looked at Amos and shook her head at him. "I can't go on like this. I can't. I'm afraid of everyone! I see conspiracy everywhere!"

"You don't have to," Benjamin promised. "Come with me and we will get away from them all. I will keep you safe."

Amos said nothing. He just followed closely, gaze locked with Emma's.

"Come on, Emma," Benjamin insisted. "We can get away from them and build a life together. We can love each other."

Emma blinked and stopped retreating. She turned and stared up at Benjamin's eyes. He was so passionate and insistent that she could not help but stare. Amos stopped walking, too, maintaining a distance several feet behind them. The darkness and the fear retreated in a wave of wonder.

"Do you love me?" Emma asked him, desperately attempting to ignore Amos' presence. He was a shadow of doubt on her dreams for the future.

Benjamin cocked his head to one side, peering into Emma's eyes. "Do I— Of course! Of course, I do, Emma. Why do you think I'm working so hard to free you from the Guild? You will be happy with me."

"Because you love me," Emma stated, clarifying. She shook her head as if trying to shake away her own doubts. "You really love me?"

Benjamin placed a hand on the side of Emma's face and he smiled gently. "Yes, I love you."

Emma held onto his words for a moment, savoring the idea of it: love in all its glory. She had never been loved before. She had never witnessed passion for anything but Guild business, and that was not true passion, anyway. It was the dark passion of crime. This was love from one person to another. Emma had no reference for it.

She looked to Amos and saw it, the look of pained compassion. He had warned her. So long ago now, back when she had just started seeing Benjamin, Amos warned her that it was all just a ruse. He warned her that the people outside the Guild would use her heart to manipulate her. *"If he says he loves you, run away."* She nodded at Amos then let her head slide down, let her gaze fall to the sidewalk in front of her. She promised Amos she would not let herself be manipulated this way.

"Come on," Benjamin ordered, glancing back at Amos. "Let's get out of here."

"I can't," Emma said decisively. She felt the cold, icy fingers of indifference wash over her heart. She stepped out of Benjamin's arms. He grabbed her wrist.

"What are you doing, Emma?" he cried in panic. "You know what they are capable of! Don't let him control you!"

Emma shrugged out of his grasp, tugging her arm free from his possessing grip. "I'm sorry," she whispered. "I can't."

Amos opened a hand to her and she moved toward it. She had to go back. The Guild was the only place where she knew exactly what was required of her. For all its dysfunction, it was the only home she knew. Benjamin's beautiful picture of the future was a nice idea, but Emma had no reason to believe it could really exist.

"Emma, don't do this!" Benjamin shouted. "Don't get sucked back into their delusion. They are trying to manipulate you."

Emma nodded as she grasped Amos' hand. She looked over her shoulder at Benjamin across the distance that separated them. It was a heavier distance than the space between them; it was a gulf of entirely diverse existences.

"I know," she told him, throat catching on the inevitability of her choice to return to the Guild. "And it sucks. But, with them, I know *how* I'm being manipulated."

"You're being abused!" Benjamin cried, opening his hands toward her, as if they could somehow close the distance.

"I'm so sorry, Benjamin," Emma whispered. She really was. She really wanted him to like her. She wanted to believe he could love her. "I never meant to ruin your mission."

Silence reigned around them for a moment while Benjamin tried to process her words.

In an instant, his expression went from concern to rage, and all of Emma's doubts flew away. It had all been true. Amos was right. To Benjamin, Emma was just a means to an end. He reached into his coat and withdrew a pistol. When others on the street saw what was happening, they screamed and ran away every direction. Amos shoved Emma away, but the barrel of the gun followed her as she stumbled over the curb and into the street.

"You will pay for this!" Benjamin screamed, aiming the gun at her. A hand clasped Emma's arm and she was jerked to the side as Benjamin pulled the trigger. She was tackled out of the way and hit the pavement hard enough to steal her breath away. The exploding gun resounded off the walls and the echo bounced all around her. It wasn't just an echo, she realized. Amos–the gentle giant who always used his words to advocate for peace–was returning gun fire.

In the moment it took to release one pained breath, it was all over. The huge weight of the man who had shoved her out of the path of the gunfire was pinning her to the ground. The smell of him gave him away. It was Leader. Where he had come from in all the pandemonium, she did not know. He didn't move away from her. He protected her from the crossfire.

The screams of bystanders echoed all across the street. The same screams as before, Emma realized. Only a heartbeat of time had passed.

"Leader," she said, struggling to breathe. The combination of his weight pressing on her and the wind being knocked out of her made it hard to catch her breath. She pushed against his weight.

"Leader," she begged. He did not move.

Then Monique was there, standing over them. With one arm, she hauled Leader off Emma by his belt and placed him face-up on the pavement beside her. She squatted beside them.

Emma sat slowly up, just in time to see Amos lowering his gun arm to his side. Emma followed the path where the bullet must have shot, and saw Benjamin sprawled across the pavement, eyes open to the sky. Involuntarily, she lifted a hand to her mouth to cover her screams. Amos killed Benjamin. *Amos killed Benjamin.* She played it over and over in her imagination.

"It was in defense," Amos insisted, so quietly she almost didn't hear. He wasn't speaking to her, anyhow. He was reassuring himself. "I couldn't let him hurt Emma."

"Your job is to protect the Guild," Monique told him briskly from her position beside Leader. "You did your duty, Amos." Amos did not answer her.

When the sting in Emma's eyes was under control enough she knew she would not start crying, she turned to Monique. She fully expected to see fury in her, but there was none. Monique's eyes and hands were occupied retrieving Leader's phone and a red card from Leader's suit pockets. Emma stared hard at them for a moment, and then she scrambled on her knees to Leader's side. There was blood all over his white shirt and now on Monique's hands. Despite the blood, Monique leaned over him and softly pressed her lips to his cheek. She reached down with one graceful hand and straightened his tie. Like she always did when they left the House.

"Oh my god," Emma gasped. "He got shot! He got shot! Is he okay? Leader? Leader, are you okay?"

He did not make any movements. He did not make any sounds.

"He's gone, Emma," Monique said sharply. She whipped the pocket square from Leader's lapel pocket and wiped the blood from her hands as she slowly stood. "He saved your life, and it cost him his."

"He's dead?" Emma whispered, crushed with the idea, disbelieving. "Because of me?"

Monique shrugged one shoulder and then reached down to grab Emma's elbow and haul her to her feet. "It's the price of disobedience," she snapped. Emma felt her knees give out again, but Monique held her upright. "We all have a final mission. His was today."

Emma felt the hot sting of tears on her face, but it was not until she sobbed out the words, "I did this to him," that she realized she was crying. Monique dragged her a few feet away from Leader's body. "*I* did this!"

"No, you didn't," Monique said sharply. "You have no control over Leader."

Monique reached down to retrieve Benjamin's phone, which had dropped on the pavement during the gun fight. She shoved it into her coat pocket and kept walking, pulling Emma behind her. Emma needed the encouragement because she was looking back over her shoulder at Leader's body, lying next to the curb in final silence. Dead. Because of her.

Monique did not even look back.

"Amos," Monique summoned the man who still stood with the gun in his hand by his side, staring in surprise at the dead form of the young man on the pavement in front of him. "Leave the gun and let's go. There are enough witnesses here to keep the locals busy for a while. We've got to make ourselves scarce before this turns into a media circus." Amos squatted and placed the gun on the ground. But he didn't move. He continued to stare at Benjamin.

Monique looked around at the scene of terrified people still running away, and the couple good Samaritans moving toward the bodies to search for signs of life. "This isn't exactly what I'd call 'cleaned up,' Eric. Fuck!"

From his squat, Amos looked up at Monique in question. Emma thought she knew the reference from the conversation Leader had had with Monique in the car yesterday. He had promised to clean up his messes before he left the Guild to her.

"Let's go, Amos," Monique ordered again and dragged Emma toward the car.

Amos cleared his throat, shaking his head as if to clear it.

"Yes, Leader," he said quietly, rising to his feet.

Emma looked back in shock at the title. Amos showed nothing on his face. He clicked the button on his key ring, starting the car and unlocking the doors in one motion. His stride was purposeful as he rounded the car and opened the driver door. Monique opened the passenger back door and said, "Get in." Emma stared up into Monique's dark eyes, searching for blame or anger. There was none. Monique raised one brow and nodded her head toward the open door.

Emma Obediently climbed in the car.

"Buckle," Amos ordered as he turned the key in the ignition. Emma reached for her safety belt. In the distance she heard the approach of emergency vehicles. It seemed like a lifetime had passed since Benjamin pulled a gun, but it had been bare moments, she realized. Everything can change in bare moments.

When Monique climbed through the passenger door and closed it, Emma stared at her back. She did not know what to make of everything.

Monique reached into the glove compartment and retrieved a small plastic bag. She emptied its contents into the compartment and passed it over the seat to Emma without looking at her. Emma was grateful for the bag because as soon as she relaxed against the seat, her stomach roiled and she emptied its contents into it repeatedly.

"*You* okay?" Monique asked Amos.

"I'll be fine," he promised in a cold voice. "What are you going to tell the Locals?"

"Nothing," she answered flatly. "I'll flash a badge, throw some glitter around, and razzle-dazzle them right out of our life."

Amos nodded as if that was what he had expected to hear.

"What will they find on him?" Amos asked. His tone was so cold as if he had not just killed a man in the middle of downtown Salt Lake City in the middle of the day.

Monique shook her head. "Nothing they haven't seen before." She held up Leader's red phone. "Everything they will be looking for is right here. We've tapped them again."

Amos nodded as if the events of the day had been scheduled and gone according to plan. He turned the car onto Cesar Chavez toward the Interstate.

"You okay?" Amos asked Emma over his shoulder.

Emma did not know how to answer that. Of course, she wasn't okay! Her boyfriend and her father had both been shot to death in the streets. And for what?

"Please tell me there was a reason," she begged him. "Please tell me this all means something! He didn't just die for nothing. Right? Amos, tell me the Guild's purpose. What are we doing here?"

Amos looked over at Monique until he caught her eye. She shook her head. "Not yet. She's not ready." And that was all Emma was likely to get in the way of answers.

She began to cry long before the car ever reached the freeway. She curled up against the back of the seat and sobbed into the interior leather. Monique reached back to retrieve the vomit bag. As she removed it from Emma's hands, she brushed the hair from Emma's face and studied her for a moment. Then she turned around, tossed the bag out the window and faced the road.

"It will be okay, Emma," she said, gently but confidently. "Do you understand me?"

Emma gathered her emotions long enough to choke, "Yes, Leader."

The End

Stay up to date!

Thank you for reading *Obedience*! If you're left wondering what's next for Emma, you won't have to wait long. *Diligence,* the second book in The Guild series is available now!

To keep up with all new releases, sign up for the newsletter at https://linktr.ee/nicholemwillden.

Enjoy the Guild? You can make a difference!

Reviews are the fastest and best way to get attention for my books. Let's face it, reviews and stars matter, and most people (me included) make choices based on feedback. I may not have the force and flex of a major advertising agency, but I do have something valuable:

A loyal bunch of readers!

Your honest review of my book will help bring it to the attention of other readers.

If you enjoyed this book, I would appreciate the gift of your review. Please spend a couple minutes leaving a review on the book's Amazon page.

Thank you so much for helping me spread the word of The Guild. (Please disregard the culty feeling of that last sentence.)

Get Exclusive FREE Content for The Guild series

Interacting with readers is the most joyful part about my writing process! My readers inspire me. Occasionally, I send out a newsletter to connect with my readers, and to offer them exclusive content from The Guild.

If you sign up for my mailing list, I will send you:
- A top secret Action Report from Arrow Guild (Book One spoilers included)

- The Guild Book Excerpts, Volume 1. Because what's a cult without a tome of doctrines?

You can get this content **for free** by signing up for my mailing list www.link-tr.ee/nicholemwillden.

ACKNOWLEDGMENTS

First of all, thank you, Reader! I appreciate that you chose to read my book, and that you stuck with Emma all the way until the end. She's not always easy to handle, trust me! I know, having spent years with her living in my head. Yet it is a pleasure whenever another reader comes on Emma's journey with me. Thank you for coming along!

Next, I must acknowledge that I in no way condone or support child abuse. Nor do I think Leader, or any other person, has the right to verbally, physically, or mentally abuse another person. That being said, Leader does a lot of things that are not okay. It would be unwise to follow his shitty example in real life.

Thank you, Amanda! I kept writing this story because you were interested in it. You helped me remember why I write and that—as frustrating as it is—it's worth it. Thanks for believing me even when I didn't believe in myself.

Thank you, as always, to my family. You're the reason my characters are broken, angry, and abusive. It's hell to live through, but it makes an interesting story I could not write without you. Thank you for torturing the artist in me until I became a writer. Additionally, thanks to you, Dad, for keeping me grounded. Thanks to you, Mom, for bringing me into the world. Thank you, brothers, for being the Bro-Club. Thank you, sisters, for *not* being the Bro-Club. My pen is mightier than my affection, I'm afraid, but my affection is not small. It roars like a lion and purrs like a kitten but is never at rest.

Jamie, I feel whelmed. Thank you for being you. That's all I need.

Amber, what in the world would I do without you? I had better never find out! Thanks for being my best. A day never goes by when I don't thank the lucky stars that put us next door to one another and separated by only a wall. Even though you've moved to another location now, I can't imagine life without you in it. How did I or Emma or Leader or any of us get along without you?

Thank you, Sam, Emily, Kate, Josh, Adam, Kami, Debb, Sandi, my team, and my class. Thank you to all my dedicated ARC readers for keeping me inspired and on my toes. Thank you, Mrs. Erickson.

And last, but not least in my head or my heart: Thank you, Wijic Et Al.

ABOUT AUTHOR

Nichole M. Willden is a poet, writer, and author of The Guild series. A survivor of indoctrination and abuse, Nichole has spent decades writing fiction that sizzles with themes of enslavement, hope, and resilience. Nichole lives and writes in the Rocky Mountains with her wife, who is helpful to the writing process, and their puppy, Potion, who is delightfully unhelpful. She works a stellar day job, reads everything she can get her hands on, and watches too much TV. If she was queen of the world, there would be no slavery, no child abuse, no loneliness, and no PowerPoint.

Find Nichole M. Willden at www.nicholemwillden.com, on Instagram www.instagram.com/nicholemwillden, on Facebook www.facebook.com/nicholemwillden, on TikTok www.tiktok.com/@nicholemwillden